M.D. JOHNSTON

Asher Paterson
and The Portal Realm

Copyright

Cover design by bookprintinguk.com.

Book design by bookprintinguk.com.

Published by Forbidden Tree Publishers.

Printed by Book Printing UK www.bookprintinguk.com,

Remus House, Coltsfoot Drive, Peterborough, PE2 9BF

Printed in Great Britain.

ISBN 978-1-3999-7456-1

Second Edition:

This paperback edition was first published in 2024.

Dedication

I would like to devote this book to everyone bold enough to come on a journey to explore the confines of my mind. Buckle up, it is going to be a wild ride.

I would especially like to dedicate this book to Martin McPhillips, who has already been petrified by what he has seen lurking there in the shadows of my thoughts. Like him, I am sure you will not be the same again.

Lastly, I would like to dedicate this book to my Mother, Jean Johnston, and Father, Michael Johnston Senior, for being my resolve in the trying times.

Contents

-Chapter 1-

7th Grade

Attempting to block out the loud noise, Asher Paterson held his polyester-filled pillow around his ears. He pressed his angular, diamond-shaped face against his soft bed mattress. His thin body wriggled side to side like a worm, as his blue striped blanket jostled back and forth.

Thump! Thump! Thump! 'It is 8.30 am, time to get ready for school, Asher. Hurry up or you will be late,' shouted his grandmother, Nancy Branning. She pounded on the kitchen ceiling with the tip of her floor brush to get his attention.

Despite his best efforts, Asher could not ignore her. 'I'll be down in a minute,' he yelled. He clinched his teeth together, he was annoyed.

'Now!' boomed Nancy, her roaring voice crackled with strain, but it was nonetheless demanding.

Groaning with utter discomfort, Asher shoved his nimble hands into his soft mattress as he forced himself to sit up straight. 'Fine, I'll be twenty minutes,' he loudly informed her, bellowing at the top of his lungs.

'Ten.' Nancy sternly howled. 'Move your skinny behind now.' She was unyielding.

'Fine, fine, alright...ok, gran.' Asher called out. He had given in. His legs dangled off the edge of his bed. His thick black hair pointed in all directions. He slowly opened the third drawer of his simple bedside dresser. His thin, set fingers clutched at non-matching socks in search of a pair, when suddenly his gaze fell upon an old, worn-out picture. Sniffle! Wiping his nose, he was caught off guard.

The timeworn image depicted a beautiful young woman with gorgeous blonde wavy hair, stunning blue eyes, and a heart-capturing smile. A smile so warm and bright, the sun's radiance paled in comparison.

'I love you, Mum,' he said softly. Banggg! Filled with sadness, he slammed the drawer shut. He wiped his teary eyes. Not only was it the eighteenth of September, his thirteenth birthday, but it had also been thirteen years since his mum, Jane Hanna Paterson, had prematurely passed away.

Despite the unlikely odds, severe complications during labour had claimed the life of Asher's mother, yet miraculously spared him. Not that he knew. His dad, Michael Anthony Paterson, better known as Mike, had hidden the stark truth from him. Misguided, he wholeheartedly believed that a fatal, incurable illness had claimed the life of his mother.

As an archaeologist, his dad, Mike, was not at home all that much. Africa, Greece, Rome, even Egypt, his dad had seen it all in his unending quest to find the undiscovered.

Rat-a-tat-tat! Rat-a-tat-tat! 'Finally, the mail!' spurted out Asher with glee. He sprang to his feet energetically. Like a kangaroo, he leapt forward.

He heard a knock on the front door of his grandmother's old wood-built house, located on 6th Avenue, Neptune City, New Jersey. He hurried toward his bedroom window. Thud! Thud! Thud! His size seven feet fell heavily upon the wooden floorboards.

'Aww, no way,' groaned Asher. He pulled the dusty blinds upward, he could see that it was just the milkman, clutching two milk bottles. His sudden outburst of enthusiasm sharply evaporated. 'Come on,' he muttered to himself in sheer disappointment. It was not the postman as he had hoped.

Each week, Asher would routinely wait for the mail. Usually, it was delivered by one grey-haired elderly gentleman, Henry, the local postman, or one red and blue striped, white, special delivery postal van. More importantly, he would wait anxiously for the arrival of the latest picture postcard sent by his dad, each with a hand-scribbled message upon the front and a carefully selected picture residing upon the back.

Some weeks, some months even, he would get no picture postcard at all. But he fully expected a postcard this week, for surely, he thought, his dad would not forget his birthday! He was disappointed that a postcard had not yet arrived.

'Where's my school bag, Gran?' howled Asher. His black hair rolled over his eyes as his head hung low. He searched under his bed. His school bag was not where he usually put it. The only thing there was a cluster of coloured socks.

'In the kitchen,' she promptly answered.

'Thanks,' he boomed. Getting to his feet, he quickly sprinted down the stairs. Peering into the living room, he could see that his grandmother stood by the fireplace. She lit a single white candle.

'I miss you, my sun, moon, and stars,' uttered Nancy with a sombre tone. She lit the remembrance candle every year on the same date. She did so in memory of her daughter, Jane.

'I miss her too,' whispered Asher. He shook his head sorrowfully. He and his grandmother never talked about his mother, Jane. He had raised the subject a few times in the past, wanting to know more about his mother, but every single time, he was met with scathing anger. With a sigh, he turned and headed toward the kitchen. His school bag rested on the kitchen counter.

Being the eighteenth of September, Asher was about to start his first day in seventh grade at Neptunica Middle School.

He left the old, shabby, wood-built house in a downbeat, sombre mood. 'I'm off then, goodbye,' he called to his grandmother, his dreary voice echoing through the dimly lit doorway.

In response, she managed to give a half-hearted groan of acknowledgement. 'Yes, goodbye, now close the door, you're letting the heat out,' she answered. Slumped in an armchair in the living room, her focus was entangled in one of her embroidery magazines.

Screechhh! As he gently closed the old oak door, its hinges whaled. He stood for a moment on the front porch. He immediately set his sights upon an old ash tree. Situated upon the front lawn, it had begun to shed its discoloured leaves.

Gasppp! He pinched his lips together before taking a deep breath. Being his very first day of term, he was feeling incredibly nervous. His stomach was doing somersaults. 'Catch a grip,' he muttered. 'I can do this,' he added, self-reassuringly. Thud! Thud! Thud! Feet racing forward, he quickly hurried off down the stone-paved path leading away from the old house.

'Watch out!' a voice called out.

Thump! 'Ouch,' yelped Asher. As he turned left, he was unexpectedly struck by a hard-jabbing object. 'What the hell…' Swooshhh! He hastily twisted his thin body. His gaze fell upon the culprit as his blue eyes widened. The tenseness in his lightly built shoulders loosened. 'That hurt! That is going to bruise,' he stated. He rubbed his side. His gaze had fallen upon a relatively short, slightly plump, dirty fair-haired boy with dangly teeth and rosy cheeks.

'Ash, sorry buddy, sorry, I didn't mean to…to…' the boy's words ran away from him like a machine gun wildly emptying its shells.

'It's ok. Slow down,' spoke Asher. 'I believe this is yours.' He took hold of a round leather-like surface. 'Catch!' Whoosh! He lobbed the spherical shape resting within his palm.

Thud! Strangling the red striped baseball within the intensity of his grip, the boy named Benjamin Mathew Wilson, better known as Ben, drifted his feet forward. 'Nice, isn't it?' In his left hand, he held up the baseball like a trophy, acting more avidly than the situation deemed necessary, before putting it in his schoolbag.

'Yes, it sure is, it's awesome,' expressed Asher with joy upon his face. He nodded excitedly, feeling thrilled to see his friend of eight years. He was mindful that Ben was left-handed, as he held out the dorsal side of his left hand at a forty-five-degree angle.

Ben Wilson was his only friend. His only human friend, that is, excluding his tail-wagging, tongue-dangling, bushy-eyed dog, Scruffy, a half breed grey and white mongrel.

Thud! Ben met him with the back of his hand before both clasped their palms together, as fingers slid away. 'Happy birthday, buddy,' he rapidly spurted out, as he finished the bespoke handshake.

'At least you remembered,' said Asher glumly. He sighed heavily.

'What do you mean?' asked Ben. Twitching his fingers, he looked a little baffled.

'There is still no word,' said Asher. His troublesome thoughts began to weigh him down like a great big anchor.

'No word! Who are you talking about?' asked Ben with a shrug of the shoulders. He did not truly understand Asher's state of mind or why he was suddenly looking rather sullen and upset.

'Oh, it doesn't matter all that much,' said Asher. He tilted his head as he dropped his gaze. 'I'd rather forget all that.' His head bobbed side to side as he quickly discarded his spontaneous, troublesome thoughts. 'Quick, let's get going before we're late for school.' He did not want to be late on his first day in seventh grade.

'Ok buddy, you got it,' replied Ben. 'By the way, you should work on those reflexes. You would make a dreadful catcher.' His voice was playful.

'It's really good to see you,' expressed Asher earnestly. He grinned, feeling truly pleased to see his dirty fair-haired friend.

'It's only been three weeks, Ash,' said Ben. He held up three fingers to affirm his point. David Wilson, Ben's dad, had taken both he, his two younger sisters, Louise and Claire, and his mother, Amanda Wilson, out of state.

'Oh, it seemed much longer,' answered Asher. 'Hope you at least had a great holiday.' He felt quite dull the last three weeks of summer. Whenever Ben was not around, he felt quite lonely.

Travelling down 6th Avenue, Neptune City, both could not stop their impulsive jabbering.

'Look, Dad also bought me this,' said Ben. Zippp! He opened his green and black zigzag patterned school bag before retrieving a superb leather baseball mitt. 'Can't wait, Dad promised me that we'd go to Red River Park after school to put my new baseball and mitt to good use.' He was thrilled by the thought.

While out of state on holiday, Ben and his family visited the National Baseball Hall of Fame and Museum in Cooperstown, New York. He had always wanted to see it first-hand.

'Oh…oh great…that's just swell.' Asher replied grimly, his tone of voice shrivelling into dismay. His unstable mood began to dip once more.

'What's wrong?' questioned Ben. For him, it was as plain as daylight that something was eating away at Asher. As a good friend, he wanted to know exactly what the problem was.

'Nothing, I'm fine as always,' Asher miserably answered. Over the years, he had built up a wall, a wall that blocked out his true emotions and feelings. He felt that no one ever really cared anyhow. No one except Ben, that is.

'Come on, you can't fool me, something is wrong,' said Ben firmly. He refused to drop the matter.

'Really, I'm fine,' said Asher. He was finding it hard to open up, to share his thoughts. He tried desperately hard to hide his true feelings, however, he did so in vain. 'It's ok, he probably just forgot!'

'You miss him, don't you?' asked Ben. He finally realised what was eating away at his dark-haired friend. He understood perfectly who 'he' was! Over the years, he was the topic of many conversations.

'I don't know what you're talking about?' lied Asher. His face went blank of all expression, he was giving nothing away. He was playing the unknowing fool.

'Your dad, of course,' said Ben. He was direct with his words. He could see right through the smoke and mirrors façade on show. Besides, Asher was a horrible liar. A horrible liar who tended to bottle up his emotions.

'Don't be foolish,' snapped Asher. He could not stop rubbing his palms together. He was feeling anxious at the hard truths he was hearing.

'Hold up one sec,' said Ben sternly. He took hold of Asher's arm. 'It's me you're talking to. Now spill, what's bugging you?'

'Dad sent no postcard or anything,' answered Asher, finally spilling the beans. He trusted no one more than his friend.

'You know the mail, it sucks,' replied Ben, trying to be positive. 'He didn't forget your birthday last year. I remember those beige socks with the pyramids stitched on them.' He thought the socks were unique.

'I…I suppose you're right,' Asher nodded in agreement. He recalled the colourful socks. Last year, for his twelfth birthday, his dad had sent him a pair of socks with an image of a pyramid stitched on each. His dad had also sent him a book outlining the history and reign of the boy pharaoh, Tutankhamun.

'I'm sure your dad didn't forget,' said Ben. He then retrieved his new baseball from his school bag. It had a National Baseball Hall of Fame sticker imprinted upon it. 'Neither did I.' He handed Asher his prized baseball, hoping it would cheer him up.

'Thank you, Ben, you're a real pal,' said Asher. He went for a hug.

'Woah! Hey now, hold up, handshake,' smiled Ben. He recoiled. Instead of a hug, he extended his hand. 'We're more accomplices than friends, we only met seven or eight years ago,' he joked.

'You're a jackass,' chuckled Asher. 'Let's go.' He hurried onward toward school.

'At least we're not the new students this year,' said Ben as they reached the outskirts of Neptunica Middle School. He watched as busloads of new and returning students pulled up outside the old building.

'Look!' said Asher frantically. He could not contain himself. 'Over there,' he wildly pointed. Something, or more to the point, someone had startled him! He had quickly spotted Tom Watson, who was a beanpole of a boy with freckles and hair so red the sun gleamed over it like gloss upon painted wood.

'He's up to all his usual tricks,' said Ben. He shook his head disapprovingly.

Now in eighth grade, Tom was undertaking his usual daily routine. He was forcefully taking money from the sixth graders. He had a bad attitude and took out his anger on others. He had been in the foster care system for most of his life. For the last six years, he lived with his adoptive parents, Mildred and Thomas Watson, on 13th Avenue. He took their surname as his own, never knowing his real parents.

'Perhaps this year he'll leave us alone,' said Asher. He was overly optimistic. Thud! Thud! Thud! His feet drummed off concrete as he slowly edged up the school steps toward the salvation of two brown, rectangular-shaped doors. His hand gently grazed against the stone wall, it slid upon it like sandpaper gliding over raggedy wood. His dazzling blue eyes hung low. Then he heard it!

'Hand over the money or else,' warned Tom. He was ruthless as he gripped the terrified sixth grader by his arm. He then forcefully searched through the boy's pockets before finding a five-dollar bill.

'Help! Help me!' The terrified boy yelped in terror.

'Ben, I can't just stand here and do nothing,' said Asher. He intervened to help the terrified boy, despite feeling petrified himself. 'Let him be,' he mustered up the courage to yell. He had put himself directly in the firing line, in the path of Tom's rage.

'Well…well…well, it is little Asher Paterson!' Tom's eyes were as sharp as any eagle on the hunt. He swiftly zoned in on Asher. His tightening lips and protruding jawbone perfectly displayed the sheer contempt he held toward him. 'Murph let that little twerp go,' he ordered. Click! Click! Click! He repeatedly snapped his scrawny fingers as if to call his pet dog to action.

A large lad known as Conor Murphy released his prey. A scared, teary-eyed sixth grader retreated from the shade of his enormous, eclipsing stature. The boy, not an inch over four and a half feet tall, barely reached the thick stump that was his bulging neckline. 'Beat it,' he grunted. A devious grin of pure delight rested upon his wide-set face as he watched the terrified sixth grader hysterically manoeuvre out of sight.

Like Tom, Conor had an attitude problem. His mother, Karen Murphy, was a cleaner at the local hospital. His dad, Sean Murphy, was a mechanic with a short fuse and a drinking problem.

'Stop wasting time. Let us say hello to our good friend,' said Tom. He was overly sarcastic. His feet began to race toward Asher, like a world-class sprinting athlete.

'Friend, but he's not our friend,' stated Conor. His stupidity radiated from his plump lips like some primitive animal not fully able to comprehend.

'Just hurry, Murph.' Tom sighed heavily at his beefy friend's sheer idiocy.

Remaining firm, Ben could foresee what was about to transpire. 'Oh boy, here we go again.' To him, the routine was all too familiar. 'It's dumb and dumber.' He detested the pair of bullies.

Rapidly, Tom advanced up several steps. His long, skinny arms dangled loosely as he went.

'Wait, wait for me,' screeched Conor. He struggled in his attempt to catch up. He trudged behind, desperately panting for air.

'Well! Well! Well!' Tom spoke slowly. His hazel eyes burned with pure hatred. He hovered over Asher like a tower block. 'Long time no see, Paterson.' He was a narcissist. He had no empathy for others, nor did he care for the misery he caused.

'What do you want?' spoke Ben. His tone was dry.

'Stay out of it!' Tom warned. 'Otherwise, things will get messy.' He pushed his finger against Ben's protruding chest in an intimidating manner.

'Yeah, stay out of it,' snarled Conor. He stood at the bottom of a row of steps. He was still a little breathless. Picking on the new kids at the school was gruelling work.

'Oh boy,' muttered Asher nervously. He bit his bottom lip as his anxiety began to overpower him. He trembled upon spotting Tom's clenched fists. He could comprehend that the lanky menace was fully intent on causing trouble. Feeling nervous and cornered, his whole complexion turned pale. His heart thudded like a kettledrum beneath his chest. Feeling goosebumps, his arm hairs stood on end like a row of matchsticks hanging disorderly from the box.

'Well, hand it over,' said Tom. His menacing snarl only added to his frightening tactics. His hand flapped back and forth as if to suggest he wanted something!

'Hand what over, what do you mean?' answered Asher. He was a little confused, to say the least.

'Don't play games! Have you got my lunch money, Paterson?' asked Tom. His voice was loud and very demanding. He deviously calculated Asher's every move.

'I…I…!' Asher struggled to respond. He felt flustered, knowing full well that he had only a few measly dollars. He had just enough money for his lunch and dreaded the idea of spending an entire day at school without a bite to eat. His hands shook. His double-strapped, blue-striped school bag wrapped around his right shoulder came loose, descending to his wrist, then to the canvas below. 'Ummm, I only have…' he began, quite unsteadily.

'Look here, we don't have to give you a damn thing!' Ben interrupted. He took a defiant stance. 'Just leave us alone.' He had bravely managed to conjure up the audacity to stand against the school predators with their fangs fully extended.

'I don't think I heard you right. Murph, sort him,' ordered Tom. He snapped his fingers, and his muscle, his overly large sidekick, shot into action.

'With pleasure,' said Conor. He made a bold lunge forward. Thud! Thud! Thud! He charged up the cobbled steps, his face beetroot red. His beefy jaws jangled as he panted for air. 'You twerp!' He rudely insulted Ben before effortlessly shoving him aside. He looked furious.

'I…I'm…I'm not afraid of you,' said Ben, fumbling his words. He was lying through his teeth. He was truly intimidated by the sight of Conor's large, overshadowing physique.

Being at least three stone heavier, Conor was colossal in comparison. He truly dominated those he preyed upon with effortless ease.

'Wait…just wait!' Asher hastily spoke. He did not see an alternative to the precarious situation. His troubled expressions continued to spill out in transparent abundance. His eyes narrowed. His dry lips tightened. He could not help but feel the noose tighten around his neck, the twine burning against his flesh, slowly draining the life from him. He was trapped, knowing full well he would have to hand his money over or have it taken by sheer force. 'Fine…fine, I'll hand it over,' he said.

'I haven't all day, Paterson,' said Tom. He tapped his feet against the ground. He watched as Asher began his search for whatever nickels, dimes, and dollars that he had. 'You're nothing.' He hurled the spiteful insult without remorse. He had a gift for making others feel small and insignificant.

'Ok…ok,' spoke Asher. Buzzz! As he searched his pocket for the green notes and coins resting within, he was unexpectedly taken by the school bell.

Ringing loudly, a cold voice bubbled above the clatter. 'Time's a ticking, everyone inside!' The firm voice came from a sharply dressed, suited man in his late forties, wearing a white shirt, stripy brown tie, and oval-shaped glasses. He immediately stamped his authority upon the situation.

Gasppp! Asher exhaled in relief. He was pleased to see Principal Emmanuel Smith.

The rule-abiding school principal was the epitome of order. He had taken over the role of principal at Neptunica Middle School the previous year. The very same year that Asher himself had started middle school.

Little was known about the new principal. He was something of an enigma. It was said that he transferred in from Milton Middle School in Delaware to be closer to his family. It was also known he had a wife and two children, though no one had ever seen them.

'You heard the chief,' said Ben. He, too, was delighted to see the school principal. He relaxed his shoulders, immediately feeling at ease. 'Back off!' He tauntingly grinned before cheekily sticking his tongue out.

'Why you…' Conor was red-faced. He simmered like a teakettle on the boil. He could do absolutely nothing. His breathing rapidly increased. He sweated profusely. He eyed his prey, unable to strike for fear of the repercussions.

It was no secret that Principal Smith was revered as a man of discipline. He took no prisoners when it came to foul play and the breaking of the school rules, which he so greatly cherished. With a contemplative glare, he spoke once again in a hollow tone. 'Mr Paterson, Mr Wilson, it's best you two get going. The bell has gone,' he said.

'Yes, sir,' replied Asher softly. He found it amazing how Principal Smith knew everyone by name, first and last. To him, anyhow, the new principal was seemingly all-knowing.

'Let's go, Murph,' said Tom. He foolishly thought that he had escaped the principal's divine wrath. He was sorely wrong.

'Not you, Mr Watson. You and Mr Murphy have been terrorising the new students,' said Principal Smith. He wagged his finger side to side, signifying his displeasure.

'Let's go, Asher,' whispered Ben. 'Before he changes his mind,' he affirmed.

'He looks very mad,' stated Asher. He was very observant of Principal Smith's body language. Observing the veins popping in his neck, he could tell the principal was not at all happy.

'Detention, three weeks!'

Slowly edging past Principal Smith's firm stature, Asher and Ben could not help but overhear the school's principal erupt with utter annoyance.

'Three whole weeks, but Sir!' Tom was not pleased one bit. His arms flopped up and down like two drowning fish. His freckled face was red with annoyance.

'Fine, if three is not enough, four then,' roared Principal Smith. He was vexed. His finger leapt forth from his greenish suit pocket. His tie swung back and forth as his head bobbed uncontrollably. 'No more, you two will leave those sixth graders alone, or it's suspension, you hear! I find it wicked that in your arrogance, you prey upon the weak.'

'But…but…' babbled Conor. He looked very uneasy as he was scolded.

'I see all, and I've records for both of you as long as my arm, it stops today,' said Principal Smith. He was firm. He had been alerted to Tom and Conor's actions by one teary-eyed sixth grader.

'Ha!' Ben whispered. 'Serves them right, too,' he added quite pleasingly.

'Shhh!' cautioned Asher. Entering the old, whitewashed building, he had to quieten his loud friend.

'Finally, they're both getting a taste of their own medicine,' said Ben. He was right, too. Both Tom and Conor made life absolutely hell for everyone at Neptunica Middle School.

'Arghhh…that sucks,' said Asher. He held his timetable in his hand. He scrolled across the columns to the day marked Wednesday. His first day of term was mid-week. It also meant his first class of the new term was mathematics.

'What room are we in?' questioned Ben. He was not particularly good at being organised.

'2a,' confirmed Asher. 'We have a full hour of math,' he grumbled. He screwed up his nose as he sighed heavily.

'It's not all that bad,' said Ben. He knew fine well that Asher hated algebra, even geometry or any other mathematical branch of study, for that matter. But still, he tried to be positive.

'It is,' protested Asher.

'It is what?' asked Ben.

'It's really all that bad,' said Asher. He had come to find the subject difficult to comprehend. $2x + 1y = 6$, what is x? Correspondingly, what is y? He had spent many wasteful mornings while in sixth grade trying to comprehend the subject to no avail.

Now in seventh grade, however, Asher felt that things would only get much harder. Though he was wrong! 'Hey, who's she?' He nudged Ben with his elbow.

'She's not Mr Ruiz,' said Ben. The previous year was the last for Mr Robert Ruiz. He had decided to retire after thirty-eight years of teaching at Neptunica Middle School.

'Real funny, pal,' said Asher. As he entered room 2a, a young woman pleasantly greeted him. She had chestnut-brown-hair, and grey eyes. He thought her to be at least in her mid-twenties.

'Hi there, my name is Miss Hamilton,' she softly spoke. 'Please take a seat.' Red scarf covering dainty neck, she wore a plain, flowery dress and white heeled shoes. She was quite young, and it was obvious that she was new to the teaching profession.

'Yes, miss,' said Asher. His preconceived assumptions about mathematics were wildly misjudged. He found to his surprise that his new mathematics teacher, Miss Claire Hamilton, was quite gentle and kind.

'Today, we will take things a little slow. I want to get to know each of you individually,' she informed the class.

She was not as strict as Principal Smith, nor was she as dull or cold as some of his other teachers in sixth grade. She most certainly was not as cold as Mr Ruiz, his prior math teacher, who let the textbooks do most of the teaching and hated answering too many questions.

'You see, it's not that hard, for example, 5b equals thirty-five, what is b?' She was all too willing to provide Asher with the help he needed.

'Well, um…' Quite naturally, he struggled at first.

'Well, Asher, five times what is thirty-five?' She simplified the question so that Asher could understand. She had a real gift for teaching.

'Seven, I suppose.'

'Therefore, b is…'

'Seven,' revealed Asher.

'Correct!' Patta! Pat! Pat! She clapped with sheer excitement.

'No way, I did it!' His spine straightened as he sat up in his chair. His cheekbones became a little more defined as a smile crept upon his face. He felt motivated by Miss Hamilton's praise.

'Gosh, it's not that hard at all,' he said, pen wedged between fingers. Reassured, he suddenly felt able to take on the difficulty that was mathematics. With Miss Hamilton to assist him, nothing seemed impossible. Well, anything mathematical that is. His dirty, fair-haired, rosy-cheeked friend, however, needed some convincing. 'Pssst!' he tried to warn him, but to no avail. 'Pssst, Ben!'

Sitting at the back of the class, Ben was busy practicing the art of paper airplane folding. Clink! Clink! Clink! Desk leg wobbling uncontrollably, his stumpy finger slid across one side of paper, and then the other. His masterpiece was launched. Unfortunately, it flew out the window and into the light morning breeze.

'Ben!' Miss Hamilton had spotted him. 'Page 234, 235, and 236 for homework,' she sternly said.

'Great,' he groaned. 'I was just having a little fun.' He slouched back in his chair with a heavy sigh.

Mathematics with Miss Hamilton was followed by science with Mr Michael Woods, preceded by art class with Mr Gareth McDonagh. The first day of the school term quickly came to an end.

Buzzz! 15:15 am arrived quickly, the school bell booming, the first day of term was over.

'Follow me,' instructed Ben. He energetically sprinted along the corridor of Neptunica Middle School, straight in the direction of the assembly hall. It was in the assembly hall that the after-school activity signups for the current term were taking place.

'Hold up,' called Asher. He struggled with his weighty school bag. He had stuffed it full of his books. For him, the first day of term had been incredibly busy.

'Hurry up slow coach,' boomed Ben. 'I don't want to be the last one to sign up for tryouts.' He hoped that this year he would finally be selected for the school's famed baseball team, the Neptunica Stingrays, coached by Jamal Jones.

On the other hand, Asher had no intention of signing up for any of the programmes on offer. He merely tagged along as a spectator of curiosity, unknowingly getting more than he had initially bargained for!

'Gosh!' His attention was instantly absorbed as he entered the assembly hall. He was immediately captivated by a girl with long, wavy, golden hair and a delightful smile. She wore a red and grey striped jumper, matching grey bottoms, and greyish shoes.

'You ok, bud?' asked Ben. He observed the tenseness on his friend's face.

'I'm…I'm just swell,' lied Asher. His arms dangled by his side. His feet tapped repeatedly on the wooden floor beneath like a river dance enthusiast. His sudden shifty posture reflected his unease. He had quite a crush on the girl with blonde hair.

'Isn't that Mandy Fleming over there?' asked Ben, all too aware of his friend's crush.

'Yes, yes, it is,' said Asher with a hard gulp.

'She's looking our way,' uttered Ben.

'Really, I didn't notice,' said Asher. He ran a hand through his thick, jet-black hair. His eyes wandered the room like a pinball machine, wildly alit with activity.

'Be rude not to say hi, we should go over and talk to her,' suggested Ben. He was trying to push his uneasy friend out of his comfort zone.

'Sure,' agreed Asher. 'I mean it would be rude,' he added.

'I'm right behind you, buddy,' said Ben.

Thud! Thud! Thud! On the march, Asher trudged forward five paces before realising that Ben had not followed his lead at all! 'Aren't you coming?' He peered back over his left shoulder. He was surprised to see that his crafty friend had totally deviated in the opposite direction.

'Say hi for both of us, the desk for baseball signups is empty, I'll only be a minute,' informed Ben.

'But, but…'

'You'll be fine,' said Ben. He held up his thumb.

'I won't be fine,' whispered Asher. His mouth dried up. His confidence dwindled as he dragged his size-seven feet onward. He did not want to lose face. He continued toward Mandy. He had the look of a terrified deer caught in the headlights. 'Oh god.' His anxiety grew with every step he took.

Thud! Thud! Thud! Crash! He, at the very last moment, before the point of no return, deflected from the task. His stomach churned. His legs wobbled like jelly. He just had to stop.

'Yoohoo, hi!' A voice suddenly caught Asher's attention.

'Ummm…hello.' He twisted his wiry-framed physique. The sight of a brass trumpet, black and silver flute and beautifully constructed violin in a mahogany metallic varnish caught his focus.

'Do you want to join the music club? It will be so much fun!'

Green eyes peered at him searchingly. A girl with dark, fuzzy brown hair, a round-shaped face, and dimples smiled at him profusely.

'Ummm…' Stunned, he was caught off guard and without an answer. His face began to glow brighter than a red fluorescent light bulb.

Leaning forward, the bubbly, dark-haired seventh grader spoke once more. 'Honestly, you'll not regret it.' She was trying her best to get students to sign up for the after-school music class. The uptake was a little lacking.

'Well, thank you, but...' he stumbled over his words. He caught sight of Mandy. She was on the move. 'Oh no!' he mumbled. Her curvy physique swayed side to side as she moved across the assembly hall toward him. Her golden hair danced back and forth from shoulder to shoulder as she went.

Screech! Screech! Screech! Her greyish shoes squeaked relentlessly against the worn-out wooden floor with each step she took.

He grew even more nervous. 'Yes, yes, I would,' he rapidly spoke. Words began to impulsively spill from his mouth. He had lost all self-control.

Pen put to paper; the girl known as Sarah Reid quickly jotted his name down in her blue notebook. She was quite thrilled. 'That's great,' she said jubilantly.

Most of the students enlisting to take up after-school activities seemed to be more interested in either the physically challenging sports activities or the more typical extracurricular topics, such as the arts and language-related subjects.

'First Tuesday of October, after school, room 9b, I'll see you there,' said Sarah. She handed him a schedule, and every Tuesday and the first and third Thursday of each month were marked out for music class. Having dished out the instructions, she then moved on to the next and only other student waiting in line.

Suddenly, the squeaking stopped. 'I didn't know you liked music, Asher.' It was her. It was Mandy Fleming! Above her lip was the faintest resemblance of a scar. It was covered with a concealer of a kind. At the age of nine, she had had a nasty accident on her bike.

'Ummm...' Pale and shaking all over, he was bewildered. 'Ummm...' Why does she want to talk to me?' he thought. In fact, in all honesty, he was amazed that she remembered his name.

'Well, say something,' she giggled. Her baby blue eyes were mesmerising. She had turned Asher's brain to mush.

'Me…I…I…I mean, I love music,' he said. His soft tone and uneven voice made him sound unconvincing.

Not believing him, she probed further. 'What instrument do you play?' she asked.

This time, he did not hesitate. 'I play the guitar,' he said. His head bobbed left and right, unable to meet her gaze. He took a deep breath to calm himself. He was telling the truth. His dad bought him a guitar two years ago as a Christmas present.

She was intrigued. She wanted to know more. As captain of the dance club, she too loved music. Her cherry-coated lips began to separate again. 'Really, the guitar, what about…'

'Tryouts here I come! This could be it, Ash, I might get on the team.' Steering into their conversation, Ben neither considered his timing nor his manners. He was simply overly excited, but rude.

'Congratulations,' said Mandy. 'Hopefully I'll see you around, Asher, but I really must go.' She had to return to her desk to sign up a few excitedly awaiting students. There was quite a bit of interest in the dance club, especially among the female students.

Seeing that Asher was standing beside the desk for music class signups, Ben had inquisitive questions of his own. 'Ash, are you thinking of joining, buddy?' he asked.

Affirming Ben's suspicions, Asher gently nodded his head. 'Yeah, we better be off,' he said gloomily. He knew he had made a right pig's ear of trying to talk to the one girl in the whole school that he had a crush on.

'Mr Paterson, may I have a word, please!' It was Principal Emmanuel Smith. He stood looming in the school corridor.

'Hi…hi Sir, what did I do?' spoke Asher softly. He began to panic. He thought himself to be in trouble of some kind.

'I'll be just over here,' informed Ben. He moved further down the corridor.

'I wanted to say thank you,' said Principal Smith. His posture eased.

'Whatever for?' responded Asher. He was truly caught off guard by the compliment.

'For standing up for Nicolas Martinez,' informed Principal Smith. He read the confusion upon Asher's diamond-shaped face. 'The sixth grader you intervened to help this morning.'

'But, how did you know?' queried Asher.

'I know all, for all I am,' said Principal Smith. He was quite cryptic in his response. 'You acted out of kindness,' he added.

'Anyone would have helped. The boy, Nicolas, was scared,' said Asher. He did not think much of it. 'Honestly, I should have done more,' he said. In truth, he felt a little shame, for he almost did not intervene at all.

'That is not true at all. It takes a pure soul to selflessly want to help another,' said Principal Smith. 'I see you for what you truly are! Yes, special indeed,' he finished.

'Thanks, Sir,' replied Asher. 'I best get going.' He quickly hurried along the school corridor.

Getting home that evening, he desperately tried to contemplate his reasoning for signing up for music class. 'Why do I get myself into these things?' he muttered, sitting on the edge of his bed.

Strangely, despite his reluctance, and while having no intention of signing up for music class, he was truly decent on the guitar. It was his characteristic shyness and sheer lack of confidence that kept him from pursuing such ends.

'Asherrr!'

Absorbing his attention, a screeching voice arose up the stairs to the summit of his room.

'Hurry yourself down these stairs this instant before your dinner gets cold.' It was his grandmother.

Trudging down the long flight of stairs to the bottom, he unenthusiastically peered into the red-themed kitchen.

'Your dinner is on the table, and yes, that no-good father of yours has sent you another postcard,' informed Nancy. 'He called to tell me not to give it to you until today.' Her silver hair dangled over her green eyes. She stood firm, giving him a long, cold look.

'So, he didn't forget after all!' Asher was excited to say the least.

She had received the postcard three days past. However, upon her son-in-law's instructions she did not inform Asher of its arrival. Mike had sent it. He had not forgotten his son's birthday.

Igniting with joy, Asher zoomed across the room like a bolt of lightning. 'Let's see,' he said with joy.

'No! Pipe down,' barked Nancy. Rolling her eyes, she raised her reading glasses to the brim of her nose. She responded quite sternly. 'You'll get it after your dinner.' She sneered as she pulled the postcard out of her fluffy white cardigan. Curious, she began reading the contents.

'Ok, Gran,' said Asher. He scurried down his roast beef and potato dinner before asking for the postcard once again, this time in a more polite manner. 'Please, may I have the postcard?' He let a row of white teeth show as his lips parted, as he attempted a forced smile.

'No,' responded Nancy once more. Exhaling, her wrinkled hands slipped into a pair of pink oven gloves. Bang! The oven door slammed open.

'What's that, Grandma?' he asked curiously.

'More than you deserve,' growled Nancy. She lifted the sponge cake out of the oven. She then proceeded to place the cake on the kitchen table. She lit up a single blue candle that she had positioned in the centre of the cake. 'Happy birthday,' she added.

'Gosh, thanks,' said Asher softly. He was a little amazed that she went to the trouble. He recalled that last year she had made no effort at all to celebrate his birthday.

'Just eat up,' groaned Nancy. Thud! She slammed a white, flower-patterned plate down upon the solid pine table. The wrinkles upon her face tightened. Screwing up her mouth, it appeared she was making more of an effort than she could bear.

'Now, may I have the postcard, please?' Asher was losing his patience. His hands drummed off the side of his thighs restlessly.

This time, his grandmother released her grip on the postcard. She set the postcard down on the kitchen table. 'Your father also sent this!' She took a brown box from atop the kitchen counter.

Asher tore the brown parcel apart and ripped the box to pieces in his excitement to see what was inside. He found a beautiful Egyptian scarab box with twenty-four tiny scarab beetles inside, fake, of course, but beautiful, nonetheless. Gold, green, blue, red, they came in a wonderful variety of colours.

Snap! He plucked the picture postcard from the kitchen table. He then hurried back up the old creaking stairs to his bedroom. Gulp! Swallowing one last chunk of dry sponge cake, he began scanning the picture on the back. 'Wow, the pyramids!' The simple picture ignited his young imagination with wonder.

He could not help but wish that he were there to see the colossus, triangular-shaped masterpieces of ancient Egyptian architecture for himself. He turned over the picture postcard and began reading the message:

Dear Asher,

Hope your new term at school is going well, staying out of trouble, I hope. Anyways, we have just come across a major discovery! Well, so the boys say. We have come across an undiscovered tomb. Who knows, perhaps we'll find some old mummies. As you know, we have been digging at a location called the Valley of the Kings for just over two years now. Anyway, just yesterday I was taking the guided tour and was fascinated by the vivid inscriptions within some of the other tombs in the valley. Some even contained within them text from the Book of the Dead! Anyway, I will be away for a while, but I hope to see you soon.

P.S. Happy birthday, hope you like the gift.

Asher felt deflated, his arms dangled loosely as he let slip the picture postcard from his grasp. His eyes welled up. The pen scribbled message jotted upon the postcard was abundantly clear. His dad would be gone even longer than he had initially expected. 'Happy birthday to me,' he mumbled sullenly.

-Chapter 2-

Baseball Tryouts

Over the next two weeks, Asher slowly adjusted to life in seventh grade at Neptunica Middle School. The adjustments were not easy either; the pests, the school bullies, Tom Watson, and Conor Murphy hounded his every movement. It was mostly crude comments or sneering, mostly words, but hurtful words, nevertheless. He was sure his unpleasant interactions with the school bullies would only escalate over the school year.

But the school bullies were not the only thing plaguing Asher's mind. One burning thought that ate away at him over the last two weeks was about his dad. The most recent picture postcard from Egypt, the very postcard that he had received on his thirteenth birthday, had not been the most welcoming of news. One question played repeatedly in his young mind: how much longer would his dad be away from home? He longed to have some sort of resemblance to a father-son relationship.

At school, the extracurricular activities were about to swing into force. Asher was to begin his music lessons in a few days. He was still entirely unsure about the whole thing.

He put his reservations about having joined the music club in the back of his mind, for today was a big day for his shorter, dirty, fair-haired friend, Ben. Being the 2nd of October, that meant that today baseball tryouts would be taking place after school.

'This is it! This is it! It is baseball time,' said Ben rapidly. He was pumped up. He could not stop thinking about the whole ordeal. Ever since he had put his name on paper in the assembly hall two weeks previously, it was the only thing he had rambled on about nonstop.

'We're late,' alluded Asher. As per usual, he and Ben were running a little late. They had just missed the school bell. Rows of empty yellow buses lined the street outside the old, whitewashed building.

'Old grumpy is up ahead,' said Ben. He panted for air as he hurried across the street.

'Hurry, hurry, let's go.' Asher was quick on his feet; he was a few paces ahead of Ben. His blue striped school bag rested on one shoulder, and a gym bag on the other. Twice a week, he had to partake in physical education with Coach Jamal Jones.

'What time do you call this?' groaned Principal Smith. He tapped his foot on the concrete beneath. He stood beside a flagpole, atop said flagpole fluttering in the morning breeze was liberty herself, the old stars and stripes.

'Sorry, Sir,' answered Asher.

'A minute and thirty seconds, you're both late, hmmm…' Principal Smith thought on the matter before waving them inside. 'I don't want to keep repeating myself, early tomorrow, both of you.' He drummed his index finger on the dial of his watch to affirm his point.

'Yes, Sir,' replied Asher. He nodded his head in agreement.

'Gosh, does he ever let up?' moaned Ben. He whispered in Asher's ear, signalling his discontent as he opened one brown door to enter the school building.

'Something to say, Mr Wilson?' Principal Smith inquired with a contemplative glare. His black framed, oval-shaped glasses rested on the tip of his nose. He pulled a notepad from his blue blazer pocket. Click! Pen in hand, he was all too ready to enforce the school rules. Indeed, many of said rules he had written himself. He was the judge, jury, and executioner at Neptunica Middle School.

'No, Sir, I was just saying what a stand-up person you are,' said Ben jestingly. He stuck up his thumb. He was pushing it. The added smile did nothing for him either.

'Insolent…rude…get a move on now, Mr Wilson,' Principal Smith thundered. He watched as Asher and Ben disappeared into the old building. 'Now, I, too, may get a move on. I've only a whole universe to tend to!' He had a lot on his mind.

The first lesson of the day for Asher was physical education. Entering the sports hall, he immediately came across Coach Jamal Jones. The dark-skinned coach was tall, being six feet six inches in height, and he towered over many of the other teachers in the school.

'Hey now, let's be getting a move on,' said Coach Jones. He began clapping his hands. 'Time's a ticking,' he added. The bald coach was competitive by nature. 'We're going to run this court end to end.' Stopwatch in hand, a silver whistle hung from his neck.

Coach Jones was already dressed for the occasion. He wore a navy tracksuit. He was thin-built, and he kept himself in decent shape. Every morning, just after seven o'clock, he hit the streets of Neptune City for a jog.

'Oh, I hope I can keep up. I've had one too many milkshakes lately,' said Ben. He rubbed his slightly round tummy. He loved to indulge a little too much at the local dinner, The Golden Spoon Diner. A lovely old couple named Jack and Rosie Crisby ran it.

'Hey now, you've got to be impressing me today,' stated Coach Jones. 'It's baseball tryouts after school.' Though competitive, he was a fair man by nature. He felt everyone deserved an opportunity to shine.

When he was younger, Coach Jones had been a baseball player himself. He knew a thing or two about the game, having played in the minor baseball leagues. He even went pro, but that did not last long after a career-derailing injury to his neck that he obtained in a car accident.

'Oh, I hope I get picked,' said Ben optimistically. He loved baseball. He wanted so much to be selected for the school's baseball team, the Neptunica Stingrays.

'You'll be great,' said Asher encouragingly. 'I'll be there to cheer you on.' In the tough spots, Ben always had his back. He only felt it right to return the favour.

'No laughing either,' said Ben. He was feeling the pressure, though he usually thrived under tough circumstances.

'Alright, alright, go get changed,' said Coach Jones. He snapped his fingers. 'We don't have all day.' He wanted to get proceedings underway.

For the next twenty minutes, Asher and Ben ran their feet off. They sprinted from one end of the sports hall to the other. With each passing run, another student dropped out, and each time, Coach Jones blew his whistle. The goal was to see who could get over the line. To see who could last the longest. It was a test of endurance.

In a way, Coach Jones had planned the exercise to get a feel for the limits of each student, especially those he coached. He was the coach of the baseball and basketball teams. He had a hand in most physical activities that took place at Neptunica Middle School. The school had been underfunded for years. Mayor Robert Adams had not improved the situation either since his election to office.

'Keep it up! Keep it up!' Coach Jones roared encouragingly. He was pushing the students to the limit.

'I...I...I just cannot go on,' wheezed Ben. His whole body ached. His lungs felt heavy. He had caved after twenty-two minutes of running. He reached into his pocket to retrieve his blue inhaler. He took a deep puff, his chest popped in and out like an accordion.

'I'm feeling it too, Ben,' said Asher. He was sweating and red in the face. But he was not done quite yet. He stuck it out until Coach Jones called time. He was one of four to go the distance.

'Great work out there, people,' praised Coach Jones. 'Now hit the showers.' One final blow on his silver whistle, and that was it. The lesson was concluded.

'I hope I didn't look too bad out there,' said Ben with worry on his face. He felt disappointed in himself. Despite trying his utmost best, he fell short. He did not last the whole thirty minutes. He was angry with himself for throwing in the towel, so to speak.

'Nobody throws a ball like you,' said Asher. 'You've a mean left hand.' He referred to the fact that Ben was left-handed, which was rare.

'You think so?' asked Ben. He felt motivated by Asher's words.

'I know so,' said Asher. 'I've got the bruise to prove it.' He began to laugh. It was just two weeks ago that he had been smacked on the side with a baseball. Not that Ben had meant to do so at all. He still had a faded bruise from the incident.

Exiting the sports hall, Asher and Ben headed toward their next lesson, which was mathematics with the new teacher, Claire Hamilton. She was highly intelligent and, most importantly, pleasant. Like Coach Jones, she pushed the students to the limit. She stretched the intellectual capacity of the students in her class, as was her goal.

'I've got to be at the top of my game today for baseball tryouts,' said Ben. 'When signing up two weeks ago, there were quite a few names on the list.' He was worried that the competition would be very stiff.

'Hey losers! Did you see any familiar names on that list?' It was the ginger-haired beanpole of a boy, Tom Watson. He had been eavesdropping on the conversation that Asher and Ben were having. He was up to his usual no-good antics. 'Get over here, Murph,' he barked.

'T…T…Tom!' Startled, Asher began to bite on his bottom lip. Suddenly, he felt very anxious. Confrontations with Tom and Conor normally did not go well for him. Since the new term had started, they had been on his back. They just would not let up.

The smaller, rounder Conor Murphy trudged forward. He was eating a chocolate bar.

'Give me that,' snapped Tom. He snatched the chocolate bar, tossing it in the bin.

'Hey, that was breakfast,' protested Conor. He moaned and groaned at losing his snack.

'Shut up,' said Tom. The freckled-faced menace was as nasty as always. 'You'll have some competition this afternoon.' Provokingly, he shoved his finger against Ben's chest.

'Oh yeah, really,' said Ben. 'Are you thinking of trying out for the baseball team?' He was curious now. He never knew Tom to be sporty at all.

'Not me, Murph here is a natural at baseball,' alluded Tom. He folded his long arms, he looked so smug with himself. He had convinced his larger accomplice, Conor Murphy, to try out for the baseball team.

'You've got to be kidding,' chuckled Ben. 'There was me thinking I was in trouble.' He was pushing his luck.

'I wouldn't, if you know what's good for you,' warned Tom. He snapped his fingers, signalling to his larger lackey.

'Yeah, if you know what's good for you,' snarled Conor. Springing into action, he gripped Ben by his shirt.

'Get off me,' struggled Ben. He wriggled, trying to break loose. 'Let go,' he said loudly. He was creating quite a bit of noise as the school corridor emptied of students.

'Leave him, let's go, Murph,' ordered Tom. 'Let these losers be.' He was suddenly alarmed by the appearance of Principal Smith. He spotted the principal at the end of the corridor. He felt a cold sweat, for he was already on the principal's radar.

'Losers,' repeated Conor. He released his grip on Ben's shirt.

'I'll be seeing you around,' said Tom. He pointed his index finger at Asher in one last act of intimidation before fleeing the scene.

'I hate those jackasses,' scolded Ben. He was annoyed, to say the least.

'Yeah, me too,' affirmed Asher. 'You know Conor is only trying out for the baseball team because of you.' He knew the school bullies better than anyone.

'Yeah, I know,' said Ben. 'It's sad, really.'

'What is?' said Asher.

'It's sad the overgrown big goon can't think for himself,' exclaimed Ben. He knew that behind the scenes, it was Tom who had put Conor up to the task.

The end of the day could not come quickly enough for Ben. Having changed clothes, he was ready for baseball tryouts.

'Wow! Cool jersey,' said Asher. 'Where did you get it?' He could see that Ben was fully kitted and prepared for tryouts.

'Dad bought me it,' answered Ben. He wore a baseball jersey with red stripes and the number one printed on the back. Of course, it was a jersey of one of his favourite local teams, named the Neptune Dirt Devils. 'Dad's been flat out practicing with me the last two weeks.' He had been training hard.

For the last two weeks, Ben had been up at Red River Park. He had been working on his pitching and a little on his batting skills. He had prepared as much as he could.

'Oh! Your dad is great. I wish my dad…' Asher's mood began to dip as he thought about his father, Mike Paterson, or lack thereof. But then he shook the thoughts off. 'Never mind all that. Just give it your all today.' He was there to support Ben, as any good friend would.

'Let's do this,' said Ben. He exited the big brown doors leading to the outside of the old, whitewashed building.

'Show them, Ben, show them what you can do.' Asher chased after Ben to the baseball field adjacent to the old building. The field was surrounded by a metal fence. He stood at the gate leading onto the field of play. He watched with the utmost curiosity.

A large group of people had gathered. Coach Jones stood in the dugout. Clipboard in hand, he was ready to get things started. He was joined by his assistant coach, Jonathan Adams.

"Alright, people, let's get this show on the road,' shouted Coach Jones. He was not one to waste time. 'We'll start with warmups.' Warmups involved static stretches and short sprints. Pretty routine stuff to say the least.

'I've got this,' said Ben, taking a deep breath. He could feel a little sweat beginning to form on his forehead. The run earlier in the day had gotten his motor running, he just hoped there was enough gas in the tank to get through baseball tryouts.

Warmups lasted less than ten minutes. Then Coach Jones blew his silver whistle. 'Alright, that'll do it, time for the sixty-yard dash.' He held up five fingers. 'I want five lines, five people to each line,' he articulated.

The twenty-four boys who had shown up for baseball tryouts were slow to get moving. Well, nearly all of them!

'Hey, bud,' said Ben. He shook one student's hand, then the hand of another. 'The name's Ben.' He quickly gathered the names of the two boys he had just met, one being Lucas, the other Sebastián. 'Let's get into a line over here.' He pointed to a white line painted onto the green grass.

'Can I join?' a third boy asked.

'Yeah, me too,' a fourth boy added.

Quite quickly, the two other boys jumped at the opportunity to join Ben and his group.

'Sure thing,' said Ben. He was more than happy to let them join. Now his group had five.

Unbeknownst to him, the other four groups followed his lead. Soon, there were five groups eager to go. The smell of competition was brewing in the air.

'Very nice, great sportsmanship,' stated Coach Jones as he observed Ben's actions. He jotted away in his notepad. He then walked down the line. 'Team one, team two, team three…' He issued each of the five teams a number. 'Team one will go on my first whistle, then team two, and so forth,' he said.

'But coach, we've only got four!' One boy waved his hand in the air.

'Who are we missing?' said Coach Jones. He began looking through a list of names. He knew for a fact that twenty-five boys had signed up for tryouts.

'Out of the way, Paterson!' It was Tom Watson, and accompanying him was Conor Murphy. They were late to the party, figuratively speaking.

'I told you we should've cut that sixth grader loose,' groaned Conor.

Of course, Tom and Conor had been held up as they had tormented another helpless student. They had garnered a reputation at the school. A reputation that Principal Smith had begun to catch on to. Their shenanigans were starting to catch his attention.

In fact, it had been on the very first day of term that Principal Smith had issued Tom and Conor with detention. It was not much of a deterrent.

'You are late. You missed warmups,' said Coach Jones. 'Get to the line.' He shook his head disapprovingly. He was not pleased at all. One thing he hated more than anything was lateness. Stopwatch in hand, he wanted to get straight down to business. 'We're going to be doing a sixty-yard dash,' he said.

'Here we go again,' moaned Ben. Running was not his forte. He was not the worst by any stretch of the imagination, but he was certainly not the best either. Adding to his worry was the fact that he was part of team one. He would be part of the first five students to sprint sixty yards.

'Ben Wilson!' Coach Jones spoke firmly, observing Ben's disgruntled reaction. 'Get with the programme, work on that speed, my man.' Not that Ben knew, but Coach Jones had been impressed with his leadership skills. But other qualities were also needed to make the cut for the baseball team.

'Hey loser, have you come to watch your pathetic friend lose?' said Tom. He was not done aggravating Asher. He took hold of his arm.

'Leave him be!' It was Mandy Fleming. She and a red-headed girl headed straight for the stands. Quite a few students had turned out to watch.

'Oh, we're just fooling around,' said Tom as if butter would not melt in his mouth. He followed her in pursuit. 'I've something to ask you! Did you see the flyers up for the dance?' Flyers had been placed all over the school. Being the start of October, the Halloween dance was fast approaching. The school committee had decided to put on some festivities for the students.

Dusting himself off, Asher remained by the gate leading to the baseball field. He did not want to be up in the stands. Not with Tom howling down his neck. No, he was happy to watch things unfold from exactly where he was.

He watched as Coach Jones pressed his silver whistle against his lips. He could see the anxiety arise on Ben's face.

'Come on,' whispered Asher. He hoped that his friend would make the baseball team. He knew how much it meant to Ben.

The whistle went! Off went the first five students. Of the five, Ben was the only one to run at an angle with his body leaning forward. Head down, he tried his hardest. Despite giving his all, he was not the quickest. His time was just under nine seconds. He was the third fastest in his group.

'You nailed that, Lucas,' praised Ben. His face was beetroot red. He shook the hand of the boy who came first. He then shook the hand of the boy who placed second.

Despite feeling a little disappointed, he could not help but praise the two boys who were faster than him. 'Don't worry, we'll get ourselves back into the running, Sebastián.' He even had time to put a smile on the face of the boy in his group who had come dead last.

'You suck!' Tom was being a pest from the stands. He knew no bounds at all.

'Sit your as…sit down!' Coach Jones was not having any of it. He shook his head disapprovingly before getting back to the task at hand. He took a few notes. Once more, Ben's conduct and behaviour impressed him. Whistle blowing again, team two went, then team three, then team four.

'Out of my way,' roared Conor. He shoved one boy who stood too close to him.

Whistle going one more time off went team five. Conor came dead last, his time being well over ten seconds.

After two more sixty-yard dashes had concluded, Coach Jones then wanted to analyse each player's ability to focus, to hit a target, and find a consistent release point.

'Alright, time to play catch,' said Coach Jones. 'Loosen those shoulders.' He instructed the students to do a few arm exercises. 'Remember, we warm up to throw, don't throw to warm up.' It was very sound advice.

He began to pair students up. 'Alright, Lucas pair up with Oliver, Conor pair up with Ben…' He went through the complete list. He paired up with the last boy of the twenty-five in attendance.

'Oh great,' groaned Ben. He did not like the idea of being paired up with Conor one little bit.

'Each person will take a mitt,' said Coach Jones. Each pair was given a baseball mitt and one ball.

'Let's go, throw it, throw it,' shouted Conor. He stuck his tongue out in an antagonising manner.

Rotating the shoulder and lifting the leg, Ben threw a soft ball with his left hand. It did not give the big brute Conor all that much trouble as it landed in his baseball mitt.

'Good, you hit the target, but work on that technique,' instructed Coach Jones. He stuck up his thumb.

'Yeah, work on your technique,' said Conor. He began to laugh. He threw the ball back without any real technique or skill himself.

'Alright, you want it, you got it!' The time for fun and games was over. Ben took the baseball and positioned his fingers across the c-shape. Middle finger and index finger stretching across the seams of the baseball, he positioned his thumb on the seam underneath the ball. 'Eat this!' He rotated his shoulder. His body movement was very fluent. He released the ball. His middle finger came off the surface of the ball at the very last moment.

His control was impeccable. He threw the baseball at great velocity.

'Oh, oh no!' All Conor could see coming towards him were four continuously rotating seams. The ball shot at him in a straight line. He was a little slow in his reaction as the ball bounced from his mitt and into his gut. He was winded a little.

'Super, that's what I'm talking about, much better,' complimented Coach Jones. Four-seam fastball was one of the most common baseball throws, but he appreciated how Ben conducted himself. He could see that the technique was there.

'You did that on purpose,' snorted Conor. He was foaming at the mouth, and he charged at Ben like a bull.

'Hey now, cut that out,' demanded Coach Jones. He intercepted him. 'There's no place for anger on the baseball field, sportsmanship is key.' He was not best pleased at all. 'Take a seat and cool off.' He pointed to the dugout.

Off trudged a very annoyed Conor. In truth, he did not care if he made the Neptunica Stingrays team. All he was concerned about was that Ben did not.

The next order of business for Coach Jones was to get specific, position-specific. Most of the players on the field he knew from sixth grade, so he had a fair idea already as to what positions each might suit.

Still, each boy got a chance to play infield and outfield positions. Each got a chance in the batting cage and the pitcher's bullpen.

'Very nice work.' Coach Jones was not so much impressed with Ben's ability in the outfield positions, but in the batting cage, he saw good skill. Though in the pitcher's bullpen, he saw Ben's potential to be great!

'Go on, you can do it,' yelled Asher. He could not help but cheer in support of Ben. His commitment was shown in the fact that he had been standing now for close to forty minutes. He hoped more than anything that Ben would make the cut.

'Alright, alright, gather around,' said Coach Jones. 'One final test! Each person will line up and throw their best pitch.' He held a hickory baseball bat. He was ready to put the young students to the test.

'Who's batting?' the boy Lucas questioned the coach.

'Well, me,' said Coach Jones. He had a grin from ear to ear. He put the students on edge. He could see the pressure arise on their young faces.

'This is going to be fun,' said Ben sarcastically. He took a hard gulp.

'Well, I'm glad you think so,' said Coach Jones. 'Because my main man John here is going to be the catcher.' The assistant coach crouched directly behind the home plate.

It was one final chance for each boy to make his mark. To etch his name onto the starting team of the Neptunica Stingrays.

The first boy went. Then the second. The numbers dwindled until there were only four left.

'Nice, Sebastián,' said Coach Jones. Baseball bat in hand, he had struck the baseball thrown by Sebastián, but still appreciated the skill behind the boy's curveball.

'Nice work, bud,' said Ben, praising Sebastián. After Sebastián, next up was Lucas. The blond-headed boy had shown his worth thus far.

'Not bad, not bad, Lucas,' said Coach Jones. He had been impressed with Lucas's batting skills, speed, and focus, but found him relatively fair at pitching.

'Give me that ball!' Next up was Conor. He snatched the baseball from one student's hand. He was very rude. It was clear he was not much of a team player.

'You better get this right,' boomed Tom, shouting from the stands. He was losing his temper. His friend was not doing very well; that much was obvious.

'Oh hell!' Coach Jones felt the cowhide slam against his hip. 'Sit yourself down, boy.' He was not impressed with Conor at all, there was no technique or skill to his throw. It took the coach a little time to get back into batting position.

'Wish me luck, Ash,' shouted Ben. He waved to Asher.

'Good luck,' yelled Asher. He was rooting for Ben. 'Oh, here, bud, use this for luck.' He quickly rummaged through his school bag. He took out a baseball. The very one Ben had given him for his birthday. The very one with the National Baseball Hall of Fame logo imprinted upon it. 'Catch!' He tossed the baseball with great velocity.

'Got…got it.' Ben caught the baseball. 'Thanks, Ash.' He waved the ball above his head.

'Wow! Your friend should have tried out for the team,' said Coach Jones. He was impressed with Asher's throw. 'Alright Ben, hopefully the best has been left to last,' he said.

Next up was none other than Ben himself! He had watched the other twenty-four contenders take their best pitch. He knew he had to give his absolute finest performance to be in contention for a spot on the Neptunica Stingrays team.

'I can do this,' said Ben. Taking a deep breath, he stepped up to the pitcher's mound. His left arm was ready to go like a well-oiled machine. He had put in the work up at Red River Park, now was the time to pursue the American Dream. He took one glance at the stars and stripes atop the flagpole, which fluttered in the distance. He was as ready as he was ever going to be.

'Come on, Ben, bring it,' challenged Coach Jones. The assistant coach, John, had been given little work to do as a catcher thus far.

'You suck!' Tom shouted another foul comment from the stands.

Two fingers split apart, Ben took a final deep breath, and then he let loose. Shoulders and feet moving fluently, he lifted his knee as he released the ball. The ball's backspin and deceptively slower velocity, followed by a sharp drop, was enough to catch Coach Jones asleep at the wheel!

The cowhide baseball slammed into the baseball mitt of the assistant coach, Jonathan Adams. 'Oh boy, oh boy, he got you, Jamal.' The assistant coach was ecstatic as he made the catch.

'Woah babe!' Coach Jones was pleased as he smiled. He was full of delight and joy.

'Holy moly!'

'You did it!'

Lucas and Sebastián returned the good sportsmanship that Ben had shown to them. The three leaped up and down at the very impressive throw.

'Yes, Ben, you blew them away.' Asher, too, was ecstatic as he watched the entire situation unfold, though he was not watching his back! Thump! He found himself face down in the mud.

'Watch your step, Paterson.' Tom was not best pleased at how things had turned out at all.

'Babe, you made the team,' informed Coach Jones. He was planning to release an official list later in the week of the Neptunica baseball team's starting lineup, but his emotions had gotten the better of him.

'Yes! Thanks, coach,' said Ben excitedly. His face lit up with utter joy. 'But why call me babe?' he asked.

'Isn't that obvious? I haven't seen a left arm like that since Ruth himself,' said Coach Jones. It was a big compliment indeed.

Retrieving his baseball, Ben rushed off the field of play. He had seen the commotion that was taking place. 'Hey, jackass, leave him alone.' He rushed forward to Asher's aid, but suddenly felt two big hands push him aside.

'Beat it!' Conor pushed him as he shoved his way past. He had a very grim face indeed. After not taking some of Coach Jones's criticism too well, he just wanted to get off the field.

'You're an imbecile, Murph.' Tom did not have any kind words for his lackey. Their plans to sabotage Ben had failed.

'Let's just go,' said Conor. His ego had taken a hard knock. He had failed miserably. In trying his best to thwart Ben's efforts to join the baseball team, he only found himself insufficient.

'Give me your hand,' said Ben. He hauled Asher to his feet.

'You were superb out there,' Asher congratulated. He dusted himself down. Despite feeling embarrassed, he praised Ben.

'Thanks, bud,' replied Ben. 'Here's your ball.' He held up in his left hand the baseball he had picked up while at the National Baseball Hall of Fame. The very one he had given to Asher as a present.

'You keep it,' said Asher. 'It will bring you good luck as a stingray.'

'Thanks, bud,' said Ben. All said and done, he had made the cut. He was now a fully-fledged player for the Neptunica Stingrays.

-Chapter 3-
Vipers

'July 28th, August 28th, September 28th, October 28th…'
Asher's weary eyes fell upon red and orange flames, and he studied one science-themed pin-up calendar of a space rocket. The pin-up calendar hung from a crooked nail wedged into his bedroom door.

'Three months,' he solemnly said. He took a firm grip of a black ballpoint pen. He marked off the 28th of October with two diagonal black lines. 'I miss you, Dad,' he whispered.

Thud! Thud! Thud! Rubbing his eyelids, his feet drummed against old, wooden floorboards as he veered across the landing. He entered a cream and blue painted, seaside-inspired bathroom. He swiftly began his daily ritual, firstly turning the sink tap. He then spread white and red toothpaste across the green and white bristled toothbrush.

Swish! Swish! Swish! Gurgle! Gurgle! Fifteen minutes of self-preparation were followed by a loud crackling roar.

'Asher!' Nancy yelled. Her voice carried up the stairs to the bathroom.

'Yes, Grandma,' he yelled. He tilted his head back to look up at the white ceiling before exhaling heavily. He found her to be irritating, as was the norm.

'Come down this instant,' she demanded. Her voice crackled with strain.

'Five minutes,' he shouted. He was almost done. He wiped away the white toothpaste clinging to the corners of his mouth.

'Now! Get your skinny behind down here,' roared Nancy. 'Best eat your breakfast before you're late for school.' She had

been getting calls from Principal Emmanuel Smith. He was
not best pleased at Asher's tardiness.

Teeth shining, hair brushed, Asher wore a blue chequered
shirt, denim jeans, and plain white trainers. He was ready.
'Fine, I'll be right there, Grandma.' Bumpety! Bumpety!
Bump! He stormed down the stairs, his hand sliding along the
wooden banister, the friction irritating his palm.

'Well, well, well, at long last…'

As he stood in the frame of the kitchen doorway, he was met
by his grandmother's solid, penetrating gaze.

'I won't tell you again, it's on the table,' growled Nancy. Her
wrinkled hands pulled her fluffy brown cardigan tight. She
slumped her plump body to one side. 'Eat up, eat up,' she
spoke with urgency, all the while looking at a clock hanging on
the wall.

'Looks tasty,' said Asher, licking his chops. He eyed up a
bowl of cereal, a banana, and a glass full of orange juice.
'Thank you,' he added.

He was overly courteous. Screechhh! He quickly took a seat.
He took hold of a stainless-steel spoon. Opening his mouth,
he then took a bite of delicious honey oats. Crunch! Crunch!
Crunch! His jaws bounced up and down, his taste buds were
pleasantly satisfied.

'You need to listen to me, boy,' snapped Nancy. The
wrinkles upon her old face tightened. 'I'm sick of shouting to
get your attention.' She wagged her finger furiously.

Six whole minutes passed upon the clock up on the wall. All
the while being scolded, Asher sat in silence, enjoying the
most important meal of the day.

'Time's ticking,' said Nancy. She lifted Asher's half-eaten bowl of cereal from the kitchen table without warning. 'Off to school with you.' She ran a tight ship.

'Hey, I wasn't done,' groaned Asher. He still held the silver spoon in his hand. He always felt uneasy around his grandmother. She could be mean at times, even if that was not her intent. He got the feeling that she did not entirely like him, as awful as that thought was.

'One more thing…' Nancy was stopped in her tracks.

Ratta tat tat! Ratta tat tat! Ratta tat tat! There was continuous knocking at the front door. Rufff! Scruffy, Asher's bushy-tailed dog, began barking loudly.

'Shush mutt.' Nancy swung a tea towel to silence the big, fluffy, half breed. It was tied up in the hall leading to the backyard.

'That'll be the postman,' said Asher with excitement. He sprang from his chair. He zoomed across the tiled kitchen, into the hall. He quickly pulled the front door open, the door hinges whaled as he did so. Creakkk! His beaming smile sharply dissolved. It was not the postman at all. 'Hi Ben,' he said unenthusiastically.

'Are you ready, buddy?' asked Ben. He spun an orange yo-yo up and down.

'Two seconds,' said Asher. He put on one navy woollen coat; he then snatched his blue striped school bag from the kitchen counter. He was quickly off. 'Goodbye, Gran,' he shouted, before slamming the front door behind him.

'Why the gloomy look?' queried Ben. He put his orange yo-yo in his school bag.

'Still no word from Dad. It's been weeks since the arrival of the last postcard,' Asher informed him. The last postcard had troubled him greatly. He knew his dad would be away longer than expected, but exactly how much longer he knew not. He had hoped at the very least to have received another postcard by now.

'How long has he been gone anyhow?' asked Ben.

'Three whole months,' confirmed Asher, quite dully. The last time he had seen his dad, Mike, was the 28th of July. His dad had only been home for a combined total of three weeks the entire year, stretching over two visits.

The two, Asher and his dad, had grown apart. Like night and day, their connection was minimal, something that Asher wished would change for the better. He wanted a father in his life.

'Gosh, that's rough, sorry,' said Ben sincerely. Crunch! He took a great big bite of a succulent green apple.

Buzzz! Asher quickly reached the outskirts of Neptunica Middle School, and the sight of anxious students scurrying toward the salvation of two brown, rectangular-shaped doors had caused him to panic. 'The bell has gone,' he gasped. His eyes bulged with alarm. 'Hurry, Ben,' he instructed.

Feet steering across the freshly cut school grass, they both raced forward.

'Look who's on patrol.' Ben pointed to the front of the school building. Thud! He tossed his half-eaten apple to the ground.

Roaring, looming at the front entrance in a grey formal suit was none other than Principal Smith. He instructed all sixth, seventh, and eighth graders to make haste inside the old, whitewashed building. 'Ten, nine, eight, hurry now, hurry,' he spoke, urging students to move quickly. His head moved back and forth. He watched the dial on his brown leather-strapped watch religiously. 'Six, five, four, hurry or you'll see me in detention, three, two, one!'

Despite their best efforts, both Asher and Ben had failed to make the cut.

'Late,' spoke Principal Smith. He raised his right hand before them like a control barrier, purposefully blocking their path. He had forcefully stopped them from entering the timeworn, whitewashed building. 'I have warned you two several times this term already,' he said.

'Come on,' Ben sighed. He threw his arms up in complete frustration.

'What was that, Mr Wilson?' Principal Smith probed. He put his hand to his ear. He disliked Ben's tone.

'We're only a minute late…'

'Shush,' intercepted Asher. He nudged his elbow against Ben's side to render him quiet.

'You know the school rules,' said Principal Smith. 'Wrote them myself. Balance must be found between the order and chaos.' He puffed out his chest, he did so with a sense of pride.

'Sorry, Sir,' apologised Asher. He understood that Principal Smith had been somewhat lenient. Both he and Ben had been late a few times this term already.

'Hmmm…' Taking another look at his watch, Principal Smith had a change of mind. 'I've warned you two before, lateness is not something I tolerate, one more time and that's it! I've already called your parents on the matter.' There was no confusion about his warning. 'This time you may go, the next I won't be so lenient, now hurry,' he said.

'You mean my grandmother,' said Asher.

'Yes, your grandmother. I know your father is a little unreachable. He is in Egypt, I believe,' said Principal Smith. He was aware that Asher's mother had long since passed.

'How…how did you know?' asked Asher, a little perplexed. He rubbed the back of his neck; he did not understand how Principal Smith knew his dad was in Egypt.

'I know all,' said Principal Smith. He smirked as he drummed his index finger on the dial of his watch. 'Well, as I mentioned, I'll overlook you being late this time.' He cherished the school rules, but that did not mean he had no compassion. He cared for the students of Neptunica Middle School.

'Thanks, Sir,' said Asher. He was quite respectful.

'Yeah, thanks,' added Ben. 'You're a lifesaver.' He squeezed down on his blue inhaler before taking a deep breath.

Thud! Thud! Thud! Feet drumming forward, Asher and Ben hurried towards a brown rectangular-shaped door and went inside. Trainers drumming on a square-patterned corridor, they rushed in the direction of the history class.

'Mr McNulty will eat us alive,' said Ben with great alarm. Worry crept upon his face.

Grouchy at the best of times, Mr Elliott McNulty was a small, grey-haired, plump man in his late fifties. He was intolerant of tardiness, even more so than the principal. He also had a Napoleon complex. He made up for his small stature by having a fiery temper and domineering behaviour.

'We're in room 3c,' said Asher. He carefully scanned his timetable. Unfortunately, he was not paying much attention to where his size-seven feet were taking him. Bang! Clumsily, his aquiline-shaped nose slammed against the shoulder of one deeply irritated student. 'Ouch,' he yelped.

He had not just slammed into any student, but the one student he had been going out of his way to avoid.

'Watch it, Paterson!'

Asher looked up to meet two burning hazel eyes looking at him. He then felt two scrawny hands take hold of his navy-blue coat. Thud! He was harshly shoved backward. His school bag dropped from his shoulder to the ground. He was consumed with fear. It was none other than Tom Watson!

'Sor…sorry,' he muttered. His tone was shaky. His blue eyes hung low in despair.

'That won't do, Paterson! Do you have my lunch money?' asked Tom. He blew his snub-shaped nose before discarding the tissue he held, throwing it in the school corridor. 'I'm a little short of funds today.' A wry grin appeared on his freckled face.

'Back off!' Ben barked. He was shorter than Tom and Asher, he looked up at the tall tower block defiantly.

'Or what?' taunted Tom. 'I'm in control.' He spoke like a true narcissist, crooked teeth showing, he boldly poked his index finger against Ben's protruding chest. 'I'll never understand how a loser like you was picked for the baseball team,' he cruelly insulted Ben.

This time, he was unwise to provoke Ben! 'Listen jackass, your friend Murphy isn't here to help this time,' he said. He was not at all fearful of Tom's intimidating tactics. Thump! He swung his fist, knocking Tom's pole-shaped arm sideways. 'You're all alone,' he continued.

'Um…um…but…!' Looking bemused, Tom was rattled. His shoes scraped off the square-patterned corridor beneath as he backed off. His eyes bulged with surprise. He took to reassessing his precarious situation. 'I'm done here anyhow; I've a class to get to,' he spoke shakily.

'Well then, get going,' said Ben firmly. He stood his ground.

Tail tucked between legs, Tom hastened down the hall. Like a cunning fox, he scuttled out of sight.

'Thanks,' expressed Asher. He rubbed the back of his neck in angst. In truth, he felt a little ashamed that again, Ben had interceded on his behalf. 'I'm lucky to have you as a friend,' he said.

'You've got that right,' smiled Ben. He put a hand on Asher's shoulder before telling it like it was. 'You shouldn't let that ginger-haired clown walk all over you. Dad always tells me to stick up for myself.' The last point hit home.

'I wish I had a dad like that,' said Asher. He sullenly dragged his feet onward down the school corridor.

Daily, Asher had to contend with Tom's sharp tongue and Conor's intimidating physique. They were ever the more persistent in making his life hell at Neptunica Middle School. His new term was overshadowed by their continuously lingering presence. Frequently, he would be confronted, and life was just easier by handing over a few dollars. Otherwise, as he had found out to his displeasure, Tom's lackey Conor would get rough.

On one specific occasion, he had found himself covered in the lunchtime special, in the middle of the school canteen. The sight of yellow custard and bits of hot chocolate fudge sliding down his shirt had sent all those in attendance into hysterics.

Of course, the big brute Conor, despite his lack of natural intellect, had managed to persuade Principal Smith that it was just a coincidental mishap.

'It was an accident,' he had said. 'Not my fault.' He was well-versed in the art of lying.

On a lighter note, with the festivities of October rapidly approaching, it meant only one thing. The school's annual Halloween fancy dress party was coming up.

'Have you asked her yet?' Ben investigated.

'I don't know what you mean,' Asher replied. He was unable to meet Ben's gaze.

'Don't play games, I mean Mandy of course, come on spill,' said Ben. He was direct and to the point.

'Well, I mean, I just haven't had a chance,' said Asher.

Hounding Asher's every movement, Ben had been unsuccessful in trying to persuade him to ask Mandy Fleming one pivotal, but simple question. Did she want to join him, Asher, that is, in going to the Halloween fancy dress party?

'So that's a no then?' Ben rolled his hazel eyes. He was frustrated.

'No,' confirmed Asher. He shook his head.

'Fine, but don't blame me when you have no one to bring to the dance,' snapped Ben. His patience was wavering. His dark-haired friend's sheer lack of confidence was proving too much for him to endure.

Although Asher would occasionally stumble across Mandy's path along the school corridor, he was always far too shy to suggest the proposal. He could never seem to articulate the right words, or any words at all, for that matter.

'Who are you taking, Ben?' asked Asher.

'Me, I've someone in mind, I've already asked them.'

Quite the opposite in his approach, Ben had no self-confidence issues. Having routinely met Asher every Tuesday after his music session and every other Thursday, he had boldly conjured up the audacity to ask Sarah Reid to the Halloween dance.

'Going to the dance then, Sarah?' he had said.

'I…I wouldn't miss it,' she had replied, the words springing from her mouth.

'Going with anyone?' he had continued to explore.

'No,' she had blushed, cheeks shining redder than a police siren.

'Great, I'll see you there then!' He was as bold as brass.

'Ok,' she had said, anxiously twisting a lock of her fuzzy brown hair.

Headstrong, Ben had put her abruptly on the spot. More to the point, his success in finding someone to bring to the Halloween dance had caused Asher to dwell evermore on his failures.

How, Asher thought, could he break the question he so desired to ask Mandy Fleming? He had neither Ben's nerve nor boldness. The question burned in his mind all through history class with Mr McNulty, mathematics class with Miss Hamilton, and even science class, so much so that he was not paying much attention to what was being taught.

'Take note of the lamp oil,' said Mr Woods. He rotated two adjoining soda bottles. 'The oil will float on the surface of the water.' His experiment was going exactly as intended.

'But why, Sir?' Hand dangling mid-air, red-framed spectacles hanging upon the edge of his box-shaped nose, one lively boy was full of curiosity.

'Because oil is less dense than water, that's why Leo,' explained Mr Woods. Being African American, for a man nearing his forties, Mr Michael Woods looked remarkably younger. His hair was short and black, as was his well-kept moustache and beard. His brown skin was vibrant, and he had the shiniest set of pearly whites you ever did see.

Banggg! Ruler snapping down upon the table, Mr Woods was not at all pleased by Asher's lack of participation. 'Is there something you wish to share with the class?' he enquired.

Lost within a daydream, Asher had spent the best part of twenty whole minutes peering out one grimy old window. 'No, Sir,' he answered. He promptly sat up right in his chair. His cheeks were red with humiliation.

'Then eyes front if you please,' said Mr Woods. 'You can only win by being focused.' When he was much younger, he had played basketball, but a bad knee injury meant he could not go professional. 'You want to go to college, earn a degree in science or whatever, like me?'

'Yes, Sir,' said Asher earnestly. He felt Mr Woods' judgemental hazel eyes burn right through him.

'Then don't spend your life looking out windows,' added Mr Woods. With his final bit of advice, he went straight back to his lesson. 'When the oil and water swirl together, the less dense oil travels down the vortex first and creates a coloured tornado-like effect, this in itself…'

Buzzz! The school bell rang loudly, and Mr Woods was cut short. 'Lunch already.' Tick! Tock! Tick! He looked at an old-fashioned, circular clock hanging upon cream cream-painted wall, he could see that the big hand was at twelve, the smaller at one. 'Right, I want three hundred words specifically on the probable causes and effects of tornadoes,' he said.

'Arghhh!' Grumbling with dissatisfaction, a horde of students scurried to the door.

'For tomorrow,' confirmed Mr Woods. He began clearing his work desk of the contents he had used during the day's lesson. 'Asher, remember to stay focused and be a winner,' he spoke, before adding a soft, reassuring smile.

'Sure thing, Sir,' answered Asher in an upbeat tone. He knew Mr Woods only meant well. He was the last among his classmates out the door. Feet swerving side to side, students brushing past left and right, he headed straight for his locker.

Clunk! Clunk! clunk! He opened his locker and jammed his books inside, emptying his blue striped school bag of its contents. 'No way,' he mumbled. Finishing the task, he slowly raised his head; eyes bulging, he could see that Mandy Fleming was doing the same thing! With just two days until the scheduled dance, this was his chance, perhaps his last. Banggg! He shut his locker with a thud before directing his unwilling feet toward her.

His white trainers slid against the square-patterned corridor of Neptunica Middle School beneath, he edged forward, right foot, left foot, right foot. 'Oh god, oh god, oh god…' He felt the pressure rise, his anxiety began to take hold. His palms began to sweat. His face went red. Like a train with no rail track left to steam ahead, his many concerns had resurfaced to stop him dead in his tracks. Would she? What if? It's impossible, isn't it? He was confused. He wanted to run.

'Hi Asher!'

But he did not get the chance to run. It was too late!

'Are you okay?' asked Mandy. She had caught sight of a very awkward-looking Asher.

'Who me?' spoke Asher softly. He pointed at himself, looking even more uneasy.

'Don't be silly, of course you,' said Mandy with a giggle. She tilted her head to one side; she caressed her lips together as she applied cherry-flavoured lip balm.

Hopelessly, he struggled to maintain control. 'I…I…was wondering if you would…would…'

She quickly probed for an answer. 'Spit it out, Asher!' Her radiant smile indicated she was curious to know what Asher had on his mind.

He failed to reply upon seeing the tall, thin tower block that was Tom Watson. Ginger hair, freckles, crooked teeth, and a scrawny composition, he was a hard individual to miss. He was rapidly advancing on their location.

'What are you doing talking to him, Mandy?' Tom roared wildly with sheer contempt, rudely interrupting them.

'Excuse me!' Mandy pushed her long, golden hair behind her slender shoulders, as her joyful exterior grew furiously serious. Her uncontained anger swiftly bubbled to the surface. 'I'm free to speak to whomever I please,' she erupted with the same velocity as a volcano.

'But why talk to him?' probed Tom. His crooked teeth showed as he eyed his prey like a rattlesnake. He was full of venomous spite.

'Why should I not?' she defiantly said.

'Um…um…um…!' Tom scratched his scalp; he was without no answer.

'Well, speak up,' she sternly said. She was strong-willed and stubborn; she was pressing him hard.

'It doesn't matter,' groaned Tom. He clenched his fists, and an overwhelming jealousy bubbled away at the centre of his malicious core. He was furiously irritated.

'Right, glad that's sorted then,' she said.

But it was not sorted, not at all! Tensions were riding high.

'Paterson!' spoke Tom.

'Yes,' said Asher, his teeth sunk into his bottom lip.

Thud! Thud! Thud! Tom edged forward, leaning his scrawny body toward Asher. 'I told you to stay out of my way,' he whispered. 'Things are going to get messy!' he warned.

Asher could feel Tom's hot, fiery breath against his skin. He was truly intimidated by the ill-tempered, ginger-haired, beanpole of an eighth grader standing before him. 'But it's not my fault, it's…'

'You'll pay, soon!' threatened Tom. He was not in the least bit concerned with whatever excuse Asher had.

'What was that?' asked Mandy.

'Oh, nothing,' said Tom, as if butter would not melt in his mouth. 'Just telling Paterson that I might have overreacted.' He was a lying git.

'Good,' she said. She foolishly believed him.

'Anyway, I'll see you at the Halloween dance,' said Tom. He chose his words very carefully to inflict as much damage as he could. Reading the situation, he had analysed that Asher liked the same girl in the school that he did too.

'Oh, oh yes, see you there,' she said. Her baby blue eyes fell, and her tone lacked enthusiasm.

'Great,' boomed Tom. He was as deceitfully cunning and just as sly as any overpaid politician running for re-election.

'No way!' Asher was left completely stunned. His initial hope departed, as if Pandora herself had reopened her sacred box. Why, he thought, would Mandy go to the Halloween dance with such an arrogant ass?

'I can't wait, already have my costume picked out,' continued Tom. He was as calculating as a professional archer, letting loose the string of his bow, he had hit his target dead centre. He had invoked the response that he had intended. 'You look a bit peaky there, Paterson,' he said, mockingly.

Sigh! Exhaling in despair, Asher was left disheartened.

'Well, I'd better get going,' said Tom. 'But I'll see you later.'

'Yes, later,' she said.

Tom trudged along the square-patterned corridor in the direction of the school canteen. His arms dangled at his side as he whistled, feeling pleased with himself.

'So, you're going to the Halloween fancy dress then?' softly spoke Asher. Gulp! He could not contain himself.

'Tom asked me to go to the dance with him a few weeks back, didn't want to say no and be left on my own,' explained Mandy. She put a finger to her lip as she thought on it. She had her insecurities to contend with. Despite being pretty, she did not think that anyone would want to ask the girl with a scar above her top lip to the dance.

'Oh…oh that's fine,' said Asher. He shrugged his shoulders; he tried in vain to restrain himself from showing his true hidden annoyance.

Perceptive of how he felt, she further attempted to highlight her reasoning. 'Was waiting on you to, well…'

'Hurry up, slow coach, or we'll be late for lunch!' It was Ben. He was making an unintentional habit of barging in on their conversations.

'I guess I'd better go,' she said. Banggg! She closed her locker before tossing her pink schoolbag over her shoulder. She began making her way toward the school canteen.

'Oh, oh sure,' replied Asher. Rubbing the back of his neck he felt quite deflated. 'Bye,' he dully added. He felt quite foolish. He could not believe his dismal situation. He could not believe that out of all people, Mandy would be going to the Halloween dance with none other than Tom Watson, the school bully.

Crafty in his approach, Tom had put Mandy on the spot. He had asked her during Ben's baseball tryouts a few weeks back.

Adding to his misfortunes, Asher's day continued to bring utter upheaval. 'I hate them both!' he said angrily.

The vipers, Tom, and Conor had returned to inflict further punishment. Causing Asher further misery, the pair had vandalised his locker. They had done so as he sat in history class listening to Mr McNulty's take on the Aztecs, an ancient tribe that had once dominated northern Mexico. Their lethal poison rapidly spread through his veins with each unkind act.

'What's going on here?' It was Principal Smith. He was hard at work attempting to get a ketchup stain out of his tie.

'Nothing, Sir,' Asher replied.

'It's not nothing, it's a mess,' said Principal Smith.

'Ha, ha, that's a really nice colour!' one sarcastic student brought attention to the situation.

'Get a move on,' snapped Principal Smith.

The colours of yellow and pink decorating Asher's locker had sent the students of Neptunica Middle School into hysterics.

'I told you that you would pay soon! Who wrote this?' asked Principal Smith. He snatched a pencil-scribbled note attached to Asher's locker.

'Ummm…' Asher was at a loss as to what to say.

'I want names,' demanded Principal Smith. He wiped his black framed, oval-shaped glasses, all the while his shiny black shoes drummed off the floor beneath. 'Well, speak up,' he said.

'I don't know, Sir,' said Asher. He lied, with a shrug of his shoulders, he refused to exploit his tormentors. He knew that if Principal Smith was to get involved that his life at Neptunica Middle School would spiral into the abyss. His life would become even more unbearable, more so than it already was.

'Fear is a powerful thing, Asher,' stated Principal Smith. He placed a hand on Asher's shoulder. 'I know who did this!' He knew fine well that it was Tom Watson and Conor Murphy. 'Truth is the purest form of being. You have to find yourself; such is the gift of free will.'

'I…I don't know who did it,' repeated Asher. He panicked.

'Fine, fine,' said Principal Smith. 'I won't press you. I'm not here to intervene, but to observe. You are special. You will do special things in your own time,' he said. His words were as cryptic as ever.

Getting home that evening, Asher had decided to reserve his ferociously terrible mood to the confines of his bedroom, his fortress of solitude. 'At least I have you, Scruffy,' he drearily said. He gently petted his tail-wagging, bushy-eyed, teddy bear of a dog. The big, lazy dog was sprawled out atop his soft bed.

'I guess we'll play a bit of music, boy,' said Asher. It was just such times, when his emotions were running high, that he would listen to his music collection. It was either rock or indie, sometimes it was a mixture of both.

'What shall it be?' he mumbled. New Age Rebels, The Knots, and Black Out were among the many superb indie bands that he would regularly listen to. On the other hand, bands such as The Stingers, Bittersweet, and The Magic Masons resembled everything he loved about rock.

'It'll have to be The Magic Masons,' he mumbled. He had first heard The Magic Masons after listening to one of his dad's old CDs. He, too, was a fan. In fact, on his bedroom wall was a picture of his dad at a Magic Masons' concert.

Click! Click! Click! He pressed the buttons of an old music player. 'It has to be this one,' he said. He decidedly played one of The Magic Masons' most famed songs. It was entitled, 'Let it all go.'

The Magic Masons' lead singer and guitarist, Razor Ryan, was one of his biggest influences. The long hair, the attitude, the powerful, hard vocals, Razor Ryan was his all-time idol.

Click! T-wang! T-wang! J-reeng! Click! While listening to his music in one ear, he listened to the sounds of his guitar with the other. Attempting to imitate greatness, for a few hours, he had managed to pluck a few soft tunes upon his worn-out, six-stringed instrument, before he heard an all too familiar voice.

'Turn that off, you silly boy, it's getting late!' yelled Nancy. She was not best pleased with the racket being created.

'OK, Grandma,' he groaned. Stubbornly, he abided by her stern demands.

The time on his alarm clock was 11:15 pm, and he quickly prepared for bed. Thud! Clunk! Bang! Rummaging through his bedside dresser, he retrieved a set of matching green striped pyjamas. He quickly changed into them.

'Good night,' he shouted. Head resting upon a soft pillow, he waited for a response, yet after sixty whole seconds, he still received none. 'I said goodnight, Grandma!' he boomed even louder.

'Yes, goodnight,' she loudly responded.

Click! Turning off his bedside lamp, Asher swiftly faded off to sleep. He fell into a deep slumber. A sleep nothing could awaken him from. Not the howling winds outside, nor the continuous cracks of thunder igniting the pitch-black sky. Not even the tree branches that thumped against the old roof slates directly above his head of black hair. No, he slept through all that Mother Nature could throw at the old wood-built house.

'Ahhhh-hhaaaaaa…' Blue eyes straining, hands providing shade from bright yellow rays, he awoke the next morning at precisely 08:15 am sharp. 'Gosh!' His blue curtains lay open as swathes of piercing sunlight flooded into his bedroom via one box-shaped window. It was as if the ancient Greek god Apollo himself had just zoomed past upon his golden chariot, raking the sun across the sky behind him.

Mother Nature's fury had conceded to a stunningly beautiful morning. 'Time to get up,' he mumbled. He tossed his blanket aside; he then steered his thin, drowsy body toward the bedroom door. Creakkk! He turned the brass handle, then veered out onto the landing before descending fourteen carpeted stairs. Bumpety! Bump! Bump!

'Ohhh…' He felt a soothing sensation as his soft, bare-skinned feet brushed against the carpet as he went.

'Yes! Finally, it's arrived,' he ignited with joy. He burst into a jubilant mood. He quickly realised that the postman had already come and gone. A parcel rested upon the kitchen table along with another carefully selected picture postcard, this time depicting an image of a sphinx, which had the body of a lion and the head of a human. Once again, the postcard had been sent from Egypt.

He did not bother to read the message scribbled on the front of the postcard. First, he wildly ripped open the brown wrapped parcel before him in sheer excitement.

'Stop it, Scruffy,' he said. Tail waggling, his bushy-eyed dog tugged away at his leg. The big, fluffy, grey, and white animal sank its teeth into his green striped pyjama trousers in a playful manner.

'Grrr!'

'Stop it, boy,' he said once again.

Chunks of brown paper drifted to the floor in abundance. To his surprise, he found a book entitled 'Valley of the Kings, The Archaeologist's Guide.' He thought the item strange. Why would his dad send him such a book?

He took hold of the latest picture postcard and began reading. 'Nooo…!' The excitement in his dazzling blue eyes sharply evaporated. Disappointment consumed his very soul. 'No, no, no, not another three months,' he said gloomily.

Dear Asher

Hope you like your present. Anyway, I've been gone longer than anticipated, and things don't look set to change. The team has been working tirelessly, but still,

Deeply angry, he began tightening his grip on the postcard. The edges began to strain. Creases began to appear upon the glossy image. He wanted to tear the postcard to shreds. But he did not. He restrained himself, decidedly continuing to read on.

Thankfully so. Loosening his grip, his bright blue eyes ignited once more with sheer enthusiasm. 'No way!' He could not believe it. His dad, Mike, wanted him to travel across the globe to be with him. He wanted him to travel to the Valley of the Kings in Egypt. The book now made perfect sense.

Simply put, my boy, I would love for you to join me here, in Egypt. Besides, it's about time you learned the tricks of the archaeology trade...

It would be over the Christmas break, as had been explained on the picture postcard, the departure date being Friday the 18th of December.

One return ticket departing from Newark Liberty International Airport has been enclosed, besides you're now of the age, lad.

I look forward to seeing you.

P.S. Love Dad.

In desperation, Asher searched anxiously for the ticket. He did so in vain. 'Hmmm, Grandma,' he called. He thought she might know something about the matter.

'Yes, Asher,' answered Nancy. She appeared in the frame of the kitchen doorway. Her silver hair was tied up in a bun, while her square-shaped spectacles dangled upon a beaded string. She moved forward slowly, her plump body swaying side to side as she went. She grinned, staring at him quite precariously.

Immediately, he could see that she was holding something in her left hand! 'What's that?' he questioned her suspiciously.

Her crinkled lips began to separate. 'Well, it's a plane ticket to Egypt, isn't that nice?' she said. She buttoned up her woollen cardigan, she then fixed her out-of-shape frilly white blouse.

Growing utterly frustrated, he asked for the ticket, relinquishing all forms of courtesy. 'Let me have it,' he insisted.

'No, no, I think I'll just mind this for you now,' she said. She took no notice of his pleas. She simply turned and steered her feet toward the living room. Irritatingly, she sneered as she went.

He did not want to induce an argument for fear that the old woman would tear the ticket up. Besides, he was running late for school.

Thud! Thud! Thud! He thundered back up the stairs to his room. He quickly hurried out of his green striped pyjamas. 'That'll do,' he said. He placed his right arm into the sleeve of a red patterned shirt, then his left. He then rummaged through his white bedside dresser. Blue denim jeans and white trainers with red stripes completed his outfit. He was all set.

Bumpety! Bump! Bump! Ready, he soared back down the stairs in a great hurry. He swerved to his left, once again entering the red-themed kitchen. The kettle, the toaster, and even the microwave were red. 'Smells nice,' he said. He immediately spotted a few rounds of toast. He stuffed a slice in his mouth. The crusts were slightly burnt, but the thick layer of strawberry jam resting on top made all the difference.

He tossed his blue striped school bag over his shoulder. He was all set to begin his short but routine journey to school. He had less than ten minutes, seven to be exact. If late, he would have to endure Principal Smith's harsh discipline.

'I'm off,' he said.

'Yes, yes, goodbye,' grumbled Nancy.

'Stay Scruffy…' he mumbled. His mouth was partially full. Banggg! He slammed the front door as he left the house. He then zoomed off down the path and out of sight.

-Chapter 4-

Festivities Underway

It was not until the following evening that Asher began his preparations for the Halloween fancy dress party. It was Friday 29th of October, the last school day of the week. 'How do I look?' He outstretched his arms, and wedged between his fingers was a black cape.

'Rufff!' Scruffy barked in response.

'Thanks, Scruffy,' he said. He petted his fluffy dog before taking hold of a silver tin canister. He sprayed his thick black hair with white mist. 'Can't forget my fangs, boy.' He opened his mouth before squeezing his shiny white pearls down upon soft plastic. 'Ouch!' In doing so, he hurt his gums.

He had put significant effort into his costume, even though he loathed the thought of going to the Halloween fancy dress party. Still, he had to, because he did not want Ben to think that he was upset at his failed attempt at asking Mandy Fleming to go with him, even if it was the whole-hearted truth. Nor did he want Tom Watson to feel he got one over on him.

Bong! Bong! Bong! Mechanical parts springing to life, his grandmother's old grandfather clock resting beyond the foot of the stairs began to chime loudly, signalling six o'clock in the evening.

Rat-a-tat-tat! Rat-a-tat-tat! Rat-a-tat-tat! Adding to the chimes coming from the old grandfather clock was a continuous knocking that fell upon the front door.

'Go away! We have no candy,' yelled Nancy. She was sitting in a flowery armchair, tea and biscuits in hand. She was watching one of her favourite soap operas on television. More to the point, she was annoyed at the sudden distraction at the door.

69

'Sorry, Miss Branning, is Asher there?' It was Ben. His eyes and mouth were painted black, while the rest of his face was painted white.

'Speak up, what did you say?' Nancy's hearing was not great. Her voice boomed down the hall as the chimes from the old grandfather clock died away.

'I said sorry, Miss Branning, is Asher there?' Ben raised his voice loudly.

'Miss!' Nancy grew furious. With a thump, she set her teacup and biscuits on her coffee table. Thud! Thud! Thud! She slowly got to her feet, her knees were not the best either. Her overweight body wobbled side to side as she stormed from the living room into the hall. Creakkk! She pulled her cardigan tight around her body. Her reading glasses dangled upon a beaded string. She was utterly irritated as she pulled the old oak door open. 'It's Mrs to you, sonny. I was married, you know,' she said.

Ben was utterly taken aback. He had not expected such a harsh response. 'So...sorry,' he uttered. He stood wearing a black and white skeleton costume with his mouth agape.

'Forty years,' continued Nancy. She held out her aged hand, showing her diamond ring to reinforce her point.

Her late husband, Asher's grandfather, John Branning, had passed away some years previous at the ripe old age of seventy-two of natural causes, five to be exact.

'No respect at all, in my day...' she continued to roar. She made a few further remarks on respect, discipline, and society's slow decline.

'I'm on the way, Ben.' Bumpety! Bump! Bump! Asher rushed from his bedroom. He struggled with his black fluttering cape as he soared down the carpet-laid stairs to the bottom.

Rufff! Scruffy wildly charged after him. Drooling at the mouth, the big teddy bear of a dog descended the stairs like an out-of-control bull.

'I'm off to the Halloween party, Grandma,' he said.

'When can I expect you home?' she asked.

'I'll be home before nine,' informed Asher. He raised his right hand high like a traffic controller, he stopped his big fluffy pet dog dead in its tracks. 'Hold it, boy, you'll be staying here.' He squeezed past his grandmother's plump stature and out the door. He zoomed off down the path. 'Ben, let's go,' he uttered.

'Bye, Miss Branning,' said Ben. He quickly followed Asher in hot pursuit.

'It's Mrs, you arrogant pup,' scolded Nancy. Banggg! She slammed the front door.

'I think your dog Scruffy wanted to go with us,' said Ben. 'Cool dog. Dad won't let me get another pet since Daisy.' He had a dog named Daisy that had passed away almost three years ago.

'I remember Daisy,' replied Asher. He screwed up his nose. He disliked the little dog. She barked at everything and would not let him pet her. 'What happened to her again?' he enquired.

'She drank gasoline,' answered Ben. He shook his head. 'Poor girl dropped running down the street.' He flicked his fingers, mimicking the running part.

'I can't believe that killed her,' gasped Asher in disbelief. He was taken with Ben's story.

'It didn't! She just ran out of gas,' said Ben, unable to keep a straight face. He began to laugh. 'She died of old age.' He patted Asher on the back.

'You're one weasel,' said Asher. He, too, could not keep a straight face as he chuckled.

'There's a sucker born every minute,' said Ben. 'You're too gullible, you trust everyone, that's your problem.'

'Alright, alright, let's hurry before the party is over,' said Asher. He broke off into a sprint.

'More running, oh great,' groaned Ben. His sarcastic comments went unnoticed. Wheeze! Wheeze! Wheeze! Huffing and puffing, he sprinted behind Asher for the rest of the journey.

It took Asher and Ben only a few minutes to reach Neptunica Middle School. It was only a few blocks away. They hurried down Sixth Avenue and took a sharp right. Soon, their destination had come into view.

'Wow!' gasped Asher. The old, whitewashed building looked utterly spectacular. 'There are so many lights,' he spurted out in sheer amazement.

Red lights, orange lights, and green lights, the old oak trees surrounding the old building shone brighter than a compilation of pelican crossings. The red, orange, and green lights even twisted around either side of the school steps.

'They…they…' Ben paused, before taking a puff of his blue inhaler. He quickly caught his breath. 'They went all out, Ash. Usually, they are a bunch of cheap skates.' The school board was notoriously always cutting back funding for something or the other.

Without delay, both proceeded to the entrance and inside to find Principal Smith looming within the corridor. He was alone.

'Trouble straight ahead,' mumbled Ben. 'Bloodsucker at twelve o'clock.'

White stripes lined Principal Smith's hair. He wore a white shirt with frills on the neck and sleeves. He also wore a black bow tie. Like Asher, he also wore a cape, which was a bright red colour. He, too, was dressed as a bloodthirsty vampire.

'Hi, Sir.' Asher found it completely uncharacteristic of Principal Smith to dress up. He always seemed a serious, disciplined man, even at the best of times.

'Good choice, can't go wrong dressed as a vampire,' approved Principal Smith.

'Thanks, Sir,' responded Asher. 'But I'm not just any creature of the night, I'm Dracula,' he said. He held out the ends of his cape. He flapped his arms like a bat.

'Begging your pardon, dark prince of Pennsylvania, I'll be sure to mind my step,' said Principal Smith, playing along. He grinned, finding the encounter with Asher quite amusing. 'You two had best hurry along, the party has already started.' He snapped his fingers, signalling for Asher and Ben to get going.

'Yes, Sir,' nodded Asher. Thud! Thud! Thud! He and Ben hastened forward.

'No running,' called out Principal Smith. 'You know the school rules.' He tutted, shaking his head.

'Yes, Sir,' responded Asher.

'Sure thing, chief,' said Ben. He gave a cheeky salute before continuing down the school corridor.

'Really,' moaned Principal Smith. He shook his head before he spoke again out of earshot of Asher and Ben. 'Everyone is subject to the governing authority, for there is no authority except that which I established!' He had an ingrained philosophy on the matter.

Both Asher and Ben headed straight in the direction of the assembly hall. Clank! Double doors pushed aside, they were both taken by surprise.

'It's more impressive than the outside,' gasped Asher. He soaked in the lively atmosphere. His eyes wandered through the assembly hall.

There were pumpkins of all shapes and sizes, many devilish skeletons, creepy ghosts, and spooky ghouls. The hall was filled with all sorts of wonderful decorations. Lights and banners dangled from the ceiling, walls, doors, and windows, while on top of three long tables, there were all sorts of delicious treats.

'Everyone seems to be here,' observed Asher. He took a hard gulp. He was not a fan of big crowds.

'No kidding, buddy,' said Ben. He was gobsmacked. 'Let's party!' He was quite brazen. He was more of an extrovert than Asher.

There were hordes of sixth graders, seventh graders, and eighth graders. It was as if a hive full of buzzing bees had been let loose.

'There are so many great costumes,' said Asher. He spotted students dressed as witches, fairies, wizards, werewolves, and even zombies, among other amazing and weird costumes. His imagination was wildly ignited.

'Look over there,' said Ben. 'Wish I'd thought of dressing like that,' he said. He pointed energetically.

Amidst the funky costumes, one of the eighth graders came dressed as a hot dog enclosed within a bun. Everywhere he went, he was stopped by a crowd of laughing admirers.

'That's cool,' said Asher. He liked the simple but funny-dressed eighth grader.

'Let's get something to drink,' said Ben. 'Loosen up and enjoy yourself.' He could sense that Asher was a little anxious.

'Sure thing,' replied Asher. He took a deep breath; he tried his best to embrace the moment.

Feet sliding along the wooden floor, both made their way forward. Bodies twisting and turning, feet jumping and tapping, arms bouncing and dangling, they eased through a horde of overly ecstatic bopping, jigging, and jiving students.

'Look who it is,' said Asher. He pointed to a girl standing at the edge of the dance floor. 'It's Sarah!' He could see she was on her own and looking quite uneasy.

'Sorry, but that's my cue, buddy,' said Ben. 'I'll have to get that drink later.' He rushed through a flock of extremely pumped-up students to greet her. 'Sarah! Sarah! Hold up,' he shouted to get her attention. He flapped his hands wildly. He looked like an out-of-control wild goose.

Her lips were smothered in black lip balm, and black netted fabric covered her hands. In addition, she wore a long, black frilled cut dress. She was as bedazzling as any magical enchantress.

'Your costume is awesome,' complimented Ben. 'Really, it's amazing.'

'Thanks,' she said. She went red in the face, her eyelashes flickered wildly. She seemed overwhelmed with uncharacteristic shyness. 'So is yours.' She quickly returned the compliment.

'Want to dance?' asked Ben. He was as bold as brass.

'Well, sure, I've been standing here ten minutes on my own,' said Sarah. She slowly extended her left hand.

'This way,' instructed Ben. He took her hand. Taking the lead, he directed her to the centre of the dance floor, just as one song had ended, and another was just about to begin.

'I'll catch up with you later,' said Asher loudly. He gave a thumbs-up to his jubilant friend.

'Yes, later, buddy,' answered Ben. He threw his hands in the air as he began jumping up and down to the funky song that had just started. He looked ridiculous, but he was having too much fun to care.

'I guess I'll get that drink on my own,' mumbled Asher. Licking his lips, he was utterly parched. He eased forward through the hordes of cheerful dancers, toward one table with a plastic punchbowl resting atop. Now on his own, he was just trying to keep his anxiety under control.

Banggg! He struggled to contain his black cape as he was knocked over before reaching the edge of the dance floor. 'My… my fangs!' His plastic vampire teeth had slipped from his mouth. He dropped to his knees, his hands rummaged along the floor, as he searched desperately to retrieve the set. 'Ouch!' As he desperately searched for his fangs, a large foot fell upon his left hand.

'Paterson!' a voice rang out.

'Get off,' Asher groaned. He took a glance up at a tall, purple monster with a long tail and lengthy plastic claws.

'Hi Asher.' Another, more feminine voice called to get his attention.

Also hovering over him was one fantastically dressed fairy clad in pink. She had glittered wings and held a star-shaped wand.

'What are you doing?' It was none other than Mandy Fleming.

'Oh, oh nothing,' said Asher. 'I just lost my teeth.' His words spilled out of his mouth. He only looked up for a moment before turning his eyes back to the dance floor.

'What?' she asked. She was deeply puzzled. 'Don't be silly.' She giggled before putting cherry-flavoured lip balm across her lips. She then retrieved a small mirror from her pink bag before inspecting her face. She ran a little concealer across the top of her lip. Her small and quite unnoticeable scar was playing on her self-confidence.

'Enough! Stop fidgeting with that mirror!' The purple monster scolded her harshly. 'You're not getting any prettier, you know.' The remark cut very deeply.

'That's not nice at all,' whispered Mandy. She looked visibly upset. She went red in the face. She looked quite uneasy as she put the small mirror back in her bag.

'I got them, I got my fangs,' bellowed Asher. 'Look, found them.' He slowly eased himself to his feet. He felt quite silly.

'You'll really lose your teeth in a minute if you don't get lost,' warned Tom. He shook his fist.

'Ttt…ttt…Tom!' screeched Asher. Suddenly, he realised that the purple monster was Tom Watson. He took note of the crooked teeth, the freckles, and two hate-filled hazel eyes. Any feelings of silliness were replaced with fear.

'Be nice,' said Mandy. 'Don't make me ask twice.' She pointed at Tom's freckled face in a commanding manner. Though having some self-conscious issues when it came to her appearance, she had a sharp tongue. She was an extrovert and more often than not was able to mask her insecurities with her bubbly personality.

'Oh alright,' grumbled Tom. He had been firmly knocked down a peg. Not too many students would get away with telling him off in such a direct manner.

'Your costume looks great, Asher,' complimented Mandy.

'Looks ridiculous,' grumbled Tom.

'Pot calling the kettle black,' said Mandy. She shook her head of blonde hair. As she did, Tom went silent. He had firmly gotten the message. 'So, Asher, are you here with anyone?' she enquired.

Asher was abruptly put on the spot. Grinding his teeth with angst, he could not hide the truth. 'No,' he sourly said.

'Too bad, Paterson, now get lost,' said Tom sharply. He was very mean.

'Tom! Stop that,' said Mandy. She did not like his behaviour at all.

'This is an awesome song and we're missing it because of Paterson,' rumbled Tom, the demon called jealousy, stirring inside his gut was rearing its ugly head again.

'Stop being rude or…'

'No, no, he's right,' interrupted Asher. 'I'm going to get a drink anyhow.' He could see that things were escalating. Tom was only getting angrier by the minute.

'You do that,' said Tom.

'Another time then,' said Mandy.

'Yeah, another time, Paterson,' snapped Tom. Showing his crooked teeth, he then stuck out his tongue provocatively.

Thud! Thud! Thud! Retreating from the dance floor, Asher took hold of a silver spoon. Scooping up a batch of red coloured punch, he filled a plastic cup to the brim. Gulp! Gulp! Gulp! He quickly devoured every little drop.

'Is the punch nice?'

While helping himself to a second serving of punch, Asher was left to fend for himself as Conor Murphy, dressed as a pumpkin, drew ever closer towards him. He was accompanied by another boy, dressed as a ghost, who went by the name of John Deeds.

Banggg! Conor blatantly slammed his shoulder against Asher, almost knocking him over.

'Arghhh!' Splashhh! Asher could not contain the red liquid within his cup, the punch drenched his hair. He felt the punch ripple down his white powdered face and seep through the fabric of his costume.

'Ha, ha, ha!' In response, Conor erupted with laughter, wrapping his hands around his enormous gut. 'Look, everyone,' he bellowed. His goal was to cause a scene.

A room full of judgemental eyes zoomed in on the situation. The lively dance floor came to a standstill. Then the laughter erupted!

'You did that on purpose,' snapped Asher. He could not help but feel a little anger beginning to simmer deep within himself.

'No, he didn't,' roared John. He was but just a little, brown-haired, green-eyed boy, with a nasty attitude. 'So, shut your mouth!' he barked, arms flopping up and down.

'It was an accidenttt…' slowly uttered Conor. His drawn-out tone was provocatively mocking. 'By the way, Tom says hello.' It was clear who had put him up to the task.

'Hope there's some punch left for me,' one student dressed as a werewolf teased.

'You better not bathe in it,' another dressed as a ghoul added.

The laughter only grew louder. The circus had just rolled into town, and Asher was the main attraction.

'Stop it!' shouted Asher. 'Just stop it.' He felt completely overwhelmed.

'Are we going to cry?' teased Conor. He was a merciless big brute with no sense of remorse. He swiped a white handkerchief from the table next to him, then he held out his right hand. 'Here, wipe away your tears,' he continued to mock.

'You're mine, jackass!' Thumppp! Ben burst into action, blindsiding Conor. He dived on top of him.

'Arghhh! Get off me, get off me,' screeched Conor. He cried as he rolled upon the floor like a plump pig put before the butcher's knife.

'You've messed with my buddy for the last time,' thundered Ben. He was sick and tired of all the antics.

'Ben!' Asher's streaky white face ignited with surprise as he watched Ben let loose. He had never seen Ben so mad.

'Help me!' shouted Conor. 'Help!' he howled.

'I'll thump him!' The pint-sized boy, John Deeds, with devilish intent, hastened forward to Conor's aid.

'Oh no, you don't.' Thwack! Asher pushed his hands forward, tossing John Deeds face first to the dance floor. He had acted quickly; Ben's boldness had spurred him on.

'Stop this instant!' It was Principal Smith. 'Up, up,' he said. He rushed across the hall, as he did, and the crowd of students parted like the Red Sea. He was accompanied by Mr Martin O'Neil, the Head of English. He was a bald, brown eyed man, with rounded shoulders, slim arms, and a bit of a tummy. He had a reputation for being playfully witty.

'Get up, Mr Wilson, you too, Mr Murphy,' Principal Smith roared. He struggled to contain his bright red cape. He looked straight at Conor Murphy with judgemental eyes. 'You had best change your ways before redemption moves beyond your reach,' he said.

'It was his fault,' sobbed Conor. He pointed at Asher. He was lying.

'It wasn't my fault,' snapped Asher. He was sick and tired of being tormented. He was feeling very emotional. Looking quite the mess, he was at his wits' end. He was feeling angry.

'He's telling the truth, chief,' added Ben. He came to Asher's defence once more.

'It was Paterson's fault, I saw it,' interrupted Tom. He emerged from the crowd of onlookers. He pointed the blame squarely at Asher's feet.

'I know who the culprits are,' stated Principal Smith. He looked at Tom, then at Conor. 'I detest wicked acts committed consciously and of free will.'

'Punish him,' groaned Conor. He moved forward, he got right in Asher's face.

Splash! 'Leave me alone,' blasted Asher. Filled with rage, he lifted the plastic punch bowl from the table. In haste, he poured the contents over Conor's head.

Giggles erupted throughout the hall as the students of Neptunica Middle School observed. The music was lowered. The lights came on.

'I…I will get you…' Conor fizzled with anger. He was shocked by Asher's actions. Punch soaked his pumpkin costume.

'You've done quite enough this evening, Mr Murphy, quite enough indeed,' said Principal Smith. 'Everyone, enjoy the party. Mr O'Neil, five weeks' detention each shall suffice.'

'I guess someone has to do the dirty work,' stated Mr O'Neil. 'Right, let's be having your names.' He took a notebook and a pen from his shirt pocket. He then jotted down the name of each convict.

'John…'

'Ben…'

'But, but…'

'No ifs, no buts, no coconuts,' said Mr O'Neil. 'Do the crime, you do the time.' He pointed his pen at the initiator of the events that had just unfolded.

'Conor…'

'That just leaves you,' said Mr O'Neil. His pen then fell before Asher's big blue eyes. 'Name, please,' he asked.

'Asher Paterson,' he replied. He neither tried to reason nor worm his way out of his sentence.

'See that's how it's done,' said Mr O'Neil. 'No squirming, short and concise.'

'I'll deal with Mr Paterson personally,' informed Principal Smith. He directed Asher across the floor and into the school corridor.

'He's really in for it now,' said Tom with glee. He was all too happy, believing Asher would be severely punished for his outburst.

'You moron, you know it wasn't his fault,' said Mandy. She had seen Tom and Conor conspiring before the evening's spectacle took place.

'I...I acted foolishly, sorry, Sir,' whispered Asher. He awaited Principal Smith's full fury. He put his head in his hands.

'I understand how tough life can be. But remember, never respond in hate. Love, forgiveness, these are much more powerful,' said Principal Smith. He hunkered down to Asher's level. 'Life shapes us. You and you alone must choose what type of person you want to be. You are unique, each individual is, but you're particularly special, you have a big purpose to play in the universe,' he said.

'But I had no choice. I was just so tired of...of...'

'The bullies. Wicked people do wicked things, but do not let that change you,' said Principal Smith. 'Events will come to pass in Egypt, unstoppable events...'

'How...how do you know about Egypt?' spurted out Asher. He was flabbergasted.

'As I've said before, I know all,' said Principal Smith. He smiled.

'So, I won't be punished?' questioned Asher.

'Now I didn't say that, Mr Paterson,' said Principal Smith. 'I believe a few weeks' detention will allow you time to reflect.'

Mondays, Wednesdays, Thursdays, and Fridays at 3.15 pm sharp, Asher would arrive in room 9d to receive his punishment. He did so for the full five weeks of his sentence. His penance, to write out the line, 'I must not fight in the assembly hall' one hundred times. A penance he had to repeat in each one-hour sitting.

Only on Tuesdays and every other Thursday was he excused to partake in his extracurricular music class. However, he still had to compose one hundred lines in addition to his homework.

October quickly turned to November, followed by December.

'How long?' queried Ben.

'Three days,' answered Asher. Excitement filled his face.

'God, wish I could go to Egypt with you,' said Ben.

Christmas break looming, sentence fully served, Friday the 18th of December was almost upon Asher. He desperately longed to spend some quality time with his dad, Mike Paterson.

'Grandma, where's my sandals?' boomed Asher. The night before his departure, Thursday the 17th of December, he packed his things, his lotions, sunglasses, shorts, and an arrangement of coloured t-shirts. 'Grandma.' He called her once more. This time, she answered him.

'You shouldn't leave things to the last minute,' she groaned.

'Arghhh Scruffy, stop chewing on that.' His big, fluffy dog had sunk its teeth into one of his leather sandals. The other rested, but only a foot away. 'It's ok, found them, Gran,' he yelled. Covered in drool, they were still intact. 'Bad dog,' he scorned.

'Rrrrr!'

Fully packed and ready, he awoke the next morning at 07.00 am sharp. His flight, destined for Luxor, Egypt, was scheduled to leave at precisely 08:45 am.

Ben had called by to see him off, explaining excitedly how he was going to watch the New Jersey Eagles with his dad, David Wilson. 'Can't wait, the Eagles have it all to play for,' he said. Gesticulating, he simulated having a hockey stick in his hands before swinging his elbows. 'Hanson will smash that puck into the back of the net,' he boomed.

Ben not only had a strong love of baseball, but he also had an ardent desire for the New Jersey Eagles. He had a love for most sports, whether it was watching ice hockey, baseball, or basketball. As a hobby, he had collected a fine array of sports cards. He cherished his collection greatly.

'That's great, Ben,' answered Asher. 'Hope you enjoy.' For the first time, he did not feel envious of Ben. He knew that he would be seeing his own dad, Mike, very soon.

'Dad managed to get us front row seats,' continued Ben.

'I don't know what I'll be getting up to with my dad,' said Asher. He could not help but wonder. He thought of tombs, sarcophaguses, wall paintings, mummies, the River Nile, and sand as far as the eye could see.

'Asher...' yelled Nancy. Her voice carried up the stairs to his bedroom.

'Yes, Gran,' he shouted.

'It's time to go,' she loudly responded.

Honkkk! Outside the old, timeworn house on 6th Avenue, Neptune City, New Jersey, a yellow taxicab hooted its horn. The taxi with the numbered plate, three eighty-eight, had just pulled up. The engine was still on, smoke escaped the yellow vehicle's exhaust pipe.

Asher headed straight for the awaiting cab; he rolled his luggage case down the path. Ben followed him.

'Oh, wish I could go to the airport and see you off,' said Ben. Both he and Asher were close. Ever since kindergarten, they have been the best of friends. Some bonds went deeper than blood.

'Hold it! Hold it!' Nancy, with purse in hand, followed in hot pursuit. 'Be a dear and get the door,' she said. She instructed Ben to open the cab door as the cab driver placed Asher's luggage in the boot.

'Yes, Miss Branning,' said Ben. He politely opened the cab door.

'It's Mrs,' groaned Nancy. She waved her wedding ring to prove her point. She slowly manoeuvred into the back seat of the cab. Age catching up to her, she was not as nimble as she once was.

'Oops, sorry,' shrugged Ben. He was a little red-faced. 'Darn it! I will never get that right,' he muttered under his breath. He did not want to warrant any further scorn from Nancy, for he knew she had a fiery temper at the best of times.

'Hey, Gran, can Ben come with us to the airport?' Asher wanted his best friend to see him off. He was already feeling quite anxious. He had never been out of the country before.

'I should think no...'

'Thanks, Miss Branning,' said Ben. He did not let Nancy finish as he jumped into the yellow cab. 'Get in, Ash, get in.' He quickly made room for Asher to sit next to him.

'Great,' expressed Asher happily. He quickly got into the cab before slamming the door shut.

'It's Mrs,' said Nancy. Before she could instruct Ben to get out, the taxicab took off down the street.

'Are you going to Newark Liberty Airport, ma'am?' The taxi driver wanted to confirm the destination.

'Yes, yes, the airport,' replied Nancy. Quite sternly, she pointed at Asher and Ben. 'I want no trouble,' she warned. She had given in. She could not very well tell the taxi driver to turn back now. 'I'll drop you off on the way back, your mother won't be pleased.' She sighed as she began to rifle through the notes in her purse. She knew Amanda Wilson, Ben's mother, well. They both went to the same bingo hall. She was a tall, brown-haired woman. A church going woman.

It did not take the taxi driver long to get to the airport, it was a routine route for him. 'Have a great trip.' He quickly unloaded Asher's luggage from the boot of the car.

'I will, thanks,' replied Asher. He took hold of his luggage case.

'This way,' howled Nancy. On arrival, she brought Asher to the check-in desk before completing an unaccompanied minor's form.

'Sign here, please.' The customer service assistant was very pleasant.

'Where do I sign?' asked Nancy. 'My eyesight isn't great, dear,' she explained. She placed her reading glasses on her fleshy, shaped nose.

'On the dotted line, please,' answered Barbara. Her name was imprinted on her name tag. 'Here's a pen,' she said, trying to be as helpful as possible. She pushed a blue pen across the desk.

'Oh, now hold on, dear,' said Nancy. 'I've got my pen right here,' she stated. She took a black ballpoint pen from her purse.

'I'm so nervous,' gasped Asher. He was feeling the pressure build. Soon, he would be up in the skies all alone, heading halfway around the world.

'You've got this,' said Ben. 'Besides, if you want, I can take your place. Oh yes, sun, sand, and sightseeing, sign me up.' He began to laugh.

'No, no, you're quite alright,' responded Asher with a grin. Ben always had a way with words, a way to put him at ease.

'Will you bring me back a duck-do?' asked Ben. 'It's Egyptian.' He could barely keep a straight face.

'What's a duck-do?' replied Asher. Scratching his head, he had no idea.

'Quack-quack.' Ben flopped his arms up and down. 'Quack, quack, quack, quack...'

'Alright, alright,' said Asher. He too laughed. 'Very funny.' He shook his head. Hook, line, and sinker, occasionally, he completely fell for Ben's jokes.

Both Ben and his grandmother remained by his side until the time came for him to board the flight.

'Now don't you be causing any trouble, you hear me,' warned Nancy. She also managed to give him a few final words of caution.

'Don't do anything I wouldn't,' said Ben. He held out his hand.

'I won't, I wouldn't be that stupid,' said Asher. He smiled as the back of his hand met Ben's. Both then clasped their palms together, as fingers slid away.

'Promise you'll look after Scruffy, Gran?' said Asher.

'Of course, what do you take me for?' barked Nancy. 'Remember one bit of trouble and there'll be hell to pay!' She shook her index finger at him.

'Bye, buddy,' said Ben. He was sad to see Asher go.

Prepared, Asher had been given instructions to meet his dad, Mike, upon his arrival in Egypt.

Microphone in hand, red-coated lips parting, a brown-haired female flight attendant wearing a green jacket issued one final message. 'Please remember all the flight safety instructions, and remain in your seats, we're about to depart,' she said.

Jet engines roaring wildly, the plane Asher was aboard slowly rotated onto a long stretch of open runway.

'Here we go.' Nervous, he had butterflies in his stomach. He could not quite believe it, it was happening, for the very first time, he was about to leave the good old United States of America.

Luggage knocking back and forth in the overhead compartment, the plane slightly rattling due to imperfections in the runway, the metal beast zoomed off before ascending upward into the air. The feeling of machinery vibrating from under the feet signalled the retraction of the plane's landing gears. Wing flaps adjusted, and the plane began to climb higher and higher.

Peering out a side window, Asher watched as Neptune City, New Jersey, slowly faded away. 'This is it, Egypt, here I come,' he whispered with delight.

-Chapter 5-

Down in Egypt

Stepping off the Boeing 747, Asher's bright blue eyes drifted upward toward the calm, cloudless sky. He quickly caught sight of an Egyptian vulture. He observed the majestic animal. It had a whitish head, back, and chest, but its primary and secondary black feathers made for a superb contrast of colour.

'Wow!' he muttered. He was truly bedazzled. His left hand rested against his brow. The bright sunlight caused his irises to constrict. He could feel the heat of the sun burn against his pale skin.

He continued to watch as the native bird glided back and forth, every part of its evolved anatomy enhancing its ability to fly. He was captivated.

Thud! Thud! Thud! He suddenly felt a light tap upon the shoulder. He awoke from his daydream, realising that he was taking too long to make his descent down the airstair to the ground below.

'Come on, let's get you sorted.' A male steward encouraged Asher to move along. 'You are creating a backlog.' A line of holidaymakers stood behind him, eager to leave the plane.

Bumpety! Bump! Bump! 'So…sorry,' spoke Asher. Placing his hand on a metal rail, he hurried down the airstairs. Clink! Clink! Clink! His feet clinked on the steps as he descended to the bottom. He headed straight for the airport terminal. He glanced back at the steward following close behind.

'Is this your first trip to Egypt, then?' The male steward named Clive spoke softly and calmly. His name tag was attached to the green jacket he wore. He had green irises and a black bushy moustache. His appearance was quite distinctive.

'Yes, this is my first trip. Dad's an archaeologist,' answered Asher. Feeling quite excited, he let his full expectations flow. 'I do hope he brings me to see the tombs later,' he said. The words raced from his mouth.

'Many a good soul has perished in those tombs over the years,' said Clive. He caressed his black, horseshoe-shaped moustache.

'Perished!' gulped Asher. His excitement quickly evaporated.

'But don't worry, you look much too smart to let some old mummies get you,' said Clive. He chuckled, indicating that he was just joking. 'Just follow the signs, you can't get lost,' he instructed.

Asher did as he was told and followed the signs. 'Excuse me, hi…hi there…' He struggled to be heard as he moved through the airport terminal. All around him at the Luxor International Airport were flocks of very loud holidaymakers. His anxiety was on the rise. 'Excuse me…excuse me, could you...' Banggg! Without intent, he clumsily slammed into one buzzing, purple-striped shirt, sunglass-wearing Aussie.

'Good day mate, are you alright?' The Aussie immediately spotted him.

'Sorry, could you point me in the direction of...'

'Asher!' A familiar voice suddenly harnessed his focus. 'Asher, my boy, over here.' It was his dad, Mike Paterson! He stood out like a sore thumb, waving a brown fedora hat above his head to garner Asher's attention.

'Dad! Asher spotted Mike immediately, running from one end of the terminal to the other. Tappity! Tap! Tap! Duck and clink! He clipped the flexible separating barrier he had hurried under without due care. Nothing could stop him. 'Dad,' he boomed. He threw his arms around his dad, squeezing him tightly.

Mike found his sturdy physique inadequate to withstand the blow. 'Whoa!' He stumbled upon impact. 'Easy now, lad, easy,' he said.

'Dad, I missed you so much,' said Asher softly. He stood on the tips of his toes, eyes closed.

'I missed you too, lad,' replied Mike in kind. He folded his arms around Asher's thin, structured body.

'It's so good to see you, Dad, it's been an eternity,' said Asher. He had not seen his dad in months, close to five months to be exact. His feelings of sheer happiness flowed through his body like electricity.

Both Asher and Mike waited a short while before retrieving Asher's luggage, which had been unloaded from the plane.

'This one is mine,' said Asher. He reached out as his luggage moved along the airport baggage carousel.

'Let me carry that,' said Mike. He wrapped his thick fingers around the handle of the large, black luggage case. 'Goodness, don't tell me you have that old bat in here, it's heavy enough,' he said.

'Old bat?' Asher scratched his head. He was a little confused.

'Sorry, I mean your grandmother,' said Mike. He could not help but smirk.

'Ha, good one,' said Asher. He chuckled. 'You know it's got wheels.' He was, of course, referring to his luggage case.

'Sure,' said Mike. 'Just flexing my muscles.'

Leaving the Luxor International Airport, Asher could not help but take note of his dad's distinctive attire. He observed his dad's brown hat, tan shirt, and cream pants. 'You remind me of someone, Dad,' he said. He could not keep a straight face. He desperately wanted to laugh.

'Go on then. Who do I remind you of?' asked Mike. He was intrigued.

'No, no, I'm wrong,' smiled Asher. 'You're missing the leather whip,' he teased.

'Oi lad, not here two minutes and you're already on my back,' replied Mike. His tone was playful. Clunk! He tossed Asher's luggage in the back of a green speckled Land Rover. Taking a key from his pocket, he then unlocked the doors. 'We haven't got all day, hop on in and tell me what you've been up to at school.'

Climbing into the passenger seat, Asher began unravelling his tales from back home, including how he was improving in his vast array of subjects, particularly his after-school music class. 'I've been brushing up on my guitar tablature, even Ben says it was a good idea to join the music club.' His initial reservations about joining the music club had been quashed.

'Hey, that is excellent. Who knows, you may be the next big thing. The next legendary six-stringer,' said Mike. 'Besides, guitarists get all the cool chicks.' He playfully nudged Asher.

'I don't think so,' said Asher softly in response. 'Mandy has gone off with a real creep,' he added. He let out a heavy sigh.

'A crush, I take it,' said Mike. As he watched, Asher fell silent. He could see the disappointment on his sullen face. 'Give it time, I met your mother as she watched me play in The Shamrock, a bar in Boston,' he alluded.

'Really, I never knew how you and Mum met,' said Asher. He sat upright in his seat. When it came to his mother, Mike never told him a great deal.

'Oh sure, coincidentally, she had told me her great grandparents were of Irish descent, they had come from the Emerald Isle itself,' said Mike. 'For goodness' sake, I could perhaps trace Irish blood in my family tree.'

'Were you in a band?' said Asher.

'Yes, I was in a band. We were smoking hot,' replied Mike. He smiled before reminiscing on his musical past. 'I played back in the so-called glory days.' One hand on the driving wheel, with the other, he caressed the stubble on his chin. His round green eyes kept fixed on the direction the vehicle was going.

'Glory days,' said Asher. 'What glory days?' He was curious.

'Back many moons ago, lad, me and a few college buds had a band, we were called The Black Thorns,' said Mike. When he was younger, he earned money by playing in a band, money and free drinks that is. He had played in lots of bars and small venues before becoming an established archaeologist.

'Cool,' replied Asher in amazement.

'Good times, lad, really good,' said Mike, radiantly.

'I know you weren't the singer with your horrid voice,' said Asher. He playfully pushed his left hand against his dad's shoulder.

'For your information, I have the voice of an angel,' said Mike. 'But no, Jerrold my bandmate was the lead singer. I played the six-string too, just like you.'

'Really, you did,' said Asher. 'Who would have thought, you never mentioned anything about playing guitar,' he said. He had no idea.

'Why did you think I bought you that guitar two Christmases ago?' asked Mike.

'I just didn't know,' said Asher. 'I mean, with you always off around the world, who would have dreamed that I would have been able to learn on my own,' he said.

'Yeah, isn't that something?' said Mike. His upbeat mood dipped. He realised that he should have been the one to teach Asher to play the guitar. He realised that there were many things that he had missed in his son's life.

'What are the odds?' said Asher. He suddenly felt an uneasy tension that had been unintentionally created. He truly did not intend to hurt his dad's feelings on purpose. For a moment, he looked along the sandy road before changing the subject. 'So, Dad, I've been reading up on the Valley of the Kings.' Asher had a passion for history, and it was only inevitable that the subject of desire soon turned to Egypt and its interwoven history dating back thousands of years.

Brushing off the prior conversation, Mike enlightened how 'the team,' in his words, had stumbled across an undiscovered tomb, even though they still had not managed to drill all the way through the thick layer of stone and rubble leading to the inside. 'We're so close. Carved deeply upon the tomb entrance are the strangest set of inscriptions me or my experienced researcher, Elisha, have ever seen,' he said.

'Inscriptions!' Asher's diamond-shaped face was filled with intrigue. He wanted to know more.

'Yes, inscriptions. But be assured, it's only a matter of time before the team and I discover their true meaning,' informed Mike. Honkkk! 'Watch…watch where you're going you bugger!' he shouted as a shabby blue vehicle hastily cut in front of him.

Lost in the ebb and flow of their conversation, Asher and his dad, Mike, soon reached the West Bank of the River Nile after crossing the Luxor Bridge. Bikes, coaches, and private hire taxis filled with tourists congested the way.

Bypassing the town of Ad Dabiyyah, Mike continued down the route of Al Mahamed Bahri Al Okser, before turning right onto Luxor Aswan Street. The open-top vehicle soon reached the Kings Valley Road.

'It's amazing, Dad,' said Asher. Grasping every ounce of his attention was approximately nine square kilometres of constant beige. He took a deep breath, he was astonished.

'Feast your eyes, lad, on the home of some of the most important archaeological sites in the world,' said Mike. Passion filled his square-shaped face. Archaeology was his life through and through. It was in his blood.

Encompassing the Valley of the Kings, the Valley of the Queens, more than five thousand nobles' tombs, countless shrines and forty-plus temples, the renowned location opposite ancient Thebes, AKA modern day Luxor, was truly spectacular to behold.

'There are so many people.' Taken aback, Asher could see flocks of people up ahead. His curiosity had been ignited like a tinderbox.

The vehicle had slowed to a crawling pace. The vehicles' four big black tyres bit into the sand and tarmac beneath.

There were hordes of locals. Most were dressed in traditional Egyptian clothing, national and religious customs playing a key factor in their choice. There were women with facial coverings and men wearing turbans, skullcaps, and fez hats. In addition, both genders, male and female, also wore traditional light robes of many varieties.

A significantly smaller segment of locals, however, wore more westernised clothing, such as denim jeans, cotton shorts, tops, and shirts, again depending on gender. Dress code norms blurring, especially among the younger generation, and growing cultural freedom was also hard at play as an influencing factor.

The only constant, whether traditional or western influenced, was that most locals had tailored their appearance to incorporate some form or combination of head, facial or neck wear.

Of course, outstripping the locals in mass numbers were hordes of vibrant tourists in great divergent variety. They swarmed the entrance gate to the Valley of the Kings like a nest of bees displaced from their hive.

American, English, French, German, Italian, a vast mixture of nationalities was present. A brew of divergent accents could be heard amongst the ecstatic crowds.

'Are we almost there yet, Dad?' queried Asher. He was anxious to see what his dad had been working on over the past two years.

'Almost, lad, it's just up ahead,' said Mike. He pointed to his destination.

The pyramid-shaped mountain, Al-Qurn, was in clear view. The Land Rover's dusty black tyres rolled to a stop. The engine ceased to hum. They had finally arrived at the exploration site. Jumping from the vehicle, they were both engulfed by a sudden flurry of intense activity!

'What the hell's going on around here?' bellowed Mike. He snatched his hat from his head. He then began rubbing the sweat off his brow. 'I leave briefly, and this is what happens,' he exclaimed. It was so hot. The sweat began to seep through his tan shirt.

Madness had utterly engulfed the exploration site. Muscles rippling, sweat caressing bald head, one of the diggers hustled forward with a dirt-covered shovel in his hand. 'Boss.' Lips flopping up and down, he was wildly frantic. 'Boss, I think you'd better see this,' he said.

'Lead the way then,' answered Mike. Swiftly, he hurried to the scene as Asher closed in behind. 'Well, well, you've managed to drill through the tomb entrance, good work, very good indeed Carl,' he said.

Without further delay, Mike made his way inside the cleared entranceway, which led to a long, shadowy corridor. The corridor itself was partially blocked by fallen debris. It was dangerously unstable, no one could get through. 'How long do you think it'll take to move this, Carl?' he queried.

He got a swift reply. 'Three, maybe four days at the very least, boss,' replied Carl Jackson, as he rubbed the back of his sweaty, bald skull.

'Look at the details!' Mike's attention was caught by the exquisite works of ancient art that rested upon the dust-ridden walls. One-eyed human figures staring back, he slowly receded out of the shady corridor. 'I've a good feeling about this one.' He was quite optimistic.

Watching his dad's every movement, Asher was equally amazed. 'Wow! It's amazing, Dad,' he gasped. Enthralled, his eyes scanned far and wide along the eerie passageway. He had only ever seen such a thing in books.

'Let's back out of here, lad,' informed Mike. 'It's too unsteady. One wrong move and crash! We're both buried under a ton of rock.' Thud! Thud! Thud! He brushed his hat against his cream pants to dislodge the dust and dirt. 'Besides, I think you and I should do some exploring, along with the tourists,' he said.

Asher felt a ginormous, blood-pumping rush of excitement. 'Where are we going, Dad?' he probed.

'To take a tour of the Valley of the Gates of the Kings,' said Mike.

Asher was initially puzzled by the phrase as he scratched his scalp. 'Where's that at then?' he queried. He was still young, just at the beginning of life's journey and the search for knowledge.

'Well, my boy, we're at it,' said Mike. He put both hands up in the air before turning three hundred and sixty degrees.

'No, Dad,' responded Asher. Acting quite smug, he spoke aloud in an attempt to correct him. 'This is the Valley of the Kings.' He even shook his index finger side to side. He was a little too overconfident. He liked to read, but his dad was ahead of him by many miles.

'That's one name to call this beautifully mysterious place,' said Mike. He went on to explain that their current location was generally known as the Valley of the Kings, but others would call it by the less-used term, as he had mentioned. 'Some have even referred to this place as the Valley of the Tombs of the Kings, really, there is little differentiation, lad,' he continued to elucidate.

'One more question, Dad,' said Asher. He held up his index finger, for he had another burning query.

'Shoot,' said Mike. He made a pistol gesture with his hand.

'Why does that man call you, boss?' asked Asher.

'You mean Carl?' answered Mike. He observed as Asher nodded. 'It's just a manner of speaking. We're good friends, besides, I'm the lead archaeologist,' he explained further.

'Wow! Lead archaeologist,' said Asher in awe. 'You're a real big shot then,' he smiled. He returned the pistol gesture.

'You better believe it. Now get in,' said Mike playfully. Jumping into the Land Rover, he twisted the key in the ignition. Brummm! Vehicle coming to life, they were soon off once again. The vehicle zoomed off, back down the valley, before coming to a screeching halt.

'We'll walk the rest, too many people, lad,' informed Mike. 'You should see tomb KV62. You haven't visited the Valley of the Kings, as you put it, unless you've seen the tomb of the boy king, Tutankhamun,' he said.

Moving further down the gorge with rigid rocks on either side, they both steered toward a flock of buzzing tourists.

Reaching their destination, they eventually attempted to enter the notorious attraction, although this took a bit of time due to the curiosity of one rather large fellow in front who could not help but stop to admire every little detail.

'Splendid Elizabeth, just splendid, isn't it?'

'We haven't seen inside yet, Albert dear.'

Captivated, Asher questioned the reasoning behind the naming of the burial site belonging to the ancient pharaoh. 'Why's it called tomb KV62, Dad?' he inquired.

'You're full of questions. Well, simply put lad, there is a sequential numbering convention used within the valley,' stated Mike. His own prized find had yet to be designated a number.

With pace, Asher stormed down several stone steps, his hand slid along a steel handrail. He then turned right, reaching the antechamber. Stripes of blue and gold-like colours directed his gaze toward a beautifully decorated facial mask. 'Gosh!' He was utterly captivated by an exquisitely carved sarcophagus. 'Dad, is that Tutankhamun's coffin?' he asked.

'Well, there's only room for one sarcophagus in here, it couldn't be anyone else's lad,' responded Mike, unable to keep a straight face. Both he and Asher let out a loud, cheerful laugh.

Scanning the images upon the chamber walls, Mike studied them with astute precision. 'Tutankhamun in the form of Osiris, Tutankhamun being greeted by the Goddess Nut and Tutankhamun's Ka further to the left, vividly beautiful,' he said. He pointed to one image after another.

'Ka! What do you mean?' asked Asher. Nose curled up; he was full of curiosity.

'His spiritual representation,' responded Mike.

Humoured by their ever-developing conversation, Mike further revealed his immediate thoughts. 'The boy King Tutankhamun Nebkheperure's tomb is believed to date from the eighteenth dynasty.' His hands fell to an iron rail separating them from the exquisitely patterned sarcophagus. 'Which of course is believed to also be one of the most prestigious and richest periods in Egyptian history,' he said.

Conveying a pleasant expression, Asher smirked uncontrollably. 'Well, I know I've heard, or should I say read, that somewhere before,' he said.

'Ha!' Mike chuckled. 'You have a selective memory.' It seemed he, too, had also read the book he had sent Asher, but a few weeks earlier, entitled 'Valley of the Kings, The Archaeologist's Guide.' Asher had a few chapters left to read. 'When first discovered, this very tomb was covered in all sorts of precious valuables,' he said.

Getting into his stride, Mike continued enlightening him that when first discovered in 1922 by a man known as Howard Carter, thousands of objects were enclosed within the chamber. 'Artefacts littered the very spot we stand upon,' he said.

However, most of which had since been put on display at the Egyptian Museum in Cairo.

'The chamber itself is quite small. The architecture is more in character with the private tombs of the West Bank rather than a royal tomb,' said Mike.

Flash! Flash! Flash! Successive bursts of bright light were quickly followed by a deep, thunderous roar.

'No, no pictures!' The tomb guard on watch quickly sprang into motion. He snatched the camera, vigorously enforcing the valley rules.

'Now…Now…' The chubby man known as Albert protested loudly. 'Now, see here, sir, give me back my camera,' he demanded. Jaws jangling, his enormous gut strained against his red shirt. It had images of pineapples on it. He was completely outraged.

'No pictures!' The tomb guard was firm.

'But…but…but…'

'No pictures!'

'Now, darling, come, we must have our camera!' The elderly woman, Elizabeth, intervened. She had grey hair and wore a flowery white dress and sandals. She held a straw hat in her wrinkled hands.

'Elizabeth, dear, I'm dealing with this,' said Albert. He looked flabbergasted. 'Now see here…' He was about to have another rant at the tan-skinned tomb guard. However, he was cut short.

'Shall we say four-fifty?' queried Elizabeth, attempting to bribe the guard. Her offer of four hundred and fifty Egyptian pounds, equivalent to just over twenty dollars, was well received.

'Yes!' The tomb guard agreed. His crooked teeth appeared from behind his shabby moustache. He let go of the camera as he wrapped his dirt-stained fingernails around the crisp notes. 'Go now,' he ordered.

'Thank you, my dear, you're too kind, come now, Albert,' said Elizabeth calmly and elegantly. She took a grip of her husband's arm.

'That was amazing, Dad,' said Asher as he exited Tutankhamun's tomb.

'It's not over yet!' Mike had other plans in mind.

'I don't like that look,' said Asher with suspicion.

Mike's mischievous facial expressions signalled that he was up to no good. 'Fancy going for a ride?'

Asher finally locked sights on a set of bushy eyebrows, two rows of long eyelashes, large tough lips, big thick footpads, and one large hump. He took note of a large camel. He could not take his eyes off the creature, he had never seen a real camel before, not in person.

'They are wonderfully majestic animals,' said Mike. 'Jump on, lad,' he said.

'You must be kidding,' gasped Asher. He pounded his feet on the sound beneath. Edgy, he would neither go near nor touch the creature.

'Well, lad, say hello,' said Mike. He forcefully took hold of Asher, lifting him high in the air. He hoisted Asher atop the camel.

'Woahhh!' Asher wriggled as he panicked. 'Dad, stop,' he yelled.

'You'll be fine, lad; the camel means you no harm,' said Mike calmly. He was sure of it. He knew the camel was well trained. He knew the camel keeper personally.

'Oh really, then where is he going?' questioned Asher. He took a tight hold of a set of leather reins as the animal stomped forward, making loud sounds as it went. His face was redder than a stop sign, his eyes looked like they were ready to pop.

'She, along with this dazzling creature, is taking us sightseeing,' Mike warmly responded. He put his hand in his pocket, turning out several colourful Egyptian notes. He had in his hand one, two, three, four, five, one-hundred-pound notes, picturing the Mosque-Madrassa of Sultan Hassan on the obverse and a sphinx on the reverse. He handed over the notes to the camel keeper. 'I owe you one, Atemu,' he said.

The dark-skinned man, wearing a white pullover tunic and grey turban, gestured in a friendly manner. 'BarakAllahu Fiykum,' he spoke, meaning 'may Allah bless you.'

Mike clambered upon the back of the second camel, taking a grip of the reins. 'Well, lad, let's go, we're burning daylight,' he said. He led the way.

Reassured by his dad's presence, Asher's nerves slowly evaporated. He grew a little curious. 'Isn't that a weird name?' he commented, referring to the camel keeper.

'His name means mythical great god of Annu,' expressed Mike. This led to another one of his intense stories. 'Ra, ancient sun god of Annu, Heliopolis to the Greeks, near modern day Cairo, is considered in some traditions to be the creator of men,' he said.

Seemingly having the gift of the gab, Mike had a flurry of interest in anything of a historical or mythical nature. Once he got started, he never seemed to stop, from the ancient gods to the Egyptian dynasties of old.

It was his lengthy outpouring of knowledge that had led to Asher's focus wavering. 'You know way too much, Dad,' he said, fleetingly.

Following a flock of tourists taking the guided tour, Asher's interests gradually wandered elsewhere. He was taken aback by the openness, the sand, and the serenity all around him. Like a sailor dislodged from his ship, he was swamped in a sea, a sea of never-ending beige.

A light breeze befell upon both Asher and his dad, as on route they had seen the Colossi of Memnon, Queen Hatshepsut's temple, and had even come within half a mile of the River Nile itself.

'Wow!' gasped Asher. He still could not get over the length of the vast body of water, which stretched as far as the eye could see. He could observe many ferry boats on the water and people, small figures as tiny as ants, manoeuvring along the riverbank. The sight was truly spectacular indeed.

Clink! Clink! Clink! Colourless liquid tumbling into his mouth, Mike took a long gulp from a silver canteen. 'Catch lad.' He then tossed the canteen mid-air.

Leaning back in a wooden-framed saddle, covered with a simple red woollen throw-over, Asher caught the silver water holder between his nimble hands.

'The River Nile, lad, it's stunning, it's the longest river in the world shared by eleven countries, originating in Burundi,' said Mike. He himself had been to some of those countries.

Glancing toward his dad, Asher could not help but think that the day so far had been one of the best in his entire life. 'I've really enjoyed today,' he said, earnestly. He felt a connection with his dad he had not felt in a long time.

'I did too,' said Mike. He was smiling from ear to ear.

'I've seen a whole other side to you,' said Asher. He reflected on the few times Mike had returned home to Neptune City, New Jersey. 'You seem a different person,' he said.

'Oh, how so?' asked Mike. He began stroking the stubble on his chin.

'Well, every time you come home, you seem gloomy; today you've been happier than I've ever seen,' said Asher.

'Well, there are just a lot of memories in that old house,' said Mike. 'Spent a lot of time with Jane and her folks there, and, well…never mind.' He shook his head. All the while, he was twisting a gold ring on his wedding finger. It appeared that after thirteen whole years, he still had not forgotten his first love.

'I'd like to know more about Mum,' said Asher softly. He grew sullen.

'Another time,' responded Mike. He did not feel like opening that can of worms. 'But unfortunately, we must get back to the exploration site,' he said.

'Oh…Ok,' whispered Asher. His Dad seemed never to want to talk about his mum, Jane Paterson.

Sun fading fast, they had to return the camels to their owner, who trusted Mike wholeheartedly with their well-being.

'Jump in, lad,' said Mike. Brummm! The engine of the Land Rover was brought to life. It was not long before he and Asher were back at the exploration site.

Smash! Bang! Thump! Thump! Thump! Hands wielding hammers, other hands pickaxes, and some chisels, Mike's small team were still pressing hard.

Sweating profusely, muscles bulging, Asher observed the man known as Carl Jackson with great interest. Light radiated off the man's brown skin as he hauled huge rocks about as if mere feathers. He was hard at work. He led a small contingent of workers.

Attentive, Mike noticed Asher's curiosity. 'You've already met Carl, he's a good man, been with me since our explorations in Africa. He is the muscle behind this small operation, along with the Egyptians,' he explained. There were ten Egyptians who were a part of the excavation. He removed his hat from his head, and he then steered his feet toward the tomb. 'On the other hand, there's Elisha Thompson, the brains.'

He continued to reveal that very few equalled her in terms of her knowledge of Egyptian history and mythology. She had also been with him for some time, in fact, since the Greek explorations, going back over eight years.

'Lastly there is Tony Richardson,' said Mike. 'The go to man,' he said.

'What do you mean, the go to man?' asked Asher. He was perplexed. He rolled his big blue eyes.

'Simple, anything you need he gets; tools, workers, expertise, he's in the know,' said Mike. Each member of his small team had a pivotal role to play.

'I'll keep that in mind,' said Asher. He grinned profusely.

'Is she shifting Carl?' probed Mike. He took a quick glance at the big man.

'Yes, boss, she'll be cleared in no time,' informed Carl, so caught up in his work, he did not even turn to look at Mike.

'Elisha, any luck?' queried Mike. He then turned to a woman with fiery red hair and hazel eyes. She was a beautiful woman in her mid-thirties. 'If anyone can decipher those markings and paintings, it's you,' he complimented.

'Come now, Mike, you know quality takes time, but there is something,' she said. She elucidated that from her translations that she had managed to decode fragments of information. Clarifying how there was a warning above the tomb entrance that read, 'death shall come swiftly to those who disturb thee!'

'The odd curse or two isn't uncommon where the ancient Egyptians of old are concerned, is there anything else?' he said.

'Please, Mike, of course there's more, on the walls of the inner corridor, there is mention of a trinket of unconceivable power,' declared Elisha. 'It's most puzzling to say the least, but I believe it to be a bracelet or wristlet of some kind,' she revealed.

'Really, are you positive?' Mike appeared baffled as he ran his hand through his dark brown hair.

'I'm quite sure,' said Elisha with confidence. 'But two figures stand out upon the wall, one shrouded in light, dressed in leopard skin and white linen, with sandals upon the feet, wearing an amulet. The other is shrouded in darkness. He appears to be a master of the bracelet, although I need more time to decipher it all.' She still had much to do.

'Of course,' said Mike. 'You just work your magic,' he said.

'I also think this particular tomb belongs to a very important noble or high priest, perhaps a pharaoh, although the structure seems to be quite simple,' said Elisha. 'I'll document and photograph what I can.'

'Be careful, for I couldn't stand anything happening to you,' said Mike, expressing concern for her. 'That inner corridor seems unsteady,' he informed her.

'Sure thing,' replied Elisha. She took him by the hand. 'I'll know more when Carl and the boys clear the rest of the debris.' She held great affection for him, too.

Listening with interest, Asher's mouth was agape in sheer fascination. He was taken with what he was hearing.

'You'd be as well closing that boy before you catch flies,' said Mike jestingly. He caught him off guard. He tapped Asher's chin with his hand.

With silver rays of moonlight radiating from overhead and countless stars twinkling in cloudless abundance, the shadow of nightfall had soon consumed them. Wood crackling, flashes of red and bright orange played with Asher's light complexion.

'Hmmm…this is nice.' Snuggled up warmly in his sleeping bag, polyester fabric brushing against his soft skin, he relaxed close to the campfire, as did his dad.

Of course, they were not alone. Mike's experienced team were situated nearby. Some were asleep, while others went about their business, bustling to and fro.

A sound, beautiful and enchanting, had arisen, each soft note full of soul, full of life. An Egyptian, wearing an orange turban and white tunic, harnessed his skill on the flute.

Mike pressed a silver steel pot to the flame of the campfire. After a while, a dark mixture started to bubble within the pot.

'Is it ready, Dad?' Asher asked. He grew impatient. He caressed his lips together; the smell of hot chocolate was all too tempting.

'Just about lad, here watch your fingers now,' instructed Mike.

'Oh, it's hot,' said Asher. He held the enamel mug tight; heat smothered his skin. He listened intently as his dad began to talk about Egypt once again. This time, however, he paid more attention.

'During the time of Egypt's New Kingdom, 1539-1075 BC, this very valley became a royal burial ground, pharaohs such as Tutankhamun, Seti I, and Ramses II are buried here, of course so are certain notable queens, high priests and other elites of the 18th, 19th, and 20th dynasties,' explained Mike. 'Egypt's last independent ruler was a queen by the name of Cleopatra. She was also the land's most celebrated pharaoh,' he said.

'Well, what happened to her?' gasped Asher. Mouth agape, he was fascinated.

'The beautiful Cleopatra committed suicide after the battle of Actium, the might of Rome had bent Egypt to her will,' said Mike. 'Although before she was captured and committed suicide, she watched her soul mate, poor old Marc Antony, die in her arms after he plunged his sword into his body,' he said.

'I would have loved to have seen Rome with you, Dad,' said Asher.

'I would have loved you to be there, but it never seemed like the right time,' informed Mike. 'When I was in Rome, you were only six.' The truth was he was so wrapped up in his work, he had no time to tend to a child. 'The plan was for me and Jane to see the world together, though she had studied psychology, not sure how that would've turned out,' he said.

'Life could have been very different had Mum lived,' said Asher. He was fed yet another piece of information about his mother's life that he did not know.

An overwhelming guilt consumed Mike once again. 'Well, you and I will be spending more time together now, oh yes, Christmas, Easter and even the summer holidays, and we'll have such fun,' he said.

'Maybe I'll get to see the Coliseum yet,' said Asher. He grew happy at the thought. It was one of his desires. Tales of gladiators and unsung heroes had captured his imagination.

'Perhaps, Rome is a beautiful city,' stated Mike. Getting to his feet, he took hold of a tin bucket. Splashhh! He threw the bucket of water over the campfire, reducing the flames to blotches of red embers. 'Come, lad, let's call it a night,' he said.

The hour had grown late. Increasingly stronger, blustering gusts of wind had sent them into retreat.

'Brhhh! It's cold,' said Asher, teeth clattering. His whole body shivered.

'Quick, inside the tent,' said Mike.

The dying melody emanating from the Egyptian flute player had signalled that he, too, had succumbed to the sudden blustery weather.

'Arghhh…' Rustling back and forth, sweating profusely, countless times throughout the night, Asher was awakened, believing he had heard strange voices! 'The Portal Realm!' The words escaped his lips as he jumped from his disturbing sleep. 'Get a grip,' he uttered. He wiped the perspiration from his forehead.

'Not again, get some shut eye,' groaned Mike. He blurted out the words as he tossed and turned. He pulled his woollen blanket over his body.

'Sure, Dad,' replied Asher. He curled up his small body before drifting back to sleep. Sent to the land of dreams, strange and unusual images began to fill his mind.

In his dream, he had entered the main chamber of a tomb. The room itself was filled with many artefacts, including jewellery of all kinds, statues, vases, and pottery. In the centre of the chamber was a sarcophagus of gold and blue colours. The sarcophagus was open. To the side of the sarcophagus stood a dark-skinned man. He was motionless, blank of all expression.

The figure in his dream wore leopard skin over white linen clothing, which was held in position by a strap over one shoulder. The figure, a male, also wore white papyrus sandals upon his feet. Most precariously, the individual was bald, with no facial hair, including brows or eyelashes.

The individual wore an amulet. It was shaped like an eye.

Upon the walls of the chamber, there were many elaborate images. Red, blue, black, and gold colours foretold of the afterlife, the underworld, and the gods of Egypt.

At one end of the chamber, there was a column of limestone. Atop the limestone column was something of immense value, a golden bracelet, with a big blue stone in the centre.

Captivated and still dreaming, Asher found his body gliding forward. He soon found the precious jewel in his hands. That is when the dream took a turn for the worse!

A blue spectacle filled the chamber. The blue swirled in a circular motion, growing brighter and brighter, bigger and bigger. Shards of a blue-like aura broke inward. Then he appeared!

'Here I come, here at last, soon you must be the one to find what was hidden in the past!' A tiny individual, an imp, appeared from the spectacle of blue, the doorway, the portal of sorts.

The little imp was three feet nine inches in height at most. He had black curly hair and wore a blue leather vest, black breeches, and boots. His clothing looked very out of place. Then he spoke yet again!

'Zippity-doo, zippy-dee, how do you do, I bet you weren't expecting me.' The little imp's eyes turned to an aura of solid, glowing white. A great many shadows filled the chamber. Dark images with horns danced upon the chamber walls. 'I say it now, I say it loud, for it's you who'll find what belongs to The Horned God!'

'Arghhh…no…no!' Asher panicked in fear.

'Oopsy-doo, oopsy me, I didn't mean to scare thee.' The imp looked just as terrified. 'I went too far, that much I can see,' he said. He reached out to Asher. 'I'm as harmless as harmless can be.'

'No, no, leave me alone!' Yelling, Asher pounced from his dream, his nightmare. His heart thudded in his chest. His hands shook uncontrollably.

'It was only a dream,' said Mike. He rushed to Asher's side.

'Yes, Dad, but it felt so real,' panted Asher. 'I…I…I stood inside, a tomb…' he started.

'Yes, but it's all in your head. Probably brought on by all the sightseeing. Not to mention what Elisha was speaking of earlier,' said Mike. 'Just tricks of the mind,' he added.

Despite his dad's reassurance, Asher still felt quite uneasy. 'Suppose so,' he mumbled. His palms were sweaty. His face was pale.

'Best get back to sleep, busy day tomorrow,' said Mike. He pulled the woollen blanket over Asher's small body.

Nodding in agreement, Asher lay back down, though the truth was he was barely able to get a wink of sleep the rest of the night.

-Chapter 6-

Intruders

'Who's in charge around this damn place?' a hoarse voice boomed.

Extremely exhausted, Asher was unexpectedly awakened the next morning by the rustling and bustling of stomping feet and loud thunderous voices. He heard a hurricane of activity erupt just outside the tent he had slept in during the night.

'Somebody better bloody well answer me!' The voice thundered once more.

Sleep-deprived, Asher listened intently for a moment. He heard an accent thicker than porridge. Little did he know the accent was Eastern European. He found it strange. 'That racket…gosh, my gran is quieter.' He was taken with the commotion; it did not sound good. He felt something was wrong!

He got to his feet. 'Dad…Dad, do you hear that...' He fell quiet as his eyes darted to the spot where Mike had slept during the night. He was not there!

'Ma…manners, my good fellow, la…ladies present,' another man interjected. He took a calmer, more rational approach. He also had a stutter.

'What, may I ask, can I do for you gentlemen?' questioned Elisha. She was composed and collected. Her soft, feminine voice broke through the air like soft silk.

Asher moved his body forward. His muscles ached. He peeked out of the tent entrance. 'Gosh, it's bright,' he muttered. His pupils narrowed. He could see that there was quite a flourish of activity by the tomb that his dad, Mike, and his team had uncovered. It seemed that another group was moving in upon his dad's prized find. Given their unprofessional behaviour, he was not entirely sure whether they were archaeologists.

'Bernard Pa…Pafford, madam, Head of the Faculty of Archaeology at the university in Luxor.' Bernard quickly introduced himself. He removed a straw hat from his head, revealing a bald patch and grey hair. He had a grey moustache too and a beard. He was tall, six feet six inches in height, and thin like a beanpole. His attire was composed of a light blue shirt, cream pants, and brown sandals.

'Sorry, Mr Pafford,' said Elisha, 'I must tell you…'

'Be…Bernard or Dr Pafford, please,' he said. His brown, patterned, oval-shaped glasses hung upon a thin black string. His accent was slightly watered down, but his English roots could still be detected, despite his clear speech impediment.

'Very well, Bernard, I'm afraid this site is already designated, I do most, if not all the research and documenting involved here,' explained Elisha. She was forced to look up at the tall, leek-shaped professor from Luxor, being only five feet, ten inches in height herself.

'I know, my colleagues have fr…friends in an official capacity,' said Bernard. He fixed his spectacles over the bridge of his nose. Without permission, he proceeded to inspect the tomb entrance way. He ran his hand along the stone, his fingers caressing embedded inscriptions. 'Be…beautiful,' he said.

'It's stunning,' said Elisha.

'It's a warning,' said Bernard as his eyes narrowed. He was fully immersed in what he was seeing. He appeared to know quite a bit about ancient Egyptian, as he expressed his first judgements about the strange markings. 'De…death shall be…befall all who disturbs thee!'

'Very good, but not uncommon,' said Elisha, not fully impressed. 'But I must ask you to leave…'

'Achooo!' Bernard's facial muscles tightened as he sneezed. He took a white hanky from the pocket of his blue, short-sleeved shirt before wiping his broad nose. 'Truly int…intriguing my dear, I must see m…more.'

Successfully, Bernard had managed to decipher fragments of information, specifically relating to the severe warning carved upon the tomb entrance, although a great deal remained elusive to him.

'That's not possible, Bernard, until all findings are officially published,' said Elisha firmly. The smile on her heart-shaped face dissolved. She rested her hands about her hips. She wore a white shirt knotted at the midsection, jean shorts, and white leather sandals.

'Th…that could take months, e…even years,' said Bernard. 'I will not sit on the si…sidelines that long, dear. Get my ca… camera and tools, Igor,' he said. With his right hand, he began stroking his grey beard.

'Of course, it will be done.' The man named Igor moved to carry out the demand. He had thighs as thick as tree trunks, his arms were large and bulky, and his neck was stocky. He had a face more unpleasant than the grim reaper. 'Shift yourselves,' he shouted with a thick accent. A vast group of accompanying men sprang into action.

'Dr Pafford, this site is designated. You cannot conduct your research here,' said Elisha. Formalities reinstated, her head energetically moved to and fro to cement her point. Her fiery red hair bounced side to side as she did so. Her nostrils began to flare as she grew irate.

'M…my dear, I can, and I w…will,' said Bernard. He was defiant.

Suffocated by an array of wild, watchful eyes and mockingly disturbing smirks, Elisha utterly struggled in her futile attempt to remain in control. 'Now, see here, this is unacceptable, Dr Pafford. You must leave now,' she warned. She scratched her fingernails together anxiously.

Bernard took no heed of Elisha's objections. He leaned his partially bald head into the tomb corridor. 'Oh b…but I wouldn't dream of leaving,' he said. He was arrogant. 'There's so much to see, be…besides I'm sure pro…professionals such as us can come to some sort of an arrangement,' he said.

'We don't want or need any more help,' said Elisha. 'Leave now.' She was stern. She waved her hand at the arrogant intruder.

'I and these fellows have ye…years of experience,' continued Bernard. 'We can only add to this ex…excavation.' He was not backing down.

'There's nothing to be gained, everything will be recorded, and tagged, most likely sent to the museums in Luxor and Cairo,' said Elisha. 'History belongs to everyone,' she said. She was a true professional.

'Yes, but hi…history doesn't need to know every little detail,' said Bernard. He was proposing something not only unethical, but illegal. Smuggling artefacts out of the country was not uncommon.

Stepping forward from the shade of the tent, Asher grew extremely concerned. 'Elisha!' He called out to her.

Brummm! Asher's soft voice was overshadowed by a loud humming sound. The unmistakable sound of an engine in motion broke over the top of the wild commotion before him. It was none other than his dad, Mike!

Mike drove the Land Rover carelessly, eventually coming to a sharp stop. Clink! He pulled up the handbrake. 'What's going on here then?' he roared. He slammed the door of the vehicle as he exited. He sought immediate answers.

'Nothing for you to worry about!' A serious-looking man interjected himself into the situation. He wore black sunglasses, blue denim jeans, and a black shirt with the top three buttons undone. 'Continue, I want to know as much as possible,' he ordered. He held a cigar between his yellow-stained fingers. It was clear that he was in command.

'Yes, Bronislav,' said Bernard obediently. He took his camera from a black bag. 'Thank you, I…Igor,' he said.

Remaining defiant, Mike was having none of it. 'This site is occupied, so I'll ask you nicely this time, move off our land,' he said. His resolve was stern.

The man named Bronislav Valadvic stood his ground. 'Take your own advice and leave before somebody gets hurt!' he threatened. Like the man, Igor, his accent was distinctively Eastern European. He was born in Saint Petersburg, Russia.

For being forty-nine years old, Bronislav was physically well built. He was six feet one inch in height, he had broad shoulders, and a defined chest. His waist was narrower than his shoulders. His black hair was combed back. He did have one obvious disability. He had a limp. As he moved, it was clear he had issues with his left leg. He had damaged his knee.

Unwavering, Mike did not take kindly to the threatening jibe. 'Call your dogs off and get lost,' he snapped fiercely. His face was red, as veins popped in his neck.

'No, I don't think so,' taunted Bronislav with a mischievous grin. He remained calm. He dropped his cigar to the sandy canvas beneath, before flattening it with his big boot. 'We're here to stay,' he alluded. He began stroking the shabby, grey-ridged stubble upon his chin as if contemplating his options. 'There could be a lot of money involved.' He rubbed his fingers together. 'We've dealt with this sort of work before, I have contacts.'

'Money, what money?' asked Mike. He was confused, to say the least.

'A friend, a governmental friend here in Luxor, says you've found something here,' said Bronislav. 'We, too, have experience in excavating and finding hidden treasures.'

'Well, get lost,' thundered Mike. 'We've been through all the proper channels, this site is ours, whatever we find will go to the museum in Cairo,' he said defiantly.

'Well, I see,' said Bronislav. He took a step back, his left leg dragging against the sandy canvas beneath, creating a cringeworthy scraping sound.

Over the years, Bronislav had been in and out of prison. More than once, he had been linked to dealings in contraband and the importing and exporting of various illegal items. While in one of Moscow's finest prisons, he was injured in a brawl. Before his descent into criminal life, he spent three years in the Russian military.

'There's only one law here,' said Bronislav. He unexpectedly, and to everyone's surprise, pulled out a long-bladed knife from a leather sheath, wedged in the back of his jeans! 'It's survival of the fittest,' he grinned.

'Oh no!' Analysing the precarious situation, Asher instantly became alight with worry. He could see that his dad was not carrying a weapon of his own. He nibbled uneasily upon his bottom lip.

'So, you're going to kill me, is that it?' asked Mike, believing that the Eastern European was bluffing. With his index finger, he flicked his brown hat upward, just a little. He was bold. He was unwilling to give way to this new cunning, arrogant, and dangerous foe.

Brought up in a disciplined household, Mike was no stranger to the military himself. His father, Michael Daniel Paterson, had served in the US military. He was a tough man. He had instilled in him tough qualities. One such quality was to never give in, to never back down.

'No, not kill, perhaps hurt a little, my boys will say it was self-defence,' spoke Bronislav. He raised his arm and the knife he held. It was hard to determine the seriousness of his intentions. 'We only want a little cooperation,' he added.

Clickkk! 'Cool it, there'll be no violence today,' howled Carl. He had been keeping a close watch on events as they had unfolded. He held in his hands a rifle. 'Let's all keep things sensible now, you hear.' He was steadfast and composed, his green eyes looked down the barrel of the gun.

'Nice timing, Carl,' said Mike. He grinned profusely.

Wisely, Carl had locked sights upon Bronislav. His unwarranted threats immediately ceased.

Bronislav's entourage of some twenty men reacted. Some revealed knives, others guns.

'Lower your weapons.' Bronislav did not want an accident. He was the one in Carl Jackson's sights after all. He raised his hand. 'Easy boys, this is just a simple misunderstanding.' His words put at ease his edgy men, who were all too ready to spring into action.

'Catch!' called out Tony shakily. He looked scared and fearful. He tossed Mike a double-barreled shotgun.

'Thanks!' Mike caught the weapon, stretching his finger across the trigger! 'Well, lad's what do you say?' he asked, looking at the aggressors. He was firm.

'Don't be foolish, you're outnumbered,' pointed out Bronislav. He snapped his black sunglasses from his face, revealing a horrid-looking scar below his right eye. It looked deep and nasty. His amber eyes were full of malice.

The fact was that Mike's team was small. In case of trouble, he could neither rely on the hired help, ten scrawny, unarmed Egyptian workers, nor could he expect that Tony Richardson, the eldest within his small group, would be anywhere near enough in terms of sheer manpower to swing the advantage in his favour. 'Well, we might be outnumbered, but I promise you one thing, if I pull my finger on this trigger there'll be a hole in you the size of the Grand Canyon,' he said.

'Ha…' cackled Bronislav. He was bold.

'Try me!' Mike's face went blank, he slowly squeezed his finger on the trigger. He was very serious.

Looking rather pale, Bronislav heeded the warning. 'Ok…ok.' He placed his long-bladed knife back within its sheath. He then raised his hands. 'Easy now, easy, remember anything happens to me and you'll be dealing with them.' He pointed to his crew.

Twenty edgy individuals observantly awaited Mike's next course of action.

'I s…say, we can work out a deal,' intervened Bernard. 'We're archaeologists too, why don't we co…combine our efforts?' He drummed his long fingers together like a cartoon villain.

'Not a chance,' said Mike. He was salivating at the mouth. He was about to blow his top. His temper was flaring to dangerous levels.

'Easy now, boys,' said Elisha. 'Put away your toys.' Placing her dainty hands upon the end of the gun barrel, she lowered the weapon that Mike held.

'We're not taking no for an answer,' said Bronislav. 'Our governmental friends have taken care of the red tape. We've permission to excavate,' he added.

'I'll need to see the paperwork,' said Elisha. She held out her hand. 'Give it here,' she said.

'Sp…splendid, I have it.' Dr Bernard Pafford reached into his black bag. 'Here it is,' he said. He took out several stamped documents.

'Why didn't you hand this over earlier?' asked Elisha. She snapped the documents he held from his fingers.

'Now my dear, you di…didn't exactly give me a ch…chance to explain,' said Bernard. 'As I said, we are archaeologists.'

'Utter rubbish,' said Mike. 'I know scum when I see it,' he scolded. He was bold.

'This doesn't add up!' Elisha studied the documents she held in detail. 'These documents clearly state a different location, and any excavation is to be conducted on behalf of the university located in Luxor,' she said.

'We can come to an arrangement,' said Bronislav. 'Everybody can win,' he said.

'Not a hope in hell,' expressed Mike. 'We've put in more than two years' hard work,' he said.

'They have approval from the proper authorities, the details are a little sketchy, but it checks out,' said Elisha. 'I'm sure we'd be willing to carve up a piece of our excavation site.' She knew that neither Mike nor Bronislav would back down. She instead sought out a temporary truce. The last thing she wanted was for Mike's pride to get him hurt.

'They've threatened us,' growled Mike. 'It smells rotten.' He spoke to her through gritted teeth.

'I know that, but they clearly have government officials in their back pocket,' whispered Elisha. Her voice was low enough to be inaudible to the intruders. 'We can't resolve anything here and now, but we can ease the tension,' she said.

'We're playing with fire here,' said Mike softly. 'We know nothing about these people.' The intruders worried him.

'Maybe, but we have to come to a resolution,' said Elisha. 'Give them something.' She knew that if government officials were involved that both Mike and the team could end up on the wrong side of their wrath.

'God damn it! Fine, fine.' Carefully analysing her words, Mike had come to an unthinkable conclusion. Options were limited; his undesirable choice was to give up a site that was pending governmental approval. He was not giving up the prized site he had been working so tirelessly on. 'Fine, you may set up, we've placed an application to excavate a few hundred feet north-east, below that cliff edge yonder, it's yours, providing the friends you speak of in government grant you approval,' he said.

'W…wonderful,' said Bernard. He clapped his hands together.

'Isn't it just?' said Bronislav. He was sour to the suggestion. He did not like the idea at all, but had no other choice. 'Well, I suppose that'll have to do then, right, get the gear boys,' he ordered. A mob of over twenty men under his command fell back. 'Igor, call the minister, get the approval.'

'Sure thing, it'll be done,' replied Igor. He moved along also.

With tensions somewhat eased, at least for now, Carl also moved on. 'Take it, you can sort the rest out, boss, just give a holler if you need me.' With a nod, he went back to work.

'Will do, Carl, will do,' responded Mike. He still felt angry as he snatched his brown hat from his head. 'God damn it!' he roared once more, sticky saliva slipping from his dry lips.

Bronislav limped forward, he boldly extended his hand. 'No hard feelings.' His eyes met Mike's. 'Well, you can't blame a guy for trying, but I suppose we'll have to get along if we're only a few hundred feet apart. You're a hard man.' He had weighed up Mike's qualities.

'These are hard times,' snarled Mike. He refused to oblige the gesture. He did not trust the crafty individual at all. But he also knew that Bronislav was not going anywhere soon. 'Keep those dogs of yours on a leash,' he said.

'Fine by me,' said Bronislav. He lowered his head. A cheeky grin appeared on his face. 'Let's go, Bernard,' he ordered.

'Ju…just give me a few more mi…minutes,' said Bernard. Unable to contain himself, he was still snooping around.

'Now!' roared Bronislav. He clicked his fingers. This time, Bernard obeyed him. Soon, both men were gone.

Irritation fully apparent, Mike turned his focus toward Elisha. He twisted his six-foot-two, well-built stature to meet her extremely worried facial expression. 'They'll be back,' he said. His dry tone signalled his discontentment toward her intervening actions.

'Sorry, Mike, but someone could have been hurt very badly,' said Elisha softly. 'They have the authority to be here,' she added.

'Doesn't matter now, just continue with your work, there's still much to be done,' said Mike.

Elisha's red lips parted; her shiny white teeth showed. Still, she could not bring herself to speak. She felt as if she had done something wrong.

'It's done, nothing can change what has happened,' continued Mike, his temper still simmering.

Falling to silence, Elisha turned her lean body toward the tomb entrance. Her fiery red hair hung over her hazel eyes; she could not help but feel utterly deflated.

'Damn it!' muffled Mike. He knew that he had acted somewhat harshly toward her. 'Wait!' he called to get her attention, feeling guilt-ridden.

'Yes, Mike?' replied Elisha.

'Thanks for the call. Without you, God knows what could have happened,' expressed Mike. He managed to suppress his feelings of deep anger.

'You're welcome, Mike,' responded Elisha. She smiled, acknowledging his unpolished attempt at an apology before continuing about her duties.

Shocked, Asher was left bewildered. He truly never thought his dad could be so daring. 'You weren't really going to shoot that horrid man, were you, Dad?' he asked nervously. He was very pale.

'Gosh, lad, I didn't notice you standing there,' said Mike, surprised. He suddenly looked rather awkward as he rubbed the back of his skull.

'You didn't answer my question, Dad,' said Asher. He was firm.

'Of course not,' answered Mike, seemingly caught off guard. Amidst his messy encounter with the Russian, he had failed to consider Asher's presence.

'Really, Dad?' said Asher.

'Yes, really,' said Mike. Clink! He opened the double-barrelled shotgun. 'Look, you'd need bullets for that.' The weapon was unloaded.

Both began to spontaneously laugh before going about their daily deeds.

'Come on, time for breakfast,' said Mike. 'Tony does make a lovely Egyptian omelette.' He diverted attention, he did not want his son to have any part of the ugly world that had just rolled in on top of him. He knew men like Bronislav were bad news.

'Yes, I do,' said Tony. He was a skinny drip of a man, of some years. He was fifty-five, to be exact.

'I love omelette,' replied Asher. He licked his chops. 'Eggs, tomatoes, cheese, ham...'

'Well, pork is off the table, fella,' interrupted Tony. 'You'll have a lot of trouble finding pork in Luxor,' he said. He handed a stainless-steel plate to Asher and another to Mike.

'What's in this then?' questioned Asher. He had never tried Egyptian omelette.

'You see, you get your pan and add a dab of olive oil,' explained Tony. 'Then add diced onions, garlic cloves, green chilli peppers, eggs, salt, red pepper, dried coriander, black pepper and parsley,' he said.

'Gran just throws honey oats in a bowl and some milk,' said Asher. 'This is nice,' he complimented. He stuck a fork full of omelette in his mouth. His taste buds danced with pure satisfaction.

'Don't forget your Lebanese pita bread,' said Mike. He set a piece of pita bread on Asher's plate before scooping up some omelette with his portion of pita bread. Both devoured the quite simple dish. Not a scrap of food was left.

'Right lad, too much time has passed as it is, I must go to work,' said Mike. He rubbed a cluster of white crumbed flakes from his dark brown pants.

'Can I have a look around?' asked Asher.

'Don't go too far,' warned Mike. 'I mean it, this place can be dangerous, lad, now more so than ever,' he said.

'Ok, Dad,' said Asher. He placed his hands behind his back, crossing his fingers. He had no intention of abiding by Mike's firm instructions. 'Dangerous, ha!' He was not taking his dad's words seriously at all.

-Chapter 7-

The Gatekeeper

Once left to his own devices, step by step, Asher drifted deeper into the heart of the Valley of the Kings and away from the exploration site. His appetite for the unknown was growing indescribably large.

'Hey there.' He politely waved at an old man wearing a white skullcap and a long white and blue robe.

'Zipit-a-dee, zipit-a-dee-doo, it's a pleasant day, how do you do?' The old man with big white bushy eyebrows and a fluffy white moustache waved at him.

'Fine, thank you,' replied Asher. He was a little perplexed. The old man seemed short of a few crackers. However, he was jolly and upbeat.

'Wonderful are the cliffs above.' The old man pointed at the surrounding sloping cliffs of limestone and other sedimentary rock. 'Stunning is the sight I see; those cliffs are great and splendid as can be.' He looked around him in awe. He was old, he held a staff for support. It was but a simple wooden stick.

Thousands of years previous, ancient Egyptian guards had been stationed atop the Valley of the Kings' wide-spanning cliff tops. Their purpose was to stop grave robbers. Unfortunately, they were not highly effective.

Many plunders have been stolen from the valley tombs over the many centuries. Over Egypt's rise and fall, the tombs residing in the Valley of the Kings were often raided.

'They sure are,' agreed Asher. 'But I prefer the tombs underneath,' he added. He tapped his fingers off a sign that read KV15.

Deep below the cliffs, the tombs of more than sixty pharaohs had been uncovered. Signs were posted all along the valley, at the entrance of each tomb. Each sign had a number and a description of which king or noble the tomb belonged to.

'Wonders are found high and low, all more fascinating than my big toe.' The old man shuffled forward. He laughed as he went. His big, bushy, white haired eyebrows danced on his time-worn face.

'You're something else,' said Asher. He, too, began to laugh. He thought the old man weird, yet intriguing.

'True, true, I'm not human like you!' He made his way toward Asher. 'Arghhh!' Tripping over his leather sandals, the old man's knees gave way. His walking aid fell from his grasp.

'Let me help!' panicked Asher. He rushed forward, before picking up the old man's walking aid, he in turn helped the old man to his feet. 'Are you ok?' he asked with concern. He was afraid the old man had seriously hurt himself.

'Dozy-do, dozy me, I keep falling like fruit from a tree.' The old man regained his composure.

'Are you sure you're ok?' asked Asher once more. He handed the old man his walking aid.

'I'm splendid Asher, as splendid as can be, but call me Geatiric, or The Gatekeeper if it suits thee,' he said. There was something quite mysterious about the old man.

'How do you know my name?' spurted out Asher. His face turned pale. He had never met the man before in his life, yet he knew there was more to the strange individual than met the eye.

'Zippitty-doo, zippitty-dee, listen closely and I'll tell thee,' said The Gatekeeper. He whispered despite no one else being around. 'All that is, and all that will be, passes its knowledge onto me,' he said.

'What?' Asher was confused. He looked dumbfounded.

'I've learnt a great deal between time and space, for millennia I've been in the cosmos,' said The Gatekeeper. He held a finger over his mouth. 'I answer to The One. Shhh! It's a secret, you see,' he said.

'Sure, ok,' nodded Asher. 'Your secret is safe with me,' he added. He ran his finger across his chest. 'Cross my heart,' he said.

'Hip-hop, bop, I can sense your thoughts,' said The Gatekeeper. 'True you are, and truer still are your words,' he said.

'Do you live close by then?' asked Asher. He was startled but not fearful. He could see with his own eyes that the old man was very fragile. He was short of a few marbles but appeared to be no threat.

'Hear this, and hear it well, beyond the stars is where I do reside,' said The Gatekeeper. He pointed up to the sky. 'A dimension between worlds is where I like to be, it's my domicile, my home.' He put a finger to his mouth. 'But shhh! It's a secret.'

'Really, between worlds.' Asher was surprised by the unusual comment, assuming, of course, that the old man was just joking. 'Then that would make you some sort of magician, wouldn't it?' he probed.

'Bipity-boo, bipity-dee, magicians play tricks, that's not me,' said The Gatekeeper. 'Listen closely and listen well, The Portal Realm is the place where I do dwell,' he said.

'The Portal Realm,' repeated Asher. He had heard the words before in his dreams. 'This is creepy.' A shiver ran up his spine. Suddenly, uneasiness washed over him.

'Now you get it, now you see, in dreams just past I've let you foresee,' said The Gatekeeper. 'I've warned you of possible things to come, and things that may pass,' he said.

'Warned me of what?' questioned Asher.

'Údra Ena Ceann has said you're special and that's enough for me, I only serve The One's decree,' said The Gatekeeper. 'The One has seen many possible futures, and all that can be; that is why The One has deemed you the key,' he said.

'The key, you're mistaken,' said Asher. 'I don't understand, I can't …'

'Zippity-do, zippity-dee, you must stop him, The Horned God is he,' said The Gatekeeper. 'It's the will of The One, that's who sent me,' he said.

'I've got to get back to my dad before he starts to worry,' said Asher. He had honestly heard enough. He had goosebumps. He was uneasy. He thought about the dream from the preceding night. Too many alarm bells were going off in his head.

'Giddy up and get you going, for I'll see you again in the dream plane,' said The Gatekeeper. He waved as he watched Asher leave. A smile lined his timeworn face.

With haste, Asher began making his way back up the valley, back toward the exploration site. 'Some people are just darn crazy,' he said. Despite his best efforts, he could not make sense of what the old man had said. Many thoughts ran through his brain as he strolled through the sun-bleached canyon, until suddenly another strange voice harnessed his focus!

'Hey boy, what are you up to?'

For the second time, Asher came across the path of a strange man. This man, though, did not look happy at all. He thought it rude not to reply. 'Nothing, mister,' he said.

'Come here, now!' The strange individual, also wearing traditional Egyptian clothing, a white robe, and a turban, gawked at him searchingly.

Caught off guard, Asher did as he was asked. He moved sheepishly toward the man. 'Can I help you, mister?' he asked.

'Have you ever seen a desert snake boy?' The Egyptian asked. He was quite serious in relation to his unusual remark. A basket rested at his feet. Straw crinkling between fingers, he removed the lid of the basket. A hissing sound began to arise from inside.

'Close it!' Asher pleaded. He received no reply from the dark-skinned Egyptian. He was paralysed as he watched the head of an Egyptian Cobra wriggle from the basket. His face grew pale as the slithering, broad-headed, broad-snouted creature with large, round eyes edged ever closer.

The Egyptian remained firm. 'Well, boy, did you lot come across anything in that old tomb yet?' he asked.

'No…nothing yet, mister,' answered Asher. Terror filled him to the core.

'Don't lie to me, boy!' The man yelled angrily.

'I'm not, I…I swear,' said Asher. He was telling the truth. He had only just arrived in Egypt and knew little. He knew nothing of the tomb his dad and team had just uncovered.

Without warning, the dark-skinned man sprang to his feet. 'You'll talk, boy, one way or another!' He clutched a tatty whip that rested by his side before raising his left hand. His devilish intent was clear.

Asher was utterly afraid to move. He was terrified by the cobra, which remained but mere inches from him. He took one glance at the Egyptian. He caught sight of the leather whip. 'Please…' He trembled with fear. He clinched his pearly whites, anticipating that his soft flesh would soon feel the inevitable.

'Hands off my boy, scum!'

'Dad!' Asher watched as his dad, Mike, took hold of the tail end of the black whip. 'Dad,' he yelled again in relief. Promptly, his dad came to his rescue.

'Pick on someone your size,' thundered Mike. Thumppp! He swung his fist, knocking the wild-eyed looking Egyptian over a wooden stool.

'Come on, lad, it's time to go,' stated Mike. Showing no fear, he carefully trapped the Egyptian Cobra within the straw-constructed basket from which it had wriggled. 'You're lucky you didn't annoy that cobra lad, you could have been blinded by its venom,' he said.

'I hate snakes,' winced Asher in disgust. 'Yuck, I don't like things with no legs,' he added.

'Ha, you're very squeamish,' said Mike. He ruffled up Asher's black hair. 'I've been searching for you, I said don't go far.' His composure eased; he was foolish to assume that all and any immediate danger had been averted. He was critically wrong!

'Watch out!' screamed Asher.

It was too late! Another dark-skinned man had unexpectedly crept up upon Mike before striking him with a hefty plank of wood. Thud! The blow to his spine was thunderous.

Mike's brown hat toppled from his head as he dropped to his knees. His hands embraced the sandy canvas below. 'Damn you!' His face filled with pain. He fell forward before progressing onto his broad back. His six-foot-two-inch, well-built physique began to curl up. 'You dirty son of a bitch,' he grumbled.

He could see that the dark-skinned man had dropped a two-by-four plank of wood, which had snapped due to the force used and now wielded a razor-sharp knife! A grin matched by a crooked set of grimy teeth expressed the man's horrid intentions as he moved ever closer.

Asher took swift action; he grabbed the basket with a cobra trapped inside. 'Leave my dad alone,' he howled. He launched the basket at the Egyptian, and as he did, the basket lid came off. The brown, patterned snake from within soared from its containment. It came loose to entangle around the grinning man's thin neck. He dropped the knife he held.

In a frenzied panic, the dark-skinned man was distracted long enough for Mike to gain the upper hand.

Clunkkk! Sweeping the man's leg, Mike sluggishly rose to his feet. 'Damn, that hurt,' he groaned. He was slow to regain his bearings. It was clear that he felt a lot of irritation along his spine.

Only temporarily stunned, the tenacious Egyptian quickly scrambled for the sharp-edged knife that had been slung from his grasp!

Despite the pain he was in, Mike was quicker of the two. He quickly analysed the man's intentions. His adrenaline was running high.

'Arghhh!' The man screamed in pain. He felt Mike's big boot crush his fingers.

Mike refused to reduce the pressure he imposed upon the Egyptian's hand. The man's flesh bit into the edge of the blade he gripped, and his blood covered the sandy canvas.

'What are you playing at then?' stated Mike. With a swift boot to the jaw, he knocked the sly figure unconscious. He showed no mercy.

It was too late however! The Egyptian's wild screams had harnessed even more undesired attention. A vast group of gravely disturbed men began closing in around Mike. Some of the men were speaking with Russian accents. Most though, by the telling of their clothing, were Egyptian workers. Wielding spades and pickaxes, they seemed edgy.

Their shrewd Russian leader, Bronislav Valadvic, limped to the front with haste. 'What's this?' he growled.

Showing no weaknesses, Mike did not quiver. 'I'll tell you what's going on, your thugs were trying to hurt my boy and if you don't control them I will,' he said.

'I see,' said Bronislav. Seemingly amused, he smiled mockingly. 'You're one ballsy American,' he said. One of the men Mike had bested groaned in agony. 'Zuberi, you're a mess,' he said.

'Pe…perhaps, we should collaborate with our neighbours,' said Bernard. 'It se…ems the fault lies with our hired help,' he said. He wiped his forehead with a hanky. The sun beat down from overhead.

'You work for me,' snapped Bronislav. He tore at Bernard's blue shirt as he pulled him closer. 'Get that straight,' he said. He pointed rudely at his face.

'I...I know th...that,' said Bernard. 'But there is a time for our p... plans to take e...effect, now is not the ti...time,' he nervously said. He was fretful. He looked like a mouse caught in the paws of a big cat.

Deciding to adhere to Dr Bernard Pafford's advice, Bronislav eased off. 'Fine, you have my assurance your boy won't be bothered again and you two I'll deal with you later,' he warned. He snapped at the two Egyptians that Mike had bested. However, only one was receptive, the other remained in an unconscious state.

With sheer anger, Mike sharply responded. 'You better, otherwise you'll be dealing with me,' he said. Knowing he was vastly outnumbered he had no other choice but to retreat. Snatching his hat off the ground he made his leave. 'Let's go lad, back toward the tomb,' he instructed.

'You don't look good at all Mike. Are you ok?' Upon seeing him, Elisha immediately grew disturbed by his tatty appearance.

'I'll live,' answered Mike. He had taken a bit of punishment but was fine. His brown pants were stained with dirt, his hairy chest was exposed from the confines of one ruffled up white shirt. Holding his hat in his hands, his brown hair looked like a mess. 'Keep your eye on that lot, in fact keep two on them and tell Carl to inform me if he and the team get that passage cleared,' he said.

'You got it,' replied Elisha. She nodded her fiery red head in acknowledgement.

Keeping out of trouble, or at least trying his best too, Asher spent the rest of the evening glancing over a vast array of pictures of Mike's travels. 'Wow! There's so many, Dad.' He was truly intrigued.

'Yes lad, I do get around you know,' said Mike. Amused, he could not help but chuckle.

'What are those?' asked Asher. He was curious as to what his dad was looking at.

'More photographs,' responded Mike.

'That's not very clear,' said Asher. He rolled his curious blue eyes.

'Well, nosy,' said Mike. 'If you must know, these photos are of the paintings and markings carved upon the inner corridor of the tomb, at least the part we can access,' he said.

'What do they mean?' asked Asher.

'That's what I'm trying to find out, lad, if I get the chance,' said Mike. With a smirk, he moved to sit down. A simple wooden table with a white cloth throw-over was his ready-made work area.

He studied each photograph individually. Seconds quickly turned into minutes, minutes into hours. Taking only short breaks to check on the team's progress, he spent the next eight hours studying the images. Before anyone knew it, day had turned to night.

Still, Mike could not find the answers he was looking for. 'I'm missing something, I just don't know what,' he said. The images were beyond anything he had ever seen before.

Two recurring figures appeared countless times, the very two Elisha had spoken of. He beheld an image of what appeared to him as an ancient Egyptian priest, perhaps a high priest wearing an amulet. The amulet was in the shape of an eye.

'The Eye of Ra, interesting,' said Mike. His first thoughts leaned toward the amulet being associated with the sun god,

Amun-Ra. He was the chief of the Egyptian gods. He was right, too.

The other one-eyed image was shrouded in darkness, and upon his wrist was a trinket or bracelet of some variety. It omitted a power of a kind. It was clear the two figures were opposing.

'I'd love to know what you lads were fighting about,' said Mike. He let out a yawn before wincing in pain. His back was bruised, and he still felt sore from his scuffle earlier in the day.

Already fast asleep, Asher's interest in photos had long evaporated. He only opened his big, blue eyes briefly as his dad, quite thoughtfully, hurled a woolly blanket atop him.

'Good night, son, you look so much like your mother,' said Mike. 'I miss Jane so very much,' he said.

Feeling the warmth of his dad's hand caressing his cheek, a few tears rolled from Asher's big blue eyes. Listening to his dad's heart-warming words, he could not help but feel emotional.

Overworked, Mike took no notice. He was completely unaware that Asher was awake at all. 'Sleep tight,' he said.

-Chapter 8-

Dreams

Lost to a land of dreams and strange imaginings, Asher had drifted back to sleep. He saw peculiar things. In his dream, he was in a sea of swirling blue. He felt the substance all over his body. It felt as if he were in the depths of the Pacific Ocean. Only he could breathe. 'This is so weird,' he said. Then suddenly, he heard it!

'Howdy-dee, howdy-do, Asher, I've come to speak to you!'

'Show yourself,' said Asher. 'Who's there?' Startled, he looked about the sea of blue. Yet he saw no one. The hairs on his neck stood on end. He was spooked.

'Zippity-do, zippity-dee, we've met before, and now again, here as I promised in the dream plane.' It was The Gatekeeper, or at least the sound of his voice.

'You're that crazy old man,' said Asher. He recognised the high-pitched tone and the bizarre speech pattern.

'Bippity-bop that's a cheap shot, I'm not crazy, just different and that's that,' spoke The Gatekeeper. 'As I said before, and say again, Geatiric or The Gatekeeper is my name,' he added.

'Where are you?' questioned Asher. 'I can't see you.' His heart began to race.

'Pippity-pop come and see, The Portal Realm is where I'll be,' informed The Gatekeeper.

'Geesh!' Asher was forced to shut his eyes as all about him, the ocean of blue light intensified. He threw his hands up over his face. 'Helppp!' he screeched as the panic consumed him.

'Sappity-dee, you're as safe as safe can be,' informed The Gatekeeper.

Bump! Asher was spit from a portal of some kind. He fell to his knees. He still wore his nightwear, a blue t-shirt, grey shorts, and stripy socks. Opening his eyes, he was in awe. He did not see an old man. 'It's you! I've seen you before,' he said. The first thing he saw was a black, curly-haired imp wearing a blue leather vest, black breeches, and black boots. It was the little person he had seen in his dreams the night before.

'Indeed-fiddly-do, twist and turn, diverse forms my body can turn,' said The Gatekeeper. The little imp turned in a circular motion. A bright white aura consumed him. In an instant, he was transformed. He stood taller, about five feet nine inches, leaner, and much older, too.

'But wait. How did you do that?' asked Asher. Astounded, his mouth lay agape. He quickly got to his feet. It was indeed the old man he had met on his wanderings through the Valley of the Kings earlier in the day.

'It's me, myself and I, for many shapes and forms I can apply,' riddled The Gatekeeper. He could change his physical form at will. More than that, it seemed he had a degree of control over matter, for his clothing was different too. Having changed his physical form, he now wore a white skullcap, white and blue robe, and sandals upon his feet.

'Where am I?' asked Asher. He was very uneasy. About him was a paradise, everything was very splendid, from the soft grass he stood upon, to the cliffs up high, to the valleys down low. There were many species of trees. There were trees with red, yellow, and even blue leaves.

There were fruits of many variants, some he recognised and others he had no idea about. There were waterfalls and there were lakes. There were lakes of blue and silver. There were many living things too.

He saw animals he recognised, such as butterflies, rabbits, and deer. However, other creatures were bizarre and unusual, including phoenixes, centaurs, and gryphons. It was surreal, to say the least.

'La-tee-da, la-tee-de, like what you see, this is home to me, a dimension between worlds, it's sublime, don't you agree?' probed The Gatekeeper. He twiddled his fingers as his big grey eyes stared at Asher in search of an answer.

'It's so peaceful,' said Asher softly. Everything about him was natural, wild, and free. Adding to that, the sky above was unnaturally mystifying, yet tranquillising. Blues, greens, reds, yellows, and oranges intertwined to create a spectacle to put even the northern lights to shame.

'Yippee! I agree, welcome to '⅄ƆႱ‑ᘔ∕Ρ⅄ꓶᴟ‑ꓑ⅄ꓶᴟ⅁.' The Gatekeeper made a sweet and beautiful sound as he spoke in the celestial language. Then he clarified. 'Or as I said before, the realm of portals, The Portal Realm,' he explained. He had a smile from ear to ear. 'Everything is designed and belongs to me, it's something spectacular, that's clear for anyone to see, tippity-tee.' He jumped about like a kangaroo, flapping his arms like a duck.

'Wait, did you not have a walking stick?' asked Asher. He recalled the old man, The Gatekeeper, being rather brittle. He recollected The Gatekeeper falling when he met him beside tomb KV15 in the Valley of the Kings earlier that day.

'He, he, he, that was all for show, don't you know,' said The Gatekeeper. 'I can walk, sing, dance, and talk.' He was full of zeal. He was not as frail as he first appeared to be.

Whoosh! 'Woah! What is that?' shrieked Asher. He quickly scrunched down. A mighty winged creature flew overhead. The figure had a fourteen-foot wingspan, the feathers brilliant white. A golden mask covered the creature's face, and pure white hair lined its head, which was great in length. Its body was humanlike in form, only it had blueish skin. White hair filled the chest area, and the legs were birdlike with brilliant white feathers, and the creature had talons instead of feet.

'Golly, gee, Guardian is thee,' stated The Gatekeeper. 'It protects the realm for jolly old me.' The term Guardian was given to bizarre creatures that served him. They were his eyes and ears. They were the janitors of his home, known as The Portal Realm.

'This can't be real,' gasped Asher. He had to pinch himself. His dream was as clear as a reflection in the mirror.

'Oh, it's real little one.' Out of the sky came a winged, furry little animal. The little creature was just over thirty-one inches in length. In addition, the creature's body was seventeen inches tall. That did not include its wings, which themselves were thirty-six inches in length and almost two-thirds that in width. It landed at The Gatekeeper's feet. 'He had a lot of help in creating all this, you know. Since I arrived, there have been a lot of changes.'

'You...you can talk,' spurted out Asher. He was astounded. He looked into the light-yellow eyes of the little creature. 'He's amazing....'

'Stop right there, kid. It's she, and the name is Vixi.' The little creature had an attitude. She also had a long snout and rusty red fur across the face, back, and sides. Her throat, chin, and belly were covered in fur of grey and white tones. She had black paws and black tipped ears that were large and pointy. She also had a rusty red tail, which had a fluffy white tip.

'Zippity-do, Vixi, be nice, be at your best for our small, but special guest,' said The Gatekeeper. He wagged his finger at the little creature.

'I'm always nice,' said Vixi. She, in turn, stuck her tongue out at him. 'Or I at least try to be.' She was a sassy little furball.

'You look remarkably like, like, a, a….'

'Spit it out, kid,' said Vixi. Her ears pricked up.

'Well, like a fox,' explained Asher. He thought that Vixi closely resembled a fox, minus the black tipped wings, of course, they were unique. He found it odd, too, that the little creature wore a green vest. In truth, though, oddities and reasoning had long evaporated. He thought that the whole situation was utterly absurd.

'Hippity-he-he, she does, I agree,' said The Gatekeeper. 'A great resemblance is there for all to see.' He found it amusing as he chuckled.

'A fox,' said Vixi. Her nose began twitching. 'Is that a compliment or an insult?' she said. She tilted her head sideways.

'It's a…a compliment,' confirmed Asher. He was a quick thinker. 'You're very dazzling,' he added. He moved forward to pet her.

'Thanks, but I know,' replied Vixi. Quickly, she turned and flicked her tail. She did not like her fur to be stroked.

'Bopttity-bo, without Vixi I'd be lost, you know,' said The Gatekeeper. 'She's precious like a diamond, and she's my dearest companion.' His head bopped up and down as he spoke.

'I agree, you would be lost if it wasn't for my genius,' said Vixi. She giggled as she shut her eyes. 'Believe me, kiddo, goodness knows where he'd be without my help, I manage The Portal Realm in many regards,' she said.

The Gatekeeper and Vixi had knowledge of the various lifeforms throughout the universe. They also had the innate knowledge to communicate with said lifeforms. A gift as part of their creation from the will of a higher power!

'Pardon me, and no offence to anyone, but this is madness,' said Asher at a pace. He wedged his fingers between the strands of his thick, black hair. He turned three hundred and sixty degrees, taking in The Portal Realm. 'All this can't possibly exist,' he said.

'Relax, kid, we're on your side,' said Vixi. She sensed his angst.

'Honestly, this is all a bit much,' said Asher, feeling overwhelmed. He threw his hands up in bemusement. His teeth sank into his bottom lip.

'Yep, yep, yep, it's as real as real can be,' said The Gatekeeper. 'Dippity-dee, what you see does exist, but you're in The Dream Realm,' he added.

'In other words, kid, you're dreaming,' said Vixi. 'But that does not mean this is not real,' she said.

'Tis true I tell you,' said The Gatekeeper. He nodded vigorously while stroking his fluffy white moustache. 'Perception is reality, I hope you do see.' He held out his hand and summoned a bright red apple. It appeared as if from nowhere in an aura of bright white light. He tossed it to Asher.

'Is it ok?' asked Asher. He held the red fruit in his palm. He was unsure if he could trust The Gatekeeper. He barely knew him. Despite The Gatekeeper's loose posture and light smile being inviting, he was not entirely sure of his motives.

'It's ripe and sweet, go on, take a bite,' replied The Gatekeeper. 'All you see are things from other worlds that are or have been.' He, too, had an apple and began eating it. His perfect row of white teeth began crunching away.

'He's been to so many worlds,' stated Vixi. 'He takes a little piece of each and incorporates it here in The Portal Realm, between worlds. I, of course, get a say in most things,' she explained.

'Wow! Other worlds,' gasped Asher. He flipped the red fruit from hand to hand. 'There must be hundreds of worlds,' he said. His mind was set ablaze thinking about the vastness of the universe.

'Trillions! But he adores your world especially,' stated Vixi. 'He copied the design of the apple from the place you hoomans call Earth.'

Everything in The Portal Realm was of Geatiric, The Gatekeeper's, design, the mountains, the cliffs, the valleys, and the creatures both big and small, his muse being the many worlds he had seen with his own two eyes. His conscience and advisor was, of course, Vixi herself.

'You mean humans,' corrected Asher.

'Clumsy-dee, clumsy you Vixi, you slipped up, you did. For well you know that the world called Earth is not the only world where living things like him dwell,' said The Gatekeeper. He began laughing giddily, all the while wagging his finger at her.

'Yes, yes, laugh it up,' blasted Vixi. Again, she stuck her tongue out at The Gatekeeper. 'We call the many sapient beings of the universe similar to, well, you in spirit, niominiums in the Riathaĺe and Breathnádol tongue, in the celestial tongue.' She spoke directly to Asher.

'Yes…sure…that's real swell,' said Asher. He nodded, not paying much attention. Instead, he eyed up the fruit in his hand.

'Upon each world, niominiums refer to themselves differently. The term 'human' is simply what your world calls your species of niominiums,' revealed Vixi. 'Honestly, having vast knowledge does not mean you get everything right all the time.'

In the grand scheme of existence, life within the walls of the universe is rare. Even rarer still are what the celestials like the Riathaĺe and Breathnádol collectively call niominiums.

Like humans, the many other niominiums in existence are sapient beings. As a cosmic collective, niominiums are similar in spiritual makeup. A lot of physical similarities also exist. For instance, some races of niominiums have two eyes, two legs and arms, and two ears. However, differences big and small also exist. Some races of niominiums have green skin or blue. Some have more than two eyes or more than two arms. Some have more than five fingers or fewer. Some species have tails. Some have two ears and some none. The races of niominiums in existence differ in shape and size, too. They differ in intelligence and longevity of life.

'It's tasty.' Asher bit into the deliciously sweet red apple. He could see, touch, taste, and smell the succulent fruit. 'Hmmm.' Mouth full of apple, his cheeks were jiggling with delight. It was the tastiest apple he had ever eaten.

'Make no fuss, as the cosmos can confuse the greatest of us,' said The Gatekeeper. He began stroking his chin. 'You must see there are beings' magnitudes greater than thee.'

'He's right, kid, beings exist out there beyond your wildest imaginings,' said Vixi. 'Beings greater in mind, spirit, and body. It was another Riathaĺe known as The Dream Keeper that helped us reach you,' she added.

'Sippitty-do, in fact, some are greater than me and my kind, too,' said The Gatekeeper. 'I only tell you what is true,' he said.

'I get that she isn't human…'

'Ahem!' Vixi cleared her throat. She sought his attention. 'She has a name.' Her nose began twitching again.

'Sorry, I get that Vixi isn't human,' alluded Asher. 'But you speak like you aren't human either.' He grew a little uneasy. From what he could tell and had seen, The Gatekeeper was something else altogether!

'Twiddle-dee-dee, I am not you see. I take this form because it is pleasing to thee,' replied The Gatekeeper. 'Time and I go hand in hand, I've been here since it started, isn't that grand?'

'The beginning of what?' asked Asher. He was further confused.

'Silly-dee-silly me, since the beginning of the cosmos, there's always been me, I think,' said The Gatekeeper. He looked confused as he caressed his white moustache. He was a celestial being. 'It's all a little fuzzy like my dear friend Vixi,' he added.

'His mind isn't what it used to be, kid,' explained Vixi. 'He lost much of himself on your world some three thousand years ago, in a land named Egypt.' Her whole demeanour was sapped of energy. Sadness washed over the little furball.

In an attempt to stop a great evil, a corrupt Breathnádol, a celestial being with immense power, Geatiric, The Gatekeeper, had lost a piece of himself. His celestial essence had been tainted. He can change into many forms, but sadly, to change into his true form causes him great agony. To change into his true form only deteriorates his spirit even quicker.

'He's whole in his true form,' declared Vixi. 'But he can't maintain his true form for long.' She knew The Gatekeeper well. She knew he had not taken his true form in three millennia.

'Wow! He visited Egypt three thousand years ago,' uttered Asher. 'That's…that's a long time.' He was flabbergasted.

'Not to beings like Geatiric, he's billions of years old,' stated Vixi. 'Might as well be yesterday in his mind,' she said.

'Bil…billions of years!' gulped Asher. He stuttered his words in shock and awe.

'Almost fifteen billion to be exact, give or take a few millennia,' said Vixi. 'I myself wasn't born yesterday either, kiddo.' She herself was many millions of years old.

Almost as old as time, as the universe itself, Geatiric, The Gatekeeper, has been the master of The Portal Realm for billions of years. He and The Portal Realm were tied in fate, as long as he existed, so too did the place between worlds.

'What are they?' asked Asher. 'Those pools of blue.' He took note of countless swirls of blue light, blue portals, which filled the landscape.

'Listen close, and listen well, portals they are, to where I'll tell,' said The Gatekeeper. 'Those gates, those portals, go to all worlds you see, throughout the cosmos, to even places I have yet to see.'

The Portal Realm itself was a dimension between time and space. It was a dimension between worlds.

'I don't get it, Gatekeeper,' shrugged Asher. 'Why am I, I…'

'Hippitty-dee, answers you seek,' said The Gatekeeper. 'Why are you here and talking to me?'

'Well, yes,' said Asher. 'But how did you know?' The Gatekeeper had outlined what was on his mind, as if opening a floodgate.

'Knockiddy-do, knockiddy-dee, I know your thoughts, that I surely do,' said The Gatekeeper.

'You get accustomed to his ways, when I first met him, I thought it was weird too,' said Vixi. 'He can read thoughts and sense emotions, it's a form of telepathy, you could say.' She flapped her wings. Up she went.

'Oopsy-do, Vixi, what did I do?" said The Gatekeeper with alarm. He had the look of an anxious child.

'I told you it's rude to listen and see the thoughts of others,' said Vixi. She was but a few inches from his aged face as she scolded him.

'Clumsy-doo, clumsy me, I'm as sorry as can be,' said The Gatekeeper. He scratched his head of fluffy white hair.

'That's all I get, kid, sorry this, sorry that,' said Vixi. 'He means well, though,' she added. She flew in circles around Asher. 'It saddens me to watch him become less as the centuries roll on.'

'Some things I don't need to know,' said Asher. He was a little freaked out. The last thing he needed was some old man, or whatever The Gatekeeper was, rummaging through his thoughts, especially one who seemed to have lost his mind.

'Tiddle-do that may be true, but some things you do,' said The Gatekeeper. 'Diddly-do, here we are and here we do be, because of a decree by The One, Ùdra Ena Ceann!'

-Chapter 9-

The Horned God

Asher was having a tough time believing what he was hearing. He still had not worked out why he was in The Portal Realm at all. Indeed, he believed the whole thing to be folly. Were Geatiric, The Gatekeeper, and Vixi even real? He thought not. A mad old celestial and a talking fox, no way he thought.

'Wake up! Wake up! Wake up!' mumbled Asher repeatedly. He was ready to get back to reality.

'Not just yet,' said Vixi. 'You're not here by accident,' she revealed.

'If I'm not here by accident, then why?' asked Asher, dumbfounded. He shrugged his shoulders.

'I've said twice before and now again, he's a creature with horns, The Horned God he is, he threatened all of the cosmos,' informed The Gatekeeper. Up went his withered hands. An aura of white shone from them, and in an instant, many images began to flow like a great river. He showed several events, several worlds. 'Diddle-dee-doo, he was a Breathnádol that much is true.'

'Brace yourself, kiddo,' warned Vixi, knowing what was to follow. 'This is going to blow you away!'

Several events flashed one after the other. The events revealed powerful celestial beings, a great many. One after the other, the powerful celestials succumbed to a hideous horned beast with golden wings and hooves. He bested celestial beings that controlled fire, lightning, water, even those that had control over other celestial aspects such as reality, matter, and time, to a degree.

'He destroyed the physical existence of many Breathnádol, those like him,' said Vixi. 'He also destroyed the physical existence of a handful of Riathaĺe, he even did something thought impossible, he destroyed the twelve cosmic enforcers, the judges of the universe, known as the Sealgairs. He was a being of great power. I should know, for I too was formerly of his kind,' she declared.

'Here in The Portal Realm, he did the deed, in leading to the fall of the Sealgairs, he did succeed,' said The Gatekeeper. He had watched the whole thing unfold three millennia ago. The twelve cosmic judges had succumbed to the being known as The Horned God.

'So, he's a god,' said Asher. He reflected on the name The Gatekeeper had uttered, 'The Horned God!'

'He calls himself The Horned God,' said Vixi. 'He's pompous, for there's only one true god, Ŭdra Ena Ceann,' she said.

Millions of years previous, before Vixi came to live in The Portal Realm, before she came to serve Geatiric, The Gatekeeper, she was a Breathnádol, a powerful celestial. She, along with several of her kind, ruled over a world known as Ariatni. Ultimately, she and her kind had their physical forms destroyed. The Breathnádol of Ariatni fought a battle with the beings known as the Sealgairs.

The Sealgairs served Ŭdra Ena Ceann and delivered The Creator's divine justice upon corrupted celestial beings. They sat above all, within the universe, in power. Or so it was thought!

In the end, Vixi's spiritual form was given a second chance. As penance, she was reincarnated in her current form to serve The Gatekeeper as his familiar. However, she was stripped of her authority and much of her power. She lost that which she loved the most, she lost her ability to change shape.

'He's so angry,' observed Asher. He watched as the horned beast tore through tens, if not hundreds, of godlike beings.

'He bested the corrupt Breathnádol of your world, Earth,' stated Vixi. 'He cut through all the self-proclaimed gods and goddesses, taking their power for his own,' she said.

'I don't understand,' said Asher. His diamond-shaped face was awash with confusion. 'Did he kill them?' he said.

'Diddly-dee, die they cannot, for immortal they are,' said The Gatekeeper.

'No, not kill. Breathnádol, like him, a Riathaĺe, cannot die,' informed Vixi. She nodded at The Gatekeeper to affirm her point. 'His spiritual makeup is eternal, sure his physical form can be destroyed and even that's no small feat, but he's powerful in spirit,' she said.

Deteriorating, Geatiric, The Gatekeeper, though, was in uncharted territory. His spiritual essence was tainted. Eventually, Vixi feared he would lose the battle. Eventually, she feared that his physical form and The Portal Realm itself would cease to exist. His spirit was immortal, but where his spirit would end up was anyone's guess. She hoped in the worst possible scenario, his spirit would find its way to a paradise named Neahmil.

Like most lifeforms in the known universe, the Riathaĺe and Breathnádol have immortal souls. However, their spiritual makeup is vastly more powerful in strength of will. If reduced to spiritual existence, they can reform physical shape or wander formless, as is their power. The Riathaĺe were created for the specific purpose of ensuring the proper functioning of the universe. The Breathnádol, on the other hand, existed to shape each world bearing life within the universe according to the will of Ůdra Ena Ceann.

'Forms we can make and forms we can shape, us Riathaĺe and the Breathnádol come from The Architect, The One, The Creator...'

'He gets it,' grumbled Vixi. 'But it's best if I do most of the talking, you'll just scramble the kid's brains,' she said.

'Actually, I don't get it,' replied Asher. 'Sorry.' He shrugged his shoulders as he shook his head of black, messed-up hair.

'Not to worry, kid, I'll break it down,' explained Vixi. 'You see all and everything in existence was created by Ůdra Ena Ceann, every blade of grass, every tree, and every element of creation, do you get the gist?' she said.

'Ůdra who?' said Asher.

'Ůdra Ena Ceann is known to some as The Architect, to others as The One, but to most, the one God is known as The Creator. The One sits beyond space and time,' said Vixi. 'The One created the Riathaĺe to oversee the cosmos, while the Breathnádol were created to fulfil The Creator's will, observe, to oversee each world they were assigned to in the cosmos,' she said.

'Nippity-dee, now do you, see?' questioned The Gatekeeper.

'Sort of,' answered Asher. He was absorbing as much as he could. 'So, what went wrong?' he asked.

'I failed. Like many other Breathnádol,' said Vixi. 'Once I ruled over a world of beautiful creatures and animals,' she said.

'How's that bad?' said Asher.

'The key word, kid, is, ruled,' responded Vixi in shame. 'My kind are meant to oversee, shape according to the will of The

Creator, but foolishly we declared ourselves gods and ruled how we pleased,' she said.

'You were a, a…'

'No kid. As I said, there's only The Creator,' asserted Vixi. 'We had incredible authority and power, but we abused that power. We were meant to observe and watch, but by interfering in Ariatni without a decree from The Creator, we committed great sacrilege,' she said.

After Ariatni was set upon by the twelve Sealgairs, Vixi, along with the other Breathnádol that lived there, were reduced to their spiritual forms.

Reduced to their spiritual forms, the Breathnádol of Ariatni were sent to Ŭdra Ena Ceann. Usually like the Riathaĺe, the Breathnádol could reform their physical shape. However, not those that were corrupt, instead, the Sealgairs brought them before The Creator to be judged.

Of the Breathnádol of Ariatni, only Vixi truly repented, and all but her were sent to the outer void, the vast darkness beyond the cosmos, beyond space and time, for eternity. To a place known as Neahimni Seachrana, known in the celestial language as ᛏᛈᛄᛃᚱᛐᛣ–ᛐᛈᚷᛃᛉᛈᛈᛐᛏ .

'So that would mean you're bad,' concluded Asher. He looked perplexed as he tried to comprehend all he was hearing.

'Once kid,' confirmed Vixi. 'Since Dorchadi, good and bad exist in all beings, all matter in the cosmos, well, almost all things,' she said.

The lifeforms that made up the universe had corrupt natures but had the capacity for good, to choose to love and obey The One. However, a Breathnádol or Riathaĺe cannot have any evil corrupt their spirits. As soon as evil enters their essence, they are no longer able to fully serve the will of Ůdra Ena Ceann. This is unique to the celestials.

Absolution was not above the Breathnádol or Riathaíe, but only The Creator could grant forgiveness. In addition, forgiveness can only be given through repentance.

'Boppity-boo, good or evil, it's up to you,' said The Gatekeeper. 'Scales will be weighed by The One,' he said.

'But why would anybody choose to be evil?' said Asher. He was a little naïve.

'It started with Dorchadi, if Ůdra Ena Ceann is The Creator, then he is The Destroyer,' said Vixi. 'He is the only being to ever challenge Ůdra Ena Ceann; he lost, of course, his spirit was cast to Neahimni Seachrana, the outer void, the vast emptiness beyond the universe, the everlasting darkness,' she said.

In the beginning, before the creation of the universe, Ůdra Ena Ceann also created the Inachta, powerful beings that serve him in his kingdom. They oversee The Creator's kingdom, known as Neahmil or, ⟨celestial script⟩, in the celestial tongue. Sitting beyond the confines of the universe, beyond time and space, Neahmil is a bastion of light. Only those souls that accept Ůdra Ena Ceann and The Creator's light of goodness, of purity, may enter.

The war started in Neahmil as Ůdra Ena Ceann was weaving the fabrics of creation, the universe itself. The Inachta named Dorchadi grew jealous that his creator had gifted, in his warped view, lesser life forms, the gift of salvation. He grew jealous of his creator's power and magnificence. He grew jealous that even though he had free will, he would always have to serve the will of Ůdra Ena Ceann.

Being the chief of the Inachta, Dorchadi was the most powerful below Ůdra Ena Ceann. He led others of his kind in rebellion against The One. Though Dorchadi failed.

'Dorchadi's essence has been piercing the veil to the universe from the outer void ever since its creation,' said Vixi. 'His evilness has been creeping into existence, tainting all creation, corrupting and tempting all life forms to reject The Creator,' she said.

'I don't follow,' replied Asher. He was not completely following the little creature's train of thought.

'So, in a way, Dorchadi corrupted he that calls himself, The Horned God. He became the greatest among the Breathnádol and the RiathaÍe, but greater still than the cosmic enforcers, the Sealgairs,' said Vixi. 'Every ounce of evil in his veins comes from Dorchadi, for he is the incarnation of evil itself.'

'This is a nightmare,' gulped Asher.

'You're telling me, kid,' said Vixi. 'The Horned God is Dorchadi's key to the universe, the key to destroying all of Ůdra Ena Ceann's creation, to tipping the scales,' she said.

Over countless millennia, a great many Breathnádol fell to the darkness, to Dorchadi. To a lesser degree, a portion of the RiathaÍe also fell from the grace of Ůdra Ena Ceann. They chose to give in to their base desires, rather than serve the will of Ůdra Ena Ceann. Many Breathnádol declared themselves gods, architects of the worlds they oversaw.

'Any moment now I'll wake up.' Asher took a deep breath and closed his blue eyes.

'Believe it, young one,' said Vixi. 'As Dorchadi was the greatest below Ůdra Ena Ceann, The Horned God became the greatest amongst the Breathnádol and the RiathaÍe. In that sense, he is an anomaly,' she said.

'I don't care,' boomed Asher. 'This all means nothing to me,' he snapped. He was getting a little frustrated.

'Tippity-tee, we only aim to help thee,' said The Gatekeeper softly. 'It's not our decree, but The One's, you must see,' he informed. He wagged his finger side to side.

'You've been chosen, kid,' declared Vixi. 'Why? Beats me to be honest,' she said. A hint of scepticism hung in her comments.

'Chosen!' thundered Asher. He grasped at his black hair with his thin fingers. 'To do what exactly?' he said, wide-eyed. He felt the air suck out of his lungs.

'The universe is in a delicate balance between good and evil,' said Vixi. 'You will ensure the Údra Ena Ceann's light of goodness is not snuffed out, for The Creator has seen that The Horned God will rise again!'

'How? I'm nobody,' said Asher. He did not feel particularly special at all.

'In every version of the future, The One saw that Soulkeeper will be found, that is the nexus event to The Horned God's release,' said Vixi. 'You must be the one to find it,' she said.

'Hope comes both great and small, you're picked by the one above all,' said The Gatekeeper.

'The Horned God took the powers of many Breathnádol, Riathaĺe, and the Sealgairs, with what he called Soulkeeper,' said Vixi. 'He defied Údra Ena Ceann by taking the souls, the essence of those he bested to enhance his power,' she said.

As soon as a world dies, a Breathnádol must return to Neahmil for their purpose is served. Likewise, when a Riathaĺe's purpose is served, they too must return to Neahmil. Though the Riathaĺe will only return to Neahmil at the end of the universe itself. For they exist at an above world level and ensure the proper functioning of the universe according to The One's will.

The Gatekeeper showed The Horned God entrapping the souls, the very essence of many living things, creatures, beasts, mortals, and beings of great power. He entrapped them within Soulkeeper, a device much like a bracelet in appearance that he wore on his wrist, and in doing so, he grew in stature.

In this instance, The Horned God broke two of the most sacred of Ůdra Ena Ceann's decrees. No Breathnádol or Riathaĺe were to destroy life. Secondly, neither should they interfere with nor manipulate a spirit. All spirits were to be brought directly before The Creator for final judgement.

'It's over to you, boss,' said Vixi. 'He needs to see what happened for himself.'

'Zippity-dee, come with me,' said The Gatekeeper. He took Asher by the arm.

'Let's do this,' said Vixi. She followed them.

A swirling pool of blue opened in thin air, and it pulled them in. The portal transported them to Earth. But they were thousands of years in the past!

'Wow! Think I'm going to be sick,' said Asher. He felt nauseous.

'Hippity-pop, here we are, in the past, in Egypt at last,' said The Gatekeeper.

'Listen now, kid, everything you see has already happened, literally no one can see us, and we can't change a thing,' said Vixi.

Another of Ůdra Ena Ceann's decrees was that no
Breathnádol or Riathaíe should interfere with or change time.
It was an extremely rare gift that few celestials possessed. Time
could only be altered by the pure of heart, for those pure of
heart were directly connected to The One, who is the master
of time and its creator.

Before Asher was a sandstone temple. Heading toward the
temple, he saw two chariots of wood and rawhide. On either
side of the chariots were two rows of sphinxes, beautiful works
of stone created by the artisans of ancient Egypt's social
pyramid. There were also several date palm trees.

Each chariot was pulled by two horses and moved at a
relaxed pace down the avenue of sphinxes. The chariots
transported five individuals. Each d-shaped chariot was
controlled by a man of dark skin, carrying a shield made from
ox hide and wood.

Each chariot also had an additional man who carried a bow,
quiver, and several arrows. Several javelins were also at the
disposal of those men in each chariot. Additionally, all men
wore helmets of bronze and leather tunics over the chest for
protection.

A vision of authority and grace, a male, a boy, was being
transported in one of the two chariots. He seemed to be of
immense importance. He was very much set apart from the
rest.

He wore a pschent, a red and white double crown, which
rested on top of his head. He was royalty. The design of the
double crown itself was inspired by two animals, the cobra and
the vulture. The double crown he wore also represented his
rule over all Egypt.

His stature was further elaborated by a blue, bearded wig. The
rest of his attire was comprised of a half-pleated kilt that

wrapped around his body, with a pleated section drawn at the front. He wore leopard skins over his shoulder, and lion's tails hung from his belt.

Behind the two chariots moving at a marching pace were over one hundred of the pharaoh's soldiers. Each had padded skullcaps, and they wore leather tunics over their chests for protection. The men of diverse skin colour also wore triangular pouches about their waists and carried large rawhide shields in addition to curved swords.

An ancient Egyptian priest greeted the young boy pharaoh as he dismounted his chariot. The priest was bald and without facial hair. He wore leopard skins over white linen and white papyrus sandals.

'His name was Asim, and Asim he was called, as high priest he did serve a corrupted Breathnádol,' said The Gatekeeper.

In another dream sequence, Asher witnessed The Gatekeeper speaking to the Egyptian high priest Asim. They spoke in ancient Egyptian. In a magnificent display, The Gatekeeper took the priest's amulet, only to infuse it with great power.

'Sippity-dee, we attempted to stop him, you see,' said The Gatekeeper. He and Vixi had sought to send The Horned God in spiritual form to The Creator for judgement.

'To stop him, we laid a trap,' said Vixi. 'Once The Horned God found out The Portal Realm existed, he wouldn't stop searching for a love that he had lost. I doubt he knew what that word 'love' meant.'

'Boppity-dee, The Portal Realm belongs to me, and I knew of everywhere he'd be,' said The Gatekeeper. Knowing that The Horned God had used the portal to Earth, he followed with Vixi.

'We were his guide between worlds, not by choice. After the fall of the Sealgairs, we fled to Neahmil,' informed Vixi. 'Geatiric did the rest,' she said.

The last flash showed a figure with pinkish skin, curled ears, and two slits, vents where a nose should reside. The figure had blond wavy hair and solid golden eyes, but no pupils. He was a vision of perfection. He was clad in black attire. He wore a black vest with gold stitched designs. He wore a black ruffled shirt and black breeches, and boots.

Blue tongue visible, his smile was radiant and inviting, as was his demeanour. He walked with confidence and moved as if gliding upon air.

He was accompanied by a servant in black robes. His servant was faceless, for his face was hidden under a black hood.

'Geatiric attempted to stop The Horned God by infusing the high priest's amulet with the power given to him by Ůdra Ena Ceann,' explained Vixi. 'After the Sealgairs fell, we had been decreed to stop The Horned God's destruction,' she said.

In a burst of darkness, the blond-haired figure dressed in black transformed. His body was distorted and twisted. Every part of his anatomy grew larger and more hideous. The six-foot-two-inch figure quickly grew to eleven feet. Two large golden horns pierced his flesh as they sprang from his head. In the centre was a stump where a third smaller horn once resided.

Standing upon two golden hooves, his legs were covered in golden fur, too. His torso resembled the human anatomy and was covered in golden hair. The pieces of flesh that did show, including the facial area, also radiated a golden aura.

He had claws and bones protruding from around his elbows. Razor-sharp teeth extended from his mouth. His nose was unnaturally shaped, animalistic-like. Most striking, though, were his red glowing eyes and large golden wings. The wings protruded from the beast's back.

'Wait…wait a minute…' Mouth agape, Asher soaked in what he was seeing with his unbelieving eyes. The vision terrified him to the core.

'Yippity-dee, it's he, the self-proclaimed god of horns, The Horned God is he,' said The Gatekeeper, his face too filled with fear.

In a horrid last flash, Asher saw the creature, The Horned God, before two large obelisks, kill the young pharaoh. The pharaoh's head cracked against one of the two obelisks. He was dead in an instant.

The Horned God then turned on the pharaoh's army. In another great show of power, he drained their souls from their bodies. Corpses littered the sand.

'At this point, Earth was in peril,' said Vixi. 'Only fitting one of its own would be its saviour,' he said.

Lastly, The Horned God turned his power on the high priest, Asim. Only something quite shocking happened! He was met with a mighty power, a power infused into the high priest's amulet. His bracelet, Soulkeeper, came loose from his wrist.

'It was meant to destroy his physical form,' stated Vixi. 'But Dorchadi interfered. You see, the amulet we infused with Údra Ena Ceann's power was off a corrupt Breathnádol, and all corruption stems from Dorchadi.'

'Stippity-do, we were duped, you know,' said The Gatekeeper. 'But weakened he was.'

'Without the abomination he called Soulkeeper, he wasn't able to resist,' said Vixi. 'Greatly weakened, we tossed him back to his world, with his little servant.'

'Aided we did in his imprisonment,' said The Gatekeeper.

'Geatiric was severely injured; he barely had enough power to send the evil beast back to his world,' stated Vixi. 'There we helped imprison him,' she said.

Spiritual essence tainted, Geatiric, The Gatekeeper, never fully recovered. To transform into his true form is an agonising, unbearable experience.

'Soulkeeper, what happened to it?' asked Asher. He feared the answer.

'Ůdra Ena Ceann has informed us that you will likely find it, that you must find it,' said Vixi. 'It's been buried with Asim's remains all these many centuries,' she said.

The truth was that The Gatekeeper left Soulkeeper buried with the high priest Asim's remains. His spiritual essence had been compromised, he feared that Soulkeeper would be enough to cast him fully into the grip of Dorchadi.

His spiritual makeup was different from other lifeforms insofar as he had to be pure and free of evil. Pure from the corruption of Dorchadi to truly serve the will of The Creator.

Vixi also feared the corruption of Soulkeeper. She had tasted corruption before.

'I...I...' Suddenly, Asher felt quite strange!

'Yes, you must find Soulkeeper,' reaffirmed Vixi. Her head bobbed up and down. She felt guilty. She knew that what Ůdra Ena Ceann had in store for him was no simple task.

'Wow! Everything is getting fuzzy,' said Asher. He heard a voice call. It was getting louder and louder.

'Asher, get out here!' It was his dad, Mike.

'Time to go, kid,' said Vixi. 'Until the next time we meet!'

'Bye for now, for now goodbye,' said The Gatekeeper. He waved with both hands.

The Gatekeeper and Vixi disappeared. They were completely gone, as was Asher's peculiar dream.

-Chapter 10-

Murphy's Inn

Shouting as he went, Mike ducked his head in through the tent entrance. 'Get up, lazy bones, I've a treat in store for today,' he spoke at a pace. He clapped his hands together, creating a racket.

Abruptly awakened, Asher's attention was quickly absorbed by the noise his dad was making. 'Give me a minute,' he said, quite shakily. He panted, his lungs emptied and then filled again rapidly like two bagpipes. His heart pounded away in his chest.

'OK, but don't take too long, lad,' replied Mike. He delivered a big thumbs-up.

Asher tried to calm himself as he took a couple of deep breaths. His dream was disturbing, but he realised the seemingly transparent truth, that it was just that, a dream. 'I have a very vivid imagination.' There was no way he thought that anything he had seen in his dream was real. 'Talking foxes, I've lost it.' He wiped the perspiration from his forehead.

'We're burning daylight,' Mike yelled as he waited impatiently outside the tent.

'I'll be ready in a minute, Dad,' said Asher. He made haste. He got to his feet, he then put on a blue chequered shirt, the sleeves rolled up to his elbow, a pair of tan shorts, and two brown leather sandals. One sandal had teeth marks, his big fluffy dog, Scruffy, being the culprit. Ready, he slowly moved forward to exit the tent.

Asher could see his dad standing by the Land Rover. He also spotted the extremely big, broad-shouldered man, Carl Jackson. The pair were chatting.

'Listen, if you get into any trouble, Richardson is about. Be sure to keep me posted if you manage to clear the rest of the passage, there is not a lot left to do,' instructed Mike. 'Today is perhaps the day.' He was radiant and full of hope.

'Yes, boss, shouldn't be long now, a few hours at the most, I've been working the lads hard.' Carl nodded in agreement. He wiped the back of his bald head and neck with a wet towel. It was another hot, dry day.

Pleased, Mike smiled before jumping into the driver's seat of the Land Rover. Brummm! Brummm! Brummm! He stepped time and again on the accelerator revving the engine. He glanced toward an observant Asher. 'Jump in, lad, this will take us part of the way,' he said. He leaned over and pushed the passenger door open.

'Coming, Dad,' responded Asher. He rushed forward and soared into the passenger seat.

Clink! Mike released the handbrake, he then stepped upon the clutch to sequentially change gear. Smoke drifted in abundance from the vehicle's part-rusted exhaust pipe. Wheels screeching, they speedily zoomed off down the valley, leaving a heap of dust behind them.

However, only a few minutes later, their only route had become blocked with hordes of people. They had come upon a flock of lively tourists, eager for the day's viewing of the valley tombs. It was quite common for hundreds, if not thousands, to visit the popular tourist attraction daily.

'You have to watch the daft fools,' said Mike. 'They'll just walk out in front without looking.' Slowly, he pressed his size twelve boot down atop the break. The wheel rotation of the vehicle began to slow. He carefully manoeuvred around tourists and locals alike before picking up speed again. He drove for a while longer before reaching the entrance to the Valley of the Kings.

'I thought we were going to see more of the tombs within the valley,' said Asher. He was extremely curious as to what his dad was up to.

'No, we're off to East Luxor, lad,' confirmed Mike.

'No way, that's awesome.' Asher jumped up and down in his seat, he was thrilled at the prospect of exploring East Luxor, situated across the River Nile. 'Cool,' he mumbled.

Coming to the West Bank of the River Nile, Asher and Mike got out of the Land Rover.

'Are we not driving, Dad?' asked Asher. He shut the passenger door of the vehicle.

'No lad,' said Mike. He pointed to the waters of the River Nile. 'We're taking the ferry, it's easier and convenient, Luxor is a madhouse for congestion, besides, I want you to enjoy yourself,' he said. He held a brown case in his hand.

'Wow! It's a boat,' said Asher. A smile brightened up his face. He saw people clamouring off, as a group waited to board.

'You're acting like you've never seen a ferry before,' said Mike.

'I have,' replied Asher. 'I have been to the beach, and, well, I've read books and stuff, but I've never been on a boat before,' he added. He was excited.

Taking the passenger ferry to East Luxor, both Asher and his dad, Mike, spent their limited time on board peering over the side rails of the shabby, red striped vessel, into the wide, vastness of the River Nile's greyish waterline.

'Gosh! It's awesome,' said Asher. 'It's truly very spectacular, all those picture postcards don't compare,' he gasped. His nimble hands glided through his jet-black hair as he peered off into the distance.

'Picture postcards, what do you mean?' asked Mike. He was a little puzzled.

'The ones you've mailed to me, back home that is,' explained Asher. He was referring to the very postcards he would wait weeks on end for Henry, the local postman man to deliver.

'Oh, I see, is that a good or bad thing then, lad?' questioned Mike. He smirked uncontrollably as he stroked his chin.

'Good,' stated Asher. 'This is an amazing place, Dad, no wonder you never want to leave,' he said. In his mind, Egypt was mysteriously wondrous and exciting.

'I see…I…' Mike was reduced to silence. His head hung low as feelings of guilt swept over him. He put a hand on Asher's shoulder. He wanted to improve his relationship with his son. 'You know, lad, never again, never that long will we be separated…' Thud! Thud! Thud! He was interrupted.

'That was quick, we've arrived,' said Asher. He watched as hordes of people hurried to the front of the ferry. The vessel had reached its port on the East Bank of the River Nile.

'Come, lad, let's go,' instructed Mike. Quickly, he scurried off the docked vessel, brown leather case in hand.

'Wait up,' called out Asher. He trailed behind. His much shorter legs struggled to keep pace.

'Come on, lad, we haven't all morning,' said Mike. He took his hat off, using it to wave Asher forward. He continued up and over a steep sandy bank. He then raised his left arm in the air, proceeding to wave down a horse-drawn carriage, known locally as a caleche. 'Al Saha, Murphy's Inn,' he said, outlining his desired destination, before jumping aboard.

'Give me a hand, Dad,' said Asher. He held out his right hand. He was hoisted up into one scruffy seat. 'Woah!' He had barely time to think, everything was happening so fast.

Without need for further instruction the horse handler zoomed off. Crack! Leather coming down upon perspiring skin, the big brown horse pulling the carriage began to move forward at a pace. Click! Clack! Click! Clack! Click! Clack! The hooves of the big brown horse thumped the ground beneath like two coconut halves coming together.

The Egyptian national, the horse handler, took a route through an open marketplace. The market resembled a beautifully orchestrated sea of colours. On display, among a variety of fruits, veggies, herbs, and spices, were fresh red tomatoes, ripe green apples, and soft yellow bananas.

East Luxor was a hive of bustling activity. An ancient place, in comparison to most cities back in the United States, but much more mysteriously astounding. It was shrouded in secrets dating back thousands of years.

On the way to Murphy's Inn, Asher spotted Luxor Temple. To the front was a three-thousand-year-old, pink-granite obelisk. It was once one of two tall, four-sided monuments that rested at the temple entrance. The second seventy-five-foot-high obelisk was moved to Place de la Concorde in Paris, France.

He also spotted two large sitting figures and one standing figure. Little did he know the three enormous stone figures were once a collection of six, all of which depicting the pharaoh, Ramses II.

'Can we stop Dad, can we?' asked Asher. Something had caught his attention. 'I think I've seen this before!' He recollected his dream the night before. The Gatekeeper and Vixi were still very much ingrained in his memory. A lot about the temple was remarkably familiar.

'Of course, you've seen it before for sure,' said Mike. 'It's in that book I sent you, it's Luxor Temple.' The book he was referring to was the very one that he had sent to Asher in the post. The one entitled 'Valley of the Kings, The Archaeologist's Guide.'

'Yes, yes, you're right,' replied Asher. He did not know what to make of it all. He simply thought his mind was playing tricks. He shook it off. He had the entire day to enjoy with his dad, and he had intentions to do so.

Deciding to relax a little, Asher took in the scenery all around him. His eyes scanned countless narrow streets, lined with old shabby buildings. He was truly taken aback by the grungy urban scenery. His big blue eyes focused upon the numerous coaches, cars and horse pulled carriages endlessly zooming past left and right, as well as the various flocks of Egyptian locals and foreign tourists covering the sidewalks.

Attentive, he took note of the three hot air balloons hovering high above in the clear blue sky, one red, one green, and one blue, each with varying Arabic patterns and symbols. He was truly captivated by the traditional and non-traditional elements at play, amidst the big city feel. 'Wow, Dad! There's so much, I mean, well, there's so much of everything,' he said.

Leather reins pulled rearward the brown skinned horse sighed loudly, and they suddenly came to an abrupt halt. 'Is this your stop?' the horse handler queried.

'Yes, this is our stop,' answered Mike. Thud! He jumped from the caleche to the ground, holding his brown case. 'This way, lad,' he instructed. He paid the horse handler before making off at pace again.

'I'm not built for this,' moaned Asher. He was sweating and breathing a little heavily, too, as he followed his dad in pursuit. It was a hot day.

They both made their way down one of the side streets before entering a print shop. Opening the brown case, Mike handed over a storage device.

'What are we doing here, Dad?' queried Asher. He had no idea as to what Mike was up to.

'I'm getting some photos developed,' explained Mike. 'The professor asked for some hard copies,' he said.

'Who's the professor?' asked Asher. Now he was bamboozled.

'The person we're here to meet,' stated Mike. After waiting a few minutes, he retrieved a handful of photos he put them in his brown case. 'Let's go,' he said. Full of zeal, he was off again.

'Here we go once more,' groaned Asher. He raced behind his dad to the end of the street.

They both entered a bar called Murphy's Inn. It was an aged, long-standing building, quite notable for the cracks in the walls.

There were not that many people in the grungy establishment. There were four, to be exact. There was one elderly, grey-haired gentleman sitting in the corner reading a newspaper and two other middle-aged men making light conversation as the barkeeper, a non-national, handed them their dark, white topped drinks.

Voice echoing throughout the dimly lit, oak-furnished public inn, Mike made his presence well known. 'Long time, Ballard, it's been what, five months?'

The elderly gentleman residing in the corner put his newspaper aside, entitled 'The Weekly News of Egypt,' to glance in his direction. In the process, his silver-framed glasses slid down the brim of his long nose. 'Well, are you going to get me a whisky, or do I die of thirst?' he chuckled. He lifted an empty glass to affirm his point.

The two men shook hands. They did so enthusiastically, like two old friends reuniting.

'It would be rude not to, seeing that I'm late,' replied Mike. Shreekkk! He pulled back a shabby oak chair, it raked across the tiled floor like uncut nails scraping across a chalkboard. He sat opposite the man named Ballard Schneider. 'This is my son Asher,' he informed the old man. He then clapped Asher on the back. 'Say hello to the professor, lad.'

'Hello, sir,' greeted Asher. He addressed Ballard as if he were speaking to one of his teachers at Neptunica Middle School.

'Hello there,' said Professor Ballard Schneider, being polite. His German accent was as clear as daylight. Being sixty-three years old and thinly built, he was sophisticatedly dressed. He wore an old-fashioned, blue-shaded, square-patterned suit. His suit jacket hung over the back of his chair.

'Two whiskies and a glass of lemonade for the boy,' Mike shouted. 'Oh, and I'll have mine on the rocks,' he said.

'Dad, aren't you driving?' questioned Asher with a little alarm. He nudged his dad with his elbow. 'Better safe than sorry,' he said. He preferred to be cautious.

'It's only one,' answered Mike. 'Not enough to take me over the limit,' he said. He fluffed up Asher's black hair.

'Be with you right away,' the ginger-bearded, ginger-moustached barkeeper stoutly replied. Setting himself to the task, he grasped one tumbler and two octagon-shaped glasses

from underneath the bar counter before briskly wiping them.
He then began the task of filling each. Cloudy coloured liquid
resting but a centimetre below the glass rim, the barkeeper
then retrieved a bottle of fine malt whisky from atop a glass
shelf.

'What do you know about this then?' asked Mike. He wasted
no time. There was a purpose as to why he was in Luxor.
Every time he needed a second opinion, the professor was his
desired choice. He trusted no one else. The old professor had
taught him while he had studied at university almost two
decades previously.

Since then, Ballard had left the United States to take up his
current post at Luxor University. He had taught at the
university in Cairo for a short while also.

Thirty-two highly detailed photos were taken from Mike's
brown leather case, only to be placed in Professor Ballard
Schneider's lined, creased hands. 'Take a look at these,' he said.

Grey, bushy eyebrows raised a little, Ballard was instantly
intrigued. 'Superb, absolutely superb, my friend,' he murmured.
He caressed his bushy, grey moustache in careful
consideration. He placed the pictures across the surface of the
table before him.

'The photos are of the tomb entrance and the walls of the
inner corridor, research conducted by Elisha Thompson, a
very talented woman,' said Mike.

'Fresh off the print,' said Ballard as he sniffed. He pressed
one photo against his nose before rubbing the surface of the
photograph with his fingers.

'The rest of my team are working hard to gain access to the
main chamber,' explained Mike. 'Once I have more, you'll be
the first person I speak to.' He delivered a warm smile.

'Good, good,' replied Ballard. 'It'll sure be something when they produce the complete findings,' he said. Tongue rustling between dry lips, he weighed up what exactly it was that he was looking at.

'I estimate a few years' work at best, depending on what we find, of course,' judged Mike. 'Recording and tagging every little detail is slow, laborious work,' he said.

Banggg! The entrance door, which was a stained-glass door, slammed shut. Another man abruptly entered the inn.

The man was tall, with a thick, distinct black moustache. The pale-skinned man was not an Egyptian local. He wore a black formal suit. His jacket hung over his arm. He also wore a white shirt with the sleeves rolled up and the top button undone. In addition, a red tie hung loosely around his scrawny neck, exposing a large Adam's apple. The pale figure slowly progressed to take a seat. He did so precariously close to Mike, the very next table to be exact!

Silently, Asher observed the pale figure. He watched as the man retrieved a cigar from his inner jacket pocket. The mysterious man inspected the cigar further with a sniff from his pointed nose.

'I don't expect a lot,' said Mike. 'Just tell me what you can,' he said. His goal was to find out who lay mummified in the old tomb. Any light on the matter would help him greatly.

'Strange, extremely mind-boggling, it appears that a doorway, a vortex of some sort, has, or should I say had, been initially opened. There's also mention of a golden trinket of some kind,' stated Ballard. His first thoughts leaned toward the old Egyptian gods.

'A vortex! Is that kind of like a portal?' gasped Asher. He twisted around in his chair. His focus had quickly shifted from the man sitting at the very next table to Ballard. His mind filled with thoughts, specifically thoughts of the strange dreams he had been having recently. He recalled the dimension between worlds, the place known as The Portal Realm!

'Yes…yes, I suppose, kid,' confirmed Ballard. He nodded his head in agreement.

'Is there mention of The Gatekeeper, an imp, or Vixi or, or…'

'Let the man speak, lad,' intervened Mike. He put his hand on Asher's back. 'Someone has not been sleeping too good lately,' he explained to his old professor. He chuckled.

'No, no, I don't believe there is,' replied Ballard. He ran his fingers across one photo at a time, carefully looking for clues.

Asher exhaled heavily with relief. 'It was all just a coincidence, that's all,' he mumbled. He knew that he had overreacted, just a little.

'Are you all done, lad?' asked Mike. He smiled as he put his hand atop Asher's head to ruffle his hair humorously.

'Ummm…oh yes, all done, Dad,' replied Asher. He nodded with a smile.

'Great, now make yourself useful,' said Mike. He took a few notes from his pocket. 'Get yourself some chips and see if our drinks are ready,' he said.

'Sure, Dad,' said Asher. He nodded before grasping the notes. He hurried toward the bar counter.

'ID kid!'

'I…I don't…'

'Relax, kid, I'm joking.' The ginger-bearded bartender held out his hand. 'The name's Brendan,' he said.

'Mine's Asher,' he said, introducing himself. He shook the barman's hand. He was no longer paying attention to his dad or the professor.

'Look at this image, Mike, do you see? One figure is holding out an arm, and the trinket in question is attached,' said Ballard. The photographs partially revealed their secrets to him.

Consumed in the moment, Mike prudently scanned the photo. 'It's nothing like what I have seen before,' he admitted.

'Peculiar, very peculiar,' said Ballard. He stroked the grey hairs on his creased chin. He fell into a lengthy, but thoughtful silence.

Tap! Tap! Tap! Mike drummed his leg against the table as he waited impatiently. He needed to know more, fast. 'Well, what else?' he asked.

'This man here is an ancient priest, perhaps a high priest,' revealed Ballard. 'The way he's depicted screams as much, hairless, leopard skin, white linen, yes, no doubt,' he said.

'Perhaps it's this fellow's tomb we've uncovered,' suggested Mike. 'He'd likely be a high priest if he's buried in the valley,' he said. He was referring to the Valley of the Kings.

'It's possible! Though do you see this other fellow, he's a pharaoh,' said Ballard. 'He wears the pschent, or double crown, signifying his rule of upper and lower Egypt,' he added.

'Really, that one slipped through the cracks,' admitted Mike. 'That's why I came to you, no one better in the business,' he complimented his old professor. He held him in very high regard.

'The head of archaeology at Luxor University would say it differently,' said Ballard. 'He's up in the Valley of the Kings himself. Bad business!' He rolled his eyes. 'In league with a nasty bunch,' he added. He shook his head.

'Is his name Bernard by any chance?' asked Mike. His fingernails drummed against the table. 'Tall fellow, with a bad stutter,' he said.

'Well…yes,' gasped Ballard. 'How did you guess that?' he inquired. He took his spectacles from his aged face. He was a little puzzled.

'He, along with some goons, tried to cause trouble for me and the team,' clarified Mike. 'He's with a man, a Russian named Bronislav,' he said.

'Keep clear of them,' said Ballard, concerned. 'They sought me out first, I told them where to go, pack of brigands,' he said. He had a look of disgust on his face.

'What do you know about them?' asked Mike. He was intrigued. He wanted to know just how dangerous the man Bronislav Valadvic was.

'They're trouble,' said Ballard. 'They've been known to bribe government officials, among others. For years, they've been selling to the black market.' He shook his head. 'A true archaeologist serves history, not themselves,' he added. It was the most important lesson that he instilled in his students.

'I thought as much, I'll need to get back soon,' said Mike, a little worried. 'Once I get back to the exploration site, I'll make a call to the chief of police, see if I can straighten everything out,' he said. He was perturbed by the news he had just heard.

'Just be careful,' expressed Ballard. 'You just don't know who's on the payroll,' he said. He was experienced not just as a lecturer, but in life. He had lived long enough to know the bad apples. He knew a vast network of people. As a professor in

Luxor, he knew a great deal, especially when it came to anything relating to archaeology.

'Is there anything else you can tell me?' asked Mike. He tapped on the photos on the table.

'Yes,' said Ballard. 'This other fellow is something else. I've never seen this before, I don't think he's a pharaoh, noble or priest. One thing is clear though: he is someone of immense importance, someone dark, someone who has committed a great offence!'

'This I have heard before,' said Mike.

'That may be so, but from this image it appears that the dark figure in question, while wielding the bracelet, the trinket of gold as mentioned, had killed the pharaoh, before turning it on the high priest,' said Ballard. His experienced eyes danced from photo to photo.

'Killed! You mean with a bladed weapon?' queried Mike. His first thoughts jumped to the obvious. He thought that the pharaoh and high priest had been killed with a knife or blade.

'No, that logical conclusion is total folly, the trinket of gold seems to have emitted a force not of man's construction, but of a higher power!' said Ballard. His eyes widened.

'You mean power that would have been wielded by beings such as the Egyptian gods of myth?' suggested Mike. 'Amun-Ra, Osiris, Horus, you get my point,' he said.

'Perhaps,' said Ballard. 'The ancient gods do usually fill the walls of the tombs of the dead,' he said.

'Well, what happened to the Egyptian high priest?' asked Mike. 'Was he killed too?' He spurted out question after question seeking evermore knowledge. His appetite for the unknown was growing insatiable.

'Eventually, he perished like the pharaoh. He was overcome by the same powerful force, and his body was simply beyond healing as it were,' revealed Ballard. 'Although he put up a fight, it would seem,' he said.

'How could this servant of Egypt, this high priest, have fought back, if this, this trinket, is as powerful as you say?' questioned Mike.

'As you know, the ancient Egyptians would commonly wear precious metals, jewellery as such, thought to restore, heal, and even protect them from black magic and evil forces,' informed Ballard.

'Your point is?' queried Mike.

'Dad, here you go,' intervened Asher. He barged in, placing two whisky glasses on the table, before heading back to the bar for his lemonade. He took a few sips from the glass while at the bar.

'Sorry, you were saying,' said Mike. He held his whisky glass in his hand.

'Look here,' said Ballard. He directed Mike's attention to one pristine photo.

'The Egyptian high priest seems to be wearing an amulet,' said Mike. 'Quite bizarre,' he said.

'Not just any amulet,' explained Ballard. 'It's an amulet in the shape of the Eye of Amun-Ra, an important Egyptian god. The eye itself is said to not only symbolise healing, restoration, and sacrifice, but also protection,' he said.

'So not even the amulet of Amun-Ra could save him,' Mike gasped. 'I've never come across a piece of mythology in which the chief of the Egyptian gods is challenged like this,' he said.

'The high priest is just a man of flesh and bone,' alluded Ballard. 'It's unusual too for a high priest to wear jewellery. Who knows, maybe he anticipated the attack,' he proposed. He shrugged his shoulders.

'This is quite something.' Mike appeared utterly bemused. Never in his entire archaeological career had he heard such a story. 'What of the golden trinket?' he asked.

'It would seem that the aggressor of the story didn't get away completely unscathed either,' replied Ballard. 'It appears that the power of the trinket he wore was forced back upon him. In the process, his trinket, his bracelet, came loose from his wrist. Not only that, in this image he even appears to have been banished!'

'Banished, what do you mean?' asked Mike.

'The doorway, the vortex that had initially been opened, the very one I mentioned, it appears he was thrown into it,' said Ballard. He fixed his silver-framed spectacles, which had slid partway down his nose.

Looking into the abyss of his whisky glass, Mike tried to draw some rational conclusion. 'Surely this is a newly uncovered story of Egyptian myth,' he said.

'Who knows, but it does seem highly likely,' agreed Ballard. He proceeded to wipe his perspiring forehead. 'I'm simply parched.' He took his whisky glass in hand.

'It's the only logical explanation,' said Mike.

'Yes,' said Ballard. 'The only logical explanation, bottoms up.' He wrapped his wrinkled fingers around his glass of whisky. He parted his crinkly lips. One swift gulp and he slammed the empty glass back down upon the oak table. Thuddd!

'I hope this tomb has the answers we seek,' said Mike. 'Mind you, a few artefacts, jewellery and ornaments would be nice to send to the Luxor Museum too, but the odds are slim.' He understood that grave robbers had ransacked many of the other burial sites situated within the Valley of the Kings over the millennia.

'Who knows?' replied Ballard. 'They didn't get everything in the case of Tutankhamun. Plus, it would be nice for one of my students to go down in the history books,' he said with pride.

'True, though we still must establish if the tomb correlates to the…' Ring! Ring! Ring! Mike was suddenly interrupted as his black cellular phone rang. He quickly pressed his index finger down upon the receive button. It was Carl Jackson. 'Already, really, good man, I'll not be long.' Face brimming with excitement, he rapidly sprang to his feet. 'Thanks, Ballard, I owe you one,' he said.

Ballard also got to his feet, a smile crept upon his timeworn face. 'You better make that two,' he said.

Ruffling through his slightly worn leather wallet, Mike pulled out some discoloured notes before placing them upon the bar counter. 'You better just give the old man the entire bottle and keep the change.' He had not touched his drink. His mind was elsewhere, so much so that he even failed to take note of Asher, who was sitting upon a stool at the bar, still sipping on his lemonade.

The barman, Brendan, finished wiping a glass before grasping at the Egyptian currency. 'Sure thing,' he said.

'Hey…hey…. Dad.' Asher was ignored as Mike made for the exit.

Mike rushed into the street outside, brown case in hand. Thuddd! A local man, caught completely unaware by his speedy emergence from the inn, crashed into his firm shoulder.

'You're a stupid man!' the angry Egyptian harshly scolded him.

'Sorry,' said Mike.

'Stupid man,' the Egyptian repeated, furiously trampling on.

'I said I'm sorry,' Mike roared, before picking up his brown leather case, which had come loose amidst the untimely incident. He dusted himself down before plodding on, when suddenly he realised that he had made yet another idiotic mistake. 'Damn it!' It took him but a matter of seconds before he realised that he had forgotten something, or more to the point, someone! He quickly scrambled back through the wooden-framed doorway of Murphy's Inn. 'Asher,' he called.

'Yes, Dad?' replied Asher. He was but a few inches from the exit.

'Let's go,' said Mike.

Hurrying out through the stained-glass door, they both scurried down the side street once more. Managing to stop a horse-drawn carriage in quick succession, they clambered aboard.

'The ferry to the West Bank, and please hurry,' said Mike. Repeatedly, he instructed the horse handler to move faster. 'Can you move quicker?' he kept repeating.

'I'm doing my best, always busy mid-day, always,' was the Egyptian's shaky response.

Asher was consumed with a more pressing matter! He glanced behind, through a tatty peephole in the carriage's folding top. He believed that someone was following them on their way back to the shabby, public vessel. He turned to his dad to alert him of the dilemma. However, he did so to his dismay. 'Dad, you know in the inn, the…'

'Not now,' said Mike firmly. Impolitely, he hushed him. He did so repeatedly. 'We must get back to the exploration site as quickly as possible, lad,' he said.

'But Dad…'

'Not now, lad, there's the ferry up ahead, it's ready to leave,' said Mike. He quickly descended from the carriage, handing over two hundred Egyptian pounds, equivalent to eleven US dollars.

'It's three hundred,' barked the horse handler.

'Nice try, fella, it was two hundred for the same journey but less than an hour ago,' said Mike. He was stern. He was not a man to be taken advantage of.

The horse handler rudely clutched the money from Mike's hand. Whip snapping off horse skin, the Egyptian zoomed off in a huff.

'Listen to me, that man's been following us from the inn,' Asher erupted. He was ready to explode like an overinflated balloon. He simply could not constrain himself any further.

Finally, Mike took the time to peer over his left shoulder.

A tall, thin, pale fellow dressed in black was in pursuit. The very same character from back at Murphy's Inn. He was descending another caleche, but just twenty feet away.

Uninterested, Mike refused to pay the man any attention, just as he had not back at the inn. 'It's your imagination, lad,' he insisted. He was ignorant of Asher's stark warning, he simply hurried onto the ferry without thinking about the matter any further. 'Keep up, lad,' he said.

Deeply irritated, Asher scrambled closely behind.

-Chapter 11-

Death and Discovery

Stomping back and forth upon the ferry's wooden deck, Mike's composure was far from calm. 'Hurry up,' he barked, teeth grinding tightly together. He desperately longed to be back at the exploration site. His angst was propelled into overdrive due to the ferry's slow movement across the River Nile. 'God damn it! This bloody boat is just too darn slow,' he grumbled.

Ring! Ring! Ring! Mike's black cellular phone rang again. He placed his brown case down before answering. 'Yes, what is it?' He listened intently. 'Yes, yes, sarcophagus, statues, artefacts, I don't believe it!' His face ignited with surprise, he clearly liked what he was hearing.

'Who is it?' asked Asher. He was curious.

'One moment, lad,' responded Mike. He put his finger to his lips, seeking silence. 'Listen, Elisha, inform Carl to make the passageway safe, I don't want anyone hurt, I'll be there soon,' he said. Hanging up, he then looked up at the clear blue sky, as if to gather his thoughts.

'Dad!' Asher said unsteadily. 'Look behind…'

'Not now.' Rubbing his hands together, Mike simply would not listen. He was consumed by his thoughts.

'But, Dad,' continued Asher, panicking. He began tugging on his dad's shirt.

'What is it that's so important?' asked Mike. Annoyed, he shook his head.

'It's that man again,' said Asher. He eyed the man dressed in black formal attire, the very man who had been following them from Murphy's Inn.

'Nonsense! You've been acting rather strangely,' said Mike. He extended his arms; he radiated a great deal of non-verbal negativity. 'You need to lighten up,' he said.

'Behind you, Dad!' Asher's tone grew to a whisper. He noted that the shifty, pale, formally dressed man was edging ever closer. He noted that the man was giving both him and his dad a great deal of attention.

'Behind me,' said Mike screwing up his face. He was dumbfounded. As he turned around, he caught sight of the man in black. He could see that the man was holding his black jacket. He seemed startled. 'What are you looking at?' he asked. He was direct. 'Do you have a problem?' His questioning instilled panic in the man.

'Easy, comrade.' The tall, wide-eyed man edged back. His angst was growing. 'No problem,' he answered. His Eastern European accent was thick.

'Are you with that thug Bronislav?' probed Mike. He was suspicious. Growing irate, he watched as the tall individual put on his black jacket. 'Bloody hell!' he boomed. Alarmed, he caught sight of a gun, a black revolver.

'Damn it!' The man in black realised what Mike had seen. He immediately went for the firearm.

'No, no you don't,' said Mike, exploding into action. His reflexes were crisp and sharp. He snatched at the bony hand of the thin, mysterious figure in black.

Brightness erupting from the gun barrel, one bullet whistled through the air! Gun then pointed downward, and another hit the wooden deck beneath. The actions of the two men spiralled wildly out of control.

'Get help!' A frenzied commuter aboard the ferry shouted.

Utter panic ensued aboard the vessel. Slow to identify the culprit, many of the startled passengers aboard the vessel quickly hastened as far away from the action as they could. They were wide-eyed and completely terrified.

'You fool,' Mike growled. His brown hat toppled from his tilted head as he gazed up at his six-foot-six-inch-tall, yellow-eyed foe. Drool slipping from his bottom lip, he was struggling to gain any sort of advantage.

'Hold on, Dad,' spurted out Asher in panic. His heart thudded in his chest; he hastened forward to take the initiative. He dropped to his knees; he then placed his hands upon the vessel's wooden deck. His small body rested just behind the mysterious man in black.

'Arghhh!' With a desperate yelp, the man fumbled, tripping over him. Clunkkk! Metal tasting wood, the deadly weapon the man held came loose to slam down upon the deck of the vessel.

'Watch out, lad.' Panting heavily, Mike smashed his fist against the pointy nose of his aggressor, rendering him dazed. The blow was worthy of any boxing champion looking for a quick knockout. Blood stained his knuckles.

'Dad, look there,' shouted Asher. He pointed to a life preserver.

'That'll do alright,' said Mike. He then quickly seized one circular, white, and red striped life preserver, to firmly place it over his foe's head. His adrenalin was running high, with a jolt of pure strength, he then tossed the mysterious man dressed in black overboard.

Splashhh! The man fell into the chilly water of the River Nile.

'Hope you can swim,' yelled out Mike. He was smug. He leaned his back up against an iron side-rail, located on the starboard side of the vessel. His red face, sweaty palms, and ruffled-up clothes told of his exhaustion. 'Well, that was bloody close lad,' he exhaled heavily. He slowly regained his composure before easing forward to retrieve his ruffled-up hat. 'That's the second time you've saved my neck.'

'He forgot this,' said Asher. He carefully wrapped his fingers around the butt of the black revolver, he then hurled it overboard. Splashhh! It sank beneath the waters of the River Nile.

'Let's go before we get into trouble,' instructed Mike. He knew there had been enough commotion aboard the ferry. He did not want to be hauled into a squabble with the police, especially if he was seeking their help. He fully intended to engage with the authorities to resolve the escalating situation with Bronislav Valadvic and his men.

'Ok, Dad,' replied Asher. He nodded as his blue eyes darted about him. He could see many frightened faces.

But only a few minutes later, the red striped ferry had docked at its port on the West Bank of the River Nile.

Not wanting to delay, both Asher and Mike quickly scrambled onto dry land. They dashed ashore among a horde of people attempting to get clear of the chaos.

'You, hey you wait, the authorities are on the way…'

Both ignored the agitated concerns of the vessel's operator.

'There's the vehicle up ahead,' said Mike. He moved quickly. Sweat seeped through his shirt. 'Shake a leg, lad,' he said.

As ever, Asher struggled to keep pace. 'Wait, Dad, wait,' he called out. Huffing and puffing, he looked like a Jack Russell trying to catch up with a greyhound.

He watched as his dad jumped into the driver's seat of the Land Rover before igniting the engine. He tossed his brown case in the back seat. Brummm! The metal beast came to life like an animal forcefully disturbed from its slumber.

'Quick, jump in lad, there's no time to lose,' spoke Mike in haste. He squeezed his foot on the accelerator, taking off. It took him no time at all to reach the entrance to the Valley of the Kings. Honk! Honk! Honk! He honked the horn repeatedly before signalling with his arm for a handful of gawking foreigners to get out of the way. 'Move you silly fools,' he said.

'Uomo pazzo!' One riled-up Italian did not take kindly to Mike's careless driving as he called him a 'crazy man' in his native language.

'Sure, buddy, just move,' responded Mike. He did not understand Italian, nor did he care for the man's protests. He simply put his foot to the accelerator once more. The way ahead was now clear.

A hive of activity awaited Mike's arrival at the excavation site. Boots and sandals clambering back and forth, his small team was utterly consumed by their work. With Carl Jackson at the helm, they were clearing the tomb of rock and rubble. A grotesque smell hung in the air. 'We're in!' He seemed incredibly pleased indeed.

Clueless, Asher had no idea what was happening. 'What's all the fuss about?' he asked.

Mike enlightened Asher with a grin of pure delight on his face. 'Well lad, the tomb passageway is finally cleared, and we do not want those damn Russian's moving in. Besides, there is no doubt it was them who sent, tall, dark, and ugly with a revolver after us,' he said.

Mike waved to get the attention of the big man, Carl. 'Over here,' he shouted. Cautiously, he informed him to be ready in case there was any further trouble. 'Keep an eye out, Carl, one of those idiots tried to take me out, or at least take what research has been gathered on our find,' he explained.

'Yes, boss,' said Carl. 'I'll get the rifle.' His bulging muscles strained against the plain white vest top that he wore.

'I'll take the shotgun too, just in case,' informed Mike. He was fully aware that Bronislav would soon find out about the ferry incident.

'Tony,' said Carl. His voice was loud, deep, and demanding.

'Yes?' answered Tony.

'The shotgun, bring it here,' instructed Carl.

Without delay, Tony disappeared for but a moment before returning with the weapon. He handed it straight to Mike. 'Is there a need for that?' he asked, displaying his distaste for the brutish weapon. Every part of his elongated facial features turned negative, his droopy hooded eyes tightened, his snub nose turned up, and his lips curled inward.

'There sure is, Tony,' affirmed Mike. 'The shells, if you please,' he said.

'This is not the answer,' replied Tony. 'We're archaeologists,' he said.

'I know,' said Mike. 'I'll call the chief of police, he'll deal with it, but first things first,' he said.

'That's all the ammunition we have,' said Tony. He took four rounds of ammunition from his slightly torn shirt pocket. His wrinkled left hand ran from the front of his extremely receded hairline to the back. 'Just make sure before the police get here that you get those weapons back to me,' he said.

Clinkkk! Mike opened the double-barrel shotgun before placing two red shells inside each of the two empty chambers. He then placed the two remaining shells within his back trouser pocket. 'Back to work, Tony, there's still much to be done,' he said.

'You're in charge," said Tony dryly. 'What do I know, but how to make a good omelette?' he groaned.

'I've been inside, boss,' said Carl. He smiled, his face brimmed with joy. He had seen wondrous things inside the tomb. 'This is it. This is the big one!' He patted Mike on the back.

'Is it safe?' asked Mike. It was his first concern. It was his job as lead archaeologist to ensure no one was hurt.

'Well, not quite,' replied Carl. He began rubbing his neck as his smile evaporated. 'The lower end of the passageway, before entering the antechamber, looks unstable,' he said.

'You shouldn't have risked it,' said Mike with concern. He wanted to scold the big man for acting so foolishly, but considering the joy of his words, he just could not. He knew that if Carl Jackson were right and indeed there were a great many artefacts inside, it would be the biggest find since nineteen twenty-two.

'You may want to speak to Elisha,' explained Carl. 'She is inside the passageway, I told her to steer clear of the unstable section,' he said.

'Thanks, Carl,' said Mike. He left the big man to tend to his work. He then turned his focus to Asher, who stood gawking with curiosity as to what all the fuss was about.

'Stay out here, lad,' instructed Mike. He did not want to put his son in a dangerous situation.

'But, but why, Dad?' protested Asher. He, too, wanted to know what was inside the tomb. Indeed, he was very eager.

'Just stay here,' said Mike. He was firm in his stance. 'I'll not be long.' With haste, he hurried forward. He quickly disappeared.

'Not a chance!' Rebelliously, Asher quickly raced after his dad. He entered the tomb corridor. To his right, he took note of the deadly shotgun. It rested up against the wall of the corridor, close to the entrance. He could also see that his dad had stopped, but just a few feet up ahead. He was talking to the fiery, red-headed, hazel-eyed Elisha.

'Carl was saying this is the big one. I hope he's right,' said Mike with hope. Many archaeologists went their whole career without such a find.

'Yes, Carl took a quick look; he's seen wonderful things. But these tunnels are still unstable, we need to get a few more support beams up, we have placed battery-powered lights along the corridor,' informed Elisha.

'Carl said the lower end of the passageway looks dodgy. I don't want anyone hurt in here, especially you,' said Mike. He had genuine feelings for her.

'You're a real sweetheart,' giggled Elisha. She softly stroked his cheek with the palm of her hand.

'I do care for you,' said Mike. He raised his hand, pushing her fiery red hair aside. He looked deep into her eyes. He wanted to kiss her, but his heart was conflicted.

'You can't keep playing with my feelings,' said Elisha. She knew he was holding back. She also knew why! 'She would want you to move on. You deserve happiness,' she said. She knew of Jane; she knew why Mike was so hesitant.

'I…I know, I'm sorry,' said Mike. He pulled his hand away. Falling to silence, he twisted the wedding band on his finger.

'What's that?' said Elisha. She took hold of his hand. 'You're bleeding!' she said with worry.

'It's not my blood,' explained Mike.

'That's reassuring,' replied Elisha. She folded her arms as she stared right through him. 'Those support beams,' she said. She snapped her fingers.

'Right, I'll see to it immediately,' said Mike. He turned and hurried back along the passageway and out of the tomb entrance to give the instruction. He had utterly failed to take notice of Asher, who had somehow managed to squeeze past both him and Elisha unnoticed.

Making little sound, Asher slowly continued along the dusty corridor. He took hold of one of the battery-powered lights along the way before clambering through one partially blocked entrance. He entered a small room. Little did he know he was in the antechamber.

Gosh, it's beautiful. Goodness, there is so much!' Asher could clearly see that the antechamber was vast, with all sorts of wondrous treasures. He could see strange animals, magnificent statues, and gold, everywhere there was the glint of gold.

Enthralled, Asher continued past all the magnificent artefacts to enter an adjoining room, which was a little bigger than the antechamber. 'Look at that!' He had found himself before a grimy, dust-ridden sarcophagus. He had entered the main burial chamber.

'This is way too familiar!' He was further amazed to find that the burial chamber resembled the very one in his dream. 'It has to be a coincidence,' he mumbled, reassuring himself.

The sarcophagus itself resided directly in the centre of the square-shaped room. Countless decorative images and symbols rested upon the burial chamber walls, and Osiris, Nut, Ra, and many of the ancient Egyptian gods and goddesses were beautifully depicted.

At the front of the room, there was a stand, a block of stone, like that which the trinket, the bracelet of gold in his recurrent nightmare, had rested atop. Only upon this column of stone there was no sign of any bracelet-like object.

Asher placed the battery-powered light he held on the ground before carelessly leaping forward. Thud! Thud! Thud! His feet drummed off the dusty floor of the burial chamber. 'Golly, look at the…oh…oh…' Thumppp! He was too fast, too reckless. He lost his footing and took a tumble to the ground. His hands landed upon the dusty, dirt-ridden canvas, exactly a foot from the base of the plain stone column.

He looked up at a splendidly decorated gold and black statue, with the body of a man and the head of what appeared to be some sort of animal. 'Didn't see you there, Anubis.' He had stumbled over the statue. He immediately recognised the part-man, part jackal statue as being a representation of the Egyptian god, Anubis. He had read about it. The statue was commonly found in ancient Egypt. Even the tourist shop, located at the entrance gate to the Valley of the Kings, sold much smaller replicas.

'It can't be!' Asher's heart almost burst from his chest, for he locked eyes upon a golden bracelet. It lay on the canvas, upon the dusty floor of the burial chamber. He put his hand out, before recoiling in fear. 'I shouldn't!' He looked back toward the exit. He considered getting up and running as fast as his legs would take him. But he did not!

He was enchanted by the bracelet's magnificence. Soon his fast-beating heart began to slow. 'There's no way this is the same bracelet,' he said. He could not resist. He took it in his hands.

'Put it on!' a voice in his head tempted him.

'I…I shouldn't really.' He was drawn in like a moth to a flame; the golden trinket was very intriguing.

Momentarily, Asher thought about the old man, The Gatekeeper. Then, about the winged creature, Vixi. He thought about the place between worlds, The Portal Realm. He thought about The Horned God. 'Nonsense!' Then he conceived the only rational thought he could. That it was all the inner workings of his over-creative imagination. A dream and nothing more.

Arising to his feet, he astutely scanned the jewel. 'Wow!' he gasped. It felt so light.

'Put it on!' He heard a voice in his head say again. 'It's yours.'

Appearing open, Asher could not resist the temptation to place the golden bracelet upon his wrist. Clink! 'What's the worst that could happen?' he naively stated.

'Yes, yes, finally!' The voice in his head boomed as the trinket closed around his skin.

'What…what the hell,' panicked Asher. His eyes were ready to spring from their sockets. To his horror, something very dark swooped over him.

Whooshhh! Asher felt a strong, unnatural gust of wind breeze past him, through the burial chamber, through the antechamber, and down the tomb passageway. 'Holy smokes!' He was surprised, he pushed aside the black strands of his hair that covered his face. 'Ok, that was weird.'

Mike's brown hat was dislodged from his head. He stood at the front of the tomb entrance. 'Asher,' he softly called. He suddenly realised that his skinny, dark-haired, blue-eyed son was nowhere to be seen. He felt the hairs on the back of his neck stand on end.

He dropped the tatty cloth he had been wiping his bloodstained knuckles with into a tin bucket full of water. His concern grew with each unanswered call. 'Lad, where are you? This isn't funny.' He grew frantic.

'Hey, boss, the boys are ready with those support beams,' said Carl.

'Where's my boy, Carl, where is he?' asked Mike with alarm. He put his hands on the shoulders of the big man.

Carl replied dumbfounded as he rubbed the back of his bald head. 'I haven't seen him, boss.' He shrugged his bulky shoulders. He was tired. He had just spent the morning inside the tomb, doing the heavy lifting. Of course, he had ten hired hands to help.

'Elisha, have you seen him?' asked Mike. He spotted the fiery, red-headed Elisha. She made her exit from the tomb entrance.

'Who?' she said.

'Asher,' stated Mike.

'No, sorry,' replied Elisha. She had not seen Asher.

Mike feared the worst as he gazed into the tomb passageway. 'Maybe, maybe he followed me inside.'

'As I said, I didn't see him pass me,' explained Elisha. She began to rub her hands anxiously, sensing that something was wrong.

'Yes, but it's easy to miss him, he's just a boy,' enlightened Mike. He hastened forward and inside the tomb entrance. 'Asher, are you in here?' he loudly yelled.

'Dad!' Asher mumbled. Already in a state of panic, he tried desperately to remove the golden bracelet from his wrist. But it would not budge. 'Darn it.' He quickly covered the jewel, not wanting to be caught. His shirt sleeve provided the perfect camouflage. He hid the bracelet just in time.

'What the hell are you playing at? I thought something had happened to you,' roared Mike. He sweated profusely as he clambered in through the partially blocked, stone-framed doorway. He found himself in the centre of the antechamber. He quickly spotted Asher. 'You are in big trouble,' he said.

'Sorry Dad,' replied Asher. His head hung low, he waited to be ferociously scolded for his actions. He sank his teeth into his bottom lip, gently caressing the pinkish flesh.

'God damn!' gasped Mike in sheer disbelief. He took a good look around the antechamber. 'I mean this place, well, it's extraordinary, wait till Elisha and the boys see this.' His eyes glistened, and his mouth was agape. His chest jumped up and down like an accordion put to work by the hands of its master. He was overcome with the greatness of the find. 'This is amazing. There hasn't been a find like this since good old Howard Carter uncovered the tomb of Tutankhamun. We'll go down in the history books.'

'It's amazing for sure,' agreed Asher. Uneasy, he was worried about what his dad would think if he found out about what he was concealing.

More than that Asher thought back on his dreams. He thought of The Gatekeeper and Vixi, and what they had told and had shown him. Said dreams were beginning to bleed out into reality.

'Well, at least the grave robbers never found their way in here,' said Mike. He could not believe his luck.

'That's not quite true,' said Asher. He pointed to a decomposed body. It was profoundly disturbing. He screwed up his nose in disgust.

'Well, I never,' said Mike. He took a good look at the skeleton. 'Poor bugger's probably been dead centuries. We should go before we end up like him.' He quickly realised the dangers the tomb posed. 'We must go, lad, it's very dangerous in here.'

'Like right now?' asked Asher.

'Yes,' said Mike. He was firm. He took Asher by the arm. He left the battery-powered light in the burial chamber, the very one Asher had taken from along the tomb passageway. He headed back toward the tomb corridor. Then he heard it. Banggg! He heard what sounded like a gunshot. 'What the bloody hell is Carl up to?'

'Do you see Dad, do you?' said Asher in haste, skinny arms flopping up and down, he was frantic. He peered in through the partially blocked entrance, across the antechamber to the adjoining burial chamber.

'Quiet for a sec,' hushed Mike. He listened carefully to the noise emanating from beyond the entrance of the tomb.

'You…you it can't be!' Fear-stricken, Asher was overcome. He set his sights on a haunting figure, the very one from his dreams. The mysterious character stood in front of the sarcophagus. The figure stood a little over thirty feet away.

'Asim,' said Asher. He whispered the name. He recognised the high priest. He first heard the name from Geatiric, The Gatekeeper. He had been shown images of how Asim had met his end.

Asim's upper body was exposed; he was bald and without facial hair. He looked just as before, just as in Asher's dreams.

He wore leopard skins over white linen, and upon his feet he wore white papyrus sandals. He had returned from the afterlife. Or at least his soul had. Around his neck was an amulet in the shape of an eye. He pointed at Asher, booming loudly in a language unbeknownst, as if in a rage.

'Dad, do you see?' Asher repeated.

'No lad,' said Mike. Slowly, he edged along the corridor, toward the exit.

'But it's right there!'

'Never mind that, Asher, keep behind me,' said Mike.

'But look,' boomed Asher. He pointed wildly. 'Arghhh!' Greatly disturbed, he could not help but screech as peering red eyes raked into the boundary of his soul. Asim's face began to decay. The flesh peeled away like paint being stripped from a wall. The sight before Asher was utterly alarming.

Battery power lights blinking continuously, pieces of debris began to fall from overhead. The unstable corridor began to give way.

'Watch out, lad!' roared Mike. Thud! Thud! Thud! Quickly, he raced back toward Asher, only to throw his considerably larger body upon his small frame. 'Arghhh! God damn it,' he screeched. His right arm was hit by falling debris. He could not help but groan in pain.

Mike's face was red, saliva oozed from his mouth. He, with all his might, began to shift a hefty piece of rock. He just about managed to wriggle his arm loose. 'Arghhh, sweet lord…' He felt excruciating pain. 'Lad, we're leaving,' he groaned through gritted teeth. He slowly managed to get back to his feet. The danger of the unstable passageway remained, but all too apparent to him.

'Are you alright, Dad?' asked Asher with concern. He was wide-eyed and pale-faced. He picked up his dad's hat. It had tumbled from his head in all the commotion.

'Yes, lad, now follow me and for god's sake don't dawdle,' instructed Mike. He placed his hat back atop his head.

This time Asher heeded his dad's words. He quickly followed him along the long corridor of the tomb.

Bursting into the open, Mike finally locked sights upon the cause of the wild commotion. 'You lot, I should've known,' he snapped. He was dismayed. Surprise ran across his face upon seeing Bronislav's thugs armed and dangerous.

Stopping but mere inches from the tomb exit, Asher himself had managed to hold back, just out of sight. With stealth, he steered his gaze toward the upheaval. He could see the cunning looking Russian, Bronislav Valadvic, with the scar below his right eye, pointing a pistol at Carl Jackson who stood firm holding his rifle.

Standing by Carl's side was Tony Richardson, rusty spade in hand. However, the hired help, ten uneasy Egyptian workers, had backed off. The big brute Igor and a band of unfriendly-looking men held them at gunpoint.

'So, what's going on here?' inquired Mike. He held his bleeding arm.

'They came from nowhere, boss,' answered Carl. Nervously, he peered at one Russian, then another.

Caught unprepared, Mike had failed to grab the shotgun, which resided back in the tomb. It was too late! There was nowhere for him to go, there was truly little that he could now do.

'I hear there is treasure in this one, oh, and a bracelet of power, I do hope it's gold, it should fetch a pretty penny,' said Bronislav, revealing his motivations. He was of the impression that he could make quick money.

The mysterious character, the man in black, the very individual who had been following both Asher and Mike from back at Murphy's Inn, suddenly appeared. His clothes were drenched, his skin soaked to the bone. He had a bloodied nose to boot for his troubles.

'I take it, your weasel filled you in,' barked Mike.

'Ahtoh does as he's told,' said Bronislav.

'You almost killed me on that ferry,' bellowed Ahtoh. He seemed dismayed by his ordeal. He looked like a rat that had just crawled from its cesspit.

Angry, Mike could not constrain his reactions. 'I should have finished the job, pulling a gun on me in front of my lad,' he spoke aloud.

'You'll die soon enough.' Ahtoh furiously threatened.

'That's for me to decide, Ahtoh,' growled Bronislav. He smacked the man in the teeth. 'You've forced my hand, I told you just to watch, nothing else. Besides, it depends on whether the American comes quietly or not.'

'Go to hell,' scorned Mike, his fury getting the better of him.

Clinkkk! 'Don't try my patience,' said Bronislav. His warning was all too chilling. He shifted his revolver in Mike's direction.

Asher was completely fearful for his dad's safety. 'I can't just do nothing,' he muttered. He spotted the loaded shotgun resting against the wall, within the tomb passageway. He acted impulsively, taking hold of the weapon. He slowly progressed from the tomb entrance. He was foolish for thinking he could make a difference. There were twenty-plus men before him, too many considering that there were only two shells in the gun he held, one bullet in each chamber.

Another dire fact was that he also had absolutely no knowledge of how to use the weapon his shaky fingers were now latched around.

'Boy!' roared Bronislav. Immediately, he caught sight of Asher, with his sharp, hate-filled eagle eyes. Without hesitation, he aimed his revolver at Asher. 'Stop, foolish boy,' he said.

'Nooo!' cried Mike. He rushed forward in a burst of energy. He acted purely on instinct.

A bright flash erupted from the barrel of Bronislav's gun! 'Very unwise,' he said. He was ruthless. He had fired his weapon without thinking twice.

Mike's body crashed to the ground in a heap. His ribs took the impact. The bullet had penetrated his broad, hairy chest. Blood spilled forth from his lips.

'You left me with no choice,' said Bronislav, justifying his actions. He moved forward. He looked down upon Mike before shaking his head. 'Look at this mess.' He gritted his teeth. Things were not quite going to plan. Not at all.

'Dad!' howled Asher. Face filled with desperation, he dropped the shotgun. He sprang to Mike's side. 'I'm sorry, Dad,' he cried. He had no time to think about his foolish actions.

At first, Mike was non-responsive. His eyes darted to and fro as life slipped away from him.

'Dad!' Asher shouted. Tears blinding him, he was utterly distraught. 'Here, Dad, get up and put your hat on.' He lifted his dad's brown hat off the sandy canvas. His distraught mind could not register the reality of what was happening.

'Easy Asher,' sobbed Elisha. She put her arms around him. Tears filled her eyes, too. She had grown close to Mike over the years. Dealing with her own emotions, she did her best to comfort Asher in the moment.

Mike was fading, the life draining from his body. He did not have long to live. He was dying! 'Listen, boy, it's not your fault, you know I love you with all my heart,' he mumbled softly. 'Elisha,' he called out.

'Yes, Mike,' she said. She took hold of his hand.

'Ensure my boy is ok.' Mike's only wish was that Asher would not be harmed in any way.

'I will,' replied Elisha. She leaned in and whispered in Mike's ear. 'I love you!' She had revealed her true feelings. She knew that these were the very last moments that they had together.

'I know,' said Mike softly. He, too, had developed great affection for Elisha over the years. He had feelings for her that went beyond friendship. Though he could never let go of Jane Paterson. He still loved Jane with all his heart; the wedding band on his finger was a testament to that. Even after thirteen years, he still had not moved on.

Sobbing uncontrollably, Asher struggled to restrain his overwhelming emotions. 'I love you, Dad, don't go, please don't go,' he hopelessly begged.

'Stay…stay strong lad,' said Mike.

'Please, please, please don't go,' repeated Asher. He rocked back and forth, with Mike's head resting upon his lap.

Gasppp! The inevitable prevailed. Mike let out his final breath.

Asher's entire world had come crashing down before him. Eye's wide and body motionless, Mike's blood covered the beige sands of the Egyptian ground that he lay upon.

Outraged by the loss of their friend, Carl and Tony put up a desperate struggle, despite the gruesome odds, but they were no match for Bronislav's vicious mob. Carl was shot in the leg, before Tony was struck across the back of the head with the butt of Bronislav's revolver, after taking a daring charge at the maniac.

Unmoved by his brutish actions, Bronislav moved quickly to achieve his goal. 'Load up the loot and make sure they don't escape,' he ordered his men.

Utterly broken, Asher remained by Mike's side for what seemed, to him, like a lifetime. He could not believe it; the one person who meant so much to him was gone within the blink of an eye.

'Asher, come with me, he's gone,' said Elisha. She threw her arms around his lean shoulders. She tried to provide him with some comfort, but there was none to be had.

It took Bronislav and his horde of men several hours before they had finished, before they had taken a great deal of the precious items contained within the tomb.

There were two trucks full of all sorts of loot, including priceless stones, invaluable artefacts, and vast amounts of gold.

Having put up the most resistance, Carl was left bloodied and bruised. Igor and two other men of Russian accent had pounded on him, while the man in black, Ahtoh, stood observantly before them. They sought to punish him before leaving.

A devilish grin rested upon Ahtoh's disturbingly entranced face. 'Slow down, Igor,' he said, before chuckling in delight.

'Move out, we must go,' ordered Bronislav. 'Damn would have liked more. But this will have to do. Company is on the way,' he revealed. He had received a call from his friends in high places.

His orders were well received. Soon, he and his horde of men were gone. They were gone before the police and the authorities showed up.

Shrewd, Bronislav left no form of transport. He even ordered one man to deflate the tyres of Mike's Land Rover.

'Easy now, easy, it's just a flesh wound,' said Elisha. She applied bandages around Carl's leg. Her cheeks were puffy and red, she was struggling to hold her own emotions together. But she had to. 'That should hold for now,' she said.

Having done all she could for Carl, she quickly moved to inspect Tony, who still lay unconscious. 'Blood!' she gasped. Surprised, she carefully placed her attention upon an open wound on the back of Tony's head. 'We need to get him to a doctor, you and you go get help, now,' she said.

She sent two Egyptian diggers who were a part of Mike's small team further down the valley in search of help. The very same that were initially held at gunpoint by Bronislav's men.

The two diggers sent for help returned, accompanied by the police and paramedics.

The paramedics were able to help Carl and Tony, who were taken to the Luxor International Hospital. Although there was nothing they could do for Mike, who had died some hours previously.

Concerned for his well-being, Elisha accompanied Asher as both went with the paramedics to the hospital. She insisted he be checked over.

It was soon after they arrived at Luxor International Hospital that the Luxor Police Department started taking statements.

Several days passed before Asher was able to make his return journey home. He was going back to Neptune City, New Jersey.

The fiery red-headed Elisha remained by his side right up until the point he went through airport security. Most puzzling was the fact that the metal detectors did not start wailing the moment he passed through. Not that Asher was in any state to notice, but there was something very mysterious about the bracelet around his wrist.

Boarding his flight home, he left Luxor broken and utterly disheartened. Awaiting his arrival at Newark Liberty International Airport was his grandmother, Nancy Branning. She had been informed about the gruesome events that had occurred in Egypt.

-Chapter 12-

Soulkeeper

Back on 6th Avenue, Neptune City, New Jersey, the atmosphere was incredibly sombre. Over one week forgone, twelve days exactly, since returning home to his grandmother's house, Asher, absolutely guilt ridden and taken with severe grief, had remained reluctant to leave the confines of his bedroom. It had become his prison of solitude.

His heart had been shattered, torn into hundreds of tiny pieces. The loss of his dad, Mike, in the most gruesome of circumstances, was simply more than he could endure.

It was not until Monday 4th of January, just two days before he would have to head out of state, just two days before he would have to make the undesirable journey to Boston for his dad's funeral proceedings, that he was eventually convinced to leave the isolation that he had rendered himself to.

'Please, Asher,' begged Nancy. More than once, her pleas had been ignored, but her persistence persevered. 'Asher, you must come down, you can't stay in your room forever,' she said. Observing his ongoing isolation, she had grown increasingly worried about his well-being. 'Asher…'

Considering recent events, her usual cold and hardened exterior had evaporated. Creakkk! Saggy, drained eyes fixed upon the twisting brass handle, she watched with silent unease as his bedroom door slowly opened. 'Asher,' she said. Her voice was soft.

Asher slowly emerged. He wiped his puffy red eyes with his green striped pyjama sleeve.

'Come on down, you can't hide away in that room forever, it's not healthy,' reaffirmed Nancy. She wiped the lenses off her glasses with a handkerchief.

Moving forward, Asher slowly descended the stairs. His hand slid along the wooden banister to the bottom. He then entered the living room.

'Your dinner is in the oven,' said Nancy. The sheer sight of his thin, pale, motionless face had caused her great concern. Not to mention that he had not been eating much ever since his return. 'Do you want me to heat it? It would only take me a few minutes,' she said. Waiting for an answer, her plump physique lingered in the frame of the kitchen doorway.

He refused to communicate. Swish! Swish! Swish! His feet brushed along the floor, and he slowly moved across the living room, past a pine table and a flowery, patterned chair, to rest his lifeless body upon the window ledge.

He sat with his face pressed up against a pane of bitterly cold glass. The unpleasantly cold sensation rapidly turned his right cheek glowing red. Outside, he watched the rain fall, it was a cold, drizzly day.

A gloomy sea of grey blanketed the city. The sight was dreary, utterly horrible. Across the street, Henry the postman was making his afternoon deliveries, though as Asher watched, he could not help but feel the ache in his heart grow, for he knew he would not be receiving any more postcards from foreign lands.

Ten, twenty, thirty, forty, fifty minutes quickly passed. Despite the growing numbness in his pole-shaped legs, he refused to move from the window ledge.

Bong! Bong! Bong! Mechanical parts springing to life, his gran's old grandfather clock, resting beyond the foot of the stairs, began to chime very loudly. The ear-pounding chimes signalling four o'clock reached the deepest, darkest corners of the old, woodworm-infested house before gradually evaporating to nothing.

Ratta tat tat! Ratta tat tat! Ratta tat tat! A sudden, but harsh and continuous knocking sound fell upon the front door.

Expressionless, Asher seemed far removed from the clutches of reality. He just did not care. It could have been the President, and he still would not have let his emotions escape. He had built a wall around his heart.

Slowly, Nancy hovered from the kitchen to answer. She placed one hand in her woolly cardigan, while with the other she turned the door handle.

'Hi Miss Branning,' said Ben. Drenched and cold, he emerged from the grasp of winter. His cheeks were rosy red.

Nancy was emotionally drained; she was too tired to correct Ben. She did not outline for the umpteenth time that she was, in fact, 'Mrs.' 'Come in, sonny,' she said. She was feeling quite sad; her poor posture and unhappy face said as much.

'Can I see him, Miss Branning?' asked Ben. He shook himself in an attempt to dislodge the droplets of rain on his clothing. He also wiped his feet on a doormat that read 'Welcome,' although he was unsure if he was indeed welcome.

'I don't think that's wise,' said Nancy. She did not need to explain to him the gruesome events of Egypt. 'As I told your mum last week, I don't think visitors at this particular time is a good idea, sonny,' she said.

Nancy had already acquired the telephone number of Ben's mother, Amanda Wilson. She had accepted Ben into her house on more than one occasion for a sleepover. Besides, she usually came across Amanda at the local bingo, but given the current circumstances, she had not left the house all that much in the last week or so.

Amanda was a tall, brown-haired woman. Nancy had called to inform her a week before the new school term was to start so that Ben himself would be aware.

'Please, I haven't seen him since he left for…' Ben paused in thoughtful consideration, before blurting out the truth. 'Well, since he left for Luxor,' he said.

'Well…I don't know…' she said, hesitating. She shook her head. The untidy strands of grey hair danced upon her wrinkled forehead.

'Please,' he begged, adding considerable pressure to her already unclear mind.

'Five minutes then,' she said. She held out all five wrinkled fingers of her right hand to cement her position. She could not bring herself to refuse.

'Thank you,' said Ben.

Clank! Clink! Clunk! Nancy slowly shuffled across the hall, her pink slippers pounding against the wooden floor as she moved. Her plump body jangled side to side.

'Oh…oh…oh…' Ben's facial muscles distorted, quite unnaturally. He could not contain himself as he followed behind Nancy. 'Achooo!' He sneezed after sniffing a strong whiff of floor polish.

'You have company, Asher,' said Nancy.

Submerged in a pool of deep depression, Asher continued to ignore his grandmother.

'Asher,' called out Nancy again. She made yet another futile attempt to gain his attention. He did not even turn his head to look at her. Knock! Knock! Knock! She tapped on the open door leading to the living room. Again, she was ignored.

'Asher, Ben is here to see you, isn't that nice?' she queried. Still, he would not budge.

Unenthused, his quietness persisted. He was doing his best to shut the entire world out.

'Come now,' said Nancy. She moved forward and placed her hand upon Asher's shoulder, only for him to shrug it off. 'I tried, sonny,' she sighed, looking back toward Ben. She looked physically defeated. She was drained and devoid of any sort of joy.

'That's alright, Miss Branning,' said Ben. Wheezy he retrieved his inhaler from his pocket. He took a puff, inhaling strongly, then exhaling through his nose.

'Hopefully he'll speak to you,' said Nancy sorrowfully. 'He hasn't spoken to me in days,' she sobbed. She threw her creased hands over her timeworn face in despair. 'Really, sonny, I just don't know what else to do.' She left the demoralising silence of the living room. She went to the foot of the stairs where she sat her tired, aged body down. She listened intently with concern.

'Alright, Ash, you've been missed, how are you holding out?' asked Ben, feeling awkward. His words fell on deaf ears. 'Was at the game,' he continued. He spurted out words, anything to cut through the silence. 'The New Jersey Eagles won, Hanson slid in before time to smash the puck in the back of the net, to um, well…'

Falling silent, Ben, too, was deeply disturbed by Asher's unresponsive, gloom-ridden exterior. 'Buddy, you just can't do this to yourself,' he said. He had quickly realised that Nancy was right, his sombre friend was indeed just not ready to see him.

Hand sliding along the wooden surface, his fingers loosened their grip. He placed a signed ice hockey card on the pine table.

An ice hockey card signed by the New Jersey Eagle's star player, Joseph Hanson himself. It was a considerate gift.

'I'm glad to finally see you,' said Ben sincerely. 'But I know that you don't want to speak to me just now, so I'll come back tomorrow after school.' He placed the hood of his maroon coat over his head. He made ready to leave. 'I am sorry about your dad,' he said. His head dangled low with awkwardness.

Breaking his silence, Asher was finally moved by his friend's heartfelt words. He finally dropped his gaze from the rectangular pane of glass. 'I…I know you care,' he said. The sorrow in Ben's voice had, at last, struck a chord.

'I mean that, buddy,' said Ben. Welling up, he trudged forward before wrapping his arms around Asher. 'I'm here for you.' Clink! Clank! Clunk! He then wiped his eyes before turning and making his way from the living room, back into the hall.

'Ben,' Asher whimpered. 'I appreciate you stopping by,' his voice cracked.

A soft smile leapt to Ben's face. Creakkk! Hinges screeching, he gently pulled the old oak door open. 'Goodbye,' he said. Banggg! As quickly as he had arrived, Ben was gone. He slipped back outside into winter's cold grasp. Back into the horrible wet weather that persisted outside.

Feet unenergetically shuffling side to side, Asher began to slowly move across the room into the hall. He edged past the old grandfather clock leading to the stairs when he was confronted by his grandmother, Nancy. There she sat at the foot of the stairs. She could not help but try to reach him once more.

'You're not alone,' said Nancy. She gently took his left hand.

'I am,' sobbed Asher. He began to well up. He had never felt more alone.

'I used to tell your mother, god rest her soul, what she meant to me, it's the same thing I'm going to tell you now,' spoke Nancy. She put her arms around him. Her fluffy cardigan smothered him. 'You're my sun, moon, and stars,' she gently whispered in his ear. She displayed a love for him that she had never shown before.

'I am?' uttered Asher, caught off guard. He looked at his grandmother as if seeing her for the first time. He always saw her as a cold, callous old woman. Now, he was unsure. 'But, but…'

'I know, I've been hard, unbearable to live with,' admitted Nancy. Her eyelids squeezed shut as she shook her head of silver hair. 'I…I…I just missed Jane so much, and I took it out on you,' she said.

'But why?' asked Asher. He did not understand. He could not, because he did not know the truth! The truth about his mother's passing.

'Because I'm an old fool,' answered Nancy, feeling guilty. 'It was never your fault,' she said. She placed a hand on his cheek. 'I'm going to be the grandmother you need, now more than ever.'

'I just need some time, Gran,' said Asher. His mind was in a hundred different places.

Ratta tat tat! Ratta tat tat! Ratta tat tat! It was the front door once again. This time it was a soft, gentle knock.

'I'll…I'll get it, Gran,' mumbled Asher. He moved to answer the door. Creakkk! He was shocked upon seeing a familiar face. 'You!' he gasped.

'Hello, Mr Paterson!' It was Principal Smith, who was smartly dressed, wearing a blue suit and tie. He held some flowers in his hand. In his other hand, he held an umbrella to shield himself from the ensuing downpour.

'What…what are you doing here?' asked Asher. He was not expecting the arbiter of rules and order at Neptunica Middle School to show up at his house.

'I've come to see how you're doing,' said Principal Smith. He was greatly concerned about Asher. Like Ben, he knew exactly what had happened down in Egypt. 'I'm so sorry,' he expressed sympathetically.

'I…I…' Asher did not know quite how to respond. He just felt like breaking apart.

'Oh, thank you, Emmanuel,' said Nancy. She shuffled forward to the door.

'These are for you,' said Principal Smith. He handed the old woman the flowers. 'I was so saddened when you called me.' He had been informed as to why Asher had not been to school.

'I…I'll be right back,' said Nancy. She shuffled into the kitchen to put the flowers in a vase. She filled the vase with water.

'I told you that unstoppable events would come to pass!' said Principal Smith. 'Do you remember our little conversation before you left for Egypt?' He took off his spectacles and wiped the lenses.

'I…I recall,' replied Asher. His face ignited with surprise and confusion. 'Unstoppable events,' he muttered. There was no way he thought Principal Smith could have known what was going to happen in Egypt. He was not God!

'Exactly so. Things are now in motion that can't be undone.'
Principal Smith spoke cryptically. 'Have no fear. Time changes
everything, in time things can be changed,' he whispered. He
knelt, he wrapped his arms around Asher, giving him a hug.
'Trust me, you'll be fine, I believe in you. You're special!'

'I…I just need some time,' sobbed Asher.

'Time is exactly what you need,' smiled Principal Smith.

'I can't thank you enough for stopping by,' said Nancy. She
emerged from the kitchen.

'Goodbye, Mr Paterson.' Turning to leave, Principal Smith
winked his eye at Asher. 'That's a splendid ash tree.' He took
note of the ash tree on the front lawn; he had a love for
creation, for nature. 'Well, goodbye then.' He took a deep
breath, then he was off.

'Yes, goodbye, sir,' said Asher sombrely. He slowly moved
across the hall and up the stairs. He disappeared back into the
seclusion of his rectangular-shaped bedroom.

'You promised me we'd see Rome together.' He ground his
teeth, his sorrow turning to anger. He began skimming over
the vivid collection of picture postcards resting upon his
bedroom wall, each one showing his dad's great adventures.

He was annoyed by the very sight of the postcards. He
glanced at a postcard of Rome in Italy, then at another
showing the wildness that was Africa. He was reminded that
each postcard was a small glimpse into the life his dad had
lived. He was starkly reminded that he had been but an
exceedingly small part of that life.

He swiped his right hand across his bedroom wall, then his
left. He tore at the picture postcards, ripping the images from
their adhesive fixture. 'You promised,' he angrily repeated.

Sobbing, he fell back upon his soft bed. He put his hands over his face, when suddenly a glint of gold caught his attention! He rolled up his stripy green pyjama sleeve. He was taken with the solid gold bracelet still attached to his scrawny wrist, upon his right arm. He had found the bracelet resting within the old tomb back in Egypt.

It was one of the few things that Bronislav Valadvic had not managed to get his thieving, murderous hands on. Although he did not take everything, as Ahtoh's actions had forced his hand, he still took a great deal contained within the old tomb. In addition to a few statues and artefacts, left behind was a sarcophagus and the mummy resting within. Perhaps not even worth the effort, considering the vast array of precious objects and gold that had been unlawfully stolen.

Asher's memories of Egypt came flooding back. He remembered the haunting moment back in the old tomb, when he believed he had seen the long-dead, high priest, Asim. He then remembered the events that followed, he recollected the gut-wrenching moment his dad was killed.

He could not shake off the guilt and grief eating away at him, deep within the pit of his stomach. Somehow, he still felt responsible. He could not help but blame himself for lifting the shotgun and for proceeding out of the tomb entrance as he had so foolishly done.

He could not help but cling to the view that if he had not acted so rashly, so stupidly, his dad, Mike, would not have been shot by the well-aimed bullet that had been fired from Bronislav's revolver. Thus, he would still be alive.

The golden jewel latched around his wrist was an unbearably disturbing reminder of events he would rather forget. A stone, a beautiful, bedazzling blue stone, the centrepiece of the stunning golden bracelet, caught his notice. Not only that, though made of pure gold, the priceless jewel strangely felt as light as a feather.

He began rubbing the dirt and grime from the bracelet's golden surface. Inscriptions, mysterious markings, started to become ever clearer. 'What do they mean?' he whispered. Dirt and grime fully removed; he still could not decipher the strange markings. They were beyond his comprehension. 'I've never seen anything quite like this,' he uttered.

To his eyes and knowledge, the markings did not even seem to be of an ancient Egyptian origin! He had read enough to know the difference. The book entitled 'Valley of the Kings, The Archaeologist's Guide' was highly informative.

More precarious was the fact that he still did not know how to remove the priceless artefact from his wrist. He could find no latch. 'Oh, forget it!' His attempt to remove the bracelet was useless. Giving up, he placed his head back upon his pillow.

'I miss you, Dad,' he said. He closed his eyes, picturing Mike in his head. He pictured his dad's silly brown hat, his smile, and recalled his all-knowing nature.

'Yes, think about what you desire most!'

'Who…' Asher slammed his palm against his temple. A voice inside his head rang out, just as before. He had heard a voice inside the tomb of Asim, though he shook it off, believing it was his frightened mind playing tricks.

'Do you wish to see him again?' The voice spoke once more.

'More than anything,' replied Asher. He thought only of his dad. He thought of the last moments he saw him in the old tomb back in Egypt.

'We shall have ourselves a little experiment, all that emotion is perfect fuel, the purest form of chaos!'

'I'm losing it,' said Asher. He shook himself.

'Let's go!' The voice would not stop. There was no off switch. 'Servo mius volantateium!' The voice recited three simple, but strange words before all sorts of chaos broke loose.

'Arghhh!' shrieked Asher. He slung his body forward as he sat upright in his bed. His eyes looked like they were about to pop out of his head. He was overcome with great alarm. 'What the hell…'

He watched as a blinding blue light surged forth from the golden bracelet upon his wrist, to create a dazzling spectacle. A portal of sorts opened right in his box-shaped room. 'Help! Help!' He called desperately for someone to help him. His pale, perplexed, diamond-shaped face expressed his utter terror.

He was ripped from his bed, and the sheets he so desperately tried to cling to came with him. He was losing all control. 'Please help!' He wrapped his fingers around wood. He held onto the bottom of his bed.

His legs soared mid-air. He was fully expecting his grandmother's plump stature to burst through the door. He was expecting her to rush into his room and rescue him. Unfortunately, she did not. No one was going to save him!

He felt the pull from the portal grow, getting stronger and stronger. Despite his determined resistance, he was slowly losing his hold. One by one, his aching fingers were plucked from their hold upon the wooden bedpost.

'Don't resist.' A voice whispered again. 'Let Soulkeeper take you to the past.'

'Nooo!' he helplessly screeched. Feet first he soared into the blue portal. He could do nothing as the portal retracted. He watched as the image of his room began to fade. He was taken without choice by the mysterious force!

-Chapter 13-

Time Portal

A blue force swamped all around Asher. His skin tingled with utterly surreal feelings. It was as if he were in the deepest, darkest depths of the Pacific Ocean, but miraculously, somehow, he could still breathe.

'This is all too familiar,' said Asher. It was not the first time he had found himself in an ocean of blue! He had encountered the same situation before. He thought of The Portal Realm, the place between worlds. He thought back to the place he had dreamt about, his second night in the Valley of the Kings. 'Wake up! Wake up! Wake up!' he kept repeating with urgency and pace.

His first thought was that he was dreaming. He desperately tried to awaken. He wriggled like a worm, but to no avail. Then he heard someone speak again!

'This is no dream!' A voice called out once more.

'Who is that?' asked Asher in panic. The voice he had been hearing was not going away. The pitch and tone were masculine. 'Show yourself,' he said.

'If only I could!' The yet-to-be-identified individual laughed quite menacingly.

Asher's eyes began to hurt as the energy, the light all about him, grew unbearably bright. He quickly closed them. 'Arghhh!' Despite doing so, he still felt a punishing irritation.

Thump! Suddenly, and without warning, instead of being pulled in, he was forcefully pushed from the portal. 'Ouch!' His hands caressed the dirt of the canvas he had fallen upon. He looked up and caught sight of a pair of scrawny legs as they raced past.

Slowly, he rose to his feet. It took a few seconds for his strained eyes to regain complete focus. 'I've seen this before.' He was puzzled as his gaze fell upon colourful, one-eyed wall paintings, distinctive symbols, and ancient inscriptions. 'It's impossible!'

'Impossible, I thought so too mortal!' The voice that he had been hearing spoke again.

'Who are you?' queried Asher. His body twisted and turned in every direction. He could see no one else, except for a boy. 'Hey, you.' Hastening forward, he called out to the boy standing before the stone-framed entrance. 'Hello.' He was ignored again. 'I'm talking to you…'

Asher was taken aback with shock and awe as a pair of dazzling blue eyes met his own. 'But this can't be real,' he gasped. He gawked at a boy with blue eyes, black hair, a diamond-shaped face, and a lightly built physique. 'Hey, that's my shirt!' He noticed that the boy wore a blue chequered shirt, and not just any blue chequered shirt, it was a shirt identical to his own. He also recognised the boy's tan shorts and leather sandals. He felt strange, as if he were looking in the mirror.

'I'm back,' said Asher disbelievingly. He realised that somehow, he was back in Egypt. He realised that he was back within the tomb in which he had first found the bracelet of gold. 'No, no, you can't!' He was stricken with utter horror as he realised what had happened or, more to the point, what was about to happen all over again.

'It's a true curse. We can see it, but not change it. Only the power of our cruel creator can.' The voice he had been hearing spoke once more.

Asher reached out and gripped his past presence by the collarbone, he was suddenly engulfed by a mysterious force. 'Whoa!' He felt an unnatural essence ripple through his entire body. Instantaneously, he had merged with his past self to become but one single entity.

'Now this is different!' The voice he had been hearing continued. The pitch was high and full of shock.

'Arghhh!' Thump! Losing his footing, Asher fell back upon his buttocks. Slowly, he crawled forward, peering outside the tomb entrance, he saw what he desired most. 'Dad!' He rubbed his eyelids disbelievingly.

He saw Mike, his arm was bloodied. He stood firm against a horde of menacing-looking men. Men who wielded weapons!

He also spotted Elisha Thompson, the bald Carl Jackson, and the tall, thin Tony Richardson. He could see the fear on each of their faces.

Then Asher saw someone he disliked entirely. 'Bronislav!' he spoke through gritted teeth. Every muscle in his face tightened in hatred. He watched as the crafty individual limped forward to confront his dad, Mike. 'I have to help,' he said. He looked to his left, up against the wall of the tomb corridor, rested a deadly shotgun.

'I suspect dashing forth into the unravelling chaos is unwise. Unless that is, you seek to bring about dear old dad's demise.' The voice spoke again.

'Right, right, I won't make the same mistake twice,' agreed Asher. His hands were shaking. 'Great, I'm talking to myself.' Inside his heart was beating fast. Lub-dub! Lub-dub! Lub-dub!

Lips cracking open, the crafty Russian, Bronislav Valadvic, proceeded just as he had done in time past. It was like déjà vu all over again.

'I hear there is treasure in this one, oh, and a bracelet of power, I do hope it's gold, it should fetch a pretty penny,' he said. He was quite arrogant.

Then, just as before, the man named Ahtoh appeared. He was the man who had attacked Mike aboard the ferry on his return from meeting Professor Ballard Schneider.

The man Ahtoh had a bloodied nose. He was soaked to the core. His clothes were ruined. Anger filled his two bulging eyes.

'I take it, your weasel filled you in,' snapped Mike.

'Ahtoh does as he's told,' replied Bronislav.

'You almost killed me on that ferry,' bellowed Ahtoh.

Bewildered, Asher could not help but mutter the next set of words to follow, as his dad thundered forward. 'I should have finished the job, pulling a gun on me in front of my lad,' he whispered. He remembered the words exactly.

'You'll die soon enough!' threatened Ahtoh.

'That's for me to decide, Ahtoh,' barked Bronislav. He smacked Ahtoh in the teeth. 'You've forced my hand, I told you just to watch, nothing else. Besides, it depends if the American comes quietly or not,' he said.

'Go to hell,' scorned Mike.

Asher quickly receded. Barely, just barely, did he escape his dad's line of vision. 'I…I…I've gone back in time! This has all happened before,' he said, reminiscently.

Once more, he hid within the corridor of the tomb, out of sight and earshot. 'A bracelet of power, that's it, it has to be, Elisha, the old man Ballard, even that conniving, dirty, no-good Russian, they're all right,' he whispered. He was momentarily entranced.

'Soulkeeper is its title!'

'Is that you, Gatekeeper?' asked Asher. Again, he heard a voice. He was picking his brains, for it did not sound like the individual that he had met in his dreams. There was a lack of rhyming in the voice's linguistic expression of words. He further recollected upon his dreams of the past. He recalled the name of The Gatekeeper's domain. 'The Portal Realm,' he whispered.

'The Gatekeeper, I'm most certainly not. On the contrary, I'm something much more prominent.' The voice seemed a little agitated. 'I shall be paying my regards to that silly fool soon and his little fur ball!' Resentment was detectable.

'Who are you then?'' asked Asher. The hairs on his arm stood on end. Unlike The Gatekeeper, whoever was speaking was well-spoken. They were clear, calm, and well-ordered in their communication. In addition, their tone was quite masculine.

'Does the name Aarus hold any meaning to you?'

'I've never heard of it,' said Asher. 'But where are you?' He looked around and saw no one.

'Splendid, then you shall refer to me as Aarus,' the voice said.

'My name is Ash…'

'I'm aware of your name, Asher,' alluded Aarus. 'Ash is better, though. I'm Soulkeeper, or should I say, Soulkeeper's a part of me. You know that little object situated upon your wrist,' he said.

What Asher was failing to grasp was that Aarus had been in his head ever since he had first found the bracelet named Soulkeeper. Ever since he had wandered into the burial chamber of the high priest named Asim. 'No way!' He looked at his wrist in bedazzlement. 'This thing talks! I'm losing my mind,' he said.

'The mortal mind can be fickle,' told Aarus. 'Though what you see and hear is reality, it's a...'

'Hold up a minute,' said Asher. He suddenly recollected what The Gatekeeper and indeed his little familiar, Vixi, had told him about a device named Soulkeeper. He had seen visions of a beast with horns using it to accumulate power throughout the universe. The Gatekeeper had shown him such visions. 'This belongs to a horned god!'

'Um...you're quite well informed, it would seem,' said Aarus. 'For being so small, you think too much.'

'I should not trust you,' said Asher uneasily. 'I...I...'

'Listen well, Ash, The Gatekeeper is a manipulator, he covets Soulkeeper's power for himself,' said Aarus. 'The silly fool showed you a place between worlds, did he not?'

'Yes,' answered Asher. 'But it was a dream.' His hands caressed his hair. He looked at his feet as concern swamped his body like a great river.

'No, no, not a dream,' continued Aarus. 'You were shown exactly what The Gatekeeper wanted you to see,' he said.

'I'm so confused,' said Asher. He held his head in his hands.

'Well, let me enlighten you, he consumes worlds to satisfy his thirst for power,' said Aarus. 'He weaves his twisted version of events to advance his agenda. He would have you do his bidding,' he said.

'I've seen a horned freak, I've seen what he's capable of,' spurted out Asher. 'He is a monster.' In said dream, The Gatekeeper had shown him a beast with golden horns and wings, a beast with golden fur and sharp teeth. He was shown a being without pity or remorse, a being that epitomised chaos.

'Freak, that's not polite, besides, he is not me,' grumbled Aarus. 'Moreover, The Gatekeeper merely presented to you only what he desired you to see; he's not to be trusted,' he said.

'I don't believe you,' said Asher shakily. Truthfully, he was having a tough time believing in anything at all.

'I can be your utmost friend, I'll prove it,' stated Aarus. 'Surprisingly, I did bring you here after all, time is a tricky business,' he said.

'How can you prove it?' asked Asher. 'You could be lying.' His gut instinct was to be wary.

'Because together we will save dear old dad,' revealed Aarus. It was clear he sought Asher's favour. For what purpose remained hidden. 'It's clear you're special!' He had just seen Asher merge with his past presence. 'I've never seen anyone interfere with time itself.'

'Dad!' gasped Asher. Fear filled his face. In a different timeline, he had seen Mike die in his arms. Now he realised he had a chance to correct that. 'So, will you help me?' Nothing else mattered more to him than his dad.

'Of course, I will,' replied Aarus. 'We're friends after all, aren't we?'

'Yes, yes, of course,' said Asher hastily.

'Then do as I say,' demanded Aarus. 'Take a look outside,' he said.

'I will,' replied Asher obediently. Once more, he began to slowly move forward. He peered outside. 'No!' Gasping with sheer disbelief, he watched helplessly as Bronislav's goons, with heavy hands, detained his frail dad.

Mike had given up; his situation was desperate. His hands were tied together by one of Bronislav's men. 'Arghhh!' He was in pain, his injured arm hurt a lot.

'Be careful,' warned Aarus. 'I'm somewhat limited in my influence,' he said.

'Limited, what do you mean?' replied Asher. He was unsure what Aarus exactly meant.

'Quite so, I've never been in this situation,' revealed Aarus. 'Not that you could fathom my position. I've always been in total control. Thus, you must allow me time to gather my thoughts,' he said.

Now, in the present moment, the only one who seemed in total control was the Russian, Bronislav. 'Take the rest,' he ordered a handful of his men.

Knowingly defeated, Carl threw down his rifle. Tony also released his hold on a part-rusted spade. The situation was utterly hopeless.

'The rest of you get the gear,' snapped Bronislav. His posse quickly dispersed.

'Seize the moment,' commanded Aarus. 'Be swift in your actions and move now,' he said.

'Where do I go?' asked Asher. He scanned the surrounding area.

'Over there, you'll find camouflage in those rocks,' said Aarus. 'But be quick about it,' he said.

Asher escaped into the open, a smokescreen of activity provided a temporary distraction. Swooshhh! His feet glided across the sandy surface like a ballet dancer in full motion. He moved quickly and quietly.

'You!' snapped Bronislav.

Heart jumping up into his throat, Asher immediately stopped dead in his tracks. Had he been caught? He surely thought the game was up.

'You have made a wise move, who knows maybe you could make it out of this one alive, if you play your cards right,' said Bronislav.

'You and your lot are nothing but scum,' said Mike scornfully. He spat. His sticky saliva splattered upon Bronislav's black, dusty boots.

'Don't cross me,' roared Bronislav. He squeezed upon Mike's wound; blood spurted forth.

'Arghhh, god damn it!' yelled Mike. He closed his round, green eyes as he clinched down hard upon his teeth. He was in total agony.

Asher was on the move once more, like a whippet avoiding capture; he quickly raced from the scene, undetected. Despite hearing his dad groan in pain, he could do nothing. If caught, he could neither help Mike nor his team.

'That's blasphemy,' growled Bronislav. He squeezed ever harder upon Mike's injured right arm. 'Bend or you'll break.' He was a narcissist by nature and felt the need to exert his control.

'I abhor subpar life forms that use sacrilegious language against me," said Aarus. 'However, the brute with a scar on his face is quite likeable.' He spat out his thoughts freely.

'Dad is in a lot of trouble,' said Asher in panic. 'That guy is the enemy.' He found Aarus's admiration questionable, to say the least.

'Then we shall thwart his efforts,' replied Aarus. 'Together we can attain greatness,' he said.

Bronislav was self-intoxicated by his merciless actions. He had a devious smile upon his shabby, scarred face. His delight was heightened by the increasing, intense pain that he caused his foe, Mike, to feel.

'Stop!' yelled Elisha. She was frantic. She found Bronislav to be a brute of a man.

'Shut it, woman…'

'Br…Bronislav…' stuttered Dr Pafford. His attempt to cut in was unwise. He looked very uneasy.

'I want you in that bloody tomb,' barked Bronislav. 'You've been well paid for your expertise, now start delivering.' He lit up a cigar. 'Well, get to it.' He was short on time.

'B…but…'

'Move your ass Doctor Pafford,' boomed Bronislav. He snapped his fingers to silence the professor. His dictatorial nature was shaped by his service in the military. While in the military, he had advanced to the rank of sergeant major. The army was most definitely not a democracy, especially the Russian military.

Scolded, Dr Bernard Pafford obeyed. Like a flogged animal, he veered across the sandy canvas and inside the tomb entrance to inspect what, or if, indeed, there were any valuable contents within.

Hiding out of sight, Asher remained concealed behind a mountain of rigid rocks. He carefully examined the unfolding situation before him with shrewd judgement. 'What can I do?' he softly said.

'Surely someone can help,' suggested Aarus. 'You're a bright niominium, or human, should I say. Think!'

Contemplating his limited options, like a bolt of lightning springing forth from the heavens, Asher had conjured up an idea! 'I'll call for help, that's it, that's what I'll do,' he said. He had formed a simple plan.

'Br…Bronislav.' After a few minutes, Dr Pafford returned.

'Tell me,' said Bronislav. He momentarily released his hellish gaze upon a worn-down, weakened Mike. 'Tell me Bernard, you son of a bitch!' He gripped the professor by the shoulders.

'I see wonderful things, ar…artefacts, statues, gold, l…lots…'

'Gold, that's good, Bernard,' interjected Bronislav. 'Do you hear that? Gold!' He mocked Mike without a slither of remorse. 'It appears Ahtoh was right in what he had heard,' he said.

'How much?' asked Bronislav. He began licking his dry lips.

'Well, a…'

'It belongs in a museum,' protested Mike. He still found the strength to resist.

'How much damn you?' asked Bronislav again. He was consumed with greed. His motivations were laid bare.

'A mo…monumental amount, more than any man could ever dream,' spoke Bernard at pace.

'You haven't long, Bernard, get a move on,' said Bronislav. He was thrilled. 'I want you lot to follow Dr Pafford, get in there now,' he ordered. A horde of men, a horde of lackeys, a horde of well-paid labourers, quickly moved to fulfil his command.

'You see my American friend, we may be the scum of the Earth, but we're going to be rich scum, you best believe there's a full house in there for the taking,' said Bronislav. 'The black market is always open for business.' He snapped his fingers together once more, he ordered one man to remove Mike from his sight.

'Chaos masks your activities," said Aarus. 'Those abhorrent filth are distracted,' he said.

'So, what do we do?' Asher shrugged his shoulders. He did not fully understand.

'Go, make haste,' said Aarus. 'Get help!' His voice was loud and demanding.

'Ok…ok,' replied Asher softly. He jumped over a pile of rocks before quickly moving across the sandy canvas once more. He had decided to put his simplistic plan into action.

He was quick and cunning. With haste, he steered his feet around his dad's Land Rover before entering one of the large triangular-shaped tents. 'There it is,' he said. He quickly found what he was looking for, a black cellular phone. The cellular phone was most likely the very same phone that Elisha Thompson had used to contact Mike aboard the ferry back on the River Nile.

Beep! Index finger striking nine, Asher then hit one before realising his idiotic blunder. 'Oh no! What's the number?' He neither knew the direct dial for the authorities situated in Luxor, nor any other contact that could help in dissolving the desperate situation he was now in. 'Who can help?' he further mumbled, pacing back and forth, from one side of the tent to the other.

'That's it!' Beep! Beep! Beep! Fingers slamming down upon buttons, he rummaged through the phone's contact list.

Suddenly, he came across a familiar name, B-Schneider. 'Yes, the old man from back at Murphy's Inn, he'll help,' he said.

'That's a fine contraption,' said Aarus. 'Nonetheless, I've seen similar, if not better, on other worlds.' Clearly, by his own words, he had travelled among the stars. 'Gadgets and gizmos have made mortals appear godly, but despite so, they still cannot hide their substandard nature.' He had a less than favourable perception of mortals, as he put it.

'Shush!' hushed Asher. His mind was set on the task of finding help. He needed to concentrate. Ringgg! Ringgg! Pushing the autodial button, he pressed the phone against his right ear. Sighing, his lungs emptied of all air. 'Pick up, please…'

'Someone approaches,' warned Aarus. 'Mask yourself from sight,' he said.

Thud! Thud! Thud! Asher was concerned by the sudden sound of footsteps. He instantly hung up. Hastily, he ran forward before dropping to the canvas. 'Ouch!' Skin tearing, small bits of stone drilled hard into his kneecaps. He struggled to remain quiet.

Swishhh! Tent fabric pushed aside, one large man entered.

Luckily, Asher was not heard. He had pounced under a table covered with a white tablecloth. He had avoided the intruder just in time. It was one of Bronislav's thugs, the large man, Igor.

Every part of the big man's anatomy was disproportionately huge. Neck, arms, torso, legs, every body part was hefty in size. He cut an intimidating figure indeed.

'Nothing but junk,' roared Igor. Banggg! Crashhh! Crackkk! He bashed, bumped, and knocked over stools, cases, and equipment as he hovered around the tent in search of precious valuables.

'Waste of time.' Whooshhh! He threw his hands across the wooden table, Asher was hiding under. He hurled a lofty pile of images to the ground beneath. The images depicted Mike's many travels across the globe.

Underneath, Asher was filled with fear. 'What if the big man found him?' he thought. He nibbled on his fingernails in angst.

Bang! Bang! Bang! Repeatedly, Igor threw his hefty hands down upon the unstable table. 'That no good, damn, damn all of it,' he snapped. He was furiously angry at finding absolutely nothing.

Losing his nerve, Asher was sweating. He bit his bottom lip. He was struggling to keep his composure. His arms and legs were shaking uncontrollably.

Bang! Igor threw his hands down upon the table once more.

'Oh!' Asher clasped his hands to his mouth; he almost alerted Igor to his presence. Terrified, he raised the white tablecloth ever so gently. He was ready to break cover.

'Come on, boys, gold of every sort, look, we're rich!'

Suddenly, a loud, crackling voice caught Igor's attention. 'Gold!' Thud! Thud! Thud! Distracted, he stormed from the tent to inspect the source of the commotion.

'Thank God,' said Asher. His relief was overwhelming.

'There's no need to express gratitude,' said Aarus.

'I'm not,' said Asher. 'Although you did help, that big brute would have torn me to threads, thanks for the heads up,' he said.

'I doubt it, Soulkeeper is protected by enchantments placed upon it by Trinity and The Horned Order,' informed Aarus. 'It would take greater power still to render that protection void,' he said.

'Horned Order,' said Asher. 'What are you rattling on about?' he asked.

'Yes, yes, I must be considerate, you do not come from Terra,' said Aarus. He was from a different place, a different planet. 'Fundamentally, little one, The Horned Order are potent individuals, they have embedded a powerful enchantment upon Soulkeeper,' he explained.

'Then why all this hiding?', asked Asher.

'Well, you can still be captured,' told Aarus. 'As I said, this entire horrendous situation is novel to me, I need time to figure things out, I never dreamed of a situation in which the will of a niominium and Soulkeeper are intertwined,' he said.

'Great, you do that,' replied Asher. He sprang to his feet before fleeing from the tent. He exited from the rear of the tent, where no one could see him.

He watched as Igor and a few of his comrades steered in the direction of the tomb, and he then moved quickly. He glided a little over ten feet before dropping to his knees yet again. He pressed his belly to the ground, he then began wriggling side to side, like a worm. He hid out of sight underneath his dad's Land Rover.

With Mike and his team in full view, he once again began to dial Professor Schneider's number. This time a man with a strong German accent and a firm voice answered.

'Hi, who's this?' It was Professor Ballard Schneider on the end of the line.

'Hi sir, it's Asher, I…'

'My class doesn't start for another hour or so,' said Ballard. He seemed confused. 'I'll speak to you then.' He believed Asher to be one of his students.

'No, it's Mike Paterson's son,' explained Asher.

'This isn't a good time. I'm doing some work here for your dad,' said Ballard. He was busy conducting research at Luxor University.

'That's what I'm calling you about,' said Asher frantically.

'But…'

'Listen!' spoke Asher firmly. He was losing his cool. 'Dad's been hurt bad, he's in a lot of trouble,' he said.

'What kind of trouble?' asked Ballard. His tone grew serious, quick.

'He's held up at the exploration site, a gang of men have taken control, and they have guns,' said Asher.

'Now, now, don't panic, I'll be there as soon as possib…'

Conversation cut short; Asher did not get the chance to reply. Unexpectedly, the phone went dead. The battery had completely depleted. Professor Ballard Schneider had become his only and last resort.

For the time being, he could do nothing but wait. Thirty minutes passed. Then an hour. Then an hour and thirty minutes. Then two hours. Still, there was no sign of help.

'Put them in the tomb and make sure they're well tied up!'

'What now?' whispered Asher.

Bursting forth from the tomb entrance, Bronislav was full of worry. 'Well, get a move on,' he roared. 'Minister Mahmoud has given us a tip off, company is coming,' he said.

'Let's go, up, up!'

Bronislav's command was promptly carried out. One man hauled Mike, weary and drained, to his feet.

'My boy.' His first concern was for Asher. His voice was waning. His eyes were heavy. Indeed, he could barely stand. 'For the love of God! What did you scum do with him?'

Neither Bronislav nor his mercenaries had any idea as to Asher's location. They could not care less either. They had bigger priorities to deal with.

'Easy, boss,' said Carl. He moved forward to Mike's aid, only to be heaved backward by two of Bronislav's lackeys. 'Let me help him,' he snapped.

'Help yourself and shut the hell up,' intervened Igor. He aggressively shook his fist at the big man, Carl.

'You're a no-good son of a bit…' Crackkk! Carl felt knuckles crash against his jaw before he could finish the sentence. Blood covered his pinkish lips. He staggered, but he remained firmly on his feet.

'Shut it now, you scum…'

Smackkk! Carl crashed his bald head against Igor's box-shaped nose, knocking him clean off his feet. He knocked Igor completely unconscious. He had harshly retaliated, but his bold actions did not go unpunished. Hands tied, he could not defend against two other men who instantly were upon him. He felt their severe wrath.

'No, stop!' Mike tried desperately to intervene. He struggled to stay upright.

Mercilessly, Ahtoh lodged a fist in Mike's gut before raising his hand again. 'We have some unfinished business,' he said.

'I can't look.' Sickened, Asher had to break his observation. He forced his eyelids shut.

'Continue observing, things are just getting interesting,' said Aarus. He seemed intoxicated with what was unfolding. Intoxicated by the chaos.

'Are you finding this amusing?' asked Asher. He grew agitated by the apparent glee in Aarus's tone.

'No, no, not at all, I'm looking for an angle, a way to help,' replied Aarus. 'Thus, I must observe,' he said.

'Please stop this madness,' begged Elisha. She grasped her fiery red hair in panic. She had no idea what to do.

'For pity's sake, he can hardly walk,' added Tony. He got a little too rowdy. He found himself knocked to the ground.

'Stop now,' ordered Bronislav. 'Get them into the tomb now,' he said. He was losing his patience. 'Idiots, they'll be dead soon enough anyhow!' His threat was all too real, for he meant to cover his tracks.

'Alright, alright, up you dog.' A man took hold of the beaten-down Carl Jackson. 'Give me a hand.' He needed help from another to move the big man.

Mike, along with the rest of his team, was forced into the tomb corridor.

'Time to go.' Bronislav, with his boot, nudged Igor. His lackey slowly regained consciousness. 'Get up,' he said. He then gave the order. 'Prepare the explosives!'

'But we've got what we came for, why not let them go?' a
hired hand questioned the actions of Bronislav. He thought his
methods were even too brutal for him.

Crackkk! Bronislav struck the defiant man, who was harshly
quietened. 'We didn't get enough! If you don't want to see the
inside of a jail cell, do as I say,' he said.

'Kill them!' murmured Asher. 'He wouldn't,' he said.
Suddenly, to his horror, his unbelieving eyes caught sight of a
black fuse. The fuse led to the inside of the tomb. Explosives
had been carefully placed in the tomb corridor. 'Where are
you?' He looked off into the distance, still there was no sign of
help. He could see no sign of Ballard or the authorities. He was
unsure if Ballard had believed him.

Ruthless, Bronislav had no intention of letting Mike and his
team live at all. 'Hurry up, damn it,' he snapped. He lit up
another cigar. He then looked at his watch.

'It's done,' replied one of his obedient men.

'How long?' he queried.

'Twenty minutes, boss,' said the compliant man.

'Ok, good work,' said Bronislav. He puffed on his cigar, and
smoke drifted upward into the atmosphere. He then took hold
of the highly flammable black fuse. He pressed his cigar to the
fuse, a bright orange spark came to life!

Ringgg! Ringgg!' Bronislav quickly answered his phone. It was
Minister Mahmoud once more. The call only lasted a few
seconds. 'Move out, we must go,' he said. Urgency hung in his
voice.

He crushed his cigar below his black, dusty boot. 'Damn, I
would've liked more, but this will do,' he said. He jumped into
the passenger seat of an awaiting vehicle. 'Pack up and follow

us.' He instructed a few of his men to follow him to the River Nile.

Five minutes, then ten passed, as time ticked by the black fuse slowly eroded. Inside the tomb, there were enough explosives to blow Fort Knox apart.

'Help, someone please help us!'

'Cut the fuse!'

Voices began echoing from within the tomb corridor, where the fuse led to, pleading for mercy. Unfortunately, the pleas of desperation fell on deaf ears.

Observant, Asher watched as the last of Bronislav's men made off down the valley before breaking cover. He hastened toward the tomb entrance.

'What do I do?' He was terrified and confused. He was also running out of time!

'The pale of water, take it,' said Aarus. 'From my familiarity, fire doesn't react particularly well to water,' he said.

'Sure thing,' answered Asher. His thin, set fingers took hold of a tin bucket; the water within was slightly discoloured red. 'I'm coming, hold on.' He sprinted forward, he eyed up the eroding fuse. 'I'll save you, Dad,' he shouted.

Thuddd! He clumsily tripped over his own feet, he crashed to the sandy canvas beneath. Splashhh! He spilled the water contained within the bucket that he held. He watched in utter horror as the water flowed forth in every direction.

'Phewww!' He sighed with relief. He raised his head of black hair to see that the fuse had luckily been put out. He then scrambled to his feet. 'The fuse is out,' he shouted.

'Then it is done,' alluded Aarus. 'Soulkeeper has fulfilled your will, you have saved dear old dad.' He simply stated the truth.

'Yes, it is done,' said Asher with joy. He smiled. He had done the unthinkable. He had changed the very course of time.

'You're pure of heart, young one,' said Aarus. He had learned a great deal, but there was still much more to learn. He had his own goals and motives to tend to. 'Servo mius volantateium.'

'We're in here, Asher, untie us!'

'Coming, I'm…' Asher failed to get the chance to respond, and an all too familiar burning sensation unexpectedly returned! His scrawny wrist tingled irritatingly. 'Arghhh! No, not again,' he said. He watched as a portal opened before his very eyes. 'Not yet, no, no…' Like before, he could not resist the mysterious, energetic force. 'Dad, Dad, where are you?' he screeched.

'Remember who aided you,' said Aarus. 'As friends, you owe me,' he said.

'Yes…yes, I won't forget,' replied Asher in haste. He owed his bizarre new friend a debt. He knew that without the help of Aarus, he might not have succeeded.

'Withered is my influence, I go for now,' said Aarus. His voice faded.

Asher was, again, forcefully taken. His essence split in two. He gawked at himself as the portal began to close. He was engulfed in a sea of bedazzling blue light once again. 'Arghhh!' His eyes hurt, just as before, as the increasing, intense blue light forced his eyelids shut.

He found himself waking up in a shabby tent, he immediately grew frantic. 'Dad!' he yelled. He quickly scrambled forth, exiting the tent. He was taken by utter shock. His dad stood but a mere few feet from him, bandaged up and giving orders. More importantly, he was alive!

'What is going on?' whispered Asher softly. He gazed blankly at a small piece of fabric entangled around his right wrist. He slowly removed the stretchy fabric to gaze at the golden bracelet. It was not big, nor bulky, it was slender. But it was noticeable. He was afraid someone would detect what he had found.

Confused, little did Asher know that past events, time in fact, had been altered. He had been returned to the exact point of time at which he had entered the portal. Only now did he find himself in a completely changed state of reality.

He was no longer in his bedroom, he was in Egypt. He was in the Valley of the Kings. It was Tuesday, the 5th of January. The time was 08.33 am. The time difference between Egypt and America, specifically New Jersey, meant he was sent to Egypt on Monday, the 4th of January, just after eleven in the evening. He had slept right through the night.

'Aarus, are you there?' He looked at his wrist. Aarus did not answer him. 'Great, I'm crazy.' He concealed the jewel upon his wrist once more. He then quickly moved to dress himself. He found a neat bundle of his clothes on the table. He put on a white long-sleeved shirt, brown shorts, and tan sandals. He then made his exit from the tent.

'Good to see you finally up and about, lad,' said Mike. He was very much alive and kicking. It was a miracle!

'Dad, you're not gone,' said Asher. He rushed forward, crashing into his dad, before throwing his arms around him. 'I love you, Dad.' He was overly emotional.

'What's all this for?' asked Mike. Surprised, he was taken aback. 'Must be the heat, lad, you've finally lost the plot,' he said.

'I haven't lost the plot,' replied Asher. A smile lined his face. 'I'm just glad you're still here, Dad,' he said. He wiped away his tears of joy.

'Well, I'm not going anywhere in a hurry,' said Mike. He was a little puzzled. He did not know what had prompted such a reaction from his son. 'I thought you had sprained your wrist.' He pointed to Asher's right arm.

'No, all good,' said Asher. He was so incredibly happy.

'Alright, boss, I'll take over things while you're gone,' interrupted Carl. 'Things are moving along smoothly,' he said.

'Great, Carl,' replied Mike. 'But don't overwork yourself,' he said.

'Where are we going, Dad?' asked Asher.

'Only to the airport lad, time to get you home, your new school term has begun already,' said Mike. 'Your gran is not pleased that you're missing the first week of your new school term, well, most of it,' he said.

'What day is it? Asher queried. He was completely mystified.

'Tuesday, of course,' chuckled Mike. 'Really, you must be losing your memory.' He took hold of Asher's fully packed luggage bag that rested by his feet. He hauled it into the back of the Land Rover. 'Elisha, are you ready?' he called out.

'Yes, Mike,' she answered. Her fiery red hair swayed to and fro, from shoulder to shoulder, as she hurried across the sandy canvas. She wore a white crop shirt tied at the midsection, jean shorts, and white sandals. 'I'm always ready,' she playfully said. Smiling, she pulled his brown hat down over his green eyes. She was being witty.

'Jump in, lad,' instructed Mike. He knocked on the hood of the vehicle. 'We're burning daylight,' he said.

'I don't want to go, Dad,' said Asher. He was reluctant to leave.

'You have to, lad, but don't worry, you'll be coming back again in the summer. I meant what I said when I told you we need to spend more time together,' reassured Mike.

'Do you promise?' asked Asher.

'Yes, now jump in,' said Mike.

Fastening her seatbelt, Elisha took to the driver's seat. 'Buckle up, boys,' she said.

'Sure thing, my lovely,' replied Mike. Injured, he took to the passenger seat next to her. There was a little chemistry in the air as his green eyes met Elisha's. Life-changing events had the strangest effects on people.

'You're not bad yourself,' said Elisha. She began to blush, as her cheeks went red.

'Seatbelt champ,' said Mike. He prompted Asher to fasten his seatbelt, as he sat dumbfounded in the back.

There were blank spaces in Asher's memory. Why, he thought, was his dad so happy? He had watched as Bronislav had made off with all that was great about his dad's most prized find. He had witnessed trucks flee with invaluable artefacts, priceless statues, and a vast amount of gold.

All the way to the airport in Luxor, Asher had tried to contemplate what had happened. He simply could not make any sense of the events that had transpired.

'We're almost there,' informed Elisha.

A little over an hour after leaving the exploration site, they had arrived at the airport. Congestion on the way had slowed them down a little.

'Quickly, lad, with me! Your flight will be leaving soon,' said Mike. He took hold of Asher's luggage.

'Goodbye hero!' said Elisha. She waved at Asher as he and Mike scuttled off.

'Hero!' Now Asher was truly bamboozled. What exactly had happened? The last thing he remembered was being sucked into a blue swirling portal.

Hastily, they scurried through the entrance of the airport before making for the check-in desk.

After the routine security checks, Asher was ready, he was heading home. Strangely, the metal detectors did not pick up the bracelet on his wrist! Stranger still was the fact that his dad had not noticed the jewel, no one had. It was as if the precious piece of metal did not want to be seen or found. Something else beyond comprehension was at work!

'Here, I thought you'd like these,' said Mike. He placed a great variety of superbly detailed images in Asher's palm. 'You can add them to your collection.'

'Thanks, Dad,' replied Asher.

'I'm glad you came to Egypt, lad, you saved all our necks back in that tomb,' said Mike, gratefully.

It was no use! Asher could not restrain himself any longer. 'But all the artefacts, the statues, the, well...'

'Safe thanks to you,' informed Mike. 'Most will be heading to the Cairo Museum for display, only fitting, I suppose,' he said.

'But Bronislav, I saw him get away,' said Asher, hastily.

'Professor Ballard Schneider turned up with the cavalry, only to catch Bronislav and his accomplices heading for the River

Nile,' said Mike. 'His friends in high places will scatter like roaches. Caught red handed the moron was,' he said.

'So that's what happened,' said Asher.

Have you hit your head or something? You rang him,' said Mike. Jokingly, he ruffled up Asher's black hair as he ran his fingers through it.

'No, just thinking,' said Asher. He was starting to make sense of everything. Now, it was all becoming much clearer. He now knew he had changed more than he had initially thought. His mind was at ease. 'I enjoyed spending Christmas with you, Dad,' he said.

'Yes, me too, lad, it was quite eventful,' said Mike. Getting quite emotional, his eyes began to get watery. 'Go on now, we'll see each other again soon enough.'

'I will miss you,' said Asher. He squeezed his dad tightly. He then headed toward the terminal. 'Hey, Dad, you were right after all.' He turned and smiled.

'Oh really! What about?' asked Mike.

'Guitarists do get all the cool chicks,' replied Asher. He smiled. 'Tell Elisha I said goodbye.' He had seen the eye contact and heard the comments in the Land Rover. He was not completely stupid. More to the point, he was happy for his dad.

'Oi, get you out of it,' said Mike. He shook his brown hat in Asher's direction. He went a little red in the face. Finally, though, he felt ready to take the next step. He was ready to explore his relationship with Elisha. The two had been toying with the notion for a long while.

With one final wave, Asher boarded the return flight back to
New Jersey. He was heading back to the good old United
States of America.

-Chapter 14-

Home Again

Thump! Thump! Thump! 'Asher, turn that off now, it's too early,' yelled Nancy Branning. She roared, her lungs emptying of air. She had grown utterly tired of the continuous loud noises echoing from her grandson's bedroom. 'It's only eight fifteen in the morning,' she boomed. Her voice crackled with strain.

Back home, on 6th Avenue, Neptune City, New Jersey, life was all too normal. Well, as normal as it was ever going to get for Asher. It was the first Thursday of the month, the 7th of January. He had missed school the day before recovering from jet lag, though in total, he had missed three days of the spring semester.

'Disregard her, Ash,' said Aarus. 'You're your own master,' he said quite rebelliously. He was no fan of rules.

'Ash! Sometimes Ben calls me that too,' said Asher. He did not mind the nickname one little bit. Twang! J-wrang! Twang! He continued practicing on his guitar despite his grandmother's objection. He had woken at seven thirty sharp to get an early start before school.

'Asher,' she roared again. Her face was beetroot red; she rested her hands upon her plump hips. 'That boy just doesn't listen,' she groaned.

'Oh alright,' yelled Asher. He just could not catch a break. He stopped playing his guitar.

'But alas,' said Aarus. 'Parents ruin everything.' Disdain simmered in his voice.

'They sure do,' answered Asher. 'My grandmother is no fun at all,' he complained. His problem with his grandmother was not so much that she was mean, which she certainly could be, it was because she emotionally distanced herself from him. Rarely did he hear a word of encouragement or support, which only made him resentful to a point.

He recalled how, before time had been altered, before he had changed his dad's fate, ho she had emotionally opened up to him. He remembered how she had called him her 'sun, moon, and stars.' If he meant that much to her, why was she always distant and sour, he thought? He just did not understand.

Unfortunately, Nancy would never recall the words she had spoken to him. The very same words she had time past, told her daughter, Jane Paterson.

'Asher,' screeched Nancy. 'Get your skinny behind down here now,' she demanded.

'I'll be right there,' howled Asher in response. Bumpety! Bumpety! Bump! He zoomed off down the stairs like a bolt of lightning, fast and full of energy. He smiled as he entered the kitchen. 'Yes, Grandma,' he said.

'Listen to me, when I say turn the music off, I mean it,' said Nancy. She was deeply annoyed. 'One more thing…' Ratta tat tat! Ratta tat tat! Ratta tat tat! She was interrupted by a loud and continuous knocking on the front door. She brushed past Asher to answer. Creakkk! 'Your friend is here,' she said. She had opened the front door to find Ben standing on the front porch.

'Hi, Miss Branning.' Ben held an orange yo-yo; he was busy practicing a few tricks.

'Mrs…it's Mrs,' she groaned. She trudged off in a mood.

'What are you here for?' said Asher. He rushed to the door.

'It's been weeks since you left for Egypt, I thought I'd get a better response,' replied Ben. Grinning profusely, his mood was playful. He placed his yo-yo in his back pocket.

'I mean it's still a bit early,' said Asher.

'Here, I wanted to give you a present,' said Ben. He placed his hand in his blue jean pocket and took out an ice hockey card.

'It's an ice hockey card,' said Asher. He had a case of *Déjà vu*.

'It's signed by…'

'By Joseph Hanson,' interjected Asher. The ice hockey card in Ben's hand looked familiar to him.

'Yes, he slid in before…'

'Before time to smash the puck in the back of the net,' said Asher. He knew the intricate details.

'But how do you know that?' asked Ben. He was puzzled.

'I watched a replay last night of the New Jersey Eagles' match,' said Asher. He was lying through his teeth, but he could not exactly tell Ben the truth. Ben would never believe him. He would never believe Asher's time-travelling undertakings. No one in their right mind would.

'Are you ready to go, buddy?' queried Ben. 'I don't want old grumpy to come down hard on us,' he said. He and Asher were already on Principal Smith's radar.

'Yes, two seconds,' answered Asher. He hurried into the kitchen, he then retrieved his navy woollen coat from the disorganised closet. Outside, winter's cold grasp had taken a firm hold. He also retrieved his school bag, as well as his guitar, needed for his after-school music class.

Asher had come to love his extracurricular music class with Mr Jerome McGrath. He was glad that Sarah Reid had forced him to sign up for the after-school class at the beginning of the year.

In his early forties, of slender build, with fuzzy brown hair and brown eyes, Mr McGrath's passion for music was immense. 'G, C, D, A, G, C, there you go, you're playing like a pro,' he said. Encouraging as always, he spent quite a lengthy period, thirty minutes to be exact, helping Asher to harness his musical skills.

'Haven't played in weeks,' noted Asher. He had spent the early part of the morning trying to catch up before his grandmother interrupted him.

'What a shame, you have talent,' complimented Mr McGrath. He stuck up his thumb to confirm his opinion.

Buzzz! Asher quickly put his guitar in his guitar bag as the school bell rang loudly.

'I'll see you tomorrow, Asher. Keep working on that new song,' said Mr McGrath. 'Be here tomorrow, everyone,' he said.

'Tomorrow! But tomorrow is Friday,' said Asher. There was no music session scheduled. Not according to his timetable.

'Well, with the Christmas break I've booked in a last-minute, extra session,' replied Mr McGrath. 'We'll need every second to prepare, big things are soon to be announced,' he said.

'Big things!' Asher had no idea as to what his fuzzy-headed schoolteacher was rambling on about.

'Yes, now keep practicing, practicing, practicing,' said Mr McGrath. The quirky music teacher snapped his fingers. 'That's how you get to Carnegie Hall,' he said.

'I will, sir,' replied Asher with a grin. He snapped his fingers right back.

After getting home, Asher did as he was asked. He spent the rest of the evening at home, practicing upon his plain, six-stringed instrument. He practiced a song that Mr McGrath had wanted him to learn, entitled 'Everything I ever wanted.' It was a classic indie song by the moderately successful band, The Blades.

'G, C, D, A, G…'

Time and again, he repeated each single guitar chord that he needed to study. He did so in exact song sequence.

'You're sublime,' complimented Aarus. 'However, a little rough around the edges,' he said.

'What would you know about music?' asked Asher. He looked at the bracelet upon his arm as he flapped his gums. He was curious.

'I ruffled a few leaves with many a wood nymph, and they are renowned flittle players,' explained Aarus. 'The greatest of the nymphs, Hamadrya, captured hearts with the very tunes she played, that's how I first met her, but she well…' Sorrow fell upon him as his words faded to silence.

'A flittle!' What's that?' asked Asher. He had never heard of such an instrument.

'Oh, it's an instrument with seven holes, made from thick reeds,' said Aarus. His attention was regained. 'The reeds thrive in wetlands and riparian habitats in Northern Iresealand,' he said.

'Where's Northern Iresealand?' asked Asher with another question. He had never heard of such a place.

'It's my birthplace,' explained Aarus. 'Terra is where I dwell,' he revealed.

'Well, flittles don't sound impressive to me,' said Asher.

'Flittles, among other instruments, were used by nymphs and other such creatures to gain the consciousness of us divine beings,' said Aarus. 'Well, that was until I ended that!'

'How?' asked Asher.

'Let's just say on Terra, no other celestial beings were left when I was done,' revealed Aarus. He chuckled.

'Wait, none were left!' said Asher. He recalled his dreams, the visions, and the downfall of godlike beings. 'The Gatekeeper showed me…'

'Well…um…let me interrupt. I simply meant they all left, after I had warned them,' said Aarus. He spoke fast and loose. He was convincing, if anything. 'The Gatekeeper was after their power, you see. He would show up from his portal, and that was that,' he said.

'I hope you're telling the truth,' said Asher. 'I still don't know what to believe.'

'Well have I not proved my friendship?' asked Aarus. 'Dad is alive and well, and life goes on,' he said.

'True,' admitted Asher. He thought about it. He had received help from Aarus alone to save his dad, Mike. He was not helped by Geatiric, The Gatekeeper, or Vixi, nor any great creator from what he could tell.

'Besides, what harm am I? I've been reduced to being but a humble voice in your head,' said Aarus. 'For now!' he mumbled.

'Alright then,' replied Asher. He rolled his eyes before plucking at the strings of his guitar. He got back to his practice. T-wang! T-wang! J-reeng! Luckily, he did not have to endure his grandmother's groans of displeasure. She had decided to go to bingo. It was her only weekly event, in addition to a few scheduled trips to the local grocery store.

The only watchful fan Asher had in attendance was his grey and white, fluffy, half-breed dog, Scruffy. 'G, C, D, A...' He stopped only for juice and comfort food. He practiced relentlessly; he did so for more than five whole hours, until his grandmother returned home. By that time, he had grown tired.

'G, C, D, A...hmmm...' He yawned as he outstretched his arms. Eventually, his sheer exhaustion had overtaken him.

His alarm clock displayed 10:45 pm; it was late. 'I best get some shut-eye, boy.' He had set the alarm clock to go off at 8.00 am sharp. He fell asleep with a blue striped blanket partially wrapped around his small body. His guitar rested on the bed by his feet. In the corner of the room, his dog, Scruffy, nibbled on a piece of exposed carpet.

A little over nine hours later, he heard a familiar, irritating voice! He heard his grandmother; her voice reached his room.

'Time to get up, school...'

'Already awake, Grandma,' interrupted Asher. His fingers were covered in blisters from the previous night's activities. He was eager to get to school early to avoid Principal Smith's wrath. The first class scheduled on his timetable was science with Mr Woods.

'Hold up, Asher!'

'Hi Sarah,' replied Asher. It was on his way to science class that he unexpectedly crossed paths with the slightly plump, brown-haired, four feet eleven-inch-tall Sarah Reid.

'Asher, you've been selected for the Rising Star Talent Show,' said Sarah excitedly. She could not stop fidgeting with her lilac-framed spectacles. 'I came up with the name,' she revealed. She nodded self-appraisingly, with a grin from ear to ear.

'No way!' gasped Asher. He was taken aback.

'It's true, the name just sprang to mind,' she said.

'No, I mean I can't believe that I've been chosen,' said Asher. Was he ready? Was he good enough to perform, he thought to himself? He now realised what his music teacher had meant when he had stated 'big things' were planned.

'It's true,' continued Sarah. 'Mr McGrath wants to see you after school, in the music room,' she explained. She nodded excitedly.

'Sarah, I don't know,' hesitated Asher. He had doubts. He was not overly social to begin with. The simple idea of performing in front of a large audience was a little terrifying.

'Come on, Asher. You're good,' said Sarah. Persistent, she was not taking no for an answer. She had seen him play on a few occasions.

'Well, thank you, but…' Asher still was not sure. His first instinct was to say 'no' outright. But he did not get the chance!

'I knew you'd be up for it,' boomed Sarah. She quickly capitalised upon his reluctance to give a firm answer. 'I'll tell Mr McGrath that you'd like to be included in the show,' she said.

'But, but…'

'See you later Asher,' said Sarah. She hastened down the school corridor and out of sight, she quickly rushed off to her art and design lesson.

'That's just swell,' groaned Asher. He knew he had just landed himself in a sticky situation, one that would be devilishly hard to get out of. 'I'm always putting my foot in my mouth,' he said.

He sulked all through science class with Mr Michael Woods and mathematics with Miss Claire Hamilton. His inclusion in the talent show weighed heavily on him.

'What's wrong? You've been sour all morning,' asked Ben. He could not help but note that Asher had a face longer than a horse.

'Nothing,' replied Asher sourly. He could not stop fidgeting with his lunch, consisting of potatoes, peas, and pie.

'Come on, you can't fool me,' probed Ben. He threw his hand forward against his friend's shoulder, demanding a response. 'Spill,' he said.

'All right, all right, I've been selected for the talent show,' informed Asher. He spoke fast and loose with his words. He let go of his fork as it fell into a chunk of potatoes. He was feeling anxious.

'That's super,' said Ben. 'I've seen the flyers in the hall. What idiot named it the Rising Star Talent Show? It's so cliché,' he said. He had no idea that it was his school crush, Sarah Reid.

'No, it's not super at all,' said Asher hastily. He put his hands in his jet-black hair, he grew a little alarmed. 'I'll have to play in front of the whole school,' he said.

'Just out of curiosity, why is that a bad thing?' queried Ben. 'If I could play guitar, I would,' he said.

'I'm not good enough. I'll be a total laughingstock,' said Asher. He disliked the idea of playing at the talent show the more he thought about it.

'You never give yourself a chance,' said Ben truthfully.

'But, but…'

'Listen, if you want out, just say something, it shouldn't be that hard,' alluded Ben. He gasped heavily as he became a little frustrated. He became frustrated as he knew his anxious friend was incredibly talented and deserved a spot in the talent show. But alas, he also knew it was not his decision to make.

'Yes…yes, you're right, it shouldn't be that hard,' responded Asher. His only thought was to find a way out of his predicament.

With the end of the day arriving, the time 3:15 pm, he hurried to music class. He had made up his mind. He would not be taking part in the talent show.

'Hi Asher,' said Mr McGrath, pleasantly greeting him. 'Ready to end the week on a high note?' he queried. He was full of zeal. A smile stretched across his face.

'Yes, sir,' responded Asher. He was half-hearted in his response, giving a weak smile to boot.

'Have a seat, we'll be starting soon,' instructed Mr McGrath.

'Listen, sir, about the talent show…'

'Yes, Sarah has already told me, I'm truly pleased that you'll be taking part,' expressed Mr McGrath happily. 'I do have high hopes this year.' His passion, his entire life centred around music, and he thoroughly enjoyed helping others excel in the subject.

'Yes, but…'

'Hold that thought one second,' said Mr McGrath. He had noticed someone lingering at the door. He hurried to the door to greet a new student, a shy plump boy stood outside unwilling to enter. 'Abraham, come on in, we don't bite,' he said. He waved the boy forward.

'Yes, sir,' said the anxious boy.

'Take a seat next to Rebecca,' informed Mr McGrath. Bang! He locked the door, he then began the lesson. 'Today I'll be holding short one-to-one sessions with each of you, so get out your instruments,' he said.

He held a colourful notebook and a blue pen in his hand. He immediately took to the task of analysing the skills of each pupil. 'I'll start with you, Joseph,' he said.

Asher placed his navy woollen coat over the back of his chair, he then began reading a book on guitar theory. He had gone over guitar scales and intervals, chord construction and musical keys. Knowledge was a big part of learning, even in music class. He would inform Mr McGrath of his decision to pull out of the talent show when it came to his individual, one-to-one session.

'Great Alex, simply great, keep it up, you're getting much better on that trumpet,' hailed Mr McGrath. He was making slow progress as he made his way around the room.

Out of eleven students, the total number making up the class, Asher was the very last to be seen.

'I've seen Joseph, Rebecca, Michael, Susie, who's next?' asked Mr McGrath. His eyes wandered the room.

'Me, sir!' Asher raised his voice, he was aware that time was running out. He simply could not wait any longer, there were only seven minutes of class left. He was restless.

'Oh yes, almost forgot you, let's see what you've been up to,' said Mr McGrath. Shreekkk! He pulled a wooden chair across the floor, and he took a seat next to Asher. He opened his notebook, pen in hand, he was ready to begin.

'Sir, about the talent show…' began Asher.

'We'll talk about that later. Show me what you've been up to,' said Mr McGrath. He tapped on Asher's guitar.

'Ok, sir,' replied Asher. His fingers slid along the frets of his six-stringed instrument, he began. 'G, C, D, A, G…' he whispered, as he played each chord.

Quite pleased, Mr McGrath listened intently. 'Perfect, the strumming, the timing, just perfect, this year you have a real chance of winning the talent show, don't let me down,' he praised.

'Really, do I?' asked Asher.

'Yes, you do.' Mr McGrath had complete faith in him.

'Golly!' Lost in the moment, Asher's two blue eyes shone like diamonds. He felt for the briefest of seconds a spark of motivation, until the doubts crept back in. 'But still, I'm unsure…'

'It's an opportunity not to be missed, everyone will be there,' added Mr McGrath. His words only added doubt.

'Everyone!' whispered Asher. He took a hard gulp. All his fears quickly resurfaced. 'Sir, I just don't think I'm ready,' he said. His teeth sank into his bottom lip.

'Nonsense,' said Mr McGrath.

'Nonsense indeed,' intervened Aarus. 'I've heard you amidst your musical undertakings, you're an acquired taste of the chaotic kind, I like it,' he said. He added his approval to the mix.

Buzzz! The school bell was booming loudly, the lesson came to a very sudden end.

'Not helping Aarus,' whispered Asher. His voice was masked by the bell. He placed his instrument in his guitar bag.

'It's a pity, without risk there's no reward,' said Aarus. 'You have to take life by the horns,' he chuckled.

Shreekkk! Mr McGrath sprang forth from his seat like a jack-in-the-box. 'I'll see everyone next Tuesday,' he said. He quickly cleared his desk of paper, pens, and whiteboard markers.

'Sir!' Asher was still hoping that somehow, he could get himself removed from the talent show. He wanted out; the idea of performing in front of the whole school was a scary prospect, one he did not want to face.

'Yes, Asher,' answered Mr McGrath. He removed his thick, red winter coat from a hook on the wall. He then covered his neck with a colourful rainbow scarf, before finally placing his fingers within a pair of thick woollen gloves. He made for the door.

Asher put his coat on. He found it a bit of a struggle as he juggled his guitar bag from one hand to the other. He followed Mr McGrath to the door. 'I…I just don't feel up to participating in the talent show,' he said.

Sharp and direct, Mr McGrath's tone grew very serious. 'Listen, Asher, these opportunities don't come along very often, Alex, Rebecca, they'll both be there performing, it'll be a real shame if you're not,' he said.

'Well…' Asher thought carefully.

'I have faith in you, but it's your decision,' continued Mr McGrath. He held out his thumb sideways, like some Roman emperor of old. His thumb dangled, tilting back and forth. He awaited Asher's answer.

'Me too,' said Aarus. 'Truly,' he said. His tone was a little sarcastic.

'I'm, I'm…' The words were on the tip of Asher's tongue.

'Yes,' probed Mr McGrath.

Tinkering on the brink of madness, Asher, to his surprise, submitted to his own deepest, darkest fears. 'I'm in,' he said.

'See, that wasn't all that hard to say,' said Aarus. 'Conquer your fears and you'll conquer all,' he said.

'Great, that's the spirit,' said Mr McGrath with delight. He put his thumb up. 'Don't forget, there is an extra music session next Tuesday, plus Wednesday and Thursday, we'll begin the hard work then,' he said. Normally, there was no music class on the second and fourth Thursday of each month.

Getting home that afternoon, Asher was greeted by an unexpected phone call. As soon as he got in the front door, the old woman was awaiting him.

'Asher, it's your father,' revealed Nancy. She placed her hand over the mouthpiece of the phone that she held before letting loose. She did not want to be heard. 'Calls when he bloody well feels like it. Forgets he has a son that one,' she said.

'Dad!' Asher quickly took the phone. 'Dad, Dad, how are things in Egypt?' He was overjoyed.

'Just swell, lad,' replied Mike. 'How has the new term at school been going?' he asked. He had not called all that much. He rarely did. He would call once a month if Asher was lucky. Though he would send him a postcard every so often in the mail.

'I've been selected for the school talent show,' said Asher. He was filled with pride as he told his dad. 'I'll be playing one of The Magic Masons' songs,' he said.

'I said you would be the next big thing. I knew it,' said Mike. 'You best get to practicing. I will send you a surprise in the mail,' he said.

'Thanks, Dad.' Asher spoke for a while longer with his dad. He then took his advice and got to practicing. Hurrying upstairs to his bedroom, it was time for the hard work to begin.

-Chapter 15-

Preparations and Confrontations

Asher practiced intensely all weekend, right up until Tuesday morning of January 12th. After school, he was to take part in the first of three music classes that had been scheduled that week. He now had a lot to live up to. The talent show was at the forefront of his mind.

Thump! Thump! Thump! Nancy lifted her broom before smacking it against the ceiling. 'Get your skinny behind down here,' she yelled.

Asher quickly placed his instrument on his bed. Clinkkk! Brass handle twisting, he then opened his bedroom door before sprinting down the stairs to the kitchen.

'I've told you once, I've told you a thousand times, no more playing that infernal instrument under this roof, that's what school is for,' said Nancy. Her temper had reached a boiling point. Her silver hair hung loosely over the brim of her spectacles.

'But Grandma, the talent show is coming up,' explained Asher. His teeth sank into his bottom lip. He rested his right hand in his black hair, his nimble fingers worked their way through the jet-black strands.

'I don't care,' replied Nancy. She was getting increasingly angry.

'You can always get rid of her,' said Aarus. His tone was all too serious.

'Oh boy.' Asher let out an uneasy chuckle, he was unsure as to whether Aarus was joking or not. 'You better be kidding.' He muttered the words softly.

'I…well, of course I am,' answered Aarus. 'Ash, I'm not some monster, at least I prefer to think so. Like a diamond, though, I can be a little rough,' he added.

'I'm not joking,' grumbled Nancy. She had overheard him.

'I need to practice…' Asher could not get a word in.

'I don't want to hear it, I'm not to be annoyed, doctor says so,' said Nancy. She had a heart condition. 'Look at the time, it's barely past eight fifteen, you've been at that infernal commotion for over thirty minutes.' She pointed to the clock on the wall.

'But, but, but…'

'No more, you hear me, no more.' Nancy was beyond reasoning.

'But Grandma…'

'Go to your room, clean up, and get ready for school,' ordered Nancy. She pointed toward the kitchen door, she was extremely firm.

'All right, all right,' replied Asher. Sulky, he had given in to her stern demands. He stormed from the kitchen in a huff, and he then quickly ascended the stairs of the old house before entering the bathroom.

He took a long, hot shower to clear his mind before completing his morning ritual. He quickly dried his hair before neatly combing the wild mess. Swish! Swish! Swish! He then, in small circular motions, cleaned his teeth with a green-bristled toothbrush. All done, he moved from the bathroom back into the seclusion of his bedroom. A grey bathrobe covered his wiry-framed physique.

'Hurry up, Asher,' boomed Nancy.

'I'll be down in a minute, grandma,' said Asher loudly.

'I'll wait right here,' replied Nancy. She stood at the bottom of the stairs. She stood like a watchful hawk eyeing his bedroom door. She waited for her target to emerge.

Asher quickly opened the drawers of his bedside dresser in search of clean clothes. He opened the second drawer and immediately fell silent at the sight of a picture he had seen many, many times. He caressed the creased photo in his hand.

'Who's this then?' asked Aarus. He was forcefully intrusive. 'That smile reminds me of Hamadrya.' He continued in a reminiscent tone. 'Her skin was much greener, as too were her eyes, but she was just as captivating,' he said.

'Who has green skin?' queried Asher. He wiped his teary eyes clean.

'You first, Ash,' said Aarus.

'It's my mother,' answered Asher. "Now it's your turn,' he said.

'Hamadrya was a beautiful forest nymph who made me feel, well, she made me feel alive inside,' responded Aarus. 'I lost her a few millennia ago,' he said.

'How can you have loved anyone?' asked Asher. He was a little too brash.

'Why? Because I am cruel, vindictive, vengeful…' Aarus, in his anger, let his feelings flow like a great raging river.

'No…no, that's not what I meant.' Asher quickly intervened. 'I never said you were any of that, I just meant that you are just a…a bracelet.'

'Oh, oh right, in that case you're pardoned,' replied Aarus, lowering his voice. 'I wasn't always confined in this state of being, I was once free to do what I wished, when I desired, and how I wanted,' he said.

Asher looked at his alarm clock, he realised he was taking a bit too long to get dressed. He needed to hurry if he did not want to be late for school. 'Gran…Gran, quick, where are my clothes?' He could not find them. He sought immediate answers.

'Everything has been washed,' informed Nancy. She suddenly remembered she had washed his clothes the night before. She had ransacked his bedside dresser.

Asher stormed from his room. 'I need my clothes for school,' he panicked. He stood at the top of the stairs, looking very annoyed.

'Hold your horses,' barked Nancy. 'They should be dried by now,' she said. She made her way into the kitchen, slowly moving toward the dryer. She then retrieved a bunch of garments from the growling, metal beast after hitting the end cycle button.

'Are they done?' asked Asher. He was growing impatient.

'Almost,' answered Nancy. 'Five more minutes, I need to iron your shirt,' she said.

'I haven't the time,' yelled Asher from atop the stairs. He was livid.

'Nonsense,' called out Nancy. She placed the ironing board in the centre of the kitchen. She then pressed the hot iron she held down upon Asher's shirt, removing the creases.

'Hurry or I'll be late,' thundered Asher. He drummed his feet off the floorboards; he was completely vexed. 'It was you who wanted me gone and out the door,' he continued to huff.

'Stop your moaning, here all done,' said Nancy. She moved into the hall, garments in hand. Ratta tat tat! Ratta tat tat! Ratta tat tat! Creakkk! She gently pulled open the front door. 'Oh, it's only you,' she said.

'Is Asher ready for school, Miss Branning?' It was Ben. His words were a little slurred as he chewed some gum.

'It's Mrs,' answered Nancy. She shook her head disapprovingly. Her unkempt, silver hair danced about her face. She had not brushed it yet.

'Sorry,' apologised Ben half-heartedly. He spun his orange yoyo up and down in his left hand, he was somewhat distracted.

'He's not ready,' informed Nancy. She shook the clothing resting on her left arm.

'I'll wait,' said Ben.

'No, you won't,' growled Nancy. 'Get yourself to school, he'll be along soon.' She slammed the front door without uttering another word.

'Why did you do that?' asked Asher. He felt that she was very rude.

'Here, put your clothes on,' said Nancy. She was not concerned in the least about how rude she had been toward Ben.

'I don't think I'll make it to school on time,' said Asher. He hurried down the stairs, grabbing his clean clothes from his grandmother's hands. He was right, too. Despite his best efforts to get to school on time, he arrived late, and much to Principal Smith's strong displeasure.

'Asher, this won't do, see me after school, at my office,' informed Principal Smith. He gazed at his brown, leather-strapped watch. 'For goodness' sake! It's twelve minutes past nine, you are twelve minutes late.' His devotion to the school rules meant that he could not let the incident slide this time.

'I've seen royalty less stuck up, compared to this one,' said Aarus. 'He should be dethroned,' he said. He was quite sarcastic.

'Stuck up!' Spontaneously, Asher chuckled as he repeated Aarus's words. He did not make eye contact with Principal Smith. Instead, he looked at his trainers as his feet moved to and fro.

'What was that?' asked Principal Smith. His face grew cold. Straightening his tie, he then buttoned up his blue blazer.

'Sorry, sir,' replied Asher. 'I meant I was stuck up at home, clothes were in the wash,' he said. He was struggling to hold both his school bag and his instrument, he was exhausted. He had jogged the entire journey to school, and for nothing.

'Well, well, you're a clever one,' said Aarus. 'You could talk yourself out of a hanging.' He was impressed by Asher's quick thinking.

This time, Asher remained quiet. He did not respond to Aarus.

'Yes, well, get a move on,' said Principal Smith. He instructed that Asher get to class. 'Remember, the school rules will bend for no one. I am the architect of the rules,' he added.

'I, too, know a tyrannical architect of rules,' told Aarus. 'Judging the rest of us from upon golden throne,' he said. He spat the words out. Whomever he was thinking of caused him great displeasure.

'Yes, sir,' said Asher. Pulling the door open, he then hurried down the school corridor and to his first class of the day with

Mr McNulty. He received a right earful for interrupting the lesson.

'Knock before disturbing my class,' boomed Mr McNulty. He did not tolerate tardiness.

'Yes, sir,' replied Asher. His head hung low amid a room full of laughter.

'Quiet!' yelled Mr McNulty. The laughter quickly evaporated. No one dared to test his patience further. 'Grab a book at the front and take a seat,' he said.

'Yes, sir,' said Asher. He retrieved a book entitled 'The Industrial Revolution, 18th and 19th Century.' He did as he was told.

'Take a seat here, buddy,' whispered Ben. 'I held this seat just for you,' he said. He pulled out a chair he had reserved for his late friend.

'Thanks, pal,' said Asher. He patted Ben on the back as he sat down.

'No sweat,' replied Ben. 'Anyhow, I called by your house, your grandmother is nasty…'

'Ben Wilson!' snapped Mr McNulty. 'Is there something you would like to share with the class?' His nostrils were flaring up. The twitch in his left eye was not a good indicator either.

'No, not that I'm aware of, chief,' said Ben cheekily. His tone was testing.

'Perhaps detention will put you at ease.' Mr McNulty looked irritated.

'I don't believe that's necessary, sir,' said Ben. He twiddled with his thumbs as he regressed into a more tolerable state.

'Stop clowning around and turn to page four then,' growled Mr McNulty. He slammed the textbook in his hand down upon his desk, he then began reading. 'The Industrial Revolution had begun in Britain during the mid-18th century, but the American colonies lagged far behind…'

Following a full forty-three minutes of reading, both Asher and Ben raced from history class. The school bell was buzzing, they could simply take no more. Their brains could not consume any more facts about waterpower, steam power, machine tools, or manufacturing processes.

'Let's get out of here, buddy,' said Ben. 'I can't take any more of old badger,' he said. He made up the nickname 'badger' to refer to his grey-haired, short-tempered history teacher.

'You don't have to tell me twice,' replied Asher. He snatched his school bag and instrument from the floor beneath, he was off. He raced along the school corridor; he passed a jeering Tom Watson. He was being a jerk as always.

'Look what we have here, the school fools,' teased Tom. He leaned his tall, slim body up against his steel locker, he seemed overly at ease. His next lesson was about to begin, not that he seemed to care.

'Shut it, Tom,' barked Ben. He shook his fist defiantly.

'Ash, your friend has some likeable qualities,' said Aarus. 'He's a brave one. Will he be fighting on your behalf? Have you no backbone?' He was pushing all the right buttons, so to speak. He sought no reply, simply to stir the anger bubbling away in Asher's core. It worked too!

'Ignore him,' said Asher firmly. 'He's an idiot!' He showed a little tenacity, which was more than usual. He never really stood up to Tom in the past. Not in the way he was presently doing.

'I'm no idiot,' snapped Tom. His hazel eyes ignited with fury. He stood upright as he clinched his fists. His annoyance was all too clear.

'Whatever you say.' Asher trudged on, he did not want to cause a scene.

'A little better,' replied Aarus. 'Nevertheless, a little physical force would be more appropriate,' he said.

'Enough!' spoke Asher. He was growing annoyed at Aarus. 'I thought you were my friend.' He was smart enough to know that Aarus was pushing him to react.

'I am,' said Ben. He looked a little puzzled. 'I'll always be there for you,' he added.

'Me too,' stated Aarus. 'I just want the best for you,' he said. His voice was a little more comforting.

'I know that,' replied Asher. It was unclear which of the two he was responding to, Ben or Aarus, or if indeed he was responding to both.

His second lesson of the day involved fractions with Miss Hamilton, while the third lesson of the day involved understanding the relationship and key differences between gases, liquids, and solids with Mr Woods. However, it was his after-school music lesson that he longed for.

'Wow! You learned that song quickly,' complimented Mr McGrath. He praised him wildly. 'You're going to blow them all away at this year's talent show,' he said.

'Thanks, sir,' replied Asher with a grin. His confidence was slowly growing.

'Is this the song you are going to perform?' asked Mr McGrath. He held a notebook and a black pen. He awaited the answer.

'It sure is,' answered Asher. He could not think of a more fitting song than one by his favourite band.

'Ok, so 'Going Down,' by The Magic Masons, it is,' said Mr McGrath. He put pen to paper as he scribbled away. 'That's us then until tomorrow,' he added.

Shriekkk! Asher jumped from his chair, he quickly packed up his things, before making for the door. He had not forgotten his appointment with Principal Smith for being late. He made a brief stop at the principal's office. Knock! Knock! Knock! 'Hello, sir, sorry I was held up.'

'In music class, I know, I was expecting your arrival, come in,' instructed Principal Smith. He sat in a black leather chair. Above his head hung a picture, a sign with the words, 'Order is nothing but an eternal friendship with chaos. Order is the stability we crave, but chaos creates the opportunities for change that we need.' He held a red book in his hand. 'The rules bend for no one, Mr Paterson, especially rule nine.' He held up the red book, pointing to said rule.

'Oh, what an insufferable bore,' said Aarus. He found the school principal quite dreary. 'Rules are made to be broken,' he added. He was rebellious by nature.

'Sorry, sir,' replied Asher. He ignored the voice in his head. He ignored Aarus. 'I had to wait on Gran ironing my shirt an…' His excuses fell on deaf ears. He was cut short.

'This is not your first late offence either,' informed Principal Smith. 'You like to put rule nine to the test,' he said. He set the red book down on his oak desk.

'Sorry, sir,' said Asher. He apologised again.

'There's more to life than rules, though,' Principal Smith stood up. He buttoned up his blazer and moved to the window. In reflection he gazed outside at creation, he gazed outside at Neptune City.

'Now we can agree on that,' said Aarus. 'Rules are meant for subservient lifeforms,' he added.

'I trust that your dad is doing well?' asked Principal Smith. Genuine concern resonated on his face. He took off his spectacles; he then wiped the lenses.

'Yes…yes, he's just fine,' replied Asher. He thought Principal Smith's words were very strange. Why, he thought, would the school principal care one little bit about his dad?

'I did say that in time things could be changed,' said Principal Smith cryptically as usual. 'I am glad your dad is doing well. I know how much he means to you,' he continued.

'Time changes everything, in time things can be changed!' whispered Asher. His big blue eyes were as wide as church doors. Did Principal Smith know of his time-altering shenanigans in Egypt? Surely not, he thought. No one else had remembered a thing except him, and of course, Aarus.

He recalled how Principal Smith had stopped by his grandmother's house after his dad's death. He remembered the words that the school principal had spoken exactly. He also recalled the events that took place shortly after and how he had altered time itself.

'This mere mortal is not all he seems to be!' said Aarus with suspicion. 'I recall that day, the day we went back in time to save your father,' he said. He, too, like Asher, recalled events to the exact detail. He could not understand how Principal Smith had seemingly remembered the very same events. 'Only certain beings can know that the timeline has been changed,' he said.

'I had read a recent article. Your dad is getting a lot of exposure,' said Principal Smith. 'The biggest find in almost a century, the experts say,' he added. He raised his eyebrows.

'Yes, he uncovered a new tomb in the Valley of the Kings,' said Asher. He looked at the school principal weirdly. He was a walking enigma. He seemed to truly know all.

'Well, isn't that something?' said Principal Smith. He stared at Asher, his gaze unyielding. 'Destiny calls for individuals like your dad, more so for special individuals like you!'

'What…' gulped Asher. 'But…but I'm not special,' he spluttered out. He was just a run-of-the-mill thirteen-year-old.

'Special! I did say that you were special too,' stated Aarus. 'No celestial I've ever come across could change the timeline!' He found the school principal strange and yet fascinating. 'Geatiric, is that you, I wonder!'

'I mean the talent show, what an opportunity to shine,' said Principal Smith. 'Your journey to do special things is set in motion. It is up to you how that journey goes,' he said.

'Thank…thank you, sir,' said Asher.

'Off you go then. But remember anymore lateness and it is a call home,' said Principal Smith. He smiled as he closed his office door behind Asher.

With haste, Asher hurried down the corridor and outside. He was spotted exiting the big brown doors to the front of the school.

'Look, Tom, look who it is!' Conor Murphy quickly spotted him. He tossed an empty chocolate wrapper to the pavement. He then cracked his knuckles.

'No, I've got this,' said Tom. Seeing that Asher was all alone, he wanted to exact a little revenge of his own doing. 'No one calls me an idiot and gets away with it.' His words were full of venomous spite. 'Paterson! Hey, I am talking to you.' He wiped his snub-shaped nose with the corner of his blue and white striped t-shirt.

Thud! Thud! Thud! Asher tried not to react as he marched on. He ignored Tom's words. His school bag dangled over his shoulder, he held his black guitar bag in his right hand. He began descending the school steps.

'Strike him, Ash,' said Aarus. 'Show strength.' His voice was demanding.

'No, I won't do it,' replied Asher. He was not a violent person by nature. He tried to avoid conflict whenever possible.

'What do you mean, no?' Tom deviously lurched his right foot forward. 'Watch yourself,' he said coldly. His hazel eyes were burning with enough hatred to power an industrial furnace. He wanted to cause Asher harm.

'Arghhh!' screeched Asher. He lost his grip on his guitar bag, face first, he went sliding down the cobblestoned steps. Though he felt no pain. His body tingled as a blue aura washed over him. Surprisingly, he did not suffer any severe injuries!

'Ha! Good one, Tom,' said Conor. His enormous gut juggled uncontrollably as he laughed.

'Next time you mock me, Paterson, it'll be ten times worse,' threatened Tom. He slammed his foot down upon Asher's guitar. Crackkk! 'Let's go, Murph, before old nosy sees us,' he said. He quickly hurried down the street.

'Wait, wait for me,' boomed Conor. He struggled to keep pace.

'Nooo!' cried Asher. He opened his guitar bag to see that the neck of his guitar was shattered. 'I'll get those two, if it's the last thing I do,' he said. He was disheartened.

'You can only respond to hate with hate,' stated Aarus. 'Thousands of years have taught me that,' he said.

'Ash…Ash…are you alright, buddy?' It was Ben. 'I seen those two lousy idiots; they deserve a taste of their own medicine,' he said. Panting a little, his plump cheeks were rosy red.

'Convenient, friends, if you can call them that, only show up when it suits,' said Aarus. He continued to stir the pot.

'Where were you?' snapped Asher. He was angry.

'I just finished practice,' said Ben. He had just finished baseball practice with Coach Jones. He had rushed to Asher's aid upon seeing the school bully's hard at work. 'Sorry, I just couldn't get here in time.' He took two puffs of his blue inhaler.

Ben was still dressed in his baseball uniform. He wore a blue cap and jersey with a cartoonish, stingray logo imprinted upon the front. He also wore white pants, with a black stripe down the side.

'No, Ben, I'm the one who should be sorry,' said Asher solemnly. He knew he had acted harshly. He was just bitterly furious. 'What will I do now? Look, they have destroyed my guitar.'

'That is not right. Those two are vicious,' muttered Ben. He shook his head in disgust.

Asher lifted his guitar bag, with the broken instrument inside. 'I'll catch you later, Ben,' he sniffled. Upset, he began the journey home.

'Do you want me to walk with you?' asked Ben. He truly felt bad for Asher.

'No, it's okay,' answered Asher. Gloomy, he could not help but think about the talent show. 'How can I practice without my guitar?' he mumbled. He miserably strode along the path, leading away from Neptunica Middle School.

He could not believe it. He felt that he had no other option, without his instrument, he could not practice for the talent show and would have to pull out. He felt horrible, believing he was letting Mr McGrath down. He also felt miserable because all his hard work thus far would amount to nothing.

Nancy did not let up either upon his arrival home. 'What happened to you?' she enquired. She also took note of the filth upon his clothes.

'I fell down a few steps and broke my guitar,' answered Asher. 'I wasn't watching where I was going,' he said. He lied bitterly.

'Should look where you're going, and don't think you're going to be getting that fixed?' groaned Nancy. Intentionally or not, she was quite scornful.

'It would appear that you are but a mere insect to be stepped upon by everyone,' said Aarus. His words struck a chord.

'I don't care!' Asher dropped his guitar bag to the ground. He ground his pearly white teeth in anger.

'Good, because my purse is shut,' said Nancy. 'Living on a pension, you know.' She had retired many years ago. She had once worked as a cook. Besides, the money your dad provides does not stretch that far,' she said.

'Would be easier getting blood from a stone,' muttered Asher. He spoke softly through gritted teeth.

'Honestly, you are a clumsy boy,' continued Nancy.

'Do you ever let up?' shouted Asher. He burst into an uncontrollable rage, he could no longer take any more. 'You're nothing but a nagging old woman with nothing better to do.' His face was red. His negative emotions spilled out.

'Superb, unleash your anger,' said Aarus. 'There's the respect I'm talking about, take it,' he said. He spurred Asher on.

'How dare you! Go to your room,' ordered Nancy. She did not take kindly to Asher's insulting temperament. 'Don't come out either until you're told, speaking to me like that,' she said, flabbergasted. Her raised voice commanded obedience.

'Fine, I will.' Asher stormed up the stairs, like he was climbing Mount Everest itself. He then entered the seclusion of his bedroom.

'The kids today,' growled Nancy with sheer distaste. 'They have no respect at all,' she said. She pulled her cardigan tight as she folded her arms. She huffed as she sat upon her flowery settee.

In solemn thought, Asher sat in his room thinking about his guitar and the talent show. Why me?' he said. His words were full of self-pity.

'No risk, no reward,' said Aarus.

'Be quiet,' snapped Asher. He did not need anyone else in his head. His head was packed with many thoughts, like a tin of sardines; there was no room for more. He listened to his music for a good while. Then he turned his gaze to his bedroom wall.

He gazed at a framed poster of his favourite band, The Magic Masons. 'That guitar right there would solve all my problems,' he sighed. He looked at Razor Ryan, the band's lead singer, who held a beautiful, V-shaped guitar of slender white and black trim.

He reached forward, taking hold of a picture that resided in the frame and a concert ticket. His dad, Mike, had purchased the ticket in nineteen eighty-seven, when The Magic Masons had played at the Giants Stadium, East Rutherford, New Jersey, during their Raging Journey Tour. 'Wish I could have seen them play, alongside you, Dad,' he said.

Clink! Asher shuffled across the room, he then opened his bedroom window to gather his thoughts. He placed the concert ticket in his pocket. Taking his time, he then observed the picture of his dad as he had done a hundred times before. 'Look at you, Dad.' He studied the photograph. The picture showed a young Mike Paterson and his friends. They stood in front of the Giant's Stadium, lights blazing in the background.

His dad, Mike, was youthful, in his early twenties. He had a lean physique and neatly cut brown hair. He also wore a stylish black leather jacket. But most striking was his comical t-shirt. The t-shirt he wore depicted Razor Ryan smashing a guitar against a falling wall. His dad looked cool. His style had changed over the years, his present, awful, scruffy hat being testament to that. 'Well, Dad, it's just not the same without you.' He was in a reflective mood.

Asher, with the photo in his hand, stuck his head out the window. He looked up into the dark night sky. He took a deep breath. He felt raindrops against his skin, it began to rain heavily. 'Brrr!' Shivers rolling down his spine, he decidedly moved to close the window. Whooshhh! But just as he tried to, a strong gust of wind swept through his room.

'Time for action!' stated Aarus. 'Not words,' he said.

Foolishly, Asher's loose grip upon the picture that he held had seen it drift out into the night. He sprang forth with concern.

'There it is,' said Asher. He could see the photo, it was wedged against a piece of chipped wood. He tried in desperation to regain it, he leaned further out the window.

'You'll have to venture outside and retrieve it, Ash,' said Aarus.

Asher felt the rain and wind batter against his soft, pink flesh. His efforts were futile, the photograph was beyond his reach. 'Fine, I'll just climb out and get it then.' He knew what he had to do. He eased out onto the ledge of the old, timeworn, wood-built house.

'I've got it!' He mustered up one careless, overstretched reach. He grasped the picture within his palm. 'Ohhh, oh, helppp!' To his dismay, however, the slippery surface had led him to lose his balance.

Clunkkk! He fell, and his slim-framed physique slid along the wet roof tiles. Bata, bump, bump, bump! 'Nooo!' he cried out. A few loose tiles went with him in the process.

He could not defy Sir Isaac Newton's law of gravity. He was descending fast. He, at the very last moment, grasped onto a shaky drainpipe. He managed to delay his bone-shattering collision with the grassy lawn beneath.

The picture that he had initially tried to recover had scampered loose yet again. He could see the photo; it was but mere inches away. He set his fears aside to retrieve the image. 'There, there, I…I can get I…' He foolishly stretched his left hand forward, he dared to try and reclaim the picture once more.

Crackkk! He heard thunder, it broke through the clouds above as a flash of light zipped across the night sky.

'You can do it,' said Aarus. He willed him on.

'Almost!' Asher could just about touch the picture with his fingertips. He nearly had it. 'What…what is going on? Arghhh!' However, to his sudden alarm, an all too familiar burning sensation had begun to irritate his wrist.

'Feel the power of Soulkeeper!' spoke Aarus. 'Servo mius volantateium.' Like before, he spoke three little words, and like before, the bracelet came to life.

'Not again,' said Asher in sheer panic. He observed helplessly as a mystical blue light had once again begun to escape from the bracelet latched upon his arm.

'Time for a little journey,' said Aarus. 'Let's go, Ash, let's see how special you are!' he said.

-Chapter 16-

The Concert of 1987

In desperation, Asher clung helplessly to the side of the old wood-built house on 6th Avenue, Neptune City, New Jersey. He was causing a great big commotion. Crackkk! Above him, another flash of lightning zipped across the sky. 'Help somebody!' he pleaded. His muscles ached, and he simply could not hold on any longer.

He felt the blue energy from Soulkeeper, he could not resist the magnetic force. 'Arghhh!' Screeching loudly, he fell, eyes closed tight.

'Wait…what…what's going on?' He did not hit the hard, wet surface of his grandmother's lawn, instead, he felt two huge hands take hold of him. 'Let go,' he protested. He squirmed like a worm caught in the beak of a blackbird.

'What are you doing hiding back here?' A muscular, bald guy yanked Asher up off the ground. 'There'll be no ticket dodgers on my watch,' he added.

'Well, we cannot blame the kid Joe. After all, it's the hottest concert of the year.' A second individual, with black hair and a goatee, spoke, adding his two cents.

'I guess you're right, Bob. I'll cut the kid some slack,' answered Joe. Like Bob, he wore black attire. He also wore a black jacket with the word 'security' imprinted upon the back.

'What do you mean by the hottest concert of the year?' asked Asher. Curious, his ears pricked up. His gaze darted back and forth between the two men.

'Forget it, playing dumb won't work with us, kid,' Bob told. He laughed in a mocking tone. 'All good out here.' He spoke into a walkie talkie.

'Beat it, kid,' said Joe. He signalled for Asher to get lost. 'I've got enough clowns to deal with this evening,' he said.

'But where am I?' queried Asher. He had been directed toward the front of a colossal building. It was lit up like the 4th of July. There were many entrances to the enormous building.

'Good luck, kid,' said Joe. He did not care to listen to another word. After all, he had thought Asher was up to no good.

'This is just perfect.' Asher was left to fend for himself, his eyes whizzing from one person to the next. He found himself lodged in the middle of a very large, excited crowd of people. He needed answers and fast. He approached a guy with long, stringy hair and black attire. 'Excuse me, what's going on?'

The eccentric figure with long hair, wearing a long black coat, a black t-shirt depicting Razor Ryan, black pants, and boots, chuckled. 'Well, my main man, this is the Masons' concert.' He held his ticket aloft for Asher to see. 'I paid top dollar for this ticket. Scalpers suck,' he stated.

'Wow!' gasped Asher. He was left in disbelief. 'The Magic Masons!' He tried to make sense of things as he made his way to the front of the overly excited crowd. 'Excuse me, sorry there, coming through.'

'Hey, kid, there's a line!' A red-haired girl protested. She wore a red cropped jacket and black skinny jeans; she placed her hands on her hips. She was not pleased with Asher cutting the line.

Ignoring the protesting girl, Asher had bigger problems to deal with. He held his wrist to his ear. 'Psttt! Are you there?'

'Put your hand down, Ash, you look like an imbecile,' stated Aarus.

'Holy moly!' Suddenly, Asher peered upward to see a vivid picture of The Magic Masons, and in flashing, bright lights, the date '09–19–1987'. 'It, it can't be!'

'Oh, but it is,' replied Aarus. 'I suspected but was unsure a mortal could withstand Soulkeeper's power. I've seen how special you truly are, indeed. Twice we've tested and twice succeeded.' The glee in his voice was amplified by its higher-than-usual pitch. 'Nothing is impossible. I'll find my way to Terra yet,' he said. He was as enigmatic as always with his words.

'What the hell, this thing is…is…unreal.' Heart pumping, Asher glanced at the priceless possession upon his wrist.

'Like before, Ash, you've gone back in time,' explained Aarus.

'Wow! Did you bring me here?' asked Asher. He could not wrap his mind around time travel one little bit.

'Yes and no,' answered Aarus. 'You're steering the ship, I merely provided a little nudge in the right direction. Believe me, though it takes its toll on me,' he said.

'Hurry up, Mike!'

Asher watched as a guy wearing all denim clothes brushed past him. He had long black hair. 'Mike!' Bemused, he quickly zoned in on a group buzzing with jubilant energy.

'Hold your horses, Jerrold.' The guy by the name of Mike hastened forward. He soared into the middle of the energetic group. He momentarily stopped to pose for a photo.

'Is that you, Dad?' whispered Asher. He developed a strange case of déjà vu. 'It's exactly like my picture,' he gasped. He found everything rather familiar, the people, the clothing, the background, the pose the group struck, it all reminded him of the photograph he had risked his life mere minutes before to regain. On reflection, he felt stupid for clambering out of his bedroom window as he had done.

'Indeed, it's dear old dad alright,' informed Aarus.

'He's so young!' gasped Asher. He looked at Mike, who looked very youthful, in his early to mid-twenties. 'This is so weird, I need to take a closer look,' he whispered. He followed the group in hot pursuit only to be halted by one snappy brunette.

'Ticket please,' she demanded. She wore pink lipstick, she repeatedly popped a piece of chewing gum in her mouth. She held her hand out.

'Ticket!' Asher was confused; in all the excitement, he forgot about the ticket in his pocket.

'Yes, ticket,' she answered. She rolled her eyes impatiently.

'They're getting away.' Asher watched as the younger Mike Paterson and a group of his friends disappeared down a long tunnel. 'I need to get in there now!' He grew frantic.

'We've got a troublemaker here, Frank.' The ticket attendant quickly called for a member of the security team.

'All right, you, out of the line, no ticket, no entry,' snapped Frank. He wore a black shirt, black pants, and had a white ID badge tied around his stumpy neck. 'You're holding up the queue.' Firmly, he placed one hand on Asher's shoulder.

'Check your pocket,' informed Aarus. He sighed; he was getting frustrated. 'Once I was the most powerful being in existence, now I'm but a mere shadow,' he said.

'Hold up, just wait, give me one sec.' Asher put his hand into his blue jean pocket, he pulled out a ticket. It was the very ticket that he had taken from the framed poster of The Magic Mason's that resided upon the wall of his bedroom. The very one that he had put into his pocket before almost plummeting to his death. 'Yes, yes, it matches!' he boomed with joy. He compared the date on the ticket with the one above him in flashing lights, everything matched perfectly.

'I'll take that,' said Frank. He scanned the ticket astutely. 'Um…well…it's all good, beat to hell, but good,' he said.

'Thought I'd lost it, sorry,' said Asher. His quick thinking just about did the trick.

'Go on through then, and make sure you have it ready in case they ask inside,' informed Frank. 'Too many ticket dodgers,' he said.

'Sure thing.' Asher grabbed the ticket before making haste forward. 'Yes! Home free. Elated, he threw up his fist in the air.

'Excuse me, aren't we forgetting something?' enquired Aarus. 'Greatness is always overlooked,' he said. He had a big part to play in current events, regardless of his motivations.

'Oh, yes, sorry,' replied Asher. 'Thanks for the help,' he added. He walked down a long concrete corridor toward the stands, somehow managing to jostle his way through the bustling crowd. 'Where do I go?' As he scanned the ticket in his hand, he had a little trouble finding which seat he was to sit in.

'Alas, Ash, I'm not quite sure,' said Aarus. 'I've used a fair deal of my influence to get you here; it's up to you to do the rest,' he said.

'I don't know where to sit,' said Asher in panic. He walked from one row to the other, and all about him, the stadium began to fill out.

'You! What are you doing here?' It was the security guard named Joe, for a second time. Unlike Frank, his ID badge was red instead of white. His muscular physique strained against the black shirt that he wore. It was a size too small, as was his black jacket.

'I…I have a ticket,' said Asher. He waved it in the air.

'Let's see your ticket then.' Inspecting the ticket, Joe could find no fault. It was valid. 'You should have shown this earlier,' he said. He rubbed his bald head as he double-checked the ticket.

'You didn't exactly give me a chance,' replied Asher. He was as sharp as usual.

'I guess so, we sure didn't, sorry kid,' apologised Joe. He realised he might have acted a bit hastily. 'This way, I'll sort you out,' he said. He wanted to make things right.

'Sure,' said Asher. He could not help but think to himself that the place was tighter than Fort Knox.

'I'm sure you're excited about this one,' said Joe. 'I'm a fan too,' he admitted.

'Can't believe I'm here, honestly,' said Asher. He followed behind the big security guard.

'Are you alone?' queried Joe. 'Usually, we get a few kids aged fourteen or fifteen in a group,' he said. This was not the first concert at which he had worked. He was doing his due diligence. It was his job after all.

'No, I'm going at this solo,' answered Asher. 'Friends bailed out at the last moment,' he said. He was very convincing.

'I see,' said Joe. He was satisfied with the response. After all, being the eighties, age limitations were a little laxer. The Magic

Masons were admired by a lot of teens. 'Follow me,' he instructed.

'Sure thing,' replied Asher. He hurried up a flight of steps.

Quickly, Joe soon found the row, then the seat. 'What, this can't be right!' Immediately, he grew puzzled by the presence of another person occupying seat number three, in row F.

'Dad!' whispered Asher. He found himself up close with his dad, Mike. He was sure it was him, the lean physique, the neat brown hair, the black leather jacket, even the t-shirt he wore depicted Razor Ryan smashing a guitar against a falling wall. It was Mike Paterson in the flesh all right! 'Wow! I wish I had that blasted photo with me,' he gasped.

The security guard, Joe, reanalysed the ticket Asher held. Seeing that it held the correct information, he was bamboozled. 'You there, you're in the wrong chair,' he boomed. He bellowed loudly in the direction of Mike.

'Who me?' asked Mike. His eyes widened as he sprang up right in his chair.

'Yes, you,' snapped Joe. He was a little sharp.

'Listen to this guy, Jerrold.' Annoyed, Mike did not take kindly to Joe's tone. 'Don't think so, pal got my ticket here somewhere, just give me a minute.' He put his hand into the pocket of his black jacket.

'Well,' said Joe. Huffing and puffing, he waited impatiently. The concert itself was about to start.

'Here got it,' said Mike. He held the ticket up.

'I'll take that,' informed Joe. He took Mike's ticket and compared it to Asher's, both were identical. 'All right, there's funny business going on here,' he said.

Joe spoke into his walkie-talkie, calling additional members of stadium security to the scene. 'Keep an eye on this lot.' He left two members of the security team to tend to the scene while he verified the tickets.

Anxious, Asher bit his bottom lip, he stared searchingly at his dad. He desperately wanted to say something. But what? He could think of nothing.

'Do you have a problem, lad?' queried Mike. He stuffed both his hands into the pockets of his black leather jacket as he slouched back in his seat. He looked a little puzzled.

'Who me?' replied Asher. He took a hard gulp.

'Yes, you kid,' said Mike. 'You look familiar, have I seen you before?' he questioned.

'I'm your...' Asher was about to blurt out the truth. But he did not get the chance.

'Perhaps not the best time to have a heart-to-heart,' alluded Aarus. 'Tell him the truth and you'll be laughed out of here like a jester,' he said. His logic was sound.

'No, I...I...' Asher recoiled. He stumbled on his words, unable to form a sentence.

'Leave the kid alone, man,' spoke Jerrold. Mike's friend, dressed in blue denim, quickly intervened.

'I'm only asking Jerrold,' said Mike. Playfully, he thumped his friend on the arm.

'There are no more seats,' informed Joe. He had swiftly returned. 'The tickets have been verified, same code, everything, god knows what has gone wrong here,' he said. He scratched his bald scalp as he contemplated his options.

'I could tell you,' said Aarus. 'But alas, no one can hear me,' he said.

'I can say what's gone wrong,' said Asher.

'I was not serious, Ash,' said Aarus hastily. 'Careful what you say,' he added.

'What do you mean, kid?' asked Joe.

'It's a…a…a mistake,' answered Asher. 'Yes, a mistake, it must be a duplicate, an error,' he said. He had almost given himself up. But once again, he proved his intellect.

'You're getting good at getting out of sticky situations, Ash,' said Aarus. He was surprised at his ability to think on the spot.

'Well, sort it out, dude,' groaned Mike. He was direct and a little vexed.

'Relax, Mike,' said Jerrold. 'Here, have a dog and bun,' he said. He handed the food to him. He then, in turn, thumped him back. 'That's us square,' he said.

Seeing that the concert was about to begin, Joe had to take immediate, affirmative action. 'Come with me,' he said.

'Arghhh! Really,' groaned Asher.

'Not to worry, kid, you're just being upgraded,' informed Joe. 'It'll have to be the VIP treatment,' he added.

'Oh, that sucks,' grumbled Asher. He was disappointed.

'Don't feel bad,' continued Joe. 'You'll have the best view of the stage, the best seating, all you can eat, and who knows, maybe a Magic Masons shirt,' he said. He was genuinely nice.

'Thanks a lot,' uttered Asher. His tone was downbeat. He did not care about the special attention, he still would have loved to have sat beside his dad, Mike, even if he did not yet know who he was.

Taking a seat, Asher placed his head back in a leather chair. He ruffled his hands through a popcorn box. He could see the stage through a pane of transparent glass as he sat in a VIP box. 'Wow!' He watched as the arena lights dimmed. 'This was it!' he thought.

'Going down, down, down, all the way down, you're out of luck, you're out of time…' Razor Ryan burst onto the stage with his 1978, custom-made, Diamond Dazzler electric guitar in hand. He sang into the microphone before ripping into an electrifying guitar solo. As he did, a multitude of different coloured lights came alive above him, like a rainbow.

Besides Razor Ryan was Slick Rick Nelson. Impressively, he held a five-neck guitar. He was known for wielding such guitars, guitars that would break a lesser musician.

Next to Rick Nelson was Tommy Keithley, the band's bass guitarist. His fingers danced upon his instrument, creating magic. Twang! Twang! J-rang!

All the while providing the rhythm and beat, Bob Moore Jr. smashed away upon his drums in the back. Bata boom! Boom! Boom!

All four members of the band were dressed in all black police uniforms. The police uniforms were ripped-up versions of course, with ripped sleeves, loosely hanging ties, and baggy pants. The four band members also wore black military style boots. The attire was the very same uniforms the band had worn, as imprinted upon their 1983, worldwide-acclaimed album, 'Against the Rule of Law.' Razor Ryan, though, was the only one to be wearing a riot police helmet.

The thousands of onlooking spectators went wild. Like waves in the ocean, a ripple effect happened as the onlooking fans stood up.

'Go Razor, go,' shouted Asher. He spilled his popcorn as he jumped from his seat. He was truly living the dream. He could feel the rush, the sounds of the music, the connection. It was his idols up on stage.

'Well, well, in all my many millennia I've never come across a situation quite like this,' said Aarus. 'The energy, the wildness, the chaos, I like it.' He approved of The Magic Masons.

'Dad!' Observing from the VIP area, Asher could see that Mike, too, was having a magical time. He jumped up and down wildly. Taking off his black leather coat, he twirled it around his head. He was without care. He sat below the VIP box, five rows down.

The Magic Masons blasted out song after song. They were a well-oiled machine. They played one song titled 'Fearsome,' then another titled 'No More Chores.' The song list included all their biggest hits.

'Oh boy, this has been one of the best days of my life,' expressed Asher. He could have listened to The Magic Masons all night, but of course, the lively performance had to end sometime. He watched the show end as Razor Ryan dropped to his knees to an avalanche of cheers.

'Hopelessly I wait, hopelessly I wait for all of time to see you once again…' Razor Ryan finished the night on yet another chartbuster, entitled 'Hopelessly.'

'Imagine if Ben could've seen this,' said Asher. He thought Ben would have appreciated The Magic Masons, even despite his preference for modern pop music.

'You'll be able to show him when you play at the music thing, the…' Aarus had a lapse in memory.

'Don't you mean the talent show?' asked Asher. He receded into his seat. His mood took a dip, he remembered what had happened to his guitar. He remembered that the vicious bully, Tom Watson, had broken it.

'Yes, the talent show,' affirmed Aarus. 'Oh, but I forgot, Ash, you have no instrument. What an absolute pity.'

'Don't remind me,' moaned Asher. He had hoped to play The Magic Masons' biggest hit, 'Going Down,' at the talent show. 'Never mind, let's go.' He watched as the stadium began to empty. He quickly rose to his feet in the search for his dad.

'Watch out!' warned Aarus.

Splashhh! 'Oh no,' groaned Asher. He was too fast, too clumsy. He was covered in orange lemonade, the liquid seeped through the green shirt that he wore.

'I did my utmost to warn you,' said Aarus. 'Oh well,' he said.

'Sorry, little guy,' apologised Joe. 'Didn't mean to soak you,' he said. Unintentionally, he spilled the large drink that he had held. 'I came to escort you outside the building,' he added.

'I'm all sticky,' said Asher. It was not the first sticky situation he had gotten himself into. Ever since he found Soulkeeper, the sticky situations had been getting more frequent.

'Um…' Joe paused in consideration for a moment. 'I can't let you go like that,' he said.

After another sincere apology, Joe escorted him backstage. 'Wait here, I'll try to get my hands on some old merchandise lying around that you can have, then you can be on your way,' he said.

'See anything you like?' asked Aarus. His tone was mischievous.

'Goodness!' Asher spotted a lot of equipment, a set of drums, amps, and a V-shaped guitar of slender white and black trim. He was overcome with sheer fascination. 'Cool guitar, it looks familiar,' he said.

'It's a one-of-a-kind, custom-made, nineteen seventy-five, six-stringed, named The Rattler,' informed Joe. 'It has been touched by some of the greats, even Razor Ryan himself.'

'Razor Ryan!' boomed Asher. His memory was jogged. 'Wait, this guitar is on the poster in my room,' he said. He could not believe it.

'Sure, this is The Magic Masons' equipment,' added Joe. 'Oh, I'll be back in a minute.' He refocused his attention on the task he had yet to complete.

'I just have to,' said Asher, giving in to the temptation. Left to his own devices, he could not resist the urge. He had to take a closer look at The Rattler. He was enchanted by the superb instrument. He outstretched his fingers.

'Easy, please don't touch,' stated Joe. 'Break that guitar, and it's my neck,' he continued. He had returned with a Magic Masons shirt. 'Here, I promised you this.' He handed the shirt to Asher.

'Cool, it's signed,' said Asher, pleased. 'Thank you,' he said. He looked at the image on the shirt, which had Razor Ryan on the front. He wore a white police uniform and a police cap with a silver star.

'Here is a bottle of water, and some tissue,' said Joe. 'It's the best I can do, clean yourself up, everyone has almost left the stadium,' he said. He informed Asher as politely as possible that he was outstaying his welcome.

'Joe, are you free?' Another member of security had shown up, to Joe's distraction.

'Yes, Garret,' responded Joe.

'The boss wants a quick word,' informed Garret. 'He asked for the head of security,' he said.

'I'll be back in a minute,' said Joe. 'Be ready to go, and for the love of god, don't touch a thing,' he said.

'Sure,' said Asher. He crossed his fingers behind his back, he was not being entirely truthful. He watched as Joe and Garret left, and he then took to inspecting the 'Rattler,' once more. Glee filled his diamond-shaped face. His eyes shone brighter than two sapphires.

He removed his long-sleeved, green shirt, he then put a dribble of water upon a tissue before wiping his sticky skin. Another dribble of water, and he began cleaning the precious bracelet upon his scrawny arm. Thankfully, the security guard, Joe, had not noticed the jewel.

He put on the shirt signed by Razor Ryan. He then wrapped his fingers around the frets of The Rattler, he felt a rush of adrenaline. 'Touched by Razor Ryan!' His imagination had taken a rollercoaster ride, and he did not want to get off.

'This is great.' Asher plucked on The Rattlers' worn strings. 'Wish I could bring this home.' He could not help but think that the beautiful guitar would nullify his talent show problems. 'With this, I could win,' he said.

'Indulge in your desires, Ash,' informed Aarus. 'No one is watching, take it,' he continued.

'Take it!' Tempted, Asher thought upon the suggestion. 'No, no, I can't, that's stealing.' He knew that it would be wrong to simply take the guitar.

'Don't you want to take it home?' asked Aarus. 'Think of it,' he said.

'Yes, I do want to take it home,' admitted Asher. He wanted more than anything to bring The Rattler home with him.

'Besides, it's only stealing if you're caught,' said Aarus. 'Time to leave, I think, servo mius volantateium.'

'Arghhh!' Head in the clouds, Asher was swiftly brought crashing back to Earth. He suddenly felt the burning sensation on his wrist again. The bright blue light surged from Soulkeeper once more. The energetic force opened into a swirling pool of blue. Glass-like shards broke inward.

'Helppp!' he screeched. The Rattler was still in his grasp. For all his resistance, it was no use. He was taken once more. He watched as the light retracted; the portal closed. He felt the blue energy all around his body, and just as before, the light grew unbearably bright, forcing his pink eyelids shut.

Soon, he found himself lying atop a wet, grassy surface. Opening his eyes, he looked up at the pale moon. 'I'll never get used to that,' he said. He was back at his grandmother's house. It was still pitch-black, and the rain was still pouring down heavily.

'What…what's this?' He felt a glossy picture land upon his face. He took hold of it. Stunned, he perceptively noticed that it was the photograph that his dad had taken at The Magic Masons' concert, their Raging Journey Tour. The concert he had just seen with his own two eyes. A sly smirk appeared on his face. 'Well, at least I got it,' he said.

'That's not all you have,' said Aarus. 'Take a look behind you, Ash,' he said.

Arising to his feet, Asher was gobsmacked as he turned around. 'No way!' He could not believe it, a superb, slender white and black guitar, The Rattler, rested in the mud, but only a few feet from where he stood. He had taken the instrument through the portal with him.

He didn't hang about to question himself, the rain was beating down upon the beautiful guitar, which lay in the dirt. 'I'll take that,' he said, with delight. He rushed forward to retrieve the instrument before sneaking into the old, wood-built house through the back door. He was not going to knock on the front door. His grandmother would have made mincemeat of him.

'Rufff!'

'Shush, Scruffy,' whispered Asher. He squeezed past the big, fluffy dog. It rested upon a blanket at the back door. He was almost done for. Almost!

He somehow managed to sneak up the stairs and into the seclusion of his bedroom, without detection. There he spent the best part of twenty minutes cleaning The Rattler, before fading off to sleep with a heart filled with sheer excitement.

-Chapter 17-

The Rattler

Ratta tat tat! Ratta tat tat! Ratta tat tat! The next morning, Asher awoke to hear a continuous, loud knocking sound at the front door. 'Who is making that racket?' Blankets tossed aside, he hurried toward the window to inspect the cause of the commotion. 'Ben!' Reality quickly struck; he was about to be late for school, yet again. He had been late several times this term alone.

'Hold your horses,' blasted Nancey. She shuffled from the living room to the hall.

In a hurry, Asher rustled about his bedroom. Thump! 'Ouch!' He accidentally slammed his big toe against The Rattler. 'It wasn't a dream!' His mouth lay agape. He lifted the white and black, slender, custom-made guitar. He was instantly reminded of events that had occurred the night before. He had indeed been at one of The Magic Masons' concerts, more specifically, the concert that had taken place on Saturday, the 19th of September 1987.

'Holy smoke, The Rattler, it's mine!' He was elated. 'Yes,' he boomed with joy.

'Ahemmm! There's no need to thank me, Ash,' interjected Aarus. 'I suppose all these favours I'm doing for you are getting taken for granted.' His tone was such that it was clear he was looking for a little gratitude to be shown.

'Yes…yes of course, thank you really,' spluttered Asher. 'I don't know what I would do without you, I owe you a lot,' he said.

'Don't forget that either,' replied Aarus. 'When the time comes, that is.' His tone grew stern.

'Asher, your friend is here,' shouted Nancy. She stood by the front door of the old wood-built house. Giving Ben a cold stare, she pulled her cardigan tight. 'Hurry, you're letting the heat out,' she moaned. Her old bones felt the bitterness of the cold morning.

'I'll be down in a minute, Gran,' yelled Asher in response. Attention refocused, he quickly managed to get dressed. He put on a blue shirt, blue jeans, and white trainers. He then enclosed The Rattler within the black guitar bag, the very one that his old, broken instrument had once occupied, and he was off. Bumpety! Bumpety! Bump! He zoomed off down the stairs. He stormed into the kitchen he put on his coat.

'You stay out of trouble,' screeched Nancy. She failed to take note of his new instrument.

'Life is nothing without a little mischief,' said Aarus.

'We're late,' informed Ben. He stood impatiently waiting by the old oak door. He had done so for more than ten whole minutes.

'Well, let's not stick around to argue about it,' said Asher. He sprang out of the front door like a frog. He had no time to complete his usual morning ritual. He had no time to brush his teeth, nor comb his thick black hair.

'Easy for you to say,' replied Ben. 'I was given a right telling off for apparently knocking on the front door too hard,' he said.

Quickly, both Asher and Ben disappeared down the street with haste. Soon, they arrived at Neptunica Middle School. The bell had already gone.

'We're almost there,' said Asher. He could see four yellow school buses parked at the front of the building, which were empty of students.

'I…I need a drink of water,' wheezed Ben. He had exhausted himself. He panted heavily.

'Just hurry,' said Asher. He had tangled with the rules in Principal Smith's big red book once too often. Especially rule nine.

Both Asher and Ben made their way up a set of cobblestoned steps, leading to the entrance of the old, whitewashed building. But they were intercepted before they could enter!

Exiting the doors was Principal Emmanuel Smith himself. 'Late again. You two, see me later,' he instructed. He wiped his black framed, oval-shaped glasses with a hanky before putting them on. He then tapped on his watch. 'Fifteen minutes, I've warned you so many times, Mr Paterson,' he said.

'Come on,' groaned Ben. He was frustrated.

'Do we have a problem, Mr Wilson?' asked Principal Smith. He radiated a stern resolve. His hands fell to his hips. His gaze of judgement almost burned a hole straight through Ben.

'No…no not at all,' gulped Ben. He felt a great uneasiness wash over him.

'Well then, get to class,' instructed Principal Smith. He snapped his fingers before pointing at the big brown doors that led to the inside of the building. 'The school rules bend for no one,' he alluded.

'Yes, sir,' said Ben. The last thing he wanted to do was get into an argument that he could not possibly win.

'Oh, and appearance is everything, Mr Paterson,' said Principal Smith. He ran a hand through his own, neat black hair, which had a few grey streaks and was very thin at the top. 'Last night must have been quite the musical affair!' he winked.

'Excuse me,' gulped Asher. He thought there was no way that Principal Smith was alluding to his time-travelling affairs at The Magic Mason's concert of nineteen eighty-seven.

'I mean you must've been practicing hard for the talent show,' said Principal Smith. He smiled softly. 'You never give up, do you?' he added.

'Oh…oh yes, sir, I was practicing all last night,' replied Asher. He patted his hair, which was sticking out in every direction.

'Good, now get going,'' said Principal Smith. He had other matters to address, like the running of a busy school.

As instructed, Asher and Ben made haste towards their first class of the day, which was mathematics, with Miss Hamilton. The young teacher was as cheerful as always.

'Nice to see you all this fine morning, now please open page two hundred and twenty-two,' said Miss Hamilton. 'We shall do some equations,' she said.

'Yes, miss.' Asher manoeuvred through his textbook. He had grown to enjoy math.

Not too serious in her ways, Miss Hamilton always managed to teach the lesson with a sense of fun and enthusiasm, plus she was always super helpful. 'Solve problems one to six,' she informed the class. She put her hand up, as her usual radiant smile sprang to her face. 'Remember, any difficulties, just raise your hand,' she added.

Mathematics with Miss Hamilton was followed by science with Mr Woods, which in turn was followed by history with Mr McNulty. Proceeding lunch was a further three lessons, art, geography, and English.

End of school day, swiftly arriving, Asher hastened toward the music room. Simply put, he could not wait to wrap his nimble fingers around the perfectly tuned guitar that he carried. He was relieved, having The Rattler meant he could still participate in the talent show.

He pounced through the door of the music room, heads quickly turned his way. He knew something was going on.

'Asher, you're just the person we wanted to see,' informed Mr McGrath. He was full of energy as he skipped across the room. 'Come in, come in,' he said. He put his hands around Asher's shoulders.

'What's going on?' asked Asher. He was directed toward the front of the room.

'Hello.' Mr Martín Garcia smiled as he greeted Asher. He wore a grey blazer, white shirt, and cream pants. He was the head of the music department. He had round, beady eyes and a goatee. He was also partially bald. 'I'm just confirming who'll be participating in the Rising Star Talent Show. I do believe that you're one of the lucky few, is that right?' he asked.

'Yes…yes, sir,' answered Asher. He nodded enthusiastically.

'Wonderful, that makes seven acts so far,' stated Mr Garcia. He scribbled away on a piece of paper, adding Asher's name to the list that he had constructed. His list contained the names of all the participants.

'Who are the seven?' asked Asher. He was a little curious.

'Well, let's see,' said Mr Garcia. 'Including you, there are Alex, Rebecca, Antonio, Susie, and two groups,' he alluded.

'Two groups,' said Asher. His tone urged further explanation.

'Yes, two groups,' informed Mr Garcia. 'One group of three, Lucía, Colleen, and Deion, the other a group of four, John, Malcolm, Tom, and Peter,' he said.

'Tom!' boomed Asher. He was shaken to the core, as surprise washed over his face.

'Yes, Tom Watson,' confirmed Mr Garcia. 'A bit of a late entry. He and his group joined just yesterday,' he said.

'Can't…can't be,' muttered Asher shakily. 'But some of the entrants are not a part of the music class,' he alluded. He did not understand. He had thought that the talent show was open only to those who attended after-school music class.

'It doesn't matter. The talent show is open to all,' said Mr Garcia. 'Besides, those who do not attend music class have been assessed separately. I oversaw two screenings yesterday, Antonio and the group consisting of Tom, Malcom, John, and Peter.'

Gobsmacked, Asher could do nothing. His nemesis would be in the talent show.

'This is bittersweet,' interjected Aarus. 'Now we know why the ginger-haired human broke your other stringed instrument, Ash,' he said.

'It makes perfect sense,' said Asher. He was responding to Aarus but spoke aloud, meaning all could hear him. It had been just yesterday that Tom had broken his guitar. The very one he had received as a Christmas present two years back from his dad.

'It does make sense, now I'll be off then,' said Mr Garcia. With the talent show sorted, he had other matters to attend to.

'I smell a conflict brewing,' said Aarus. 'Well, at least a small clash.' He had a nose for trouble. Indeed, he seemed to revel in it.

'Let's begin practice,' informed Mr McGrath. He clapped his hands. 'Everyone to their seat,' he instructed. He was eager to begin the lesson. He understood that there was no time to lose; the talent show was fast approaching.

'Yes, sir,' said Asher. He opened his guitar bag to reveal his newly acquired slender white and black guitar.

'Goodness me! That is a fine piece of equipment,' stated Mr McGrath. 'If you don't mind me asking, where did you get it?' he said. He could tell straight away that it was no cheap instrument.

'Think fast, Ash,' said Aarus. 'You can't tell him the truth,' he added.

'It was a present from my dad,' replied Asher. His teeth caressed his bottom lip, and he thought out his story, putting the pieces together like a jigsaw. 'It was his. He was in a band, The Black Thorns,' he said.

'I see, is he a musician then?' asked Mr McGrath. 'Talent clearly runs in the family,' he said.

'He was, but that was a long time ago,' informed Asher. 'He's now an archaeologist working in the Valley of the Kings, near Luxor,' he said.

'Very quick,' said Aarus. 'You are getting very good at this.' Of course, he was referring to Asher's growing ability to get out of troubling situations.

'Egypt's a wonderful country, culturally rich,' said Mr McGrath. 'Been once myself, Cairo to be precise, it is truly a beautiful place.'

'Yes, Egypt is great,' said Asher. His head bobbed up and down in agreement.

'While visiting Tahrir Square, both me and the wife saw the stunning Egyptian Museum, and a trove of antiquities including the royal mummies of old, and even gilded Tutankhamun artefacts,' stated Mr McGrath.

'No way!' gasped Asher. 'My Dad and I visited Tutankhamun's tomb, while in the Valley of the Kings, it was awesome.' In truth, he hoped his dad would keep his promise and that he would be back in Egypt soon.

'Almost as stunning as that guitar, now let's practice,' said Mr McGrath.

It was just two weeks until the big show, and Asher knew he had to brush up on his guitar skills and fast. He spent the next hour or so harnessing his skill. He was very pleased, the new instrument sounded great. 'G, D, C, A, G…' he whispered, as his fingers worked their way from one chord to the next in cohesion.

'That's just swell,' said Mr McGrath, sticking his thumbs up in approval. 'You get better every day,' he complimented.

'Thanks, sir, I've been practicing a lot,' said Asher. He had truly been putting in the work.

'Oh, look at the time,' said Mr McGrath as he gazed at his watch, which had a bright yellow strap. He had gotten carried away; the lesson had exceeded the scheduled time.

'Good to see you, bud.' Ben straddled into the music room, looking rather pleased with himself. 'You should have seen us today, the game went right down to the wire, but we won, the Neptunica Stingrays sting once again,' he spoke with glee. He rotated his left arm. 'Nothing can stop this cannon.' His ego was inflated.

The baseball game had been scheduled to begin during school hours and had lasted just over two hours. It showed, too, Ben looked beat.

'That's great,' congratulated Asher.

'Don't leave me hanging,' said Ben. He extended his left hand high.

Clap! Jubilantly, Asher met the gesture with a left of his own.

The pair then clasped their palms together. Then, sequentially, fingers slid away to conclude the handshake.

'Are you ready to go then?' asked Ben. Having changed out of his dirty baseball uniform, he wore a red t-shirt, jeans, and trainers.

'I sure am,' answered Asher. 'Just give me a minute to pack up,' he said.

'Who did you steal that from?' gasped Ben. 'That's superb, not like that old piece of garbage you had,' he said. He spotted The Rattler for the first time.

'I…I didn't steal it,' said Asher uneasily. 'It was my dad's.'

'Relax, I was joking,' said Ben. He patted Asher on the back. 'You take everything too seriously,' he said.

'Don't forget to change those strings,' informed Mr McGrath. 'They look a bit worn,' he said. He had a keen eye for detail.

'Yes, sir,' answered Asher. He grabbed his things and headed for the door.

Both Asher and Ben strode down the long corridor of Neptunica Middle School. They jabbered as they went, until they spotted Tom Watson and Conor Murphy. The pair stood at the end of the long hall. The vipers were ready to strike their prey.

'That'll be for us then,' said Ben. 'What are they even doing here? School finished over an hour ago.' His radiant mood swiftly sank.

'This is your chance, Ash,' Aarus said. 'It's time for revenge.' His intentions were clear. He seemed gleeful at the prospect of a full-on confrontation.

'I believe they're waiting for me. You don't have to be a part of this, Ben,' said Asher. 'It's me they detest.' He trudged forward toward his impending doom, knowing that his fate was inevitable.

'Let anger fill you, let it drive you to overcome those who would do you wrong,' said Aarus. He could sense that Asher had already given up. 'Fight, seize the moment.' He seemed to like the prospect of conflict a little too much.

'Leave me alone,' snapped Asher. On the other hand, conflict had always been something that he had tried to avoid at all costs.

'You have to be joking,' said Ben. 'We're both in it up to our necks.' He followed Asher in close pursuit.

'Hey, what kept you? We've been waiting,' sneered Tom. His sly grin was patronising. He was up to no good, as per usual.

'Clear off,' barked Ben. He was bold, yet the sweat on his perspiring forehead told that he was not completely free of fear.

'Don't let others fight your battles,' continued Aarus. He was pressing Asher hard. 'Take matters into your own hands. You're on your own. No one cares for you...you…' He could not let it go. He had a superiority complex.

'Stop!' snapped Asher. He was loud. He was growing annoyed at Aarus. But his annoyance was inadvertently deflected toward the school bullies.

'Sure thing,' said Tom. 'Step aside, Murph,' he ordered his lackey.

The big brute did as commanded. With a grunt, he moved out of the way.

'Just put the finishing touches to it, what do you think?' queried Tom. He banged his palm on Asher's locker. 'Murph and I took a little trip to the art storeroom,' he said.

'Do something, Ash,' roared Aarus. He was losing control.

'You're a fool,' boomed Asher. His locker was covered in paint. He grew deeply irritated at the sight.

'That's it, that's it,' said Aarus. 'A little spark is all it takes,' he said.

'Well, well, well, look who's talking back. I thought you had no bottle, Paterson,' said Tom. He pointed his finger at Asher's face. 'I told you it would be ten times worse if you called me names,' he said.

'Let me at him,' growled Conor. He clinched his fists, ready to strike.

'Hit the ginger one in the snout,' spoke Aarus with wicked intent. 'Before the big one gets involved.' He was spurring Asher on. He was hungry for the fight. It was like he fed on all the anger and rage, all the chaos that was unfolding.

'I suppose the two of you think that you're tough guys,' said Asher. 'You're nothing but bullies.' His blue eyes narrowed in anger. His jawline tightened. His diamond-shaped face was filled with fury.

'Trust me,' Aarus told. 'I know the squealers, hit the ginger one and the other will run,' he said.

'Shut your mouth.' Caught off guard, Tom was shocked by the defiance on display. He was not used to Asher being so bold.

'Or what?' replied Asher. He showed a fierce tenacity, a newfound tenacity.

'Let him have it, Murph,' said Tom. He was unwilling to get his own hands dirty.

Thud! Thud! Thud! Obedient, Conor moved in, foaming at the mouth, he was all too ready and willing to put a hurting on Asher.

'See, now it is too late,' said Aarus.

'What do you think you're playing at?' Boom! Ben charged shoulder-first into the devilish Conor Murphy, pushing him back and almost off his feet.

'Stay out of this,' growled Tom. He shook his fist.

'No way,' yelled Ben. His resolve had hardened immensely, made so by Asher's show of courage.

'Well, well, I see your bodyguard is saving the day once more,' said Aarus. He continued to provoke Asher, spurring him to act.

'I see that you got a new guitar there, maybe we should have a closer look at it,' said Tom. He eyed the guitar bag hanging over Asher's shoulder.

'Sounds about right,' said Conor. Regaining his footing, he charged for the precious instrument like a raging bull.

'Hands off,' boomed Asher. He could not avoid the big brute.

'Give me it,' shouted Conor. He put his hands on Asher, gripping him by the coat. He was used to getting his way. He intimidated others with effortless ease.

'Leave him be,' said Ben. He took hold of Conor's arm, only to be pushed against a locker. He hit the locker hard with a thump. Holding the back of his head, he took quite a bump.

'I said give it here,' growled Conor. He raised a fist. He was intent on causing further harm.

'No way,' resisted Asher. He was insistent on putting up a fight. Then it unexpectedly happened! Zoom! An aura of blue sent the big brute crashing to the floor in a heap.

'He pushed me, he pushed me,' moaned Conor. He squirmed wildly on the ground.

'I believe I did mention the protection enchantment that The Horned Order placed on Soulkeeper. Oh well,' said Aarus flippantly. He knew exactly what would happen if someone attacked Asher. 'Now watch the ginger one,' he said.

'Hey,' snapped Tom. He was unsure of exactly what had just happened. He moved forward, fists clenched.

'Go for it, if you think you can,' said Asher. He was angry, angrier than he had ever been. His voice carried along the corridor. He raised his right fist, fully prepared to strike.

'Well, I...' Tom stopped dead in his tracks. He took to recalculating his situation. Fear bubbled away at him under the surface. For the first time, he was truly scared of Asher. He saw Conor drop like a ton of bricks.

'Look into his eyes, the gateway to the soul, do you see that?' stated Aarus. 'That is pure fear, now finish it!' He was pushing extremely hard.

'Easy Ash, easy bud,' said Ben. 'Cool the jets.' He put a hand on Asher's shoulder. 'He's not worth it.' He was shocked more than anything, having never seen Asher so unhinged.

'Don't listen, hit him,' said Aarus. He was full of malice.

'Both of you get out of my head,' shouted Asher. He was being torn in two directions. He was torn between Ben and Aarus's words.

'What is going on here?' It was Principal Smith. He hastened down the corridor toward the upheaval. He was attracted by all the noise. 'What is going on?'' He repeated.

'Um…nothing, sir, we were talking,' lied Tom. He was glad to see Principal Smith for a change.

'Yes, and pigs fly too,' said Principal Smith sarcastically. 'Then what happened to him?' He pointed to Conor Murphy, who was still lying on the floor.

'Murph fell accidentally,' said Tom. 'Isn't that so, Murph?'

'Fell sir, fell,' screeched Conor. He struggled to get to his feet, his gut weighed him down.

'Get up,' said Tom. He helped Conor to his feet, if only to save face.

'Hmmm…I see,' said Principal Smith. 'What about this locker, did it vandalise itself?'

'Yes, I mean no!' Tongue-tied, Tom found himself entangled in knots. He had walked blindly into a pit of quicksand, and he was sinking fast.

'Well, which is it, yes or no?' questioned Principal Smith. Like a locksmith, he picked away to unlock the lies, sort of speak.

'We didn't mean to do it,' interjected Conor. He was a gullible fool. He had admitted where the fault lay.

'Shut it, you idiot,' snapped Tom. With his elbow, he nudged Conor to render him quiet.

'Enough!' Principal Smith had snapped. 'You two make your way to my office now,' he demanded. He had lost his cool.

'But…but sir.' Red-faced, Tom squabbled under the pressure he now found himself engulfed by.

'Now,' said Principal Smith. He pointed to a room at the end of the hall.

Both did as they were told; neither Tom nor Conor dared to protest any further. They were deep in it.

'I was expecting both of you,' said Principal Smith. He turned his focus to Asher and Ben.

'Apologies, chief, we were…' Ben did not get the chance to explain himself.

'I know Mr Wilson, a very impressive win today,' complimented Principal Smith. 'You have talent. That left arm will find its way to the major league one day,' he added.

'Thanks, chief,' replied Ben. He had a grin from ear to ear.

'I was in music…' Similarly, to Ben, Asher too was interjected.

'In music class,' said Principal Smith. 'That new instrument does you credit,' he said.

'Thanks, sir,' replied Asher. He looked rather confused as to how the school principal knew about The Rattler. 'About being late this morning…'

'Well, that hardly matters now,' intercepted Principal Smith. 'I have these two to deal with now, you got lucky,' he said. He straightened his tie.

'Lucky…' Asher was not exactly sure what Principal Smith meant.

'Yes! Lucky,' replied Principal Smith. 'The only rule that trumps rule nine is rule one, no bullying. I have got eyes, those two are wicked.' He tapped on Asher's locker. He then shook his head. 'I do hope that they change their ways and repent,' he added.

'So, just to clarify, can we go?' queried Ben. He could hardly believe that they were being let off the hook.

'Yes, I've got my hands full,' answered Principal Smith. 'Now go, before I change my mind,' he said.

'Yes, sir,' stated Asher.

'Oh, two more things,' said Principal Smith. He held up two fingers. 'Firstly, anger is a vice that leads to damnation. Keep that anger in check, Mr Paterson,' he advised.

'Yes, sir.' Asher nodded, agreeing. His anger had gotten the better of him.

'Secondly, be careful of new friends. They may not be all that they seem!' said Principal Smith. With his final bit of advice given, he headed toward his office.

'Sir, excuse me…' Asher was baffled. New instrument, new friend, did the school principal know more than he was letting on? he thought.

'Get going, Mr Paterson, you too, Mr Wilson,' said Principal Smith. He closed his office door as he entered.

'Let's go, bud,' suggested Ben. He did not want to hang about in the school corridor.

Soon, both Asher and Ben were gone. They exited the big brown rectangular doors to the front of the school, before descending several steps.

'What happened back there? I've never known you to stand up to Tom like that,' said Ben with surprise. He simply could not hold in his amazement any longer.

'Well, bullies like him and Bronislav only get away with it if no one stands up to them,' replied Asher. He could not help but feel pleased. He had taken a stand.

'Who's Bronislav?' asked Ben. He was puzzled. The past two weeks or so, he had heard quite a bit about Egypt, tombs, the River Nile, and Luxor, but not a man named Bronislav.

'Oh, that doesn't matter,' said Asher. 'All that matters is that those two are finally getting what they deserve.' A smile simmered on his face.

'Amen,' agreed Ben. 'But I think you went a little too far,' he said. He agreed with Principal Emmanuel Smith. He had never seen Asher so embroiled in anger.

'Ash, whose side is your friend on?' questioned Aarus. He was manipulating Asher.

'They deserved it,' snapped Asher through gritted teeth. 'Besides, whose friend are you anyway, mine or theirs?' he asked. He looked Ben in the eyes. His face filled with anger once more.

'I've known you since kindergarten,' said Ben. 'I've always stood by you, even when being your friend meant a target being placed on my back.' He placed a hand upon Asher's shoulder. 'But I've never seen you get that angry,' he said.

'Anger leads to chaos, and chaos can be used to stomp your enemies into oblivion,' said Aarus. He was a little dark in his philosophical outlook.

'That's not me,' said Asher softly. 'I don't want to hurt anyone,' he said. He reflected upon Aarus's words. He shook his head.

'Now, hey, I didn't say you can't stand up for yourself,' said Ben. 'But there is a time, place, and way to go about things.' He took his blue inhaler from his pocket, he took a puff. He took a deep breath, closing his mouth, before breathing out through his nose.

'Who rolled over and died to make you so wise?' asked Asher. He listened carefully. He found a lot of wisdom in Ben's words.

'Now listen, you may do better than me in tests and pop quizzes, but remember...' Ben fell silent.

'Remember what?' asked Asher.

'Remember that is because I let you,' replied Ben. 'I don't want to make you look bad.' He burst into laughter.

'That's good jackass,' said Asher. He, too, began to laugh.

Returning home, Asher spent all night practicing his song for the Rising Star Talent Show. He spent the next couple of nights practicing. His big fluffy dog, Scruffy, and of course Aarus, were his only audience.

'Exquisite Ash,' praised Aarus. 'There's no stopping you now,' he said.

The song he had chosen was 'Going Down,' by The Magic Masons, as intended. A fitting tribute, he thought, seeing that the song would be played on The Rattler, as done by his idol Razor Ryan himself.

'Going down, down, down, all the way down, you're out of luck, you're out of time…'

Twang! Jang! J-rang! His fingers burst along the frets of the V-shaped guitar before his lips cracked open once more. 'Lightning strikes through the air, as the one you love lies in despair, there isn't one thing she will hear, for her heart has been torn as the smoke begins to clear…'

It was like the instrument possessed a kind of magic!

Over the next two weeks leading up to the Rising Star Talent Show, the seven billed acts had each been given a test run. At Asher's rehearsal, Mr Garcia was truly awestruck. 'Very impressive,' were his exact words.

Each of the seven acts to perform had been given a separate rehearsal. The talent show was a competition after all. There was even a trophy for the winning act.

-Chapter 18-

Rising Star Talent Show

With the big day finally upon him, Asher was as ready as he was ever going to be. 'This is it.' His feelings were playing havoc. He was excited, yet fearful. He knew that everyone from Neptunica Middle School would likely be at the talent show.

'Don't worry, you couldn't be any worse than Tom,' said Ben. He waited by Asher's bedroom door. He was there to accompany his emotional friend to the much-anticipated event. He was the moral support, just as Asher had been for him during baseball tryouts at the start of the year.

'I suppose you're right,' agreed Asher. 'He's only participating to get one over on me,' he said. He assumed, like Ben, that Tom would be dreadful. He had never known him to be into music. He did not even know that Tom would be a part of the talent show until Mr Martín Garcia had highlighted the fact.

He polished The Rattler down before placing it in his guitar bag. 'Let's go, Ben,' he said. He had to hurry, as usual, he was running late. 'Oops, almost forgot!' He opened the second drawer of his bedside dresser. 'I couldn't do this without you, Mum,' he said. He placed her picture in his back pocket.

Asher hurried down the stairs toward the front door, he could see that his grandmother was already prepared. She wore a knitted lilac hat, a woollen coat, and held a flowery handbag. A grin resided upon her aged face.

'Are you coming to the talent show, Gran?' sighed Asher. He was not enthused by the prospect.

'I wouldn't miss this. All the parents are going to be there,' said Nancy. She was missing a night at the bingo to attend. 'I spoke to that nice man, Emmanuel, he called to say you were having some trouble at school,' she explained.

'That's not true, my parents are not going to be there,' whispered Asher sullenly. His Dad would be absent. To boot, he never knew what having a mother felt like, just that not having a mother was horrible. He pulled open the front door. Creakkk! He was met by a stiff, cold breeze.

'Wait, hold your horses,' said Nancy. 'I almost forgot there is a parcel on the kitchen table for you,' she said.

'Gran!' screeched Asher. 'We're running late,' he said. He rushed into the kitchen before ripping open the brown wrapped parcel. He found inside a Magic Mason's guitar strap and guitar picks, with a letter that his dad, Mike, had sent from Egypt. He began reading:

Dear Asher,

Sorry, I couldn't be there for the big show, but I know you'll be great. I know that I haven't been around much, but I promise I will make it up to you, lad. I know your mum would have loved to have been there, God rest her soul. She'd have been as proud of you as I am.

P.S.

Love dad, good luck, and give'em hell. Enjoy the gift that I promised!

'I love you, Dad,' whispered Asher. He held the letter tightly in his grasp; the words his dad had written had meant a great deal to him. He wiped his teary eyes. He put the letter on the kitchen table, and he then quickly hurried back toward the door. 'Let's go,' he instructed.

A little over ten minutes later, Asher, Ben, and Nancy had arrived at Neptunica Middle School. All three hurried inside and not a second too soon. The Rising Star Talent Show had already begun!

'You'd be late to your death burial,' said Aarus. 'Make haste,' he said.

'Quick, this way,' instructed Asher. Suddenly, as he was making his way down the school corridor, a sea of lively music washed over him. His ears were pleasantly appeased by what they were hearing. 'Wow! That sounds great, sounds like an angel,' he said, admiringly.

'It sure does, buddy,' agreed Ben. 'That voice is something else,' he said.

'Will there be tea and biscuits?' asked Nancy. Her brown, flowery handbag swung at her side, she was going as fast as her plump legs would allow.

'After Gran,' said Asher. 'Through here.' He dashed into the overflowing assembly hall. 'No way!' Stunned, he could see that up on stage, there was none other than Tom Watson and his group.

Banging away upon the drums was Tom himself. In front of him was John Deeds, who played the bass guitar. Thirdly, Malcolm Rafferty was playing the guitar. The fourth member, however, took him by complete surprise.

'Mandy!' Asher could see that she was the band's lead singer. He was taken aback with utter horror. She stood centre stage, her long blonde hair hanging over her shoulders, as she sang to perfection. 'No, no, no!' His very foundations were shaken. His nimble hands began to tremble, and his eyes widened. A pool of sweat clung to his forehead. It affected him that, yet again, she was with his rival, that she was with such a nasty person.

'I fell victim to the poison of love's cruel grasp once, Ash,' spoke Aarus. 'Hamadrya made me feel the same way.' He could sense that Asher had feelings for Mandy. 'Alas, she was ripped from me, along with any ideals of love,' he said.

'Oh no, things have just taken a turn for the worse,' grumbled Ben. He, too, was completely bamboozled. 'Shake it off, buddy, just shake it off.' He placed his hands on Asher's lean shoulders, he tried to calm him.

'She, she, she…'

'I know, I know,' said Ben. 'Nothing for it now,' he said.

'But…but…' Asher was caught off guard.

'Snap out of it! You must get on that stage and play,' said Ben firmly. 'Besides, it's not like you two were a thing,' he said.

'Not helping,' said Asher. 'Would you say the same thing if it were Sarah up there?' he asked. His point hit home hard.

'No, no, I wouldn't,' replied Ben. He hung his head low. 'But if Mandy is with that clown, then you should forget her.' He only had Asher's best interests at heart.

'I thought she was better than that,' said Asher. He spoke softly, before shaking his head. 'She was always so nice.' He just could not get it.

'Come on, let's get backstage,' said Ben. He took hold of the guitar bag strapped around Asher's shoulder. 'We can't stand here all night.'

'Asher, you're just in time.' It was Mr McGrath. 'Quick, you're up soon.' His tone carried a sense of urgency.

'Why is Mandy Fleming on stage?' questioned Asher. He asked the question with a sigh. His motivation had deflated quicker than a flat tyre.

'A late replacement, Peter had to pull out, came down with the flu,' informed Mr McGrath. 'Now get a move on backstage,' he said.

'Yes…yes, sir,' replied Asher. His tone was downbeat, he was still bedazzled as all his nightmares sprang to life on stage.

'You heard the man, move,' ordered Ben. He was a rock, but a rock was needed in challenging times.

'Where do I sit?' asked Nancy. She made herself heard amongst the noisy audience. 'Nobody has manners anymore,' she groaned. Her feet were sore, and there were very limited seats. She was not as nimble as she used to be.

'Hello there, Mrs Branning, it's lovely to see you.' It was Principal Smith. He took the old woman by the arm. 'Just take a seat right here,' he said. He was extremely pleasant.

'Oh, thank you,' said Nancy. 'It's so rare to meet a man with manners these days,' she added.

'Mr Paterson, hold up just a second, I need to have a chat,' said Principal Smith. He rushed forward toward Asher and Ben. His black formal shoes beat against the wooden floor beneath. 'I would appreciate a bit of privacy, Mr Wilson.'

'Sure, you got it, chief,' replied Ben. He continued toward the school stage.

'I wanted to wish you luck, Mr Paterson,' said Principal Smith. He had a very grave look on his face.

'Well, thank you, sir,' answered Asher.

'I also wanted to say that whatever you do next is up to you,' said Principal Smith. 'I chose you, don't let me down.' He put his hands upon Asher's shoulders. 'You're very special!'

'Oh, Geatiric, you old fool. I see that you're up to your usual tricks!' Aarus had inclinations of his own. He believed Principal Emmanuel Smith to be a very old friend, turned nemesis. 'Hiding your true form, you thought I wouldn't notice,' he said with suspicion.

'Geatiric!' whispered Asher. He thought back to the old man whom he had met in the Valley of the Kings. He thought of the old man of his dreams, The Gatekeeper of The Portal Realm.

'Geatiric! Oh, that reminds me, I have a very important appointment to attend,' spoke Principal Smith. 'I must depart,' he added.

'Sure thing, sir,' replied Asher. Like Aarus, he was confused.

'Goodbye, Mr Paterson,' said Principal Smith. He turned to make his leave. 'Oh, just one more thing, do you remember what I said?' he asked.

'No, sir,' admitted Asher, puzzled.

'Be careful of new friends!' said Principal Smith. With those his final words, he hurried across the hall and out the doors leading to the school corridor. He seemed to be in a rush.

'Hurry up, bud,' shouted Ben. He waited impatiently.

'Yes…yes, I'm coming,' yelled Asher. His feet raced past countless rows of people. He raced up a flight of steps and backstage.

The backstage area was a mess. There were many instruments scattered about, scenery backdrops, boxes, and props.

'What now?' asked Asher. He peeked through a pair of long red curtains, he watched as Tom, Mandy, John, and Malcolm finished their performance to an avalanche of cheers.

'The way I perceive the situation, you have two choices,' said Aarus. He had to get his say in.

'Give me a minute,' said Ben. 'I'm thinking,' he said. Clicking his fingers repeatedly, he tried to produce an answer.

'We don't have a minute,' said Asher. 'Think faster!' His heart thudded like a kettle drum. 'What are my choices?' He was simultaneously speaking to both Aarus and Ben.

'Option one: face the mob,' answered Aarus. 'Or you could avoid the embarrassment,' he said. He knew exactly what he was playing at. He knew the second choice was much more appealing.

'How can I avoid the humiliation?' asked Asher. His teeth sank into his bottom lip.

'Soulkeeper!' answered Aarus. 'For alas, twice now it has benefited your desires. Your will is what Soulkeeper bends to, however, I can influence its workings just like before,' he said. He was manipulating more than just Soulkeeper.

'Um…' Asher thought about what Aarus was saying. He was proposing a way out of his current predicament. A tempting idea. 'I think that…' He was cut short by the presence of a familiar seventh grader.

'Sarah! Thank goodness,' boomed Ben with relief. He was pleased to see that it was none other than Sarah Reid. 'Help us out here, what do we do?' he asked her.

'He needs to prepare for his routine,' informed Sarah. She twisted a lock of her fuzzy, brown hair as she marched towards the red stage curtains. 'I'm surprised so many turned up,' she said as she peeked out into the crowd.

The talent show had thus far been an enormous success. Parents, aunts, uncles, friends, and students, so many had shown up to support the acts performing.

'Prepare…can you be a little more specific?' asked Ben sarcastically. He shrugged his shoulders.

'Prepare your instrument, Asher,' explained Sarah. 'I'll address the audience before I announce you up onto the stage.' She took a deep breath and then off she went. She glided across the stage.

'Ok, sure,' replied Asher. 'I'll do that,' he said.

'I'll help,' said Ben. He took The Rattler from Asher's black guitar bag. 'Hey buddy, does this need tuning?' He held the guitar in his hands.

'Um, what?' Asher's mind was obliterated by countless thoughts, he was struggling to come to terms with the fact that he had to go up on stage, and soon. He was the very next act to grace the whole school with his talents.

'Wake up!' boomed Ben. He snapped his fingers repeatedly before Asher's pale face. 'Now does your guitar need tuning?' he asked again.

'No,' answered Asher. 'I tuned it before I left home,' he said. His arms dangled by his side, and he appeared distant. He was busy looking across to the other side of the stage. 'Mandy!' He spotted her standing there. A sea of obstacles separated them. 'Tom!' Then he spotted his arch nemesis, Tom did not look all that happy as his arms flapped about. He ruthlessly had a go at his bandmates.

'You idiot,' snapped Tom. 'You messed up part of the song,' he said. He was fuming despite receiving an enormous round of applause from the audience. He had to have control, it was his nature.

'She messed up too,' the small boy named John Deeds answered back.

'Yes, you did,' barked Tom. He turned his burning focus to Mandy Fleming. 'Why did you just stand there? You made me look bad.' He began rudely pointing at her.

'Sorry,' said Mandy, looking awkward. She had frozen as the song had begun. The song itself had to be restarted. It was not a big deal either, because she sang perfectly. 'I didn't want to be here anyhow,' she said. She pushed her blonde hair back. She stood up straight. She defended herself.

'Oh, I know. You didn't want to sing because of that scar above your lip,' revealed Tom. 'You told me,' he said. He pushed too hard and too far. He was very mean to her.

'Leave her alone, you...you clown,' yelled Asher. He shouted across the stage. He could see tears welling up in Mandy's eyes. She immediately spotted him, too.

'Hey...hey...forget him,' said Ben. He finally noticed what it was that Asher was focused on. 'Leave it, it's not worth it.' He understood that there were many more pressing matters to deal with.

'Clown! Clown!' Tom looked like he was ready to blow his top. He and his band hurried off the stage. He took the steps on the opposite end of the backstage area.

'Is there anything else you need to do?' asked Ben.

'Yes, yes, there is,' replied Asher. His words spilled out slowly.

'We'll get to it,' said Ben. He was losing his cool.

'Sure, sure,' said Asher. He refocused his attention. He lifted his guitar, attaching the Magic Masons guitar strap, the very one his dad had sent him. He then put a pick between the strings. 'Oh god! What if they boo me off the stage?'

'You've practiced for hours, days, no weeks, you are ready, buddy,' answered Ben. He tried his best to instill some courage in Asher. 'You've got this,' he said.

'We could just leave,' said Asher. 'We won't be missed.'

'No way,' refused Ben. 'I believe in you, you can do this,' he said.

'Hear me now, Ash,' said Aarus. 'Save face, let's escape,' he said. He had garnered profound influence over Asher. 'If Geatiric is here, he's not in The Portal Realm. Yes, now is the perfect chance.' He had his motivations.

'I can't perform,' said Asher. 'I'll look the fool,' he said.

'Fools don't face their fears,' said Ben. 'You will.' He was trying his utmost to help.

'You'll always look the fool!' It was Conor Murphy. Abruptly, he appeared from the shadows to rudely interrupt. 'Principal Smith came down hard, four weeks detention,' he said. He knocked over a few boxes as he marched across the backstage area.

'You deserved it,' snapped Ben.

'Go away,' said Asher. He placed the Magic Mason's guitar strap over his head. He was ready to be called up on stage.

'You're a joke,' Conor insulted. He was trying his utmost to provoke a reaction. 'You're the clown,' he said. It was clear that an infuriated Tom had sent his lackey to do his bidding.

Thumppp! 'I said get the hell out of here,' roared Asher. He threw his hands against Conor's large chest, teeth clenched, cheeks red, he was tired of the intimidation, the scare tactics, the bullying. He was not taking it anymore.

'That's the spirit,' said Aarus. 'Stand your ground, stand and fight.' He was manipulative, he seemed to want Asher to act out angrily.

'Just leave us alone,' said Ben. 'If you know what's good for you.' He edged his way between Asher and Conor, defusing the situation.

'Alright, alright, have it your way,' replied Conor. He backed off.

'Right now, get out of here,' demanded Ben. He pointed at the stage exit.

'Ok, this is it,' said Asher. He took a deep breath before exhaling with a gust of unease. Foolishly, he did not wait to see Conor take his leave. He was up to no good!

The big brute was not done. Infuriated, he took hold of a red firehose! 'Hey, you have no chance of winning, you won't even make it up on stage,' he said.

'Woah, easy now, big fella, easy,' said Ben.

'Calm down,' said Asher. He set The Rattler in the corner, before raising his arms to reason with the mindless brute. 'Think about this, you'll be expelled,' he warned.

'You can't negotiate with this imbecile,' said Aarus.

'That idiot Smith will never find out,' said Conor. Clatter! Clatter! Clatter! He twisted the nozzle on the fire hose, he let loose; water erupted into a free-flowing stream.

'Nooo!' screeched Asher. Thuddd! His body crashed to the floor, he found himself lying in a pool of cold water. 'Great, this shirt was signed by Razor Ryan,' he moaned. The t-shirt he wore under his blue chequered shirt had Razor Ryan on the front. He held his Diamond Dazzler guitar and wore a white police uniform with a silver cap.

'I'll get you for this,' groaned Ben. He, too was drenched to the very core. Water seeped through his grey woollen zipper coat, red shirt, and light blue jeans.

'You two have a nice day now,' mocked Conor. Squeakkk! He twisted the nozzle on the fire hose again, stemming the flow of water, before dropping the fire hose. Thud! Thud! Thud! He then made his hasty escape. Sniggering, his gut jangled as he went.

Turning quickly, Asher could see that his slick-looking guitar, The Rattler, was fine. But how was he going to play with his clothes all soaked? he thought. 'I wish I didn't have to perform,' he sighed. He threw his arms up in despair.

'You could still escape,' suggested Aarus. 'You just have to use a little imagination,' he said. He was very convincing.

'You have to go out there,' said Ben. He wanted Asher to perform, win or lose. He knew how hard Asher had practiced the last few weeks. He believed that he deserved a chance.

'Yes, how can I get out of here?' said Asher. His fight-or-flight instincts kicked in, and he chose the latter. He was a mess. He also had the wind knocked out of his sails, having just seen Mandy perform alongside his nemesis.

'You can't leave,' said Ben. His words now fell on deaf ears.

'Do you remember The Gatekeeper and that place between worlds?' asked Aarus. 'He called it...he called it...'

'The Portal Realm,' answered Asher. He would not easily forget the place filled with beauty and wondrous things. It was a paradise. 'I wish I were there now instead of here, anywhere but here…'

'Servo mius volantateium,' said Aarus. 'Your will shall be done,' he said.

Asher barely had time to think when a familiar burning sensation began irritating his skin once again. He pulled the sleeve of his blue chequered shirt back, looking at his wrist, he could see that the bracelet had leapt into life. 'No, not again,' he grumbled. He began to shake his arm frantically. 'Aarus, what is happening?' he asked.

'This is what you wanted,' replied Aarus. It seemed he knew exactly how Soulkeeper worked!

'I need this to stop,' said Asher. He began to panic as a stream of bright blue burst from the golden jewel. He knew what was to follow.

'Remember, Ash,' said Aarus. 'You wanted to escape. I've just provided a little nudge in the right direction!'

'Stop!' whimpered Asher. It was no use; he could feel the all-too-familiar magnetic force as it started to take hold of his lean physique.

'Terra, I'm coming!' Elated, Aarus began to chuckle in the chaos of the moment. He seemed to have full awareness of what was happening. His motives were still not fully transparent to Asher.

'Somebody helppp!' cried Asher. His feet began to rise from the canvas. 'What, what the…' Just as he was dragged inward, into the portal, he felt a hand grab onto him!

-Chapter 19-

The Portal Realm

Heart pounding, Asher was taken once again without the luxury of choice. He was swallowed up by the portal. He felt a blanket of blue energy all around his small body. He was forced to shut his blue eyes as the ocean of light grew intensely bright. 'Arghhh!' Screeching in panic, he then felt himself hurtling forward.

Bump! Unceremoniously, he was tossed from the portal. He fell upon a murky, dirt-ridden canvas with a thud. 'Ouch, that hurt,' he moaned. He fell directly on his backside.

'You're telling me, bud!'

Immediately, Asher heard a familiar voice ring out. 'Ben, what are you doing here?' His fingernails bit into the dirt as he got to his knees. He gazed at a dazed Ben in surprise.

'Oh, my head, that was some ride,' groaned Ben. 'I think I'm going to be sick,' he said. He was feeling dizzy, his hands caressed his plump tummy. His dirty fair hair resembled a bird's nest. His plump cheeks were rosy.

'Ben!' said Asher. He placed his hands around Ben's shoulders, he shook him to gain his attention.

'Yes…yes, what is it?' asked Ben. Regaining his senses, his hazel eyes zoned in on Asher.

'How are you here?' queried Asher. He repeated himself once more.

'This is very unexpected,' uttered Aarus. 'He's not part of the equation.' He spoke as if referring to a plan, clearly one of his own making!

'I don't know, I just grabbed onto you, and what was the swirling blue light?' enquired Ben. He remained sitting on the ground, he took his inhaler from his jean pocket. He took a puff before holding his breath for a moment, then exhaling through his nose. His chest popped in and out like an accordion.

'I'm still trying to work that out myself,' answered Asher truthfully. He rose to his feet before dusting himself down. His clothes were still wet.

'Oh no,' panicked Ben. It looked like his eyes were going to pop from their sockets.

'What…what is it?' asked Asher.

'The talent show will be nearly over,' alluded Ben. 'You'll be missing your performance, the…the…' His words ran away from him wildly.

'Cool it, Ben,' said Asher. He snapped his fingers, drawing Ben's undivided attention. 'That's the least of our problems now, look around,' he said.

'Where in the hell are we?' asked Ben. He took in the gravity of the situation. He felt a little lightheaded as he jumped to his feet a little too quickly. He could not believe what he was seeing.

'Hell is about right,' gasped Asher. His eyes wandered, scanning the area. 'Well, one thing's for sure, we're not in Neptune City anymore,' he said. He looked up, and the sky above was thundery grey. He then looked left and right. The ground below was muddy and lifeless, and as far as the eye could see, there were countless portals.

He spotted numerous energetic auras of blue that were cast into cliff sides, into unnatural stone structures, into large trees. 'There are so many,' he said. He took note of the many portals, each one was different in shape and size. He glanced at several portals that were quite close by. One portal was only a few feet away. It rested between three lifeless trees.

'So many what?' said Ben.

'It's real after all,' gasped Asher. He had a stark revelation. 'Aarus, this is The Portal Realm,' he said.

'Hey, bud…,' said Ben. He tried to get a word in. Though he found Asher somewhat, he zoned out. 'Hello, portal, what?' He waved his arms about his head before sighing. He did not like that Asher was ignoring him.

'Indeed, it is Ash,' confirmed Aarus. He was not surprised to be in the place between worlds, almost like it was his intention! 'As I suspected, Geatiric is not home. He is too busy masquerading in human flesh, the fool.' The absence of The Gatekeeper seemed to confirm his beliefs. He believed that Principal Smith was indeed Geatiric!

'It's so different to what The Gatekeeper had shown me, to what I had dreamt, this place is horrid,' said Asher. He rubbed his forehead. He tried to make some rational sense of what he was seeing.

'Were you here before?' asked Ben. Still, he was ignored.

'I'm not sure exactly how much time has passed, possibly many centuries,' said Aarus. 'Nonetheless, I recall a green and lavish utopia. I suppose without Geatiric, this place becomes lifeless, just as before when he fled my wrath. An improvement if you ask me,' he added. He concluded that every time Geatiric, The Gatekeeper left The Portal Realm, it became devoid of life, beauty, and colour.

'Improvement! You have lost it,' Asher said. He was a little confused. 'This place is just awful.'

'Absolutely…you're…you're quite right,' articulated Aarus. 'I simply meant we're fortunate that Geatiric isn't here, the fool is a master of deception,' he said.

'He seemed nice,' recalled Asher. He remembered Geatiric, the old man from the Valley of the Kings, the old man from his dreams. 'He…he called himself The Gatekeeper.' To him, Geatiric seemed harmless, short a few marbles, but no real threat. 'I never imagined the dreams real…'

'Real! Oh yes, he is real alright,' intercepted Aarus. He knew Geatiric on a more personal level.

'Um… yes, I know he's real, I've seen him. I meant the dreams, they were just dreams, weren't they?' he asked.

'The visions you were shown were nothing but deceptions,' informed Aarus. 'Given the chance, Geatiric will ensnare you within his grasp with his lies. He's a master manipulator,' he added.

'Yo!' Ben placed his fingers between his lips, and he whistled loudly.

'One moment,' answered Asher. He quietened a rather worried-looking Ben.

'Geatiric is quite deceiving indeed,' said Aarus. 'Given the opportunity, he'll trap you here for eternity. He will take Soulkeeper.' His words were gloom-ridden. 'However, remember this and remember well, only you can give up Soulkeeper willingly,' he said.

'Nope, that does not work for me. We must get out of here,' stated Asher. He did not want to spend forever in the lifeless place he now found himself in.

'Hey buddy,' said Ben. 'Have you lost your mind?' he asked.

'What do you mean?' questioned Asher. He was absent as to how Ben was perceiving the current situation.

'Who are you talking to?' asked Ben. 'You've been outright ignoring me,' he said. He was more confused than anyone. Taking a hard gulp, he looked very shaken.

'Sorry, Ben. I've been talking to Aarus,' informed Asher. He held up his arm, showing the bracelet of gold. 'He's trapped in this,' he explained.

'It's called Soulkeeper,' said Aarus. 'The problem is nobody listens anymore.'

'Soulkeeper is its name,' said Asher. 'Are you happy now, Aarus?' he asked. He was sarcastic in his response.

'I'm just splendid,' answered Aarus. He teased Asher in an equally lively manner.

'Wow! Holy smoke, where did you get that?' asked Ben. He ran his fingers along Soulkeeper. 'It's real!' His eyes widened as his mouth lay agape in awe.

'Egypt,' replied Asher. 'And yes, it is real,' he said.

'You reveal a great deal,' said Aarus. 'You can't trust anyone, just like I couldn't trust The Gatekeeper.'

'The Gatekeeper had told me that this was his home,' said Asher.

'Indeed, it is,' confirmed Aarus. 'He is a trickster, a shapeshifter who controls this, this realm of portals between worlds,' he explained. His voice rose as he began to get angry.

'The Gatekeeper!' gulped Ben. Rubbing his hands together uncontrollably, it was clear he was barely holding himself together. 'Who is…'

'I met him in Egypt, Ben,' interrupted Asher. 'He lives here. He is kind of like a magician,' he explained. It was the best way that he could understand The Gatekeeper. He had seen him change form and manipulate matter, but that was while dreaming. In truth, The Gatekeeper, though not apparently harmful, was still a mystery to him. If Aarus was right, he believed he was in a lot of danger.

'He's a Riathaĺe, a race of beings with divergent powers,' said Aarus. 'They can change form, manipulate matter, and control the elements. A select few can even influence time, those tied to the false god that is.' He spoke as if he had experience of dealing with the Riathaĺe. 'Geatiric is by far in the upper echelons of skills and abilities amongst his kind,' he added.

The gift of influencing time was connected directly to a higher power. Only those beings pure of heart with a direct spiritual connection to The One had such authority.

Even then, time itself was a tricky business. It was not plain sailing. The greatest gift from The One was not to be meddled with, and that gift was free will itself! Changing time could change fates, change outcomes, and meddle in the choices of sapient beings that inherited the universe.

'Wait, Aarus, you said you've been here before,' said Asher. A thought suddenly jumped to his mind.

'Yes,' confirmed Aarus. 'A long time ago,' he said.

'Well, if you were here before, you must know a way out,' said Asher. 'How can we get back to the talent show?' he asked.

'Are you talking to the thingy ma bob?' questioned Ben. He was still wide-eyed and somewhat sceptical. He had a few questions to say the least. 'You sure it's not in your mind?' His knees were shaking like leaves in the wind.

'Take a look around,' said Asher. 'Does this place look real to you?' he asked. His trainers scraped against the mud and dirt below as he turned in a circular motion.

'Well…um…yes,' replied Ben. He stomped on the ground to make sure.

'Well, this brought us here,' said Asher. He held up Soulkeeper. 'Believe me, Aarus is in here,' he said. He shook Soulkeeper before Ben's hazel eyes.

'Why can't I hear him?' asked Ben. He flapped his ears back and forth with his fingers.

'Only I can hear him, big ears,' replied Asher screwing up his nose. 'Somehow I'm connected to Soulkeeper, perhaps because it's on my arm and not yours,' he said. He shrugged his shoulders. He was not entirely sure himself.

'Stupid name if you ask me,' replied Ben. He stuck out his pink tongue. He did not like the reference to his ears.

'I no longer find the plump one amusing,' said Aarus. 'He'll hinder our progress,' he said.

'Never mind all that,' said Asher. His blue eyes darted high and low. 'Where do I go?' he asked. The Portal Realm was vast. It was greater than the Sahara Desert, larger than any ocean.

'I don't know,' shrugged Ben.

'I'm speaking to Aarus,' informed Asher. 'You must know if you were here before,' he said.

'It's been a very long time,' said Aarus. 'Nothing is coming to mind yet.'

'While you try to remember, I'll take a look around, maybe something will jog your memory,' said Asher. He urged his friend forward. 'Follow me, Ben,' he instructed.

'Asher!'

'Yes, Ben,' answered Asher.

'Are you sure we are not dead?' asked Ben.

'Don't think so,' replied Asher. 'No one, not even us, could have been that bad to end up in a place like this,' he said.

'I don't know about that,' responded Ben. 'Tom and Conor have definitely earned a spot in this place,' he joked. A fleeting grin appeared on his face.

'This way, wise guy,' chuckled Asher. His feet began to move forward at a rapid pace. Thud! Thud! Thud! His shoes slapped against the muddy canvas beneath with each step.

'Hold up!' shouted Ben, face beaming red. He began to pant a little as he hurried in hot pursuit. He could not get his words out.

'Watch out, Ash!' boomed Aarus. 'Mind the cliff edge,' he warned.

Arms swinging wildly by his side, Asher was not paying much attention to where his size-seven feet were taking him. Thumppp! He tripped over a hefty rock, he stumbled forward. He came to the edge of a huge cliff. 'Woah!' he screeched in fear. He struggled to keep his balance.

'It's…it's alright buddy,' said Ben. He wrapped his arms around Asher's slender frame, allowing him to regain his footing. He watched as a few rocks took a tumble, sliding down a few hundred feet or more, before hitting the bottom of the cliff. 'Watch where you…you're going,' he wheezed. He looked like a clogged-up vacuum unable to take in any air.

Reaching into his pocket, he retrieved his blue inhaler. He took another puff.

'Thanks, Ben, thanks, you…you saved my life,' Asher spoke in a panic. He rolled his fingers through his jet-black hair. The thought of his body hitting the rocks below made him shudder.

'I'm…I'm always saving your behind. You'd be lo…lost without me,' said Ben. 'Besides…' looking quite rough, he struggled for air.

'Besides what?' asked Asher.

'Besides, I…I just don't want to be stuck here on my own,' stated Ben. He shakily smiled.

'You're a real pal,' said Asher. 'Doesn't matter if I'd died or anything.' He was offhand in his response, knowing just how lucky he was not to fall. His heart was racing faster than a locomotive.

'I doubt the plunge would have been your end,' informed Aarus. 'Take heed, as I mentioned to you before, Soulkeeper protects its wearer,' he explained.

'Aarus, then why the concern?' questioned Asher.

'Time is against us,' replied Aarus. 'Geatiric could appear at any moment,' he said.

'Oh, that feels a little better,' said Ben. He took a few deep breaths, the medicine from his inhaler had done the trick. He placed his inhaler back in his blue jean pocket.

'Are you going to be okay?' asked Asher. He placed a hand on Ben's back. 'You've got worse lungs than my grandma,' he said.

'I'll be fine,' answered Ben. 'It only happens when I get overly excited, and, well, this place is all the excitement I need in my life right now,' he said.

The vast landscape was devilish. Depending on which direction you took, it rose high up into the sky and down low into bottomless canyons.

'That dead tree up there looks familiar,' said Aarus. He spotted a lifeless tree with many branches. 'Inspect it further, Ash,' he said. He encouraged Asher to take a closer look in a bid to escape The Portal Realm.

'We have to go up there.' Looking up, Asher saw the lifeless tree. It rested atop a steep rock face, at least thirty feet up.

'You have to be kidding,' gasped Ben. 'That's not going to be easy.' He rolled his eyes as he grunted.

'We've no choice,' informed Asher. He reached out with his right hand, then his left, and he began to climb. 'Hurry up, slow coach,' he shouted.

'Ok…ok fine,' grumbled Ben. He too began the climb. He was slower, and it took him a little longer to reach the top. 'Give me a hand,' he said.

'Sure thing,' said Asher. He reached out and pulled Ben forward to the summit.

'I need to take gym more seriously,' said Ben. He was breathing heavily and sweating, he rested his buttocks in the mud. He did not care if his jeans got dirty. He had to take another puff from his blue inhaler.

'I'm not a stingray, but that's just pathetic.' Asher made fun of the fact that Ben was in the school baseball team, the Neptunica Stingrays, but was less fit than he.

'Hey now, no one pitches like me, I bat pretty well too, Coach Jones says so,' alluded Ben. 'Keep it up and you'll be experiencing my swing firsthand,' he said before sticking out his tongue in jest.

'Aarus, the tree, it's right there,' said Asher. He sprinted toward the tree, which overlooked miles and miles of lifeless terrain below. He reached out slowly. The tip of his index finger just about touched the bark of the tree when he felt it. 'Woah! That felt strange.' He felt a spark.

'Careful now, Ash,' warned Aarus. 'Don't touch that tree, it's forbidden,' he said. He could comprehend that something else was at play.

'Sure…sure ok,' replied Asher. Fearful, he pulled his hand back.

'Great, you talk to your new friend,' said Ben. 'I'll just sit here.' He remained sitting in the mud. He was feeling worn out.

'This tree was once alive. Yes, alive. It used to have red, round fruit,' stated Aarus as he recollected his memories. It was all coming back to him, his past, every detail. 'Geatiric prohibited anyone from eating from that tree. Like some slave, he takes his orders from up on high,' he added quite resentfully. He seemed to have a great deal of knowledge of the place between worlds and its occupier.

'Why was no one allowed to eat the fruit?' asked Asher. He found nothing extraordinary about the tree. 'It doesn't look all that special to me,' he spoke aloud, his thoughts spilling out.

'Special! Funny you should mention that. Lately, I've realised that even the most seemingly insignificant things can be special, just look at you, Ash,' said Aarus. 'Geatiric said the sweet, crunchy fruit was not to be eaten. He said it was a gift, the tree was created by The One. Even the most important universal decisions can come down to a simple apple, or one small human boy like you!'

'I'm hardly special,' said Asher. 'Well, what happened? Why did the tree die?' he asked. He looked up at many sprawling branches devoid of leaves.

'Let's just say that I and Geatiric had a disagreement,' told Aarus. 'A disagreement that means no one will ever eat from this tree again.'

'Hey, bud, are you seeing this?' asked Ben. He rose to his feet. Something had caught his attention. 'Look, the inscriptions carved upon that doorway are shining bright blue,' he said.

'Wow! You're right,' replied Asher. He quickly refocused his attention. He spotted a portal. It was buried deep in rock and earth. Inscriptions in an unknown language were etched into the rocky surface around the portal.

'Would you look at those two,' said Ben. 'What are they?' he asked. He saw two nine-foot-tall statues, they were positioned on either side of the portal.

'Those wings, the hair, the masks, the bird feet, I've seen this before,' informed Asher. He was electrified. His dreams were bleeding into reality.

'As too have I, Ash. More of my memories of this place are resurfacing,' revealed Aarus. 'There's an army of them throughout the realm of portals,' he said.

'They are Guardians,' said Asher. He ran his fingers across one of the decorative masks. 'The Gatekeeper said they protect his realm.' He recalled his dreams.

' ⅅᒪᒋᏟᎮᚷᒪᒋᎦᏴ!.' Aarus made an extremely sweet whistling sound. A sound not too dissimilar to sweet music.

'Wow!' gasped Asher. He did not understand the noise that Aarus was making, but he thought it very pleasant to his ears.

'They are Geatiric's detestable beasts. They serve him and him alone, for they are of him,' revealed Aarus. 'They are cheap imitations of his true form. Yet he and that little furball have the gumption to call me the pompous one,' he said.

'Gotcha,' gulped Asher, feeling rather uneasy. 'But what was that sound? It's beautiful…it's…'

'It's a language that I'm very familiar with,' replied Aarus. 'It's spoken by Geatiric and our kind. I, too inherited a great deal of knowledge of the universe.'

As part of his birthright, as a celestial being, Aarus was gifted with knowledge and power. Gifts given by his divine creator. A creator he had grown to resent. He knew many languages and methods of communication. He even knew of the complicated workings of the universe itself to a vast degree.

'It's a good thing they're not real,' gulped Ben. He began prodding the statues. He was curious.

'You better believe it,' replied Asher. He was truly astonished by the sheer size of the Guardians. 'In a dream I had, they were very real.' He recollected how one whizzed overhead as he spoke to Geatiric, The Gatekeeper, and his winged familiar, Vixi.

'Be careful of those creatures, Ash,' warned Aarus. A little fear resonated in his voice. 'They can spring to life at The Gatekeeper's command, that's if he were here,' he said.

'How do you know that The Gatekeeper isn't here?' asked Asher. He quickly glanced over his right shoulder, then his left. 'I mean, what if he's watching?' he whispered. He had more questions than answers. A cold shudder shot up his spine.

'As I have already stated, Geatiric is busy elsewhere,' assumed Aarus. He believed Geatiric to be back on Earth, more specifically, Neptunica Middle School! 'No, if he were here, he would have intercepted us. He would try to take Soulkeeper and thwart our plans. We must go through that doorway. I recall now, it leads to Terra,' he said.

'What plans? Terra, what's that…' Asher was cut short.

'There's no time for any more questions. Do as I say, through that portal is salvation itself,' boomed Aarus. 'If you desire to see home again, then that portal is the only way,' he lied.

'I don't know,' said Asher with caution. 'I mean it could be dangerous.' He had seen fragments of what Soulkeeper could do. Well, he had travelled through time twice, after all. Now, though, it was different. He had never experienced anything quite like The Portal Realm. The lifeless place did not match his expectations one little bit. In the Dream Realm, he saw colour, beauty, and wonderous things.

'It's either that or we wait for Geatiric to come for us,' said Aarus. He was sharp and direct. 'Do it now, Ash!' He grew quite demanding.

'Fine…fine, I'll do it,' submitted Asher, feeling that he was out of options. 'Ben, hold onto my arm, we're going in.' He wanted to ensure his dirty fair-haired friend was with him every step of the way.

'You must be crazy! I'm not going in there,' groaned Ben. Worry befell his face. He began to rub his wide-set nose as he shook his head.

'Do you really want to stay here?' asked Asher. 'Let's face it, you couldn't go a day alone in this place,' he said.

'Oh, alright,' said Ben, giving in. He grabbed onto Asher's arm. 'But if anything happens to me, you tell Aarus he's getting a knuckle sandwich,' he said.

'Here goes nothing,' gasped Asher. He cautiously edged his way toward the portal. He reached out to the blue aura. But he did not get the chance to go through!

'I wouldn't do that, kiddo!' a feminine voice rang out.

'Who's there?' asked Asher. He looked like a startled cat, ready to scurry off to safety.

'Over there,' said Ben. He spotted the source of the noise. He was startled. On the move once more, he moved back toward the tall, lifeless tree. 'It's a…a…'

'It's Vixi!' Asher spotted a familiar-looking creature. She sat atop the lifeless tree, upon one of its many outstretched branches. He had not forgotten the little creature with rusty red wings, black tipped ears, and most distinctly a rusty red tail with a fluffy white tip. She also wore a green vest. It was The Gatekeeper's associate, all right.

'Hey kiddo,' said Vixi.

'I didn't think you were real,' said Asher. He had followed Ben in pursuit. He looked up at her.

'Oh, believe it, kid, I'm the real deal,' stated Vixi. She descended from the sky to land at Asher's feet. Her waggling tail indicated she was pleased to see Asher. 'I've been looking for you,' she explained.

'Hey buddy, is that fox talking?' asked Ben. Speaking from the side of his mouth, he nudged Asher in the ribs.

'She is…' Asher attempted to explain.

'Ahem! She has a name,' said Vixi. She was sassy.

'Sorry, Vixi is not a fox,' informed Asher. 'She is…well, I don't quite know what she is,' he admitted. As he thought about it further, he realised that he did not know what, or who, Vixi was at all.

'Oh, ok then, never mind me,' replied Ben. He shook his head, he then took his orange yo-yo from his jean pocket, and he began to pace back and forth. 'Voices and talking animals…' he mumbled away to himself.

'Be done with her,' told Aarus. 'She's trouble. She's a vindictive little creature.' He had no liking for Vixi at all.

'Aarus, she doesn't seem dangerous,' whispered Asher. He could not see how Vixi was something to fear. He did find her strange, but he also found her quite likable.

'Aarus!' Alarmed, Vixi shrieked, as her yellow eyes widened. 'That name, where did you hear it?' she asked. She looked beset with fear.

'Oh, Aarus is a friend,' replied Asher. He held up Soulkeeper. 'He talks to me, he's in here,' he explained. His head bobbed up and down to reaffirm his point.

'Are you crazy?' snapped Vixi. Her wings flapped wildly as she soared up into the air. She began to circle Asher's head. 'Geatiric is right. He sent me here to warn you,' she said.

'Don't listen, Ash,' Aarus said in panic. 'She's manipulative, she will curse my name and seek to take Soulkeeper,' he said.

'Warn me, don't be silly,' said Asher. He grew nervous. 'I'm not in any danger.' He was a little naïve for all that had occurred of late.

'Aarus, he is the evil I and Geatiric warned you of,' revealed Vixi. 'He's The Horned God!' Her voice grew loud.

'No way! I…I…don't believe you,' spluttered out Asher. He shook his head distrustfully. 'Aarus helped me to save my dad, he wouldn't hurt me.' He was not open to accepting Vixi's bold accusation. He viewed Aarus as someone he could trust. After all he had done, enough to earn it.

'Exactly, Ash. Where was Geatiric, The Gatekeeper or Vixi for that matter, when it counted?' said Aarus hastily. 'No one but me intervened on your behalf.' He was quite convincing, too.

'Trust me, kid, that horned freak is evil and like bad fruit, rotten to the core,' blasted Vixi. She did her best to reason with Asher.

'You're mistaken,' said Asher. He was having a tough time believing her.

'Hey buddy, we should get going,' said Ben, feeling rather overwhelmed. 'Ditch the fox and let's go home,' he said. He had seen and heard enough. His hazel eyes were wide with worry. Anxiously, he rubbed his hands together.

'Listen to your friend, Ash,' stated Aarus. 'That portal is our ticket, go through it,' he said.

'Kid, you must wait for Geatiric,' said Vixi. 'He'll know what to do with Soulkeeper, he's been summoned by…well…he's in a very important meeting with The One!' She seemed hesitant to give the information.

In his prior dreams, the very dreams he had while camping in the Valley of the Kings, Asher had been told of The One. 'The One, what does that even mean?' he asked. He did not fully understand.

'As it were, The One is the creator of all, including the universe, the stars, the planets, and all matter in existence,' said

Vixi. 'The One, of course, has many names, chief among them is Údra Ena Ceann.'

'The One!' bellowed Aarus. His elated pitch indicated that the name resonated with him. 'The Creator, the force that dwells beyond space and time, does not merely summon anyone; greater forces are at play here.' He was alarmed.

'Aarus, I don't know what to do,' uttered Asher. He was confused. His teeth caressed his bottom lip. So many thoughts were running through his mind. Like a runaway train, he was ready to derail.

'Soulkeeper must not leave The Portal Realm,' growled Vixi. Her voice grew loud and more serious. 'You'll stay put.' She grew very demanding.

'Trust me, Ash, I've not let you down thus far,' reasoned Aarus. 'Leave now or Geatiric will trap us all here.' He panicked.

'Ok…ok…I trust you,' replied Asher. 'Just tell me what to do,' he said.

'Don't listen,' pleaded Vixi. All her efforts were futile.

'Perfect Ash,' spoke Aarus with glee. 'Now focus on finding help,' he said.

'I…I…don't know,' replied Asher. 'Is there anyone who can help us?'

'Oh, I know just the slithering sikze that can help,' answered Aarus. 'Servo mius volantateium. Atumi is who I seek,' he said. A sikze was a reptilian species that Aarus had quite a bit of knowledge of. They dwelt on a planet named Terra.

'Fiddly do, fiddly dee, arrived in time did jolly old me!' A portal opened out of thin air, its core was oozing white purity. Through it came Geatiric, The Gatekeeper. He stood five feet nine inches tall, wearing a white skullcap, white and blue robes, and sandals.

Almost instantly, the grey clouds above succumbed to a rainbow of colours as the sky came alive like an artist's palette. The landscape transformed into a sea of greens. Life itself sporadically burst into motion, as all types of creatures came into existence. The trees flourished with many different coloured leaves and fruits. It was a utopia!

Inside The Portal Realm, The Gatekeeper was rivalled by almost no one. His power was immense. Only one ever superseded him in his own realm, and that being was Aarus, The Horned God himself! However, even then, Aarus had only bested him with the aid of Soulkeeper.

The One, Ůdra Ena Ceann, had shown The Gatekeeper several possible futures, two alternate futures prominent among them. One where Asher would succeed, and The Horned God would be removed from the universe along with Soulkeeper's influence.

The second future, The Gatekeeper, was shown was very sobering. He had seen The Horned God take over the universe, creating chaos and darkness. He had seen Dorchadi breach the veil to the universe. He had seen creation's ultimate destruction. He had foreseen a future in which The Portal Realm itself ceased to exist.

Unshackled, the Guardians broke forth into life. No longer were they idle. Huge, feathered wings expanded outward as they soared up into the sky. The light danced upon their golden masks.

'Go Ash, go now, run before the Guardians capture you,' demanded Aarus. This was his chance. 'Geatiric is not to be trusted,' he barked.

'Kiddo no!' Vixi pleaded with Asher once more. She was not giving up so easily. 'Don't leave,' she begged. She then looked at Geatiric, The Gatekeeper. 'Do something, this is not the plan,' she said.

'You're as wrong as wrong can be,' replied The Gatekeeper. 'All is going to plan as should be.' He bounced about like a kangaroo. He had a lot of zeal.

'This is not the plan,' grumbled Vixi. 'The kid has Soulkeeper, and The Horned God has his ear,' she explained.

'Hopity-dee, I know, I've seen,' revealed The Gatekeeper. 'I've been informed by Ůdra Ena Ceann.' He had just returned from Neahmil, the true paradise beyond the universe.

'If the kid leaves, he is on his own,' sighed Vixi. 'Your power is greatly diminished outside The Portal Realm,' she said. She was truly concerned. She was filled with great uncertainty.

'Nopity-do, we'll be there in the end, me and you,' revealed The Gatekeeper.

'Don't let him leave,' stated Vixi. She raced towards Asher and Ben.

'Tipity-tee, I have to, it's The One's will you see, he was chosen, for little Asher is as special as special can be,' said The Gatekeeper. 'It's forbidden, I can't go against a decree from Ůdra Ena Ceann!'

'Stay back,' said Asher. He stamped his feet at Vixi.

'You, Asher, will decide! The fate of the universe rests with you to make,' revealed The Gatekeeper.

'I'm not listening to you,' snapped Asher. He was fully under Aarus's influence. He edged ever closer to the portal. 'That's our cue, Ben, let's leave this awful place.' He took Ben by the arm.

'Oh crap!' Ben closed his hazel eyes as he plunged feet first into the portal.

In the blink of an eye, Asher and Ben were gone. Both were swallowed by the portal leading to Terra, a place neither knew. 'Final judgement is at hand, and the champions of good and evil hold all at stake,' said The Gatekeeper.

Appendix

Language of the Celestials

A B C D E F G

H I J K L M N

O P Q R S T U

V W X Y Z

Laws of the Celestials

The Formation of the Universe

Ůdra Ena Ceann spoke, bringing the universe and life into existence. The exact words of The Creator are as follows:

⟨constructed script glyphs⟩

'Order and chaos manifest in the creation of light and life, let balance be found in between.'

A big bang of unimaginable magnitudes sparked the start of the universe. The will of Ůdra Ena Ceann was brought to bear. The Creator's grand design had begun. Following the universe's creation came the chosen, the self-conscious. The inheritors of the gift of salvation and free will, the inheritors of the universe. Those life forms moulded in the image of their creator.

Creation

Outside the walls of the universe, there is a place, in a parallel realm, named Neahmil, which is translated in the celestial language. Neahmil is the kingdom of the one true god. The one true god named Ůdra Ena Ceann.

Also known as The Creator, The One, and The Architect, among other names, Ůdra Ena Ceann is both order and chaos, for all creation must have elements of both to exist. Thus, creation walks the delicate line of balance between both concepts.

Ůdra Ena Ceann is the father and mother of all that has been and all that ever will be. The One is often referred to as he or she, but in essence is a purely divine spiritless form embodying both masculinity and femininity. The one God has no beginning and will have no end.

There in Neahmil, a kingdom of light and beauty, the one true god dwells on a throne of golden purity. A throne showered in white flowers blossomed from the seeds of life, the very seeds of creation. There, the divine creator is master of all. The Creator is the omnipotent, all-knowing, all-seeing, and all-powerful ruler of all creation in its vast manifestations.

The Creator's kingdom of Neahmil is eternal. Neahmil is boundless and without limits, it's a place of the divine, of purity and light, it came into existence before the very creation of the universe. Exactly when that is unknown, for time does not exist in Neahmil. Time does not exist beyond the walls of the universe.

After the creation of the paradise, Neahmil, and before the universe leapt into existence, came the creation of the Inachta. The Inachta are a race of celestial beings only surpassed in power by their creator. The Inachta are beings great in spirit and power, more so than a billion neutron stars. The Inachta are servants of light, they are servants of Ůdra Ena Ceann.

The Inachta's purpose is to serve and glorify Ůdra Ena Ceann, to spread their creator's divine truth, to record all of creation and bring all spirits before their creator for divine judgement.

As was Ůdra Ena Ceann's will, from the darkness came an ever-expanding burst of light and the creation of the universe itself. With said creation came the stars, the planets, and all matter. With said creation came time itself as a concept. Almost fifteen billion Earth years have passed since the universe itself leapt into existence.

In creating the universe, Ůdra Ena Ceann created three further races of celestial beings. The first among them was the Sealgairs, the judges and enforcers within the walls of the universe. The Sealgairs' sole purpose is to act according to their creator's will and to uniquely execute The Creator's justice. They oversee all life and formless spirits in the universe. They also exist to ensure that said formless spirits are brought to Neahmil for judgement. In this way, the Sealgairs and the Inachta work hand in hand.

Secondly, the Sealgairs were created to ensure that the next two races of celestials did not deviate from The Creator's plans. The Sealgairs are special because they can traverse between the veil of the universe to Neahmil itself. The only celestials permitted to do so unless decreed otherwise by The Creator.

The Sealgairs are less than the Inachta in sheer magnificence, but they are the singular, greatest force within the walls of the universe itself. The Sealgairs are formless beings constructed of pure divine energy. They are spirits without physical bodies.

The Inachta in their true form are far too magnificent to cross the veil into the universe itself. Such an act is forbidden, for the universe and all its diverse life forms could be tainted or, at worst, destroyed as a result of such action.

Next to be brought into existence was the Riathaĺe. Their purpose is to ensure the proper functioning of the universe. First among the Riathaĺe was Geatiric, The Gatekeeper.

The Gatekeeper's function is to observe in a place between worlds, a place known as The Portal Realm. His function is to record the many worlds in existence. To record, observe and serve The Creator's will.

Both The Gatekeeper and The Portal Realm were created simultaneously. Both are eternally connected. The Gatekeeper and The Portal Realm were created to last until the end of the universe itself. One cannot exist without the other.

After the creation of the Sealgairs and the Riathaĺe came the Breathnádol, the world shepherds. The Breathnádol, like the Riathaĺe, are great in spirit and power. The Breathnádol are assigned to planets capable of bearing life. Their purpose is to oversee, record and, as decreed, carry out the will of Ůdra Ena Ceann.

The Breathnádol exist to ensure that all non-celestial, sapient beings follow their creator's design, that all sapient beings glorify their creator. The Breathnádol shape the worlds they oversee so that life can thrive. Those worlds that are located in the Goldilocks zone of each star or stars they orbit.

In bringing life into existence, in creating the universe, Ůdra Ena Ceann bestowed a gift. The gift of free will. The One bestowed said gift upon all sapient lifeforms, including the Sealgairs, the Riathaĺe and the Breathnádol. Created before time itself, even the Inachta have free will. Though they are the enlightened. They have seen the purity of Neahmil and the full glory of Ůdra Ena Ceann.

Like the other, lesser celestial races, the Inachta are spiritually immortal, although greater in spiritual essence. Apart from spiritual essence, the Inachta contrast with the other celestial races in other ways, too. For one, they dwell in Neahmil with Ůdra Ena Ceann. Secondly, there is no salvation for the Inachta should they taint their spiritual make-up. This gift was reserved for those within the walls of the universe, including the Riathaĺe and Breathnádol.

One Inachta, the greatest of his kind, named Dorchadi, was given a seat at the right hand of Ůdra Ena Ceann. He was once the leader of the celestials that dwell in Neahmil. His purpose was to record the deeds of all sapient lifeforms that had begun to spring up across the universe. He was the master of the Book of Life.

However, Dorchadi grew jealous on his thrown of silver. He grew jealous of the gift of salvation. He grew jealous that, although having free will himself, he would eternally be bound to serve the will of Ůdra Ena Ceann. He desired only to serve his own will.

Furthermore, he grew jealous that with the birth of the universe, and the creation of self-conscious lifeforms, non-celestial beings, that only those lifeforms within the walls of the universe were created in the image of Ůdra Ena Ceann. He grew jealous that Ůdra Ena Ceann had granted such a gift to those he considered much lesser than he.

He began to deviate from his purpose. He went against the forbidden rule that had been set by his creator that no Inachta should enter or influence life within the walls of the universe unless decreed so by The One. Even if decreed, an Inachta could only traverse the veil of the universe as a lesser incarnation of what they truly were.

He began to sow evil into the fabric of creation. He began to sow disorder into the universe itself. Then he tried to taint Neahmil itself with his corrupt nature.

Then it happened! A rebellion broke out in Neahmil. Dorchadi and his followers found themselves cast from Neahmil. They were cast beyond the veil of the universe. There, Dorchadi dwells in his kingdom of darkness known as Neahimni Seachrana. To the celestials, it is oblivion, a sea of eternal darkness. To many of the celestials, Dorchadi is referred to as The Destroyer.

Ever since his fall from grace, Dorchadi has been trying to pierce said veil to the universe. In his kingdom of shadows and darkness, he craves for his chance to be master of all, to usurp the will of Ủdra Ena Ceann.

In his absence, within the universe, the evil he introduced has taken root. It exists in all matter, to the core of every atom, and in all life forms. Thus, he is eternally connected to the universe. There in Neahimni Seachrana, his evilness, like a poison, surrounds the veil to the universe, slowly seeping in.

At the end of time and creation, at the very end of the universe itself, Dorchadi will be left in the darkness for eternity. His desires will die in the darkness with him.

There in the darkness, too, will be cast those celestial beings that have severed their ties with their true creator. Those who reject salvation. There in the darkness at the end of the universe and time will be the spirits of the damned, all those lifeforms that reject Ủdra Ena Ceann. Only the pure and the redeemed can enter The Creator's kingdom.

Life in the Universe

Over time, many sapient lifeforms of the universe, the creations of Ůdra Ena Ceann, have come to call their creator by many names. Knowledge of The One is passed on by the world shepherds, the Breathnádol, as is part of their purpose. Often, the Breathnádol do this in very subtle ways to guide the sapient life forms of the worlds to which they are assigned.

Just like the celestials, the great many life forms of the universe have adapted names such as The One, The Creator, and The Architect, even the God of Light among them.

Of course, throughout the universe, there are billions of languages and ways of communicating. There are billions of worlds overseen by Breathnádol that have not deviated from the will of The Creator.

Likewise, billions of worlds have at one point or another been led by corrupted Breathnádol. Many worlds are still led by corrupted Breathnádol. Many worlds follow only Dorchadi, knowingly or not.

Some lifeforms in the universe refer to The Creator as the father, while others refer to The Creator as the mother. Just as The Creator is both order and chaos, The Creator is also both masculine and feminine. Thus, you could say life is reflected in The Creator.

For almost fifteen billion years, the universe has continually expanded according to The Creator's will. Many sapient lifeforms have come into existence, and many sapient lifeforms have been extinguished in that time also.

The Creator names all sapient lifeforms as niominiums. All niominiums are similar in spirit, all are given the gift of free will, and all can choose between good and evil. This makes niominiums sovereign to make their own choices. They can connect spiritually with Ủdra Ena Ceann or choose not to. Regardless, each soul will be judged in the end, and unlike the Inachta, niominiums have been granted the gift of salvation, should they choose to repent.

The sapient lifeforms of the universe can choose between Ủdra Ena Ceann's love and mercy or Dorchadi's hate, anger, and destruction.

Not all niominiums appear the same physically either. Some have pale skin, some dark, some green, some blue. Not all niominiums have two eyes either, some have three or more. Likewise, some have more than two arms or legs, some have none. Creation is such that diversity runs rampant across the entire universe.

Life within the veil, within the walls of the universe, is rare. Rare that is in the grand design of things. Most planets in the universe are inhospitable. Even when life does form, often the life forms are not sapient. The odds of intelligent life forming are incredibly low.

Though, in the grand scheme of the universe, that still means billions of sapient life forms that have existed, do exist, and that will come into existence.

A God with Horns

There is, existing between time and space, between worlds, a place known to Ủdra Ena Ceann and the Inachta as The Portal Realm. There, too, in the place between worlds, exists a powerful celestial named Geatiric, The Gatekeeper.

His function as a RiathaÍe, as decreed by Ủdra Ena Ceann, is to oversee the many worlds in the universe. For that is what the RiathaÍe were created for, to oversee the very functioning of the universe. Each RiathaÍe, of course, had slightly distinct parts to play in the grand design of things.

‘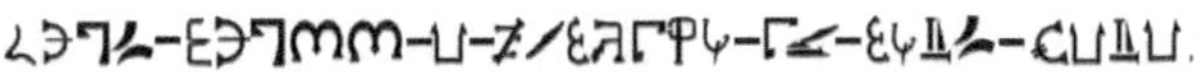’

He spoke in the celestial tongue, though The Gatekeeper knew all languages and had vast knowledge on almost all things within the walls of the universe. This knowledge had been granted to him by The Creator.

‘What shall I conjure up next, Vixi?’ said The Gatekeeper. He was a splendid-looking creature. He was full of happiness, hope, and love, full of purity.

Standing eleven feet tall, The Gatekeeper was majestic. An aura of white, an aura of purity, shrouded his entire body. Whiter still were his eyes, which were solid in colour. Antlers protruded from his head, and he had a snub nose, a very inhuman-looking nose. His nose was rosy.

Long, brilliant white hair flowed from his head down his back. Huge white feathered wings protruded from his back, too. He had two arms and white claws. His legs, too, were animalistic in nature, covered in brilliant white feathers. Instead of feet, he had large talons.

‘Makes no difference, Geatiric.’ Wearing a green vest, a four-legged creature with wings, much smaller in stature, flew overhead. ‘You’ll only change your mind, eventually,’ she sighed. She shook her head. The little creature had a sassy attitude. She, too, knew the celestial language. She also had a great understanding of the inner workings of the universe.

The little creature had black tipped ears, four legs and four black paws. She had a big bushy tail, reddish in colour, with a white tip. Her fur coat had two tones, a reddish colour and a greyish white that mostly covered her underbelly.

The most distinct thing about the little creature was her magnificent wings. Her wings were at least thirty-six inches in length, and almost two-thirds that in width.

'Ripples it will be, Vixi. I came across them on a world named Keplora,' said The Gatekeeper. Up went his arms, waving his white claws, and he adjusted the matter, the very reality about him. Upon a yellow-leaved tree burst forth a type of purple fruit.

Having control over matter and all that went on within The Portal Realm, Geatiric, The Gatekeeper, was busy at work in designing the utopia that was his home. Like all celestial beings, he had great power.

He did, however, not wield the power of true creation! To create physical life, entities with souls, is a power only Údra Ena Ceann wielded. Any living animal or entity that Geatiric created was a simple imitation of the divine. He was an artist, The Portal Realm his canvas. His palette was filled with the colourful ideas of his very own imagination, an imagination inspired by the many millions of worlds that he had seen and visited.

His home, The Portal Realm, was a vision of electrifying beauty. The sky above was a bedazzling sea of colour, filled with reds, blues, greens, and yellows, it was quite the spectacle. Colours too flooded the very landscape as all manner of trees, bushes, and living things flourished in great abundance.

There were bedazzling lakes of blues and silvers. The very air itself smelled sweet and delightful like honey, the aroma was quite enticing.

Scattered throughout the sky and landscape, there were animals in various shapes and sizes. They were a wonderful sight to behold. There were purple, furry little animals with six legs, there were red two-headed animals with long snouts, and there were rainbow-coloured creatures that flew up high overhead. There were even phoenixes and griffons, centaurs, and nymphs. There were beings with musical instruments dancing amongst the trees and foliage. It was quite majestic.

Above in the sky, there were numerous entities similar in shape to The Gatekeeper. The faceless beings wore golden masks. Like The Gatekeeper, the faceless beings had brilliant white wings. They had long white hair stretching down their backs and large bird-like legs and talons instead of feet. They had two arms and claws instead of fingers. They were wondrous-looking. Less magnificent than The Gatekeeper, but beautiful, nonetheless. They were the Guardians, entities created by The Gatekeeper to watch over The Portal Realm, to guard his home. They were his very own army of watchers. They were his eyes and ears.

They were not celestials, they did not emit the same white aura, the same purity that The Gatekeeper did. Instead, they had blueish skin, most noticeable around the neck, arms, and torso. They were less than him. They were soulless entities.

Vast, The Portal Realm stretched indefinitely in every direction. In every direction, there were doorways, portals that led to other worlds; millions, billions, the number of portals was unfathomable.

'What about that tree?' said Vixi. She took note of one beautiful tree, a tree that emitted an aura of celestial purity.

From its branches hung many ripe red fruits, which were sweet and succulent.

'I don't have the authority to touch even one branch on that tree. It was created along with me, that is, the Forbidden Tree,' revealed The Gatekeeper. The tree was gifted to him from The Creator, along with guardianship of The Portal Realm. It embodied true creation. The tree overlooked a portal, a doorway to another world.

'It's a pity.' The Gatekeeper said softly. He shook his head. Sadness filled him.

'What is a pity?' questioned Vixi. Taking flight, she landed atop the tree. Her light-yellow eyes looked down upon The Gatekeeper as she curiously awaited a response from him.

'That's the doorway to Lauriel, now called Terra by the fallen,' informed The Gatekeeper. He had been to the world of Terra numerous times. Over millennia, he had seen many of the world's Breathnádol fall and become corrupted by their selfish ambitions. He had seen many of the Breathnádol of Terra declare themselves gods and abandon The Creator. 'I lost many brothers and sisters on that world to Dorchadi.' Sucking in a deep breath, the very thought troubled him deeply.

The last time he had visited Terra was a few centuries ago, which to a celestial was insignificant. Time held no meaning to The Gatekeeper, he being billions of years old. His hope rested in a handful of Breathnádol that were still pure, still kind, still connected to the divine.

'Wouldn't be the first,' said Vixi. She spoke with a sense of regret, for she too had once been counted among the fallen. Many millions of years previous, she was once a powerful celestial being. She had originated from a world named Ariatni.

At one time, she could take many forms. Her true form was as brilliant in nature and as majestic as The Gatekeeper himself.

She had once taken on a more feminine form, quite different to her current physical appearance. Once she had stood eleven feet tall and had much larger, much more splendid white wings. Once she had fiery red hair that flowed down her back. She had larger, pointed ears, too.

Once her eyes were yellow, quite alike to her current appearance, but they shone brightly like two burning stars. She had a much longer, bushy red and white tail, too. Like The Gatekeeper, she too had two arms and long claws, though her legs were covered in red fur instead of brilliant white feathers. Once, she was a vision of electrifying beauty. She was once a wild and free being.

Then he came! Dorchadi, or at least his avatar. A formless cloud of darkness. He introduced temptation to the celestial beings of Vixi's world and many others. One by one, many celestials fell and became corrupted in nature.

Even after Dorchadi's expulsion to the great sea of darkness, Neahimni Seachrana, a place beyond the walls of the universe, his dark influence persisted. His introduction of evil, of temptation, took root and tainted all creation.

Then came a decree! Ùdra Ena Ceann sent forth the Sealgairs. The universal judges were sent to the world Ariatni to carry out The Creator's divine justice. They brought to heel the corrupted Breathnádol of the world Ariatni, including Vixi herself.

The Sealgairs relinquished the Breathnádol of the world Ariatni of their physical forms. Then, in their formless states, said Breathnádol were brought beyond the walls of the universe to Neahmil for divine judgement. The Inachta opened the Book of Life, and in it was recorded all the deeds of those Breathnádol of Ariatni.

In the end, only Vixi was forgiven; only she repented. All but her were sent to Neahimni Seachrana, the great sea of darkness, to dwell for eternity with Dorchadi.

As a second chance, she was sent back to the universe, being allowed to take her current form. She was permitted to serve as The Gatekeeper's familiar. Her repentance would last until the end of the universe itself. At which point she would be judged a final time.

'I may plan on another trip soon, my little friend,' suggested The Gatekeeper. He had not been away from The Portal Realm in a while, at least one hundred Earth years. It was a long spell, considering he was used to making hundreds, if not thousands, of trips within that time. He was an explorer at heart. Not only that, but it was also his function as a Riathaĺe to observe the universe and all its many splendours. 'I wouldn't want to be accused of neglecting my duties,' he added.

In his visits to countless worlds, a few had become his favourites. Some worlds he visited more frequently than others.

'Oh goody, off to another world then,' said Vixi. 'Wherever shall we go?' She often accompanied him on his many travels between worlds.

'Olora could be rather nice, be great to see what the Otilas have been up to,' said The Gatekeeper. The Otilas are a peaceful species of niominiums from the world they call Olora. They are a green-skinned species. They are advanced, with great cities and technology.

The Breathnádol of that world had remained faithful to Ŭdra Ena Ceann. They were obedient in serving their creator's will in all things.

'Or Graxalora, peaceful but beautiful,' said The Gatekeeper. That world had yet to develop any sapient life, but it was wild and wonderful. A green utopia.

The Breathnádol of that world were still sowing the seeds of Ůdra Ena Ceann's will. Much had yet to be done.

'Speaking of travelling, when's the last time we've had any visitors?' stated Vixi as her yellow eyes widened. She hovered over the portal that led to the world of Terra. Suddenly, it had come alive! A blue surge of energy began to twirl, inscriptions began to light up surrounding the portal.

'We have never had any visitors! Well, none that were not sanctioned by me first.' The Gatekeeper was very puzzled. The Portal Realm was hidden between time and space. It was one of the best-kept secrets. Only a handful of celestials knew of it. Even fewer had the means or power to reach it.

After a short while, a figure dressed in black robes came tumbling forward. He had pinkish skin and curled ears. Where a nose should be were two slits, vents. He had solid, emerald green eyes.

The black robed figure wore a horned pendant around his neck, and in his right hand was a staff. The staff had a name. It was called the Breithira Staff. It took its name from a species of winged serpent of the world now called Terra.

'Sss…seot àitel sss…si gi hului sss…salarach!' The black robed figure spoke in a language he had learned back on Terra. He spoke the language of a race of niominiums known on Terra as neenius's. They were Gaililians of the Dominion of Gaililand. He hissed loudly as the words oozed from his mouth.

'I don't think it's detestable,' protested The Gatekeeper. He understood the words perfectly. He found the insult unwarranted. 'Quite puzzling, how did a neenu like you get here?' he questioned the unexpected visitor.

'Sata di agagul!' Another figure leapt from the portal. He looked more eloquent. He had blond wavy hair, curled ears, solid gold eyes, a blue tongue, and vents in the place of a nose. His skin was a pinkish, inhuman tone. He advised his black-robed accomplice to stop his whining. Pushing him aside, he glided forward with grace.

His dress sense was grand. Over a black sleeved shirt with ruffles at the neck, the figure wore a black vest with gold buttons and intricate gold engravings. The vest had an open collar and was wide at the shoulders. He wore black breeches and black leather boots with three golden buckles on each boot.

'What do you want?' Wary, Vixi flew over the head of the well-dressed figure in black. She, too, knew the language of the Gaililians from the world of Terra. She, like The Gatekeeper, knew all languages and forms of communication throughout the universe.

' ப-∠٦٤ᒪ-ப∠-٦ᄱᄱ -ப-∠٦٤ᒪ-Ә٦ᄀ٦XΡ☉٦ .'

The figure then spoke a language known only to the celestials. He strode forward with an air of confidence. He used a black cane of sorts topped with a silver handle. 'Well, this place just splendid. I never truly believed my mother Terrial. I never believed that this place existed.' He took a deep breath as he scanned the landscape. Many portals fell into his view. 'I shall find her!' Running his hand through his blond hair, he smiled with a sense of hope. It was immediately apparent that he was in search of someone.

'Who are you?'' asked The Gatekeeper. He could sense he was talking to an entity of similar standing. A celestial! Though the celestial before him was cloaked. Cloaked in the form of a neenu. The term for a male neenius of the world, Terra.

'Do not test me, Geatiric! We have met before. I am in search of Hamadrya,' he said.

'Aarus!' The Gatekeeper quickly realised that, submerged in pink flesh, was a powerful spirit. Suddenly, he could see very clearly. He could see Aarus's true form. He had met the celestial now standing before him many centuries previously. He had met him on the world now known as Terra. More specifically, he had met him in a wild forest called Gloomwood Forest.

There, too, in said forest, The Gatekeeper had met the green-skinned forest nymph known as Hamadrya. She was a peace-loving being of the forest. She loved wild things, and she especially loved music.

Both Aarus and Hamadrya were immortal. Both were in love. Both, though, were not cut from the same cloth! Though immortal Hamadrya was not a celestial. She could die as easily as all living things could. She could not reform like a celestial could.

'Indeed, it is I,' said Aarus. He strode across the soft green canopy. He took note of The Forbidden Tree, the tree of purity, the tree gifted to The Gatekeeper from Údra Ena Ceann. 'I shall taste its fruit.' He reached forth with his pink fingers.

'None shall!' boomed The Gatekeeper. In panic, he warned Aarus to refrain from taking such action. 'It's decreed so. I do apologise.' With the creation of The Gatekeeper and The Portal Realm also came the creation of The Forbidden Tree. With the creation of said tree came one strict instruction from Údra Ena Ceann. That one instruction, that one decree, was that no one should eat the fruit its branches did bear.

'Is that so?' said Aarus. Smirking, he placed a hand on the tree.

'Where is she?' asked The Gatekeeper. A smile arose on his face. He talked to the celestial Aarus as if greeting a friend. He remembered Aarus fondly. He was one of a handful of Breathnádol of the world, Terra still filled with kindness. Still filled with love of wild things. Still filled with hope.

'They took her from me!' snapped Aarus. Anger washed over his face. His pink flesh began to peel away in a shroud of blackness. His grand attire began to give way to something wilder and more animalistic! 'I go by The Horned God now.' He grew to eleven feet in stature. Two large golden horns and a golden stump projected from his head. Golden wings burst from his back. He had a golden spiked tail, red eyes, razor-sharp teeth, and an inhuman nose. He looked devilish as his true form revealed itself.

Bone protruded from his arms. He had huge claws. Like the rest of his body, his torso emitted a golden aura. His legs were animalistic with golden hair. His two golden hooves bit into the dirt beneath.

'You've defiled yourself,' said The Gatekeeper. He recalled a being with three golden horns. He could see that one golden horn had been cut from Aarus's head!

'Look what you've done,' groaned Vixi. She stuck her tongue out at Aarus. The fruit upon the Forbidden Tree that he had touched began to turn black and fall to the green canopy beneath. The incredibly special tree, filled with purity, the tree gifted by the divine, began to wither and die.

'Kill them masss…ster!' The cloaked figure wriggled forward, blue tongue slithering from between the cracks in his teeth. He was full of anger. 'Soon they will come!' Fear filled him.

'Shut it Atumi,' commanded Aarus. He harshly struck the black robed figure, silencing him.

'So, you've fallen from the light,' The Gatekeeper spoke with sadness in his voice. A sparkling white tear rolled down his cheek as he slowly realised the truth. For a celestial, the greatest of losses was the loss of the connection that they had to The One, Ůdra Ena Ceann.

'It's so,' alluded Aarus. 'I serve no one but I.' It was boldly apparent that he had indeed rebelled against Ůdra Ena Ceann's will.

'Only Dorchadi's seed of darkness could destroy something so pure,' said The Gatekeeper. Evil in the beginning of creation of the universe had but a nebulous existence. It was Dorchadi that planted the seed of evil, of temptation, of pain, of suffering.

Once a celestial became impure, they could never regain their connection with Ůdra Ena Ceann. Not without giving up their physical form and surrendering to The Creator's divine judgement in Neahmil.

Those celestials in Neahmil known as the Inachta were not granted this gift of salvation. Once fallen, they could not be redeemed. Such was their spiritual essence. In this sense, they were unique amongst the races of celestials.

'I was the God of Order when we had first met, you didn't mind then,' said Aarus. He was quite smug as he sized up The Gatekeeper. 'Did that not go against the code, against the law?' He was antagonising The Gatekeeper.

Indeed, the corrupted Breathnádol of Terra had bestowed upon Aarus the title, God of Order. He was one of nineteen Breathnádol that sat upon the Omniscient Council, a council of the most powerful Breathnádol of Terra, five of which were known as the Elemental Gods. Two of the Elemental Gods, Terrial and Ignis, were Aarus's mother and father. Unlike his parents, he was indirectly created by The One.

'You never liked that title,' said The Gatekeeper. 'You were pure and had a love of living things like her, like Hamadrya.' He was finding it hard to understand the dark change that had taken root within Aarus.

'Indeed, I didn't like that title, so I took the title God of Chaos, then those lowly races of Terra called me The Horned God,' said Aarus. 'The name has grown on me.' He drummed his sharp claws upon one golden horn.

'So foolish,' said The Gatekeeper. He shook his head. He was not angry but saddened. He felt only sorrow for Aarus. For Aarus had almost certainly doomed himself to an eternity of darkness.

Of all the fallen celestials that had been brought to Neahmil for judgement, only one, only Vixi, was ever given a second chance! The Sealgairs had brought thousands, if not millions, of corrupt Breathnádol to face judgement. All now dwell in oblivion with Dorchadi.

'I've spent so long in the darkness, I'm now blind to the light,' said Aarus. He looked at The Gatekeeper with disgust. 'Where was the light, where was The One when she was taken?' Rage filled him. He was beyond reasoning. Like an intoxicating drug, Dorchadi's greatest creation, evil, now took root in his veins.

'I would never have imagined you would fall so low,' said The Gatekeeper. He grew stout. 'The fallen are not welcome here, in The Portal Realm.' He wanted Aarus to leave.

'You kept this place well hidden,' said Aarus. 'At her end, she spoke of this place! She tried to reason with me. She tried to save her own skin.'

'She!' The Gatekeeper was truly puzzled. 'Who was this she?' he thought.

'Terrial, my mother. Don't you know of her?' asked Aarus. An evil grin rested upon his inhuman face.

'Of course I do, she was one of the first Breathnádol, we were once close friends,' revealed The Gatekeeper. 'That was until she too fell.' Over the millennia, he had watched many celestials fall from grace. He had watched many celestials that he had once called friends deviate from The One.

'Not anymore,' said Aarus. He began to laugh. 'She, like the others of my world, is gone, or should I say out of the way!' Smoke flared from his nostrils. His bulging red eyes were full of hateful intent.

'She's gone,' said The Gatekeeper. 'The Sealgairs, did they finally come for her?' He had assumed that the Sealgairs, the cosmic judges, had come for the corrupted Breathnádol of Terra.

'No…no, they did not, but I did!' declared Aarus. He clinched his razor-sharp teeth together. 'Now I've come here, to you. I will be going to each world. I will find her, and I will take all their power.' His evil intentions were becoming ever clearer.

On the world Terra, Aarus, The Horned God, was worshipped by many and feared by all. The horned pendant around the neck of his servant, Atumi, is a symbol of worship. It's the symbol of an order that follows him alone, The Horned Order!

He had rid the world Terra of all the Breathnádol that had called it home. He had rid Terra of the Elemental Gods, including his mother, Terrial and his father Ignis.

He, alongside The Horned Order, had forged a weapon like no other, a weapon named Soulkeeper. He had used one of his three golden horns in forging the celestial object.

He took from the Breathnádol's known as Past, Present, and Future, the Elixir Cup. Contained within were the seeds of creation, seeds taken from the flowers that covered The One's golden throne of purity in Neahmil.

Deceitfully, Aarus had promised the naïve Breathnádol named Past, Present, and Future rule over Terra in exchange. The three Breathnádol in agreeing lost their connection with Ůdra Ena Ceann. They were blinded by their selfish ambitions.

He took the celestial purity of the cup to forge his instrument. Then, from the shadows, he heard a voice! The voice cracked through the veil of the universe. It was Dorchadi!

Seeing his opportunity, Dorchadi poured his essence into the celestial tool that Aarus had created. His connection to Aarus was formed the very moment that Aarus had lost his connection to Ůdra Ena Ceann.

Bitter and twisted, Dorchadi's goal was to use Aarus as an instrument. A way to remake creation in his image and will.

Later, after the fall of the Breathnádol of Terra, Aarus, The Horned God added a special piece to Soulkeeper! He added a reminder of what he had lost, what was taken from him. He added a blue stone, the very heart of the celestial Vellium, God of the Void. The very Breathnádol that had destroyed Hamadrya's body and cast her soul out into the universe.

The hardest thing he had to do was to destroy the physical presence of his mother, Terrial. He destroyed her form. In doing so, he used Soulkeeper to entrap her essence and power for him alone to wield.

He had once loved his mother Terrial very deeply. Even though she was already counted among the fallen. She had betrayed him! She had alerted the other corrupt Breathnádol of his love for Hamadrya.

He blamed his father Ignis, too, God of Fire, just as much, for he did nothing. Nothing but laugh when the God of the Void, Vellium, ripped Hamadrya's soul from her body and cast it out into the dark void, into the universe.

The corrupted Breathnádol, Vellium, took a great deal of pleasure in doing so, for Aarus had been promised to the Goddess of Love, Astemi. She was his daughter. Aarus had committed a great offence in hiding his love for Hamadrya for many centuries.

'You were always different from the rest,' said The Gatekeeper. Last time he met Aarus, he was not yet counted among the fallen. Of course, he sat with the other self-proclaimed gods. They had even bestowed upon him the title, God of Order. But back then, Aarus never cared for titles, nor power. He only cared for Hamadrya. Perhaps she was the only thing keeping him in the light. Now, though she was gone!

'Enough talk,' thundered Aarus. He had grown restless. There was no time to lose. 'I will go to each world. I will find her.' His intent was quite clear.

'Why would I help you?' questioned The Gatekeeper. He had no intent to aid one of the fallen. To do so willingly would compromise his spirit.

'Oh, but I don't need you, old friend,' answered Aarus. 'Servio mius volantateium.' As he spoke, he held up his arm, and upon it was the celestial weapon, Soulkeeper. It sprang to life. A river of blue oozed from it.

'Back off, you big goon,' yelled Vixi. She had seen enough. She zoomed at him like a lightning bolt. She bit into one golden wing. She had snapped viciously at The Horned God, but he barely noticed.

'Bow down, you vermin,' demanded Atumi. His staff came to life, a red bolt knocked Vixi out of the sky. Fear kept him loyal to The Horned God. He was the figurehead of The Horned Order. He held the position of The Voice, the direct word and will of The Horned God himself.

'Arghhh!' With a horrendous yelp, Vixi fell to the green canopy. Thuddd! Her small body hit the ground hard. She struggled to lift her head. She had taken quite a hit.

'What is this?' boomed The Gatekeeper in sheer panic. The blue aura swamped his physical form. He struggled mightily, but the power was too great. The power of The Horned God contained him.

'It's useless to resist,' said Aarus.

'How's this even possible?' shrieked The Gatekeeper in panic. He was a Riathaĺe, he was a being as great, if not greater, than the Breathnádol before him. He was created at the beginning of the universe, billions of years before Aarus had even come into existence. He was created directly by The One, Ủdra Ena Ceann.

Little did The Gatekeeper know that the combined power of all the Breathnádol of Terra had been brought to bear upon him. He couldn't resist. He was brought to his knees before Aarus, The Horned God.

Many golden-masked, white winged Guardians sensing The Gatekeeper's vulnerability rushed to his aid. Hundreds came from every direction, stretching as far as the eye could see. 'These cheap imitations won't stop me,' said Aarus. 'Servio mius volantateium.' He spoke again and again he displayed great raw power. The Guardians became lifeless. Turning to stone, they fell from the sky to the colourful canvas of The Portal Realm.

'This is impossible for one Breathnádol!' proclaimed The Gatekeeper. He was shaken by the raw display of power.

'For one of our kind, yes, for many, no,' said Aarus. 'With Soulkeeper, I shall take from you what I took from the Breathnádol of my world!' He held up the golden bracelet attached to his right arm. 'Servio mius volantateium.' The words he spoke were old Ireseaian. It was an ancient language once spoken by the ancestors of the Gaililians, a sapient race of the world Terra.

The bracelet of gold had been forged with the help of The Horned Order. Some of its servants were magic users, like Atumi. Many had even learned from the Goddess Trinity. Upon the world Terra, she was the self-proclaimed goddess of magic.

The first servants of The Horned Order were defectors from The Elemental Order, the order that had once served the Breathnádol of Terra, particularly the five most powerful that had control over the elements.

The Horned Order had placed a protection enchantment upon Soulkeeper. In addition to activate Soulkeeper, the words 'servio mius volantateium' had to be spoken. In old Ireseaian, those words meant 'serve thy will.' Soulkeeper was an instrument that served the will of its user.

Present in Soulkeeper's forging, Trinity had added her celestial knowledge and power to the creation of the celestial tool.

In the end, Aarus turned on his sister, Trinity, like all the other Breathnádol of his world, even those who chose to follow him. Like all the rest, he took her power for himself.

The blue aura wrapping around The Gatekeeper's body like folds of silk began to drain his essence. The Horned God was draining his purity and power. His form began to deteriorate.

'No Geatiric!' In pain, Vixi crawled toward The Gatekeeper. Her four paws edged toward someone she held dear and had come to call a friend. She was powerless to help him.

'Know this, to destroy me means to destroy your desires,' said The Gatekeeper. He began to laugh. Then, all around him, The Portal Realm began to shake. The ground beneath began to crack. All matter and all things within The Portal Realm began to deteriorate also.

'What's this?' cried Aarus. Startled, his golden hooves twisted and turned upon the green canopy as his red eyes wondered about the place between worlds. It was ceasing to exist!

'We musss…st leave.' Fear taking hold of him, Atumi grew quite alarmed. His solid green eyes were wide with fear and awe. The sickly black robed figure hurried toward the portal that led back to the world of Terra. Then, suddenly, the portal went dark. There was no escape!

'To destroy me is to destroy The Portal Realm!' revealed The Gatekeeper. He and The Portal Realm were connected. The Fate of The Portal Realm and The Gatekeeper were entwined until the end of the universe itself.

'Servio mius volantateium.' Aarus spoke again. The Gatekeeper had been spared. In doing so, The Portal Realm had also been spared. 'I shall keep you around for the time being to serve me.' He had no choice but to keep The Gatekeeper around just a little while longer.

'You are despicable,' howled Vixi. Her yellow eyes were filled with scorn for Aarus, The Horned God.

'As I was saying, where does that portal lead?' asked Aarus. He had no time to lose. Back on the world Terra, the Sealgairs had shown up. They had sensed Dorchadi's influence. He had taken his leave of the universal judges.

He would need more power to confront them. His motives were now twofold: the first to find Hamadrya's spirit, and secondly to eliminate every Breathnádol and Riathaĺe he could find, to amalgamate power from every viable source, to remove the Sealgairs from the equation.

For the next forty Earth years, he plundered the universe. Many thousands of Breathnádol fell to his wrath. The Horned God did not distinguish between good and evil, those serving the will of Ŭdra Ena Ceann or those that had fallen to Dorchadi.

He used Soulkeeper to imprison spirits both great and small. Entire worlds were wiped of life at his merciless hands.

For forty years, he searched and for forty years he did not find Hamadrya. Then it happened, by chance, he came upon one particular doorway!

'Tell me, Geatiric, where does this one lead?' said Aarus. He had seen hundreds of worlds. Thousands of his kind had succumbed to his vicious fury.

'Earth,' said The Gatekeeper. He was losing hope and fast. Another of his most beloved worlds was about to succumb to The Horned God!

The Sealgairs and the Decree

Over the course of forty Earth years, The Portal Realm had become a means for Aarus, The Horned God, to reach other worlds, many thousands in fact, with relative ease. A whole ocean of planets awaited him. In his mind, there was no time to lose. His next stop was planet Earth itself! A blue planet. A spherical ball that was home to many powerful Breathnádol.

'Well, what are we waiting for?' boomed Aarus with glee in his eyes. He had been relentless in his quest to find Hamadrya's essence.

'End this madness!' pleaded The Gatekeeper. He had seen countless atrocities take place. He had seen the fall of many Breathnádol, a score of Riathaĺe those like him, as well as many wicked and ferocious beasts, animals, and lesser lifeforms. He had witnessed many he called friends succumb to Aarus, The Horned God, unable to help.

Though most sickening, The Gatekeeper had seen the destruction of many niominiums, many lifeforms of different creeds. They were crushed like ants beneath a boot. They had no means to defend themselves.

'It's useless to beg Geatiric. That sicko's spirit is black to the core,' snapped Vixi. She understood the nature of tyrannical psychopaths. She had descended from a world filled with corrupted celestials.

'Hold your tongue, vermin, or you'll lose it,' threatened Aarus. He was losing his temper with Vixi. 'Know this, I will never stop until Hamadrya is with me.' Despite his extensive search thus far, he had not found her soul. The universe was a big place. He feared that he would never find her. He feared that she had transcended beyond the veil of the universe. That she was in Neahmil.

He also knew that if indeed her soul had transcended beyond the great veil of the universe to Neahmil, that she was truly beyond his reach.

'This is no longer about Hamadrya,' said Vixi. 'This is about power!' The little winged creature sat on the shoulder of The Gatekeeper. The pair were equally helpless to stop The Horned God.

'Just so, just so vermin,' uttered Aarus through sharp gritted teeth. 'If I can't have her, then everything else will do!' If he could not have Hamadrya, then he would turn his malice fully toward The Creator, Ůdra Ena Ceann. 'The One has the power to give her back to me.'

'If she's been judged before the twelve gates to Neahmil, she's beyond your reach,' alluded The Gatekeeper. There was truth in his words.

'Atumi, follow me,' commanded Aarus. He instructed his sickly, black-robed servant onward toward the portal that led to Earth. His golden hooves bit into the green canopy beneath. His solid red eyes fixed upon the doorway. Surrounding the portal was a hive of colourful trees with yellow, blue, and red leaves.

'We're no longer alone!' spoke The Gatekeeper as he looked upward at the sky in awe. The colourful canvas above cracked with thunder. The beautiful colours in the sky above began to run until there was only a soulless grey. Piercing the sky were twelve celestial auras. Formless auras of celestial white.

'The Sealgairs have come!' blurted out Vixi. Delight filled her yellow eyes. They were a vision of hope. 'I never thought I'd be glad to see them.' The last time she had seen the Sealgairs millions of years previous, she had been stripped of her physical form and celestial gifts.

'So, they've finally caught up with me,' said Aarus softly. He contemplated his next actions briefly. It didn't take him long. He put his arms up, then stretched out his claws, before booming loudly. 'I will run from you no more!' He looked very menacing. Smoke flared from his nostrils.

'Oh, you're in trouble now,' said Vixi. She, herself, had witnessed the power of the celestials known as the Sealgairs. The entire cohort of Breathnádol of her world, Ariatni, had fallen to their very power.

'Isss it wisss…se to confront them?' hissed Atumi as he questioned his master. He put a hand upon The Horned God, only to be thrown back. With a thump, he fell to the ground. Like a snake, he recoiled in fear.

'We've evaded the Sealgairs long enough,' stated Aarus. He outstretched his golden wings and soared upward high into the sky to meet the Sealgairs head-on in direct challenge. Twelve auras of purity quickly surrounded him.

'It's finally over,' gasped The Gatekeeper with relief. He took comfort believing that no more worlds would have to succumb to The Horned God's greed for power.

The Sealgairs, though not in physical form, took on many different shapes. One Sealgair had the head of what appeared to be a feline of some kind, much like a lion. A second Sealgair took on a more reptilian-like shape. The rest were equally strange.

One of the twelve formless Sealgairs began to speak. The Sealgair spoke in the celestial tongue.

'Let judgement be passed upon the wicked,' the lion-headed Sealgair spoke.

'So be it, pass your judgement, you fools!' raged Aarus. If found guilty, he knew that he would be stripped of his physical form and celestial gifts. Unable to reform, he would then be sent to Neahmil and be judged before the twelve gates to the everlasting paradise.

The second formless aura then spoke. This Sealgair had a reptilian face with scales and had narrow pupils. Two great horns protruded from the Sealgair's head. But this Sealgair's form, like the others, was like smoke.

'Cast your vote, let justice roll on like a great river, just and true like a never-failing stream.'

[illegible]
[illegible]

'Vote then. Vote, you shills of The Creator.' Seemingly unbothered by his impending doom, Aarus slung insults at the Sealgairs in open defiance. 'Servio mius volantateium,' he whispered. An aura of blue oozed from the golden instrument upon his wrist. It washed over his body. Golden wings fluttering wildly, he looked devilish.

'Guilty!

[illegible]

Twelve times the word guilty was spoken, and twelve times a ray of light surged from each of the twelve Sealgairs. With judgement passed, The Horned God was to be stripped of his physical form and brought naked in his spiritual form to Neahmil. There in Neahmil, the final judgement would be passed. No doubt the great sea of darkness awaited him. He would be sent to Dorchadi's kingdom, Neahimni Seachrana. He would be sent to oblivion.

'I shall be with you!' a voice rang out. It was Dorchadi himself, from beyond the veil. 'You will be my herald, you will break the seals imprisoning me here in the darkness,' he said.

Then it happened! Something unthinkable, something thought completely impossible. Each of the twelve beams of pure energy failed, not having the desired effect. The Sealgairs did not destroy The Horned God's physical form. Instead, each of the twelve Sealgairs fell, one by one.

'This cannot be!' gasped The Gatekeeper in sheer disbelief. He had been shaken to the very core.

The lion-headed Sealgair was absorbed into Soulkeeper. Then the reptilian-headed Sealgair. Each one of the cosmic judges fell for the first time in the universe's nearly fifteen-billion-year existence.

'We're doomed!' cried Vixi. She knew that with the fall of the Sealgairs, The Horned God could not be stopped. They were the most powerful force within the walls of the universe.

'Earth, it doesn't stand a chance!' The Gatekeeper knew the fate of the blue planet was now sealed. He believed it would fall, just like the countless other planets that had fallen before it.

Hope lost, he thought it all over. But it was not over, not yet! A portal of celestial white purity opened. It opened directly beneath the branches of The Forbidden Tree.

Then something happened that few celestial beings other than the Inachta had experienced. The voice of Ůdra Ena Ceann called out to The Gatekeeper.

'I summon thee to Neahmil.'

'Masss…ster they are esss…scaping!' Wildly, Atumi, the sickly, black-robed figure, shook his staff.

'Crawl back to your master.' The Gatekeeper easily deflected Atumi's feeble attempts to stop him. He took the black robed, bald-headed, pink-skinned weasel off his feet.

'Servio mius volantateium,' yelled Aarus. After devouring the essence of all the Sealgair's he brought his fury down upon The Gatekeeper and Vixi. Wings flapping wildly, he soared through the sky toward them like a great tornado.

'Quick, we must take our leave,' said Vixi in panic. Rustic red wings flapping, she darted toward the portal to Neahmil.

Talons pushing into the canopy beneath, The Gatekeeper's enormous white wings sprang open. Bending his knees, he then pushed with all his might. Up in the air he went, and he too quickly headed for the portal to Neahmil. He headed for the portal that led beyond the veil of the universe. The one portal that even he could not summon or access of his own accord.

'They have escaped me! No matter,' said Aarus, as The Portal Realm transformed into a barren, desolate place. Absent of The Gatekeeper, The Portal Realm grew very cold and colourless. 'Atumi, get up, you fool; we make leave for the planet they call Earth!' Undeterred, he still had work to complete.